Maru and the Maple Leaf

Maru and the Maple Leaf

Uma Parameswaran

Dedicated to Maru, who adopted my writings as her own, nurtured and brought them to maturity

Decades ago. I, a boy in years but a man withal,
left my village home....
....The opening lines of an autobiography. An autobiography was the
last failing of a successful man, an irresistible temptation. A
temptation, and therefore to be resisted, fought, overcome. And yet a
well-written autobiography...

from Uma Parameswaran's A Cycle of the Moon

Maru and the Maple Leaf

© Uma Parameswaran. 2016

This book is a work of fiction. Characters, places and incidents are a product of the author's imagination or are used fictitiously.

National Library of Canada Cataloguing in Publication Data

Maru and the Maple Leaf
Uma Parameswaran
ISBN: 978-0-9808881-9-5

Larkuma: <larkumapublishing@gmail.com>

September 2016

This novel was first published in July 2016
by Manipal University Press

Printed and bound in Canada by Art Bookbindery

ONE

It is strange to be sitting here after so long. Nothing has changed; the huge picture window still has Crayola smudges in one corner, made by Arvind when he was a child. Aunty Maru told me she started to clean it the day Arvind smudged it there but it wouldn't get erased with wet tissue, and then she decided it had to stay. Superstition, I said, when I heard the story in Ottawa, and this was when Arvind was already twenty six and married, but she laughed and said, Memories are important; check the den of your dad's house and see if there isn't a pencilled height chart that records your height from the time you were two years old. And next time I came home to Winnipeg, I checked and sure enough it was there. The wall had been painted yea times but someone (Dad of course, I can't see Ma doing it) had made sure it wasn't wholly painted over and had marked it over again before the second coat each time, and then again, I guess, for the lines were clear as daylight. I seemed to have had my biggest spurt of growth between my eleventh birthday and twelve years six months and two days, on Krish's birthday. The dates are there against mine and Vithal's and Krish's. Jyoti and Jayant are recorded only twice but they were Vithal's age, and I can't remember any birthday parties with them, which was usually when Dad lined us up against the wall. Krish was about my age and we spent an awful lot of time together.

Parents can be weird, I guess, when it comes to their kids. Crayola marks and height charts, what next?

I wonder if I too will have some nut-case idiosyncrasy when it comes my time to have kids. My biological clock is ticking. I have done some crazy things. Has Aunty Maru written a story about it, me?

So what am I to do with my inheritance, these three cartons containing most likely her writings and photographs and stuff? Not too many knew about her writings though she had published a few here and there. I knew a lot about it, having lived at her house and heard her reading them out to me - fit audience though few, as she often said from her rocker-recliner while I lolled on the couch. First, I would much rather not have all this, just yet, anyway. I would give all I have not to be here taking office, Lyndon Johnson said words to that effect, I must look it up. I'd never thought much of the old geezer in my contemporary history course, but my trip to Dallas last year changed my view of him somewhat - just the sight of him on the video screen at the Kennedy Museum, hand upraised, taking the oath of office in the airplane and the caption under one of the photographs, "All I have I would have given gladly not to be standing here today."

I don't know if I can honestly say that. I have too much to give it all up. But yes, I'd give a lot to have Aunty Maru here. When did I start calling her Aunty again? When I was seventeen, I dropped the Aunty. When I entered the Collegiate, I decided I needed a new image, and changed around certain things - haircut and favourite dress and some habit or other - and when I was entering university, I started to call Aunty Maru just Maru. I also put my hair in an Afro, no that was when I entered medschool. By the time I entered University, I was five foot six to her five two, and wanted to prove something, I guess. But then at some later point, I went back to the Aunty bit, after the time I spent at her place because I didn't want to stay at home, another of those proving-something things, I guess. Maru said that she would welcome a boarder, with all the boys gone to different universities across the country, and she living within walking distance from the university. Now that I think on it, it was probably a plot hatched by her to keep an eye on me at my parents' request, but I was too naïve to figure it out at the time. During that year we became real close, too close I suppose but in the final count Aunty Maru didn't hold anything against me; and here is the proof - her legacy to me, and the responsibility of doing something with it.

I still can't believe it. When Uncle Siv called me that Friday evening, I greeted him with surprise. Because he had called me on my birthday the previous week. And on that day, my first question was to ask where Aunty Maru was. If she had been in Winnipeg, she was the one who would have called. Uncle Siv left all such matters to her - birthday, Christmas, Diwali cards and replies - and she would have said he joins her in wishing me all the best etc. But if either was not in town, both called, she early morning, he during the morning coffee break. As they had, on my twenty eighth birthday. But she had called from Edmonton and said she'd be home next Friday. And Uncle Siv had called earlier that morning. And so when he called again a week later, my hands started trembling after the first expression of pleased surprise. His calls were always scheduled - New Year's, birthday, and Diwali; he never called on his own though whenever Maru called and he happened to be home, he would take the phone to say a little something, leaving us to do all the talking.

"She's gone," he said, and paused. I started trembling, waiting for him to say something that it was not what I thought it was. But the silence continued and I knew what it meant. I could imagine his Adam's apple bobbing up and down as he swallowed sobs. He had come home a little earlier, knowing she always made a point of not driving after dark and so would be home by five, and she had, except that her van was in the driveway and she was slumped over the steering wheel. Later, they found out that she had had a mild heart attack an hour or so earlier but had just picked herself together and driven home. And then it had been a major one. The ignition was turned off, and the door ajar. That woman was quite something. Maru, my Aunty Maru.

So like her, to die with her boots on so to say, in the saddle, sword unsheathed ... in the van that had been her home on wheels for two months every year as she drove across the continent, oh the sheer exuberance of it, as she often said. I flew in the morning of the funeral and flew out again the same day. I was on call all nights that week, it was all I could do to get away for the day.

And then after months, Uncle Siv had called and said could I come some weekend and look into something she'd left for me. He was putting the house up for sale, and had come across "all this" as he said vaguely, and I could see his long tapering fingers weaving a circle as they often did during our debates.   As always he spoke in slow measured tones, his rich baritone cresting over the vowels. I interrupted him in my usual breathless way.

It was more than two weeks before I could arrange to take time off and now here I was, in this living room with its large picture window outside which the ornamental crabapple tree is breaking out into blossom as it has every third week of June as far back as I can remember. Maru never let us forget it - even after we'd left Winnipeg she'd call us the week the tree blossomed and tell us it was in bloom. Stupid tree. For precisely three days every year it is one big spray of gorgeous pink, and then for another four days it whitens and then it sheds it all.   All that growing and reaching out for a three-day extravaganza. The reason why I could not come earlier was Michael-John; born with a faulty heart, he had challenged all of us, and we thought we were up to it. We were just waiting to get him ready for surgery. But then, he was gone.

Each carton is numbered – P1, P2, P3. Taped to one of the cartons is a sheet. "These three boxes are for Priti Moghe," it says, in her bold handwriting and familiar black-ink felt pen. That carton had been the middle one.   All three cartons were taped together with one long strip of duct tape, and Uncle Siv had not untaped them. So typical of him. Aunty Maru had always opened all the letters delivered at home, no matter whether they were addressed to him or her (anyone who wants to write only to him should address it to the university, she maintained) but he never opened any that had her name on it. Of course he never bothered to open any that had his name or both their names either. That too had been her job. Behind every successful man is a good secretary, she always laughed away his assumption that she would keep everything running while he did little to help around the house, it seemed to me.

These three boxes are for Priti. Uncle Siv has gone to the university in the morning, as he has for the last god knows how many years, leaving me to attend to my work. I miss her so terribly I lie on the carpet and stare at the ceiling; and then I cry; I want her back; I want her back; I want her back. And my thoughts tumble each time over what "back" meant, back to which time of my life. There had never been a time when she hadn't been a part of my life, but there had been so many phases of our relationship that my thoughts tumbled, like Tshirts in the laundromat dryer, a kaleidoscope of colours, and black, black, black. I wanted her back. I wanted her back. It has taken me two hours to bring myself to open the cartons. These three boxes are for Priti.

~

And then I opened the carton on which the sheet had been taped because on the side, written with a felt pen, were the words – For Priti.

On top was a photograph album, one of those old ones with black paper and photo corners, with an embossed tracing paper between each page. It was wrapped in thin plastic, Saran Wrap, all stuck together. I didn't bother to open it. I didn't want to see old photographs. People did that all the time. Trains and photographs are part of the Canadian psyche, Maru used to say any time Uncle Siv brought home the developed spool after one of his trips and passed it around at the dining table. Every Canadian author has to stick them in somewhere, she said once. Like every poet has to write a poem about losing his poetic inspiration, Uncle Siv said, with that faint undertone of sarcasm that coloured his view of poetry. And I had said, "slash her," because that is what I said to everyone all the time during that phase of my life, his slash her. Sounds so ghastly even though it is a mere aural transcription of the written his/her, she said. We used to have these arguments all the time, about changing the language to make it less masculinist and all that. And Uncle Siv would look over his reading glasses and shake his head. Anyone listening only to the sound of your voices would think you two were not in agreement, he'd say, or something like that.

I took the album out of the carton and placed it on the carpet. Under it was a thick pile of unused lined-paper. Aunty Maru had a weakness for buying reams and reams of three-hole lined-paper every August when the school-reopening sales were on. Not to mention ballpoint pens, most of which dried up unused and had to be thrown out after a year or two. No one used lined-paper once the boys had left home, and Maru got used to the computer, and Uncle Siv never brought any of his university work home. One of these days, Uncle Siv would probably come across more of these packages of lined-paper in some corner, stacked up to the top of some shelf. However is he going to sort out the contents of this house to fit into an apartment, I thought. We must get together one last time, I thought, Arvind, Nari, Giri and their families, and me and Vith and Donna and the kids; Jayant, Krish, Jyoti and their families, or never mind their families, at least just us who were kids together and had spent so many weekends here in this house.

Under the lined sheets was a stack of computer sheets, each filled with computer garbage. Sometimes Maru's earlier computer did that, just filled the sheet with slashes or squares or some strange characters until it was switched off and rebooted. She couldn't bear to throw them away. She kept them as one-side paper next to the telephone, next to her bed, next to the computer.

Under them was a set of computer sheets, clipped together.

Maru and the Maple Leaf
by Maru Sivaraman

December 28, 1993

I started on my memoirs in the Fall. Why write? who's interested in your memoirs, they said, especially with the elections around the corner who has the time to see anything but television news, they said, unless, ah unless, have you had an affair with Kim Campbell, or with Jean Chretien, or both, sequentially, concurrently, they said. Or at least, are you a tightlipped nun or priest who taught at a native reserve or residential Catholic school, they said. If not, forget it, memoirs huh, they said.

But I started on it anyway; and by the end of November, I had reeled out a whole lot of stories from the time I came to Canada, a blushing bride, the henna scarce dried on my hands and feet.

My writing was going really well. I had found my voice, voice, ah that magic word that my Creative Writing instructors used - yes I took several of those courses at the University because secretaries are encouraged to get professional development, and our strict regimen at our desk could be made a little more flexible to accommodate courses as long as we made up for it some other time - so where was I, yes voice, I had found my voice, the light-hearted voice with which I had arrived at this true North strong and free. More important, I'd found whom I was addressing. It is so vital in any writing - not only the eyes through which you see something, not only the words which you choose to relate an experience, but a sense of the ear into which you drip your story drop by honey drop. No, wrong associations, that is what Manthara did to Kaikeyi, except it was poison and not honey; more literally, that is how Hamlet Senior was done in.

Priti, I am writing all this for Priti. Priti, whom I love dearly. An intelligent young woman, with a social conscience, the kind that volunteers at the women's shelter and Aids Alert, a thinker, she wanted me to tape Noam Chomsky from PBS for her, can anyone imagine that? and a sensitive reader. Caught in a bind like so many Indo-Canadians of her generation. Brainwashed into thinking that medicine is the only respectable profession in the world; that anyone who did not get into medicine, dentistry, business management, in that order, was a moron. Intelligent enough to realize that she's been brainwashed but the pressures are too great. She would have excelled at anything she wanted to but at that age one does not always know just what one wants; this country offers such limitless options, unlike my college days in that other land, where we'd better figure out where we were headed by the time we were fifteen, or else. But here, one can wait and dip into the smorgasbord before doing anything, and many end up not making up their minds ever. Me this unchartered freedom tires.... She applied for medicine because everyone else in her peer group did, and unlike most of them, she got in. Now she's stuck. She has to be there else she'll be letting down a lot of people - or so she thinks.

I see her every time I open my computer and start writing. Her reclining form on the living room couch under the large

picture window through which the sun shines between branches
of my crabapple tree, my sole reason Sivaram thinks, for us
buying this house is this large window; the television on PBS,
and she discussing women's issues with me and politics with
Sivaram - when he's around she doesn't loll, though she doesn't
always sit with knees together the way Sister Mary Angeline
would approve. I told her so once, and then I had to tell her all
about my Convent school back in India, its grey walls and flower
beds in the grotto at the centre of which was the Mater Dolorosa,
her blue robe so real one could see it moving in the breeze, and
how we stole her flowers anyway. Priti loved stories. Her laugh,
spontaneous, contagious. And in thy voice I catch the language
of my former heart, and read my former pleasures in the
shooting lights of thy wild eyes. Her loves – that side could do
with some restraint, oh well.

Some day soon may be, I will show her all this. Or maybe
she will inherit these diskettes along with my women's lit library
and she'll read it then. But are floppy diskettes the way to go?
May be by then these computer systems will be totally outdated,
like eight track cassettes now or 8mm movies on which we have
reels and reels of the children when they were toddlers. I should
make sure there is a printout, neatly filed in a three ring binder,
so Priti can read it some day. May be the printed word is the
only thing that will last, and not computers, Star Trek and all its
successors notwithstanding. May be it will be sooner than I think,
floppies and me, who knows, I might drop dead tomorrow.
Now, is that likely? I doubt. But I just might be blown to
smithereens, and that is not at all unlikely, the way air travel is
going.

I wrote about my community work experiences - the time
Folklorama was first started and my work for the India Pavilion,
the time I started all those dance courses in the late seventies, the
time I had a weekly television show "Helping Indo-Canadians
stand tall" sort of thing, and then the heady days of my work
with the Immigrant Women's Association which took me to
Ottawa and all that, and then whoa, the headiest perhaps of them
all in that it gave me the most humungous headache ever - the
time I was President of the local writers' guild. I wrote all these
and more, with just the right mix of satire and fun, and then

came December, and that month has a way of cutting into everything else.

Preempting everything, every single thing, including my voice. Gone, all gone. The other day I had this feeling in the pit of my guts that the computer had eaten, chewed up and spit out all my files, that like Chanakya it had taken its revenge on my lethargy of years. The files were, however, intact and I spent two days making two copies of back-up diskettes of every blessed word I'd typed, but my inspiration was gone. All gone.

~~~~~

So that is what she wants me to do, I thought. She loved to tell stories, and she was good at it. And I loved to hear her stories. I loved her voice, her accent which had never lost that Indian lilt despite three plus decades in Canada. And the ache came over me again. I want her back. I want her back. And I realized that it was her voice, her accents, I'd heard as I read what I'd just read. I am writing all this for Priti, she had said. And my heart soared. But that was in December 1993. Much had happened since then. Would she have said that now? I felt ill. I was poaching. All this wasn't really for me.

I might just as well look at the album into some distant past that was safely and forever the same. The phone rang. From the coffee table, I picked up the cordless that Uncle Siv had given me from his study table that morning.

It was Uncle Siv. Would it be all right if he came home for lunch, he asked. I'd love that, I said. I'd love that. I left everything the way they were and busied myself in the kitchen. The cupboards were all quite bare, but the bottle of cream-of-wheat was in its usual place, and though the bag of mixed vegetables in the freezer had clearly been there a long time, and the onions and potatoes in the pantry had started sprouting, I managed to cook some *uppuma* that tasted reasonably good. I perked fresh coffee, the bag of coffee seeds was the only thing that I could be sure of being fresh in Uncle Siv's kitchen.

Uncle Siv's Volvo rolled up the driveway at five past twelve, and I ran to open the door for him. He had singled out the door key from his bunch, and was pleasantly surprised to see me opening the door. He pocketed his keys, and came in. "I can smell something good," he said, drawing in his breath. He was that kind of person, always saying something nice. I was there the first time Arvind and Kathy had come after their wedding, it was Diwali and I was staying with Maru because Dad and Ma had gone some place, Frisco I think for a conference, and Maru said there was no way she'd let me spend Diwali day all by myself poring over books, and Kathy had made some *rasmalai*, and when Kathy's parents called that evening, Uncle Siv had told her mother how delicious Kathy's *rasmalai* had been; all of us knew they had fallen apart instead of staying as firm spongy balls, but that is Uncle Siv.

I had already set the table, knowing he would want to go back at five to one; sometimes I feel you are the secretary and not I, Aunty Maru would say to him, the way your body clock follows all the coffee and lunch breaks to the minute. He went to wash his hands, and also combed his hair, which had thinned even more since I last remembered. We sat down to eat, and he polished off the first serving in two minutes flat and then slowed down. I asked him about his research, and he told me but I wasn't quite listening, all that technical language. May be that is what happens with me and my patients too, I try to make it simple but I don't want to be seen as talking down at them and anyway we do have to use medical terms. I'd like to finish all my projects by the end of next year, he said, and that would be it, F I N I S. What will you do, I wanted to ask him, what can you possibly do without your lab, your research, your students? But I didn't. "And time you did too," I said. "Though I can't quite think of you as a babysitter to your grandchildren."

"So, did you find anything?" he asked.

"In those boxes?" I didn't want to talk about it; I wasn't ready yet. "As a matter of fact, I did," I laughed. "You've gypped me of my books. Aunty Maru wanted me to have all her women's writings library."

"Glory be," he said, also laughing. That was Maru's phrase, I thought. "That would be twenty cartons less to carry to the Children's Hospital Book Market bins." Then, more seriously, he said, "I should have thought about it sooner. Who else would she have had in mind for her treasures? Just tell me when and where, and I will send them to you."

"Not just yet, Uncle Siv," I said, "You've seen my apartment."

"Time you moved into a bigger one," he said. "Let's make a switch. You move in here and I'll move into your apartment."

"I'd love to move back but ... like you'll move to Ottawa? Huh."

"Why not," he said. "We had a wonderful time there. The number of parties we had! And you would always come the day after the party to eat all the leftovers, remember? With all your odd friends; that lovely Caribbean girl who kept us in fits with her mimicking of dialect, 'Ah'm tellin yu sistah girl' and 'youslissening chile?' where is she now?   You remember the time I bought that cottage in the Gatineaus?"

Suddenly I was annoyed. He was away so much of the time. If he had been around a little more....

"She loved Ottawa," he said.   "That's when she appropriated my computer and was at it night and day." He still couldn't bring himself to name her. He used to be forever calling her, Roo or My-roo; Maroo-Maaroo was his favourite sing-song when he came from his study into the kitchen or living room.

So he knew about her writing.   "What do you think she wrote?" I asked.

"Isn't that what you've been going through all morning?"

"I cried for about two hours, if you want to know." I don't know why I said that.

He didn't look at me; he helped himself to a third serving.   "Good stuff," he said, "thank you."

"As though you didn't hear me," I said. "For a scientist your glossing over basic rules of manners leaves much to be desired."

"For a surgeon, I do hope your fingers are more sensitive than your understanding of human responses."

"Physician heal thyself," we both said at the same time and laughed. It was like old times.

"So tell me, what are you planning to do with the stuff?" he asked.

"She was a great storyteller."

"None better."

"What do you want me to do?"

"Hasn't she said anything somewhere?"

"I don't know. I'll have to go through them all."

"I hope you'll find the time."

"Meaning I'd better find the time?"

"Something like that."

"I don't know. Should I take all of them now? They weigh a ton."

"I could send them to you. Courier."

"Why? what's the hurry? You may not even want me to read it all; all the personal stuff between the two of you, for instance. You don't mind me knowing all that?"

"What makes you think there is any?   These are mostly her attempts at fiction, I would think. Good stuff, everything she did was good."

"I wouldn't want anyone to read what she's written about me. So if I were you, I wouldn't want anyone to read it, period."

"May be I trust you so much," he said it with a smile.

"May be you shouldn't. I'll sell all your bedtime secrets and mint a fortune. I can see the headlines - Wind Tunnel Expert's windy past."

"There won't be any dark secrets. You forget I knew her well," he said. "Thirty plus years."

"*Because I would not stop for Death, he kindly stopped for me.*"

He nodded. "That was the only way he could have taken her," he said. "But it is hard. Thirty five years and she left without so much as a good bye." Tears rose to my eyes, as I am sure to his. Eight months but it was like we were going through it all over again.

"There is a sense of urgency about certain matters," he said. "I wish she had started earlier. There were so many things she need not have got into. All that community work, new immigrants, women's shelter on and on.... Mainly though, we never let her become the writer she was born to be, with all our demands on her time, her energy. If you'd say the word, I could take charge of them. I owe that much at least to her."

"No," I said quickly. I knew she'd written about him, and so she would have written about me, too. And suddenly I felt a pang of panic. I would take all three cartons with me.

~~~~~

TWO

Stephen met me at the airport baggage carousel. "I missed you," he said, handing me nine yellow roses. "This is for yesterday." It was nine months since we had first made love. "And this is for today." He leaned over and gave me a quick peck on the cheek. "Oh, please," I said. I never was one for kissing in public. "Whatever are you going to do when they clink their wine glasses at the wedding reception?" he said. "Aren't we a little presumptuous?" I said. "I am good at waiting," he said, "Just to get rid of me as insistent suitor, you are going to say yes sooner than you think." He went for a cart when he saw how much luggage I had. "Oh no," he said, heaving the cartons on to the cart. "I'd better get some good sturdy shelves for all your books else they'll kill us one of these nights I trip against that rickety bookshelf. So how was the trip? How's DocSiv?"

"Okay," I said, not wanting to talk about anything of that. "Tell me how much you missed me."

"That would take me half the night," he said. And it did.

~

Next evening, Stephen came in with his tool kit, having stubbed his toes on the cartons on his way out wee hours of the morning to get ready for his all-day shift. He puttered around the almost-floor-to-ceiling bookshelf in the bedroom, and said all he could do was to drive a bracket on either side and into the wall to make it safe. I said the landlord wouldn't like that and he said the landlord wouldn't ever find out because he would putty and paint it when it was time for me to leave the apartment, and may be it was time already, if we would just move in together into a bigger place. I said, No thanks, this was just fine, and he said it was miserable walking back to his digs on cold nights, and I said that was okay because who knows where he or I would be next year. He threw up his hands and shrugged in mock despair. I'll get the brackets this weekend, he said.

He said he could open the cartons and stack the books on the lowest shelf, that way the weight will keep the shelf stable, and I said they weren't books but papers, and I told him all about Maru's bequest and how I would have to start working on them. I untaped a carton and picked out a sheaf of computer paper. The sheets had not been separated, and they had been folded the wrong way, with the blank pages outside. There were actually two sheaves and I gave one to

Stephen and took the other. We flipped the pages the right way so that the typescript scrolled out in front of us. I put mine away, and sat on Stephen's lap on the sofa and we read the script he had in his hand.

Jo Paquette, I miss you
By/par Maru Sivaraman

[note to myself: I wrote this on one of my flights back after attending a National Council meeting of the ACW.]

Jo Paquette, I miss you
By/par Uma Parameswaran
[Should I use my pseudonym for everything I write? After all, the little I've published to date has been under my pseudonym, and I do like it, it sounds so right, using almost all the letters, and also a good combination of first and last names, the Importance of being Earnest, not that anyone would notice these details if I published it here in Canada. Would it make sense to publish anything in India? Must think about that. Leave out the name for now.]

Jo Paquette, I miss you

As I sit at Gate 73 waiting for my flight to be called, my mind brimmed with ideas on how to get airline passengers to appreciate Canadian writers as much as I did. I had just completed a weekend of planning for the seminars and workshops that would be held at the annual meeting of my writing organization. I thought how good it would be if the in-flight CBC News could be followed by fifteen minutes of readings from a Canadian writer's work. When W.O.Mitchell ascended the podium two years ago, there was electricity in the auditorium, and we knew we were watching and hearing an icon who had been adored from coast to coast for two generations, that an age was passing even as we looked and heard. It would be good too to see others – Margaret Atwood, with her frizzy hair, Elizabethan forehead, and laconic smile.... Or even just a voice-over of some lines with the cover of a book on the screen, for those who had passed on, like Margaret Laurence, for example, surely the CBC would have enough tapes with the voice of the matriarch of Canadian Literature; in short, not to make an expensive production of it but just to present an interlude of our Canadian literary heritage, not only the known names but the not-so-known as well.

The flight was called, and passengers obediently herded themselves single file through the doors and into the aircraft. The child in the row just in front of me was one of those super-hyper kids, but within minutes the air-hostess, no sorry she is to be called a flight attendant these days, had brought a colouring book and crayons, and the child was appeased. That is what had won my loyalty to Air Canada all these twenty plus years. Years ago, when my daughter was a child, if anyone treated her like a princess, I fell for them pronto. I had fallen for Air Canada, which always had milk and cookies and colouring books, unlike some other airlines that concentrated on serving booze to businessmen, or gave priority boarding not to passengers with crutches or children but to those who had large carry-ons. Yes, there are airlines that do that, especially when flying out of Singapore which people in India used to visit just to do their duty-free (and dutied-too) shopping. I could write a ream about one of those flights, when half the passengers were already drunk by the time the plane left the tarmac (yes, airlines served drinks on the ground to keep their passengers happy) and kept drinking, (who can resist free booze?) for the entire trip, which luckily was only an hour and a half.

Another attendant was rearranging bags in the overhead compartment for a heavy carry-on brought in by a latecomer.

The usual pre-flight announcements came on – seat in the upright position, fasten your seat belts, in-case-of-emergency instructions about oxygen masks, what meal would be served when etcetera; that passengers should refrain from using cellular phones and laptops etcetera until we reached cruising altitude etcetera. The plane took off.

I could hear the wheels being retracted. Then the itch that had been pulsing from the minute I had fastened my seat belt started in right earnest. The businessmen on either side of me itched to open their laptops; I frantically thumbed through *En Route*, the in-flight magazine, for my pastime. I knew it had been discontinued for some time now, but hope springs eternal in the human breast, and I hoped to see it once again – Air-o-gram by/par Jo Paquette. It wasn't there.

I was in a panic. Two and a half hours to go and nothing to do. Don't they know we all need our colouring books, something inane and mindless to do while the aircraft ascended through the clouds into cerulean blue? My hands itched, my forehead sweated, my mind raced to the imminent crash ahead; with nothing to do, I conjured up all the lurid details of what lay ahead – from the moment those heavy hand-baggages stowed overhead came down, to the crash, to Peter Mansbridge covering the disaster on another inflight CBC news – would they do that? really report an air disaster on an in-flight news-break? – to the long dark eternity of my own silence.

We had reached cruising altitude and my neighbours' agony was over. They whipped out their laptops and started to work. I had always felt business people only pretended they were deep in important earth-shaking decisions. Now I knew for sure. The guy to my left was transferring names and addresses from a stack of business cards on to his computer. The guy to his left was entering his business expenses; the guy across the aisle was playing a game. The guy next to him was reading the *Globe and Mail*. For some time now, the custom of giving newspapers to passengers before take-off had been discontinued on most flights. Siv said the newspapers were stacked somewhere on the way to boarding, for passengers to pick up if they so wanted, but I had never figured out just where the stack was. I looked at *En Route* again. Budget cuts seemed to have affected that too. The cover was drab, not glossy. So what if John Irving was on the cover and interviewed inside? Without Air-o-gram by/par Jo Paquette, the magazine was not worth the ink. Oh to spend an hour or more squinting up-down-diagonally to figure out where the words on the list fit into the checkered block!!! May be poor Jo was gone because of the cutbacks. Anyone who could spin out those inane blocks of words month after month was worth his/her weight in gold. And Air Canada was only making three times the profit it had made five years ago. How could they afford Jo Paquette?

Jo Paquette, please come back. Please, please.

My head was beginning to throb; the beginnings of a panic headache. I had to do something, anything. I leaned over my neighbour, and got the attention of the man with the *Globe and Mail*. Could I please have the crossword section? I begged. Please, please? He gave it to me, with a sneer. Some women, he seemed to say. I breathed again. The *Globe* crossword is not like my hometown paper's. One almost needs to think to get the answers. The sight of white and black squares helped the throbbing subside. But not enough to drive away my mourning for Air-o-gram by/par Jo Paquette.

"I would have enjoyed meeting your Aunt Maru. I didn't know she was on the national executive of ACW." Stephen said.

"She was on all kinds of committees and councils," I said, "what is ACW?"

"The Association of Canadian Writers," Stephen said. "Impressive."

"I think she was really afraid she'd die in an air crash," I said.

"Could be a spillover from the Air India tragedy, I think every Indo-Canadian has that event stamped on his psyche, his/her psyche," Stephen said. "I think the name was Jo Ouellet though. I used to fly a lot in those days, with Dad away on assignment and us staying where we were till the end of the school year and joining Dad for long weekends."

"If she says it is Jo Paquette, I'd think it IS Jo Paquette," I said, reflexively defending Maru as though I had to.

"Writers usually intentionally change names of real characters to avoid legalese, I think," he said.

"Oh sheesh, legalese," I said, "she can't use the name Air-o-gram then, I bet it is patented."

"Copyrighted," Stephen corrected me, and went on so I wouldn't fly at him for his one-up-manship, so what is the big difference between the two words anyway, "It could be that Paquette came naturally to mind because she has referred to Margaret Laurence, and Piquette was her character in *The Diviners*, remember?"

I didn't remember even though it was a novel I had read, so what if I read it because I had to, back in freshman English, the only English course I had taken and only because one had to take it to get into medicine. But I wasn't going to give myself away. Stephen was quite disgustingly familiar with all kinds of fiction and even poetry. Where does he get all that time? I barely get to keep up with my evening TV soap nowadays.

But of course, that was why I had fallen for Stephen – his knowledge of literature and the arts, which he seemed to have soaked in from his crib onwards. He is so like Uncle Siv and Dad and that generation, like, he not only reads but retains everything in his head. It is not that he has deep knowledge, rather he knows a little bit about a great many things. I used to read a lot of non-fiction once, but when I joined medschool, it was as though everything else had to be thrown out to make room in my head for textbooks.

Next day, I phoned *En Route* magazine, meaning to ask how I could find out which issue had the John Irving cover. If I knew that, I could date the piece – that is what I had to do, date each piece so I could arrange them chronologically. Instead, I asked about Jo Paquette and Air-o-gram. It took the woman at the other end of the line a while to figure out what I wanted, and when she did, she asked me to hold on for a minute while she checked it out with someone who might know. She told me the person whom she had consulted thought they had stopped including that puzzle once Jo Ouellet left them for CPAir, and that regrettably Jo Ouellet had died soon after, around 1998. She could be totally wrong about the date, she added.

After I hung up, I realized I had not asked about the John Irving issue. I jotted down notes of the telephone conversation to settle myself. Jo had died, god that was upsetting, and even though I didn't know her Air-o-gram from Adam, Maru had appreciated her and Maru was gone and Jo was gone and Michael John was gone.

I so thought he was okay. But something was wrong with his heart and he was gone. I had not got used to it yet, and I had to. I am a doctor, and I would excel in anything I took up. I had Maru's assurance on that.

Why me, why had she chosen me to be her literary executor? What did I know about writing and all that stuff? Sure I read, but mostly non-fiction, political stuff and global warming etcetera stuff, what would I know about how to get stories together? But I had to. I would excel in anything I take up. But there was something weird about the way she had everything so neatly packed up. Had she been ill? Been given a warning of what was coming?

I phoned Uncle Siv that evening. He was an early sleeper, a fact I remembered only when I heard him pick up the phone within a ring. He was already in bed.

"Listen," I said, "how come she packed it all up so neatly and wrote me that note? Do you think she knew something? Did she have any medical problems? I mean, it is spooky, that she should tape everything so neatly and label it and all." I guess I was kind of spooked, and so went on and on.

Uncle Siv said, "Cool it, Priti, she could have done all that years ago for all you know."

"She's dated her entries. December 1993, that's when she started all this. I've read only some of it, and so I don't know when she stopped writing, but it seems such a deliberate thing to do, to pack it and label it and all."

"May be you should read more before you get all upset with unnecessary speculations," he said. "Maru was ultra-organized about some things. Like some people get all hyper about shopping before a long weekend to stock the kitchen, she used to throw out any number of garbage bags stuffed with who knows what just before leaving on her summer trips."

"Oh, I don't know." I wanted to believe there was something supernatural about the way Maru died, but Uncle Siv brought me to earth.

~

I had left that carton open, with papers stacked, or so I thought, in some order. I had read at random, thinking I should figure out some system to classify all this. Should it be chronological? Themes? Genre? Chronology made sense. It almost looked like she had done some kind of sorting out herself. Except for the top layer of computer sheets with her Memoirs, everything else in that carton was handwritten or typed on single sheets and stapled, or letters or photographs, or small notebooks. Anything I had read seemed to be from the 1970s or earlier. I re-taped the other two cartons to make sure Stephen didn't get to them before I had taken a look. When Stephen started rummaging through the open carton that weekend, I didn't stop him but warned him to put things back exactly the way I had left them. 1970s was before my time, long before my problem-years. There couldn't be any telltale tellall stuff about me. While I was getting my books off the dining table so we could have dinner, Stephen waved some sheets, quite excited. "Heh," he said, "look at this! Letters from Kamala Markandaya, just imagine, Maru knew Markandaya in person!"

"How do you know her, Markandaya?" I asked, rather peeved that he should have recognized the importance of letters that I had probably seen but not seen.

"Grandad subscribed to the Book of the Month Club, and he had shelves and shelves of those neatly bound hardcovers, and *Nectar in a Sieve* was one of them and I loved it, absolutely loved it."

I too had read the novel at Maru's insistence and I remember I cried because it was so beautiful and sad but now I don't remember much except that it was about peasants – Storms of Nature, Winds of Change was how Maru called the story. But I remembered another title that would help me get one over Stephen. "Maru's favourite was *A Silence of Desire*," I said, "she said it so brilliantly articulates the inarticulateness of the middle class." I was rather pleased I remembered her words – Stephen appreciated well-turned out phrases.

"Never heard of it," Stephen said. "I read *The Coffer Dams* after *Nectar*, that was the only title I could get at the time - "But just look at this – Preetums, just look at them."

I grabbed the folder from him.

The folder was marked Letters from Friends. Yes, I had seen it while reading from the carton. I had read a couple from P. Lal, struck by his calligraphic handwriting that jumped off the page absolutely demanding to be read. Yes, I had noticed Markandaya's letters too but only because the handwriting was so opposite of Lal's, so tiny it just demanded to be passed over and I had not realized who the writer was. I was mad at myself for letting Stephen get one over me on this important discovery.

The handwritten one that Stephen held was dated 12th April, 1975, on a Wessex Hotel letterhead.

"I felt quite sad seeing you drive off into the night outside Geddes House en route for Winnipeg. It had been so pleasant having your company, I know I would have been lost (I am not the most competent person in the world as you might have noticed) if you had not been at Stirling. I would also have enjoyed myself less. You have a marvellous quiet charm that appeals to the quiet person that, in a way, I am."

I squinted to read the two pages, for the ink was already fading. Stephen passed me another letter as I was reading the second page. It was typed, dated 7th May, 1977, and it started off, "For the third time I had to see you whirl off in a cab to your destination. I was quite sad, you have a quiet, warm personality which appeals so much to me – a kind of serenity almost....The onyx book-ends you brought for me – I'm a traveller too and I appreciate with what difficulty – are exquisite. You could not have brought me anything I liked better, or that were more useful. They have a lovely calm feel to them, touching them itself is a pleasure."

I read it to the end, where she had signed off in ink – All the best, Kamala.

There were several others. Stephen read them all while the dinner got cold on the table. As I reheated the stew in the microwave, Stephen was at the computer, Googling as usual.

"Aw shucks," he said, "since there is a postcard of a waterfall in India, I thought she wrote to Maru when she was researching for *The Coffer Dams* but the dates don't tally." He held up a postcard of Jog Falls near Shimoga, and the date was 4th October 1976. In even smaller print than her usual, Markandaya had squeezed in no fewer than twenty lines on the back of the postcard, and written about how she was happy to have escaped a wannabee biographer who had written he was coming to England to tape his projected interview with her, but thankfully she was in India. "I just find it too embarrassing to talk about myself.... I feel like an oyster – the poor thing merely tried to cover up a grain of sand and found itself lumbered with a pearl."

"I think you should make a copy of them before the ink fades," Stephen said, "Really, I didn't know Maru was a quiet person, from what you've said I thought she was a lively chatty person."

Yes, it was strange that Markandaya should have said that of Maru. I always thought of her as a live wire sparking people into animated conversation. The way she laughed!! The way she would march into the house without notice, pass on some gossip or the other or drop off some Indian grocery – Ma never had time to do that kind of shopping – she was always on the go, the Maru I knew.

Stephen was mightily impressed that Maru had Kamala Markandaya as a friend. He told me what some of the letters were about. Maru had carbon copies of letters she herself had written, not all but enough to make out the back and forth conversation. There was just one letter, he said, where Markandaya sounded light-hearted, a letter that started, "Shake: you are obviously a Brahmin and so obviously am I." It went on to say she had double checked that the restaurant she had in mind for their lunch-meeting could serve vegetarian food. Was that their first meeting? Should I figure out more details than were in the letters?

Apparently, Stephen went on to say, Maru had wanted to write a critical biography of her and she had refused to give an interview. Then Maru found out that some other wannabee biographer had said he had a contract with TWAYNE for a biography and wanted details about her personal life. At which Maru had written that Kamala with her usual courtesy just might agree to meet him and if so she, Maru, would feel like "dancing on her remains with hobnailed boots," and if the volume were published "may it be such that you daily regret saying no to me and then being talked into it by someone else."

Stephen and I argued, on different sides as usual, about letters, to whom did they belong? To the writer or to the receiver? Are they private, should they be placed in the public domain? The legality of it, the ethics of it.

The Maru-Markandaya connection impressed Stephen, and the Wodehouse reference too, I could tell, for he was now really keen to join me in my job of sorting through the cartons. Next day, I was at work all day but Stephen got off early and dinner was on the table when I came back. He seemed quite excited about the number of writers Maru seemed to have known. There were several letters from June Callwood, one of Canada's pioneer activists and ground breaking journalists, he added. Stephen is a gem the way he preempts silly questions from me, as to who and what people or events are, by explaining it without making me feel an ignoramus. Apparently Maru wrote for some photo-book about Canada's multiculturalism. He read aloud from a couple of letters, one dated Nov. 24, 1998 where she said, "Your story is very powerful and I am touched that you shared it with me. That final comment about men losing their survival skills when they are transplanted will haunt me." And another from one dated May 11, 1997: "Your contribution caused that melting feeling in me that readers get when a writer pulls it off. Thank you … for the line, 'Our rainbow smiles arcing from sea to sea' …. The photographers are about to fan out across the country and I'll give that line to them as a mantra." Stephen added his own comment about how the sentence would mean something else now since rainbows had been taken over as banner by gays.

As we chomped on our nut-filled dessert, he asked me if I knew anything about one of Maru's friends, Attia. "Give me a hint," I said, "in Winnipeg? Could be one of the women at the Immigrant Women's Association."

"Oh no, someone she met in England, whose address she got from Markandaya, so I am wondering if it was the Attia Hosain that Google mentions. If so," Stephen whistled. "I wish I could have met Maru," he said, "I don't know why you just won't let me meet your family. You are so mean, what are you afraid of? really. They've got to meet me some time dammit, I ain't going anywhere and we are going to be together forever as you damn well know." He was getting steamed up as usual about the topic. I calmed him down. "Lover boy, I am afraid that if they meet you, they'll nag me into getting married." That cooled him and he quietly helped himself to more dessert.

I remembered the name. Attia Hosain, a wonderful writer of that wonderful Partition novel about a Muslim family, another book Maru had forced on me, but I couldn't remember the title. I said, "She wrote a novel that tells us about Muslim India as beautifully as *Nectar* is about peasant India, the title is a famous line from some famous poem, but I can't remember."

Then he got excited again. "That is what I thought. She is the same – *Sunlight on a Broken Column*. Went to England early in 1947 and lived there till her death in 1998. Maru met her, did you know that? It couldn't be any Attia other than Attia Hosain right?" He took a sheet he had left on a chair and held it out to me.

The Day I met Attia.

I had the honour and pleasure of spending an evening with Attia in the early 1980s. I want to place this on record now, after some soul searching on the ethics of whether I should or should not. Should I share with the world, where many are often unthinking, insensitive, with their own axe to grind? I decided I would because I have a little detail that says something about this author and a lot about what is valuable in life, and perhaps it will inspire others. But could it instead just make one cynical on the workings of destiny?

It was on one of my visits to London. I had spent an afternoon with Kamala Markandaya who cordially agreed to meet with me any time I was in London (I first met her at a conference in Stirling, Scotland in the 1970s.) Kamala gave me Attia's phone number. I phoned her and she graciously invited me to her flat the next day.

The most memorable point of this memorable meeting consisted of a question from me and her answer to it. She told me of her life, of how she had come to England with her diplomat-husband, and how her husband had taken up with the Muslim League, and how when on partition Indian diplomats had to choose between serving India or Pakistan, he had opted for Pakistan. She had argued against it. Lucknow was home, and Lucknow was in India. How could one turn one's back on one's home? He went to Pakistan, and she would not. She stayed on in London. She earned her living working part time for the B.B.C. and with the school system. Her son and daughter stayed with her in England. Life was not easy, but she managed.

I thought it was ironic that she had not only exiled herself from the homeland she loved but had broken up her marital life for a principle, perhaps an ephemeral principle of where was home. Was it worth doing that? I asked. She said, "When we are young, we are so idealistic, we think we know exactly what is right, what needs to be done."

There was yet another irony. I record it separately because it came later in the conversation. But I record it because it seems very connected to me. Her husband, disillusioned with General Ayub Khan's Pakistan, left the Pakistani diplomatic service and returned to India, starting a horse-farm near Bangalore.

Stephen was very moved by the story. "What's the big deal?" I said, "they went their different ways, and that is that."

He said, "You have to set it in context. We are talking about the 1940s, people didn't split up even here in those days, especially if there were children. She must have felt really strongly about her ideals, but I don't know why she stayed on in England instead of going back home. Life in Britain is much tougher than here even now, and must have been really hard then, all that post-war trauma and destitution. I must find out about her books. Hope the Library has them."

So like Stephen, always reading books, where does he have the time, me I haven't watched even my evening soaps the way work is killing me, and endless exams. Now, why was this sheet in the 1970s box when it was clearly written in the 80s or later? It is in the Friends folder, that's why – so would it make sense after all to sort out all this stuff thematically instead of chronologically?

Stapled to it is a comment on *Sunlight*, actually on novels of that kind I guess:

The novels that delineate those times have priceless archival value. *Sunlight, The Princes, Some Inner Fury, Remember the House, Labyrinth* … give us not only a visual archival picture but a deeper experience of an age that is irrevocably irretrievably past. Somewhat sentimentalized and romanticized no doubt but until another Naipaul comes along to paint a palimpsest over it to make it another *Area of Darkness,* the old dispensation, the century between 1845 and 1945 will be the repository and expression of a collective need and desire for an idealized culture that evokes more than mere nostalgia.

This is followed by a page of notes that starts off:

Re-reading Attia H. one realizes that Rushdie is not fabricating but merely exaggerating.

And then she has page references from *Sunlight* and *Shame* to prove her point.

~~~~~

THREE

In the 1970s box, I came across a heading that of course drew my attention – The Hijrahs. I knew who they were but was surprised that Maru would write about them. This piece had Maru's first Winnipeg address on the top - 892 Grosvenor Avenue - so it must have been written soon after she came I guess. Why was the address on top, like it was a letter? And why does she misspell even her pseudonym to Uta instead of Uma? Trying out different pseudonyms?

The Hijrahs
I was in Delhi that summer, with my sister (this has been scratched out and replaced with "sister-in-law") Divya who had just had her first baby. We were in her bedroom, the coolest room in the house. Divya was changing the baby's diaper. Munni, a bright-eyed teenager who did the washing for the tenants in the block, was talking cheerfully about the woman in the upstairs apartment, "She lets the cradle stay messy till I come, and you know I can't be there all the time, all yellow and messy, just imagine, and her third baby too! Not as though it is her first." I was amused. Munni's standard of personal cleanliness was minimal – her hair was dry and matted, her clothes had a stale odour of sweat – but her distaste and concern about the other woman's messiness was genuine. "Imagine," she said, and her hands and expressive eyes described it even more vividly than her words. Just then we heard the front gate being opened and voices saying in an oddly accented Hindi, "Greetings, greetings and congratulations."

Munni picked up the diaper pail and said matter-of-factly, "It is the Hijrahs, how quickly news of a new-born spreads." Divya was beyond speech. She collected her baby into her arms and clung to him. "God, god! tell them to go away,"

"It is only the hijrahs," Munni said, "and you know they'd rather abduct the baby than go away empty-handed." That placid statement sent Divya into near-hysterics. This educated modern young woman was transformed into a shaking mass of terror. The voices outside continued singing their chant, "Greetings, we bring greetings and congratulations."

"Send them away, please send them away," Divya pushed me out of the room and shut the door, securing the safety chain. I stepped out to the front veranda.

The leader was a tall well-built woman with large hands and feet. She wore a bright yellow printed gharara-kameez. She had an odd assortment of costume jewellery on her and held a tambourine in her left hand, which she jingled gently. "We have come to greet the newborn and congratulate the happy mother," she said. Her voice was unnaturally bass. One of the others had a small face, chiselled features and a pearly set of teeth. I looked at her beautiful face and suddenly realized it was clean shaven. I started trembling.

The leader jingled her tambourine and the others, there were five of them, cleared their throats. "Now they will sing," Munni said, squatting on the floor. Divya opened the door with the safety chain still secured, and said, "Please, please."

"Okay," I said, "what do you want?"

They spoke one after another.

"We come to greet the newborn."

"The first born, a son, thrice happy the occasion."

"We will sing for you."

"We will dance for him."

"And see if, may be, he is one of our own."

"And then accept your gifts of clothes and money, as is the custom."

"We did not invite you," I said.

"It is our custom to come to you, we need no invitation."

"We are from the south," I said, "and we have no such custom."

"But you have chosen to live here," she said, "it is the custom here."

"That is true," Munni said, greatly to my chagrin. "it is the custom here."

"Whenever a child is born, we come to you, and we never go away empty-handed. At marriages, we dance in front of the bridegroom's carriage, at funerals we walk behind and weep."

"So you will come everyday and pester us for money?" I said.

The others were getting restless, but the leader continued to be patient.

"We come only once. Neither we nor any other of our groups will come again. We have our code and our territory."

"You want me to believe that?"

"A hijrah never breaks code."

The others started moving forward towards Divya's bedroom window.

"Why do you grudge us a sari? You who have everything."

Divya screamed.

"Just a sari and twenty three rupees," the leader said implacably.

"If you bargain, they might settle for eleven," Munni said.

"A sari and twenty three rupees, that's not much for a first child, and a son."

The clean shaven one came forward. "We can never have a child," she said, pointing to her belly.

The baby started crying. A moment later, the cries stopped.

Another, not so clean shaven, said, "Nor can we silence a baby's cries with our breasts, we have none."

"Nor breasts nor babies," the fourth one said, smoothfaced and young. "Don't you believe it? We can show you."

"We don't want your congratulations," I said.

"Do you want our curses then?" the leader said, her voice suddenly soft, sibilant.

She tapped her fingers on the tambourine. The others clapped their hands and started swaying.

"Now they'll take off their clothes," Munni said, at last excited, "that is the biggest insult they can offer. That pretty one has falsies. You will see."

The dupatta was dropped to the ground by the leader and her long flat figure loomed in the doorway. Then her hands went to the buttons of her shirt. The three who wore saris fumbled at their waist cloth. Another ran her hands over her shoulder length hair and twisted her body in a dance movement. The leader moved towards the window.

I was hypnotized by the sweep of the yellow skirt. I thought the hijrahs would shed their saris and rip open their blouses. I thought they would rush into the house. I have never felt so paralysed.

Suddenly the music ceased, the song faded, the veil went back on the flat bosom, the swaying stopped. The leader walked to where three ten-rupee bills and a blue silk sari floated to the ground from the bedroom window. The party left, shutting the gate noiselessly behind them.

~

I left the sheets on the table, and wondered what Stephen would have to say about it. He had only one comment. Why didn't they check the baby? he asked, "isn't that why they come? To see if the new baby is one of them? I've heard they can recognize these birth defects and so offer to take the baby away."

"How do you know so much about it," I said, exasperated at his knowledge of everything. He patiently replied, "Do you remember there was a story a few years ago from your Winnipeg about a boy, David Reimer I think his name was, who was made to live as a girl by a Baltimore psychologist (the way he experimented with these poor twins, he should have been shot dead if you ask me) and at that time I got myself to read up on all this. By the way, I am off to see my parents this weekend. Guess we'll have to miss Bob's party night."

~

It has been a hectic day at work. Lot of speaking through the teeth and exasperated shaking of heads. Everyone seemed mad at everyone else even though everyone worked with utmost decorum and stopped short of biting each other's head off. I took my lunch break at two o'clock, and brought out my sandwich and apple juice. I had also stuffed some of Maru's sheets into my bag that morning; riffling through the sheafs, I came across the first line of an opening page which was titled "Prologue" and mentioned Fall 1993. It seemed the same as the other one I had read in Winnipeg, but only the first paragraph was the same. It absolutely demanded to be read. I carefully took a small bite of my sandwich because I have a tendency to eat fast and I really needed something to chew on whenever I read. I was glad I had brought a bag of chips and some Smarties, one at a time would go a long way. Sheesh, these juice cartons hardly hold a mouthful.

Prologue

Yes, I'm starting on my memoirs.

Why, you ask, why at all, why now? What's so special about the late Fall of 1993? With the election around the corner, who has the time or interest in your memoirs? you ask... unless, ah unless ... have you had a steamy affair with Kim Campbell or Jean Chretien or both? or at least, have you been beaten black and blue by your mommy dearest? or maybe you are a now-penitent or still-tightlipped nun or priest who taught in a residential school in the sixties ...

No to all, but wait, I am a Canadian eh? and this is the twentieth century still - and so the reason is much diviner than the sordid rationales you proffer. By reliving my life, I am delving into the ethos of my people, the diaspora flung far and wide on the Sargasso Sea, and also purging myself of some deep dark secrets that have been eating up my soul. How do you expect me to tell you right now what those secrets are? I don't know about them any more than you do. They'll no doubt surface as I tell my tale; at some point I'll go into a primal scream and voila, I shall be cleansed and made whole.

So let us begin. Om Ganesaya Namaha. What would that be? you ask. Titles, mottoes, first lines, they are always important. Om Ganesaya Namaha; it is a traditional invocation to the god of wisdom, but you are sure there's got to be more since you've been steeped in LitCrit reading strategies. Never take anything at face value. Like Ganesa was my father's name ah ha, the old Oedipal complex bit, aching and yearning for father's approval etc. etc. Always consider all the different takes there could be without getting fixated on something. So what else? Ganesa is the god with an elephant's head, elephant, six blind men, vegetarian, South Asian habitat, ivory, right on, the trunk of course, proboscis, everything hangs together, you say. Look at any text with a Freudian lens, and voila.

Oh yes, we are conscientious immigrant Canadians eh? All of us are immigrants here, so says Margaret Atwood, none other, and I know my French, excuse moi, there used to be an old idiom about pardoning one's French, may be there's something there waiting to surface. But the beginning of my story is quite simple,

really. It starts in the mid-sixties, just before the maple leaf and
our true North strong and free.

******

I O Canada Here We Come

Okay, I know I said my story starts in the mid-sixties, but if
you think I'm about to give you a chronological record the way
people on CBC do, think again. We first go to the mid-seventies
in order to reach the late sixties. Why, you ask? Maybe because
that is the page at which the book fell open, like the Sikhs have a
custom of naming an infant according to the first syllable on the
page of the *Granth Sahib* that is randomly opened. Let me tell you
right now that I am in the habit of keeping a notebook or diary,
or a journal as it is called nowadays. Like gymnasts warming up
with routine stretches and jumps, I'll get my narrative muscles
going by dipping into old familiar stuff first.   Loosens up
memory chords, limbers up the thesaurus stashed away in the
attic for years.

In those early days, I used to write every day and the stacks
grew under my bed, loaded in envelope cartons, which were the
only size that could be stashed under the bed. Back in India, one
could and did stash large suitcases and steel trunks under the
cots, which is what we did in the school and college dormitories.
Here it would make sense to store it in regular sized cartons in
the basement, you say, but there's something about under the
bed that is appealing. Who would bother to look under the bed,
right? Not even the cleaning lady I used to have when the boys
were at home.   Closets are the place for skeletons, not the
underside of the bed.

Yes, I plan to use some of those old journal entries and
letters in this magnum opus. Should I revise them? I spent long
hours thinking about this; you can rest assured I am
conscientious about this project. Then I decided, no I wouldn't
do much rewriting; one can see the changes in me and my jargon
as I evolved over the years. Take "girls" for instance. I used to
call the other secretaries girls, but I wouldn't now. Not just
because I am not a secretary any more, but because I have gone

through a feminist awakening etc. Every female is a woman; the other day I told someone at work how I'd promised to take my neighbour's teenager out shopping for panty-hose because she was in a new job where the girls wore skirts and pantyhose, and this person said, "Why do you call them girls and not young women?" Gives one a bit of jolt, you know, when one is caught falling from grace. It happens once in a while, when I forget to adjust to the company; perhaps because I play badminton and tennis with women who still say "girls" and "cleaning ladies."

So maybe I should toss between my sports friends and feminist friends and decide whether to revise my wording when using old journals, but hey, let us use some common sense here; it would be a pretty dumb thing to do, to write about the early seventies in my 1990s voice. So here's a journal entry from those early days.

~

I lost my handbag today. It was there at 10:20 when I came back after coffee break because I distinctly remember placing it on the table, fully intending to put it in its usual place in the drawer under the typewriter, but the phone was ringing when I'd come in and you know how it is if you don't give the phone top priority. If secretaries aren't at their desks pronto at 10.20 after the coffee break, you may be sure someone or other of the million people to whom we are accountable would bitch about it. So I'd answered the phone and probably had left my handbag on the table all morning. It was gone at noon, when I set out for my lunch break. I expected it to turn up by the time I got back from lunch. After all, I work at a university, and surely I would get it back, perhaps minus the cash but that was okay. I found enough change for coffee, took my sandwich bag and headed for the cafeteria. When I told the girls about the handbag that had disappeared, they sent me right back before I could take so much as a bite of my sandwich. Cancel your credit cards, they said, what with Christmas around the corner, the thief will freeload to the credit line before you have time to put on your lipstick. That would be a long while since I don't have any lipstick to put on, it having gone with the bag, I wanted to say, but I'd learnt long ago that word-play didn't get across if it came from me. Everyone around me knew that I had to correct as many spelling and syntax errors as any of them in the handwritten scrawls that came to our typing desks, and that I knew the ins and outs of my second language more thoroughly than they who had only been born with it, but simply because I looked and dressed a little differently, they assumed I didn't know their idiom, and my word jokes had fallen flat so often that I had quit indulging in them. They meant well, though, and were now genuinely concerned about me. So I was packed off to report my loss pronto to the credit card places.

Back at my office desk, since it was still lunch hour, I locked the door to keep out the endless stream of students who wanted to hand in their papers or pick them up; I love them, these kids with their smiles and worries and snarky asides, but this was my lunch hour and I needed some respite from "Maru, could I use your stapler please?" or "Maru, I had an appointment with Prof. X and he doesn't seem to be here." I duly notified Eaton's and Sears. Then I dialled the first number for credit-card-loss reporting, and answered the usual questions about my name and address and what have you. And then came a question that knocked me cold. What was my mother's maiden name? On no, I groaned, oh no, do you really need all that? The voice was still polite, but with an icy edge: would I please try? It was necessary for identification. I'll call you back, I said, and hung up. She probably thought I was an amateur con artist. Thank god, those telephones that register the source number are only in science fiction as of now.

I knew my mother's name, of course, but I was keeping a step ahead of my inquisitor and knew she'd ask me for her date of birth and that I did not know. I should know it as well as I know the back of my hand that moves above the keyboards in front of me six hours a day. But I don't. And that's because I spent two months searching for it and found it too and have used it time and again, as when getting this credit card. It doesn't make sense, you might say, but that's what is called a mental block. Before I moved to the English department, I was with Psychology.

Yes, I spent two months tracking down my mother's date of birth so I could come to Canada.

~

"Winnipeg ? Where is Winnipeg ?"

"Ridiculous ! We are not so poorly off that you have to go to the back of beyond in search of a livelihood."

"If at all you have to go to the barbaric west why don't you choose some place that is on the map ?"

So said my aunt, great-aunt and uncle when they first heard that Sivaram and I were planning to come to Winnipeg.

The whole family, all who lived in Madras that is, were at my uncle's celebrating the first birthday of his first grandchild. My uncle made the announcement about my trip with pontifical solemnity soon after lunch, one of those heavy six course lunches that makes one want to sleep away the rest of the day; he loves to be sensational and has the tone and bearing of a tragic actor, which is probably the reason he could make his million as a lawyer. The immediate family reaction immensely gratified his theatrical sense. Everyone was roused, some to sympathy, some to disgust, most to wonder.   Where on earth, literally, was Winnipeg ?

"The wheat granary of the world," a niece shrieked breathlessly, eager to beat everyone to the answer.

Her younger brother, not to be outdone, recited in a sing-song classroom-voice, "The Canadian National Railway runs right across Canada from Halifax..."

A younger niece disappointedly said, "Oh, I thought Winnie was a Pooh not a pig."

My sister, her baby in her lap, softly crooned, "The innocuous land of the lost and the damned..."

"If all the bright young people leave the country that has educated them and brought them to manhood" an older uncle started to say but another uncle cut him short with an oratorical, "Let them go, let all self-respecting people go, let everyone who can get away from this regime of blackguards leave before he himself becomes one." Whereupon the men turned to discuss the state of the Republic and whether, how and why the country was going to the dogs.

The general reaction among the women was touching at first but became quite exasperating soon after. They surrounded my mother to condole with her. That we would get an immigrant-visa status if we went to Canada connoted some dire and irrevocable finality to them. We were as good as lost to the family. We would never return. Moreover we would throw our heritage to the winds, take to meat-eating and liquor-drinking and other habits they said they dreaded to mention but went on just the same to describe in graphic detail. Yes, it was a sad thing to have one's daughter go away and never return (they had no doubt at all on that point) but live all her life in some god-forsaken land if ever she reached it, that is; only the other day a jetliner had crashed into the Alps with our best atomic scientist on board, had it not? and a few months earlier another had killed three of our best generals, do you remember ? And if she survived the journey there were all those terrible highway accidents one heard about; and even if she never ventured out on the highway there were all those electrical gadgets right at home any of which could electrocute her to death without a moment's warning. Ah me, ah me, it was a sad thing to be sure. And who knows what will happen there? Do you remember how so-and so went to Burma in the thirties and never returned, poisoned on the plantation he was by some disgruntled labourer. Which reminds me of whatshisname who deserted his wife in Singapore and lived in open sin with.... The raconteuring became more lurid as with many headshakes and sighs of foreboding and macabre enjoyment the neighbours joined my aunts and older cousins in 'condoling' with my mother.

My younger cousins, city-bred and of affluent parents as they were, belonged to a type of teenagers that runs wild in Madras today; somewhat behind their North American contemporaries, but not, I am sorry to say, very far behind. (They were avid James Bond-Monkees fans when I left.) These cousins were riled that I should be leaving for Canada. It was galling enough that dithering politicians and doddering administrators should be sent on free tours round the world - as disgusting a waste as gifting a confectionery store to a diabetic. But that I, a nincompoop with no talent and less go, should be flying by Super DC 10 (that leaves the sound behind) to fantabulous Canada, darn, how blind can Dame Fortune get?

One of them stuck his thumbs in the pockets of his drainpipe-cut trousers and said out of the corner of his mouth, "Fellows out there must be darned ignorant indeed if they are willing to be taught by you." Those were the days when I'd hoped to be a university teacher and didn't know my degrees wouldn't be recognized. Another cousin, on hearing how much Sivaram's salary would be, said, "I warn you, they are going to pitch a set of retarded kids on you. Guys who teach kids ninepence to the shilling are always paid more, you know." He looked at me pityingly but I knew his vitals were churning with envy. And so, as soon as we bought our first car, with sisterly thoughtfulness I sent him a colour photograph of our sky blue, power-equipped, eight cylinder, bucket-seat... oh well this is not a commercial.

~

We in India are not obsessed with the idea of Time the Tyrant. We are not over-particular about punctuality though most of us do get corrupted somewhat on coming to the west. Incidents are always correlated to other incidents and are seldom remembered by their calendar dates. No wonder then that my aunts and great-aunts were exasperated by my questions when I was engaged in filling out the application form for my visa to Canada.

How ignorant of whoever-it-was-to-whom-we-were-applying to ask if and when I had had measles, diphtheria, whooping cough and chicken pox! Of course every child goes through these fevers, and always in childhood, didn't they know these simple facts? And how dared they ask if there was insanity or venereal diseases in the family, what a personal affront! What a blot on the family escutcheon! how dared they insinuate such things...

I confess that even I, accustomed to the data-loving ways of the western world, was made impatient when it came to writing down when and where (date, month, year, town, province, country) my father and mother were born. No one seemed to know the date of my mother's birth though most knew her birthstar birthday. Some were very sure it was the end of January and others adamant that it was February. Her horoscope, duly charted when she was born, had been lost along the way. I thought of leaving the column blank but I feared that a machine somewhere would return the application as incomplete. I thought of concocting a birthdate for my mother but frightening visions of being charged with unlawful entry into the country and of being deported rose in front of me and I hastened to find out the date.

In India births and marriages and deaths are not so promptly and systematically recorded as here. I was quite flabbergasted at being given an assignment in an English class the other day concerning the dates of Milton's birth and death. Yes, I am a student, at the other university; I thought taking a few graduate courses would admit me back into the profession for which I had trained in India. Not only does it seem immaterial as to whether he died on the eighth of November or the ninth but it seemed an impossibility that one can ever find out the day of death of someone who lived three centuries ago. That Church Registers have these records was quite beyond my imagination until I was told about it by a friendly fellow-student. Nothing of the kind is found in our temples. Even the names of the sculptors of the exquisite statues that fill our temples are nowhere to be found except sometimes as little squiggles that make no sense to anyone; so self-effacing is the outlook.

My parents could not help me. My father volunteered to tell me the date of their wedding. My mother smiled her beatific smile and went off to some household chore. I turned to my aunts and great-aunts. They were willing to testify that my mother had been born, oh yes, they were sure of that. What did it matter whether it was in January, or February ? It was by such hair-splitting distinctions that the younger generation was losing its sense of values, always looking at the clock, becoming slaves to Time for all the wrong things instead of thinking of different phases of one's life.

I wrote to the Municipal Office nearest my grandfather's village. After many frantic reminders to different offices (because the village had been transferred from one area of jurisdiction to another several times in the last forty years) I got an answer. On deciphering the handwritten letter on the brown paper that smaller offices use, it read that my grandmother "had been delivered of a male child on September 4, 1917." Since my mother had been born a female child, I handed the letter over to my uncle in case any of his sons should ever need it.

Another week passed. I took courage. I knew that a prisoner is deemed innocent until proven guilty, and I felt that if I could not find the record, Canadian Immigration would not either. I thought that the thirty first of January, almost February, was a suitable date of birth for my mother. This date I would have entered on the form, but Sivaram is meticulous and uncomfortably honest.

"Try," he said, "keep trying".

After several more days of rambling reminiscences my aunts directed me to the eldest of their aunts who had been present at the birth. She lives in a village sixty miles from Madras, and there I went one Saturday morning. She was pathetically delighted that I should have come to take her blessings (she could think of no other reason) before leaving for distant lands. She was sure I would spend a week with her. I could not bluntly ask my question and so I had to stay with her that night. Next morning I led up to the subject, rather tactfully I thought, but not tactfully enough as I found very shortly. My mother was about forty five now and that was all one need know. It was not by years that a woman's life is measured but by her achievements - how many children she had borne, how well she brought them up, how successfully she had married off her daughters and how much dowry she had taken for her sons. Only till a woman is married are her date of birth and horoscope important. And since it was more than twenty five years that my mother, by the grace of the gods, had been wife and parent, what need to be so fastidious about when she was born ? It was because of being obsessed with hair-splitting distinctions that the younger generation was losing its sense of values. To get up with the sun, to work till sundown, that was the Brahmin's life as ordained by the Law-Giver, whereas these younger folk..."

Just about this time the boy next door came in to share the morning's adventure with my nephew. His great-grandfather had woken up in the middle of the night, seen that the sky was bright, had gone to the riverside for his ablutions and prayers as was his custom and had woken the others on his return - at half past three in the morning.

It took another hour to steer the conversation back to dates of birth. Then my great-aunt with amazing felicity drew out wads of mental notes and pictures from her ninety years of memories and tracked down the day, date, and hour of the birth of my mother. Each of the landmarks she used had a secondary and tertiary anecdote but however circumlocutious, her reminiscences led surely towards the goal.

That was the year after the plague and the plague came three monsoons after the granary caught fire, that summer two years before the drought...it was the tenth month of the Tamil year because the harvest had just come in and they had celebrated the new-grain festival in style because it had been a bumper crop. Yes, it was about two weeks after the festival that so and so's baby had fallen into the well and been rescued by whatshisname by the good Lord's grace, and it was a day or two later that the baby was born, the night grandfather flew into a temper because the food had been too hot and had burnt his tongue and he had gone away fuming and had not been there to call the midwife and old Chellamma's husband next door had to hobble all the way to the other side of the village on that dark night for it was just a day or two before the new moon, but the birth was an easy one, praise be to our household goddess. I thought of verifying the accuracy of the old lady's memory by asking her to trace my uncle's date of birth (the one born on September 4, 1917) but I had only four hours to spare before my train's scheduled departure and so I refrained.

By coordinating my mother's birth star with the tenth month etcetera our family priest arrived at Tuesday the twenty eighth of January as the correct date.

~

II   More Trains

Canadian psyche, as we know, is all tied up with the railways. The last spike, the whistle of an engine, pioneer songs and covered wagons of tough men and women building the railroad from the east coast to the prairies etc. We now know that things got rather messy once the railroad started moving west of Manitoba, with workers from China etc., but in the sixties, when I first arrived in this our home and our children's native land, we didn't know much about the Yellow Peril and the Brown Plague, about how our fellow Asians had been mistreated by those who happened to have come earlier. Wilfrid Laurier and Mackenzie King were still heroes since their part in the Komagatamaru incident and aboriginal exploitation was little known. No, back then, the sound of an engine whistle and the sight of the train chugging across the country had a romantic aura that encapsulated the best of everything Canadian.

Having been a regular train traveller since two or three months before my birth (yes, I must tell you at some point about the reasons why our women went to their parents' house for birthing their children) and having been an obsessive journal writer, my first train journey in Canada was certainly something buried somewhere in my cartons of notes and journals, I thought. No memoirs can be complete without it, I said to myself. The other day, when I realized it was to date my last train journey as well, I nostalgically hunted for those journals and here is what I found. Not much. Had I known my first train journey in Canada would also be my last, I would surely have written more. I wish I could paste up the entries into my computer page; it is so interesting to see how my handwriting has changed: neat rounded letters getting more and more angular and impatient with the years until now it is such a scrawl as would make poor Sister Mary Angeline, my Third Standard teacher, weep with frustration.

~

For some reason known only to our travel agent and God we did the last lap of our Madras-Winnipeg journey by train. We arrived at the station just fifteen minutes before the train was to leave, yet the place was quite empty; so like a catacomb even without comparing it to India where the station becomes a bubbling cauldron of activity an hour before a train comes in. A man in a blue uniform and badges on his sleeve and cap directed us to a door. I peeked down and saw steps leading to the netherworld. I touched Sivaram's sleeve. In a new place one can never be too careful, and uniform and badge notwithstanding, a stranger is a stranger. But Sivaram went through the door and Alcestis-like I followed him.

The platform (you call it a track here) had only thirty odd persons and a funereal gloom. There were no porters carrying pyramids of steel trunks on their heads, no vendors selling cigarette-matches, no jostling passengers, no sound, nothing. I stared back at the door expecting it to spout a stream of passengers. The train sneaked up on us just then. I swivelled round, instantly on guard. Everything here was highly suspect. In India trains don't sneak in silently; blowing balloons of black smoke they roar in to the clanging of bells and the shouting of a surging mass of passengers, seers-off, receivers, vendors, porters.

"Next car, please," a conductor said.

"What car?" I said.

"Compartment," Sivaram explained, helping me into the carriage.

"Might as well call it an airplane," I said, looking at the rows and rows of cushioned seats and inhaling the musty-pungent air with its whorls of cigarette-smoke, body odour and air freshener.

Minutes later the train slithered out of the station and sprinted up into the sunshine. I relaxed. It was a September morning, the sun was shining and all was sure to be right with the world.

"It is not like home though," I said nostalgically.

"True. Much more comfortable," my husband said, opening a newspaper. "Fine landscape too. Might turn out to be a ride on the Deccan Queen." He was thinking of the Bombay-Poona train. That route is famous for its landscape, an aesthetic experience in itself, tourists are told, exquisite scenery, tall slender palms set against a wool-cloud sky, sleepy hamlets, rounded hilltops, exciting tunnels, breathtaking ravines on either side of the train that zooms along on air etc. etc. and tourists agree, tourists travelling in the air-conditioned aristocracy of a first class compartment. "You idle rich," I muttered to the back of my husband's head, "ask me, a third class commuter all the days of my student life."

In India we used to call a spade a spade. We categorised almost everything into three classes. We didn't have under-achievers; we called them third class students. We don't have low-income brackets; we have 'Government Service, Class III.' So also in the railways. We had a first class: some coupes, but mostly four-berthers with cushioned berths and footstools and mirrors and ceiling fans and car-service; we had a second class with harder cushions and narrower berths; and we had a third class which was about the same size as the first but seated ten times as many persons and had benches running perpendicular to an aisle that ran parallel to the side of the train. And on these wooden benches I travelled an average of four thousand miles a year for six years when I was in college. I have never been on a horse but I am sure I can take even the first few days of bareback riding without a whimper.

Yet it was with nostalgia that I recalled my first Bombay-Poona journey as this train silently sped into the setting Canadian sun.

The summer I was twelve, my aunt, Chikkamma we used to call her though I am sure she had a real name, wanted to visit some old friends she had gone to school with and she took me along to Bombay and Poona to carry her suitcases and water jug. She was a school principal and so was used to having a girl or two to do such chores every day at school. I had always found her intriguing, a feisty lady with a history that we as children were never told, and I loved her big Chevrolet - one of those huge hump-backed ones the last of which disappeared sometime in the sixties after being on the road as taxis during the fifties. So when she came to our home one day - she always came with the speed of lightning - and told my mother she wanted one of her daughters for a couple of weeks, I raised my hand; she had a way of making me feel I was in class and so I raised my hand and was duly packed off with her.

The Deccan Queen, the gold letters shone emblazoned on the black face of the engine. It had such a ring to it! The Deccan Queen. Inside the compartment, a sign read, 'To seat 40.' Now, in an inter-city bus that seats forty the doors are closed when the number reaches around sixty, but not so in a train that is considered to be an expanding sponge, and by Jove it is ! When the train started we were stacked in several layers - rows of adults with rows of children squeezed in between and an assortment of infants and handbags on our laps. There is a technique for third class travel as there is for everything else. In India railway platforms are always overground and the windows are always open. As soon as the train slows down, and there are stations every thirty minutes if you take a passenger train and not an express, those inside quickly pull down the window shutters and hang close to the doors so no can come in. But at Kalyan, the only stop for the Deccan Queen, we were a little slow with our window. A strong arm held the shutter up, another threw a child in, and in a matter of seconds three women had oozed in with two steel trunks   (and each trunk had four sharp corners), a hold-all, two shoulder-bags, four kids and an earful of advice from the man who was seeing them off. We bounced the hold-all and bags off our laps and had it thrown right back; there was quite a battle royal, and help me if the two schoolgirls and I who had led the fray did not end up with a child each on our laps ! If you want to reinforce your faith in the essential goodness of the human heart just take a trip in a third class compartment.

As for the exciting tunnels, the girls cooied out of the window once and it acted as a signal for everyone of the thirty odd infants in the carriage to set music to a witch dance.

And if I sandwiched my head between the big behind of a woman and the bony shoulder of a boy, both of whom were standing, I could see a patch of the window frame. Once when the behind bounced off balance for a second, I saw the outside world; a big black crow flew in and out of my sight and the sky was blue!

Okay, there wasn't much about Canada in that piece you may say, and I'd be the first to agree. But absence is as significant as presence, silence as articulate as speech as we know who have gone through politicians' trapeze acts in the MeechLake, Oka and Free Trade circuses.

I haven't lived all these years doing all the different things I have done without making analyses and conclusions about Canadian attitudes and immigrant experiences. For the first little while, the immigrant's heart and mind are habituated to looking back at where one comes from. The landscape of spruce and maple don't mean a diddly for the first little while anyway to one who grew up in the shade of the neem and mango.

You don't like my philosophizing. You are waiting to hear more about my life under the Maple Leaf. It was quite a shock, my first sight of downtown Winnipeg. I came here before we got our flag, as I told you already.

III Arriving in Winnipeg

We arrived in Winnipeg one September day, the man I had recently married, and I a blushing bride with the wedding henna scarcely faded on my palms and feet. Note how I am trying to set up a romantic aura, two young people starting a new life in a new land and all that. A shrink would read a lot in that. But don't go for shrinks; just get the aura right - a young bride in a young country etc. The other day, I was on television, and the interviewer wanted old photographs taken just before or after we arrived, and they appeared along with me as I am now, on prime time CBC no less, and twenty nine of the thirty friends who told me they'd seen the show said, O you looked gorgeous when you were young, or words to that effect, and most of them usually followed up on this left-handed compliment with a salve to take the edge off the faux pas, and I'll quote the one I liked best, "Oh didn't we all?" This was in the locker room after our Saturday swim-before-lunch and you can imagine how apt that statement was in light of our various stages of undress that displayed what we were now. The thirtieth was Sivaram and he asked me how and why I gave the interviewer photographs of him without so much as a may I. But that's another story.

So there we were in Winnipeg that September morning, met by a colleague-to-be at the railway station, and duly deposited at a downtown hotel, called Gordon Downtowner Motor Hotel. Next morning, Sivaram and I took a walk down Portage Avenue, and bless me if the first thing I saw wasn't the Union Jack flying over the Bay! the flag to remove which our fathers had marched up and down the streets and fields of India, and though beaten with police batons, had not bowed or stopped shouting those forbidden words "Vande Mataram" but had marched to the tunes that movie moghuls had caught for us on His Master's Voice and the silver screen: *khilenge phool oos jagah pe tu jahaan shaheed ho* ... flowers will bloom where falls the blood of these martyrs.... So this is where we had come, to the land of the Union Jack. I remembered the old man I had seen in my teens at the flagpole in my town back in India (where flags can be flown only in designated places unlike here where the Maple Leaf and Stars & Stripes jostle with flags of fast food joints) who had tears in his eyes and said, "So often, during the Raj, I have stood here looking at the Union Jack and praying for the day when it will be replaced by the tricolour, and it gives me so much joy that I lived long enough to see it happen that I come here everyday to raise my voice in thanks."

Now in the Fall of 1993 , after many November 11s, I can see how the Union Jack could have meant the same thing for many of us, including turbaned Sikhs who stood shoulder to shoulder with Brits and are now denied entry into RCMP and Legion lounges, what the tricolour meant for that old man, but you asked for an honest reminiscence and so you have it - I saw the Union Jack on Hudson's Bay Company, that trading company which like the camel asked for a wee bit of shelter on Indian soil and soon drove everyone else out of the tent, and I almost freaked out.

But not for long. Heh, I was starting a new life in a new land with a husband who was as new to me as everything else around me, and I was ready to dive head first into Canadian culture, and who could blame me for being a tad dismayed to see the Union Jack flying over Hudson's Bay store?

~

This had taken me a lot longer than my usual break. I quickly crushed the juice carton and chips bag into balls, wrapped them with the piece of Saran Wrap of the sandwich, and threw them in the bin as I ran to the wards. Everything seemed to have calmed down; no one seemed to have noticed my long lunch break; or may be it was I who had been all uptight in the morning and had been put into good humour by Maru's pieces.

I read over some of the pages again that evening to check on something. Yes, this was not written for me after all. The person she was addressing was some white Canadian, all those explanations about India and an apologetic note here and there. I took out the sheets I had read in Winnipeg. Both were clearly part of the same manuscript – Fall 1993, December 1993 – but I wasn't in one and was in the other. Now, what does that mean?

Why did they take a train? From where? Toronto? Montreal? Minneapolis?

I phoned Uncle Siv and asked him whether they took the train from Toronto or Montreal or may be Minneapolis. What train, he asked. The train by which you first arrived in Winnipeg, I said. "Why would we take a train?" he said, "after being en route thirty four hours already including the wait at Bombay airport, you think we'd have opted for a train? All anyone would want to do is to reach the destination as fast as one can and hit the pillow. Of course we flew from Montreal. Roy, you remember my colleague Roy? met us at the airport and brought excuses from the Head of the Department, who couldn't come to welcome us because it was Rosh Hashana, the 24th of September 1966 or was it the 23rd?"

Stephen and I read the rest of the piece next evening after dinner.

IV Diving Head First into Canadian Culture: A-Curling we did go.

We arrived one late September day, as I said. Two friends we made in the first week of our need were friends indeed, let's call them Roy and Brent because I don't want to be calling names; I leave that to politicians seeking to get elected and their many rival campaign managers who'd rather they weren't. Roy, who'd met us at the station, helped find another and cheaper hotel on finding that Sivaram's thousand dollar moving expenses had already been spent twice over on our travel. Brent drove us around to see apartment blocks and finally helped us decide on a furnished apartment on Wellington Crescent, an address that gave us an open sesame whenever we wrote a cheque or asked for a bank loan. We didn't know at the time that Winnipeg society too was as class conscious as they come. So we had this swanky two bedroom apartment furnished with the choicest furniture, sublet by a dowager who spent four months in Winnipeg and eight in Florida, for which we paid what others thought was a prince's ransom, all of one hundred and eighty dollars a month.

Brent introduced us to Curling. And so I wrote about that. In those days I used to write long letters with a carbon copy to boot, that were more like serial stories, and I wrote them in a neat convent-school handwriting that I now often see among the native Indian students. Missionary links of the colonial age. Someday I should tell you about the many common phrases and nursery rhymes between Australian, Nigerian and Indo-English literatures that I culled for one of my term papers in Anthropology. Anglo Canadians seem to have missed out on that linkage.

~

Curling, that rock-throwing game

.... I first heard of curling two weeks after Sivaram and I arrived in Winnipeg from India last September. Jack, one of Sivaram's colleagues, took us for a drive through the city that weekend. As we passed a huge, closed-up structure, I asked, "What's that?"

"That's a curling club," Jack said. "I'll take you there once the season starts."

"Curling is a game where you throw rocks," his wife Mary explained. I looked up at the building. It didn't seem battered. Rock-proof walls, I told myself, admiring Canadian building technology.

"There are several sheets of ice, see, and you have a house at either end of each sheet, and the idea is to get your rock into the house..." Mary was saying. I sighed. I knew civilization had been regressing during the last decade or two since my grandfather said so at least twice a day, but I was sorry to learn that Canadians were already back in the Stone Age.

But then I found method in their madness. Modern psychologists were always advocating the-safety-valve practices:

don't bottle up tensions... blow your top off once in a while so they don't blow you up once and for all.   Instead of the punching bags we use back home, Canadians release tension in a big way. I imagined one-room log cabins inside that giant barn, and men in animal hides hurling rocks at each other while whooping war songs.

I next heard of curling on a Saturday morning about a month later. I was about to curl up with a book when the phone rang. It was Jack, who asked if I had any plans for the afternoon. I hadn't. "How would you like to experience the major Canadian pastime of curling this afternoon?" he asked. By then I had forgotten about the rock-throwing game; looking at my book, I said that's just what I was thinking.

"Wonderful. We'll curl together," he said enthusiastically. "I'll be there in half an hour. Right?"

I was rather staggered at his suggestion that I substitute him for my book. If that was a major Canadian pastime, I had no quarrels about that, live and let live, but not for me;   I was brought up on another set of do's and don'ts. I was about to slam down the receiver when I heard him say, "Hey Mary, isn't that great? Maru says they can join us at curling."

I sank to the carpet, the receiver dangling from its cord over my arm. So it was to be a cuddly foursome. "We don't know anything about such things," I said weakly.

"Don't worry," Mary said (they have an extension phone and they spoke alternately now) "there isn't anything about curling that Jack can't teach you."

"Thank you, honey, but I'm not really that good."

"Oh you are, sweetheart."

"It's fun, Maru, you'll see for yourself."

"And we can have dinner after curling at the Club."

"Yes, and watch other people curl. The new lounge area is great for that."

"You'll like the club, people are friendly."

I thought of the last days of the Roman Empire being reenacted, long tables laden with food, men and women sprawled all over the place, now curling now dining. Yes, I could imagine they would be friendly.

Fortunately, before I made a fool of myself, Sivaram came in and I handed the phone to him. I was appalled all over again when he started to gush as enthusiastically as Jack and Mary. Then I came to my senses and realized what the whole thing was about; we were only going to throw rocks at each other's houses. I could cope with that, even though my uncles are all Gandhians and believe in non-violence and all that.

At the Curling Club, I finally found out what they meant by rocks and houses. The sheets of ice were oh so beautiful, and the houses with their concentric circles of blue, white, red and green were so neatly marked and the rocks felt so heavy and strong, I forgot how cold the rink was. Jack told us how to play. Sivaram, as usual, understood everything, I as usual nothing. I was rather flattered that I was going to be the lead.

I was left alone with a tall, lanky Adam's-appled youth who encouragingly placed a rock at my feet. "Slide it down the sheet," he said. I did. It stopped halfway.

Life is full of disillusionments, I told myself. But it was a hard blow, this realization that Newton's theories had been disproved. I distinctly remembered our science teacher explaining the first law of motion and saying we could understand it more clearly by rolling a wooden disc on a sheet of ice. Having never seen ice except as cubes in the refrigerator or sawdust covered blocks sold by vendors in summer, the example made no sense to any of us but we accepted it as the word of science, and therefore infallible.

Sometime during the last few years, I surmised, Newton had been shot down in flames and I hadn't known about it. Here was the sheet of ice and here the equivalent of a wooden disc and no obstacle of any kind but the rock had stopped, very definitely stopped. One of these days the bottom would be knocked out of his theory of gravity and we'd all be rocketing skyward, I thought.

"You need more weight," my companion said.

"Look who's talking," I wanted to say; I'd wager that if it weren't for the heavy sweater, his ribs would be protruding as pathetically as any urchin's on the streets back home.

I watched him carefully as he threw his first rock. He cleaned the underside of the rock and scrupulously swept the ice in front of him. Then he threw his right glove behind him, knelt and squinted. I couldn't guess whether he was praying or looking for ants on the ice. Then he tucked his broom under his left arm and doubled over, hanging on to the rock as though loth to let go. He finally released it but followed the rock with his nose about an inch away from it.

So that's the secret, I told myself, though it did seem absurd trying to blow a heavy thing like that. Absurd or no, I'd blow the rock on its way if that's what was needed to get it into the house.

I lifted the rock, ran my broom underside and almost dropped it on my toes. Then I squinted till I saw two of everything. Then I doubled over. The rock flew out of my hand. And I flew after it. The others swept vigorously, the straw from their brooms flying. I told myself that handmaidens in olden days used to sweep and strew flowers along the queen's paths. But I felt more like a witch as I flew along the ice, broom tucked between my legs.

"All the way, all the way," the skip kept yelling.

I'd been told to do at all times what the skip told me to. But, I said to myself, I'm not going to be the Light Brigade, say what Tennyson may, not if I can help it. But I couldn't. I kept on my giddy way, and when at last I came to a stop, I was glad that Newton was a phony after all.

~

I sure hope you liked that story. It may even have some fodder for social anthropologists. When we first come, we keep remembering where we came from but we also love the new world around us and can't wait to experience it, rocks and all.

"A good enough read. That's one sport I have never tried," was all Stephen had to say.

He seemed more taken up with a little poem he found in the pre-1970s tray. "I remember reading that she had been a train traveler all her life, and here is proof, and also a premonition of sorts that she would be going away from India." He handed it to me:

When I am far away
I shall think of this with nostalgic tears –

The sand-shrub vast flaming into fields
Fresh, pale green corn, bribed cows,
Naked brown children waving to our train,
Patches of the sea, blue, cool, d i s t a n t.
Hawkers selling badaam milk (rotten nuts)
Dosa, "Puri plate char anna, pav anna do,"
Gravel piled for the new railroad,
Workers in once-white loincloths
Downing ragi kanji in the noonday sun,
My land, my dear loved land.

But now,
God, am I sick of this
endless humid hot
train jolting, slow, swaying
like the village maid's waterpot.
Flies, coal dust, crying babies
Pissing on the floor and worse,
God, I sure am sick.

I remembered Maru's laughter and silly jokes but it was no use talking
of that to Stephen. Does Arvind think of Maru as often as I do? We
must get together some time. Keep in touch. Last I spoke to him, he
said they might move to Europe for some time.

~~~~~

FOUR

December 1967, she has a blank page with just those words – December 1967.

I can see something. December, so many of her memos to herself were written in December. There is something about the end of the year that rattles one. A diagnostic report. I've spent quite a few hours on my off days at these cartons. I've got a bit done, the 60s, and it sounds okay. It was easy enough to know where to start, "a blushing bride, the henna scarce dried on my hands and feet." What a dress up! The album in that box – I unwrapped it and yes, it had wedding photos but she didn't have henna at her wedding and I can't imagine her blushing at any time, though she did look pretty fragile and babyish. Uncle Siv was one good-looking guy when he had more of his hair, I must say.

There were a great many handwritten pages. One sheet fell out because it was of a different colour – blue, from a letter pad probably. But it had what seemed like class notes on the first few lines. But the bottom half has a strange entry:

Went to the Bolshoi ballet. I've never liked men in ballet costume and on stage. But this made me change my views. The men were magnificent; though they still looked like horses whenever they jumped, they were magnificent. The Bolshoi after all. As I walked back across the campus, the news from V's letter hit me at last, and I cried, in loud heaving sobs I cried all the way back to my room thinking of Ashok crashing into the sea.

I could sort them out later, I said to myself, may be the handwriting will help me figure out the years they were written. The handwriting on the blue paper was definitely an earlier hand as in some of the notes I have read in what seems to be the 1960s. I was glad to see several pages with the dates clearly written in that earlier handwriting, and these I read.

~

1st to 4th November, 1966

I looked out the drawing room window this morning. I was thrilled. A colourless coat of ice had formed on the river. Winter was here.

First, the October sun had seared leaves to the ground; men came in little machines to mow the grass, and ground the yellow, dry leaves, and the wind carried away the dust.

The wind carried away the ice crust too.

The sun usually rises at the corner of Wellington Towers, and the bleak blackwalled glass dome of St. Mary's Academy flashes back the red ball and I could see the sun reflected on to my eyes. Today there is no sunrise and no sunset, only a luminous cloud moving across the southern horizon.

The next day the ice crust was not colourless but white. But the river still reflected light by night.

The next day the crust was thick and white except for the far edge and near the bank. Neither sun nor wind shall bring to life those petrified ripples and currents that streak whiter against the white surface of the Assiniboine.

Tuesday, 8th November

This afternoon I went for a walk. The sun was shining brightly, the snow piled high on the sidewalks. I went down McMillan thinking I'd walk down Dorchester and buy buttermilk on my way back at Mini Mart that is at Dorchester and Lilac. I kept on but met neither Dorchester nor Lilac, so I turned off towards Corydon, where I turned left, resolving to return by the familiar roads now that I had my coordinates, for the cold was seeping into my snow boots through my leotards on to my toes. We'd just have to do without buttermilk for the time being. I met an old lady with some grocery bags in her hand.

"Can you tell me where I am," she asked me.

"This is Corydon, and that is Arbuthnot," I said, "Where do you want to go?"

"Oh dear, oh dear. I've come too far, I think," she said, and the way she said it sounded to me like something out of *Alice in Wonderland*. She was a non-descript old woman in a faded blue coat, who had a rather well-featured face. Her mouth looked shrunk as though she had no teeth, but she did. Her dentures were yellow.

"What is the address you are looking for?" I asked.

"Lilac," she said.

I told her Lilac was a couple of blocks away, and pointed out. "Ah yes," she said, "I believe you are right, ah yes," and she started walking in that direction. I decided to join her.

"They steal," she said, "where I stay, they steal little things every day. I don't mind giving, but they steal and that I don't like."

I was surprised. "That's too bad," I commiserated.

We walked on.

"Cold, eh?" she said.

"Oh yes," I said.

"I had to wear my cotton coat," she said. "They stole my fur coat yesterday." Indeed, she was wearing only a cotton coat, a blue one with minute checks. She must have been quite cold.

"Do you have an apartment?" I asked, wondering if she lived in an old folks' home.

"I am sick and tired of Leila," she said.

"Leila?" I asked, surprised. Leila was a street in the north end of town, or maybe it was the name of one of her friends.

"Yes, Lilac," she said peevishly. "I am sick and tired of it. We are leaving. We'll go back to Winnipeg."

By then we had reached Lilac, and parted ways.

[Surely there is a story in this. So hilarious that she should ask me, barely six weeks here, for the way, and so sad that she had on only a cotton coat. I sure hope she reached all right. Should I have walked with her to make sure she entered her apartment block?]

And then in a red ink pen, at some later point obviously, she had added "had I known then about dementia I would not have laughed."

15th November

We had an appointment with A and B last Friday. They were to take us shopping for a car. Siv has passed his road test and we are ready for a car. A has been very kindly driving Siv back and forth from the University every day, and it is time to stop imposing on him. A is a non-stop talker, as I found out the few days I went with them so I could spend the day at the Library and have some company at lunch. He has jokes for every occasion. He is also a chain smoker. That was another reason to get our own car.

Around 4:15 we went to their apartment, just across the street, in an apartment block I thought beautiful because it had a brick face and there was a walk along the river behind the block. I did not want to climb four flights of stairs and so we hung around. Then we went up saying we might as well see their new bookcases. We rang the bell. He opened the door. He was fully dressed, topcoat and all. He invited us in, "You want to see a body?" I wondered what dirty joke he was about to unfold. We walked along the corridor and entered the hall, and sure enough there was a body. B. sat up and I saw that she was in her panties and a blouse with all buttons undone. She made no effort to cover herself, merely putting her red slacks across her knees. I looked away. Siv backed out into the corridor. I turned my back to her and appreciated their new bookcases. A sat on the sofa and said he had been shifting shelves all day to suit her whims. She sat on. I did not look back. I ignored her. And I talked on. I wonder how one is expected to behave.

He poured himself another glass. She left the room, slacks in hand. I felt her leaving. I did not see. I wonder what Siv was doing when she got up, bare below her waist except for her panties and almost bare on top as well.

We then saw a hurling game of TV. He kept repeating it was very like field hockey, only that they had no rules, they could jab at each other. And he kept calling her endearing names, asking her to get ready.

At last she came, but she had to have a smoke. She invited me to their den, to see the playboy calendar full of lumpy, busty women in cartoon poses. We rose to leave. I went ahead. I thought he was a bit tipsy but still okay. "Everything is open late on Fridays," he said, opening the car door for me.

We got into the car. He reversed it over the log embedded in the ground to prevent cars from rolling down the incline to the river. When he got out I realized he was quite drunk. We pushed the car over and sat again. He was sleepy. She offered to help. He said it was okay. I thought the stinging air would bring him back. But it did not. He reversed and went over the log again. We got out and pushed it back over the log. He raced the engine. Then he slept at the wheel. Then he woke. He staggered out. She got upset. She walked off saying she'd phone for a taxi. We shoved and pushed. He went back to sleep, woke up every two minutes, raced the engine and slept again.

Some ten minutes later we left the car, in which we were getting choked with cigarette smoke. Siv and he walked into the house. I came back. Siv returned home fifteen minutes after I did, having seen him back into the apartment.

I wonder how one is expected to behave, how one is supposed to refer to the incident. We did not phone or contact them all Sunday. We have not referred to that incident.

I wonder, I do wonder how one is supposed to handle such a situation.

[Okay material for U and R, they'll have a good laugh.]

January 1967

At Safeway today, I stood at the express counter behind three other customers. Siv waited in the car, since I had to buy just buttermilk, milk and bread. The second customer ahead of me was a bearded young man in his late 20s, who had stacked his purchases in an empty carton – he had several baby-food bottles, some sliced meat and/or chicken packages (I just don't notice meats, a survival ploy) and a half-gallon carton of homogenized milk. He placed everything on the counter except for the milk, which was behind the carton. I leaned past the person in front of me and said, "Excuse me, your milk carton is still here.' The woman in front of me took the milk carton and placed it along with his other things. He did not smile or thank me. Suddenly it struck me that may be he meant to leave it in the cart and wheel it away without paying for it. No wonder he didn't thank me for pointing out his "inadvertent" error. Was that his intent?

~

I found some more lined sheets from the 1970s. They were right between computer sheets, obviously from the 90s, – did they have computer sheets in the 1980s? must check. Wow, my idea about sorting stuff out chronologically might work, thanks to these journal-like writings. Stephen thinks I should check about this Dutch East India thing, did it really exist in the war years?

May 28th, 1970

I had lunch with M.H. She said she could not bear to waste a morsel of food, and this came from her war experience. When the Japanese took over Indonesia in 1942, all Europeans including her father, who was with Dutch East India Company, were interned. She was ten, her brothers six and three. As was the custom at the concentration camps, all males over the age of twelve were kept separate from their families, while male children under twelve and all the girls were allowed to live with their mother.

They were made to work in a vegetable garden. It had no fences, and foxes and ferrets destroyed everything periodically. They never got to eat so much as a stalk or a bean from the vegetable patches. It was clearly just something to keep them busy.

At first, they got enough to eat every day. But in the second year, rations were drastically decreased. If the servants of the Japanese officers were kind, they threw food into the garbage cans, and children who were assigned to clean the garbage cans could get some leftovers. Till the age of twelve, girls were assigned to babysitting duties. At age twelve, girls were assigned to kitchen duty. Their work was to scour the pots and pans in which the meals were cooked. M was small and thin (she did not gain an ounce of weight in the three years) and she could get right into the huge pots and pans. She got to scrape food off the walls of the pots, and though it was not much it was a welcome addition to their daily ration.

She never got to see her father again. He died before the end of the war. It was only three months after Armistice Day that they came to know the war was over.

She grew up in Holland and became a pathologist. An older friend who had come to Canada offered her a job and she accepted. But her boss thought it was a breach of professional ethics for anyone to have offered her a job without consulting him and even more unforgivable that she should have accepted it. He would not release her. So she resigned and even though the friend had returned to Holland meanwhile, she emigrated to Canada. Her friend Nel got the original job.

(I met Nel too, and indeed, the dining table I bought from her was handmade by her father, or was it father-in-law?)

~

Here are two dreams Maru has recorded in 1970 or is it 1960? Surely, they will tell me something about her early days. It was all very juvenile, like storylines for a teenage detective story. But it did mean she was writing all the time, doesn't it? The date is smudged over but it is February and the year ends in 0, or is it 9? 1959? 1969?

What a dream! Chasing a gang of liquor smugglers in Nagpur, though the scenes were from here.

I was visiting a house, some kind of tourist attraction because there were several groups being led around. I too was part of a conducted tour. The house was big and had a huge compound. It was a hotel, may be. No other house or habitation in sight. I caught on quickly that some fishy business was in progress. At a snack bar, I saw the girl behind the counter making signs to a girl (both teenagers, like college students) beside me. They were waiting for me to leave, I could see. The girl next to me had a small piece of paper that she was rolling around her finger. When she thought I wasn't looking, she slipped it into a hole on the counter, a hole like you see for wooden nails in furniture. It stuck out. And I edged towards it, pretending I hadn't seen it, and then I suddenly reached for it. I shouldn't have done so, nor should I have shown my glee at having got the paper. But I did. The girl behind the counter said nothing. I ran out. Lots of people on the veranda. Is there any plain clothes policeman here? I asked. Two men stepped out. "How do I know you are genuine," I asked. I don't remember what they said to convince me. Maybe I didn't even wait. I showed them the slip. It was a grocery bill such as we get here, just a long row of figures with the total. But on the top of the paper was a faint drawing of a bird or some such sign. The plainclothes men pointed to it and said, "Yes, that's them all right." And they set out to arrest the girls. But the girls had vanished.

~

Dream re: Godu Tai [this is written on the same sheet as the above.]

This was some nights ago.
A group of us were walking, Once again a picnic spot. This scene recurs so often in my dreams – pebbles, uneven ground, flowing water somewhere (in the smuggler dream there was a stream near the house). We started going down to the water in the distance. J. was with me and she and I were talking about dance and culture or something. Our destination was a temple on the other side of the river. Our guide was reluctant to take us there. It was getting dark and he said we might not be able to get a boat back. He was dissuading us indirectly. But we went just the same. I don't remember taking a boat or anything. In fact the temple and the big house beyond (the temple was part of this rich man's compound) were on the same side of the water as we were. And we went to the temple. It had many pillars and a shrine in the centre and beyond was the house which was our destination. Hurry, hurry, J said, this place is so deserted. But I went around and saw an old woman near one of the pillars. I went forward saying, "I knew this wasn't totally deserted." And I saw the woman. It was Godu Tai! "Why," I cried joyfully, "it is Godu Tai. Isn't that wonderful!" and I went forward with one arm outstretched. She was equally joyful at seeing me. "Back from Canada!" she cried and stretched both arms. And just as I was about to touch her hand, I remembered with a ghastly fear that she was dead. I retreated telling myself she was dead and if she was dead, oh god, no wonder the guide ... and yet so like alive, the same....

~

I wanted Stephen to tell me what he thought the dreams meant. He dismissed them altogether. "Just teenage stuff," he said. I was not pleased. "The big house, meeting with the dead, meeting smugglers and fake policemen, surely it means something," I insisted. "Fear, she was afraid something terrible was going to hit her."

"Nah," Stephen said, "both dreams end with her being okay. Must be some residue from her childhood about being lost and then being found. Or just Nancy Drew stuff. Nothing of literary merit anyway." Seeing I was disappointed, he added, "She does mention Tai, a name Rushdie has for the old man with prodigious memory – may be that is what it means, memory or history or something?" "Sheesh," I said, "it just means elder sister." "Thought that was *behn,* my friend Dilip used to call his sister that," he said. "In Hindi," I said, "but in Marathi it is *tai.*"

"But I thought Maru was from South India, I know your parents speak Marathi but…"

"Maru grew up in central India, I thought I've told you that."

"Okay, okay, unless I meet your people, how am I ever going to know all these details?"

Stephen is forever angling for an introduction to my family. But I am not biting. I spoke about Maru instead. About how she read detective novels when she was a tween – she had told me all about it, about the summer holidays when she read a Sexton Blake mystery each day, and had to finish it before going to bed because the murderer couldn't be on the loose prowling at night but had to be safe in custody caught by the police, thanks to the detective, Sexton Blake. They were a stack of paperbacks – I forget if her older brothers borrowed them from their friend Raja Marwaha or got them from the circulating library – always 64 pages long, and already the pages were yellow or brown and the print fading. She told me too of the comics borrowed from the same friend, one called *Film Fun* that had strips of Laurel and Hardy and Bud Abbott and Lou Costello, and at least one mystery or thriller story each issue. She had read John Dickson Carr and Agatha Christie but more than that she loved horror and ghost thrillers. Which were scarier, especially since they slept under the stars on steel cots with thin cotton mattresses on the front lawn of their house in the boondocks of a college campus in Jabalpur, and the mosquito-proof nets they slept under were certainly not enough to keep out ghosts, though she tucked in the edge of the netting ever so carefully under the mattress.

~

Next day was a long day for me but it was Stephen's day off. Over the dinner that Stephen had made, he told me he found something that proved Maru had indeed gone through the detective novel phase. "You don't need proof to something I told you as a fact," I said, irritated at his observation. "Calm down, sweetums, always a bit of internal substantiation works when you are writing a biography."

"No way I am doing that," I said, "no way. I am a doctor, not a writer."

"One can be both, you know. Abraham Verghese is a doctor from India who has written a powerful book about his experience treating AIDS patients. There is Andrew Greeley who is a Roman Catholic priest, who writes mystery thrillers."

"Oh for heavens' sake, where do you find all this trivia? So do I care?"

"There was a review of his latest mystery about the bishop and the missing L-Train, and it said he writes two novels each year. Sure, we can be both doctors and writers, can't we?

"Sorry I asked," I said, "what is Maru's story about?"

"Just juvenilia, actually, but may be you can find her teenage friends through it – it starts off, with," he picked up a sheaf of foolscap papers and read:

Planned on a walk (Y-RadioStn-Pavilion-BishopCottonSchool) on the 5th of August 1959 and written on 6th and 8th of August 1959

The characters in this story are entirely real and most observations on life in the Y are not purely coincidental. The theme, the victim and murderer are, however, purely imaginary. Allusions to traits and character of persons figuring in the story are recorded without malice where applicable to their real selves. It is in short a phantasia built around the humdrum life at the Y.

Stephen continued, "Then it goes on to kill off a new girl at the Y Hostel. Of course any of the narrator's friends, she is named Nandini by the way, does that mean anything? any of her friends could have done it. It has clues, Gold Flake cigarette stubs, poison residue in a glass of milk, a figure in white who appears on the hostel yard along which flows a little stream. The main suspect is Veejala, someone everyone likes, who is studying to be a pharmacist and provides them with aspirin and codopyrin for their headaches, and also has a stash of pharmaceutical powders and carries poison tablets in a Sucrets lozenge box, and she flushes something down the toilet soon after the body is found; but as in all good murder mysteries it could be anyone at all - one of the girls disapproves of the victim spending so much time in bed, especially because she likes the dorm to herself when she is having an afternoon nap, another has political connections and the victim happens to be a Muslim from a princely state. There are all kinds of details about the maintenance staff at the hostel and the warden whom nobody seems to like, a lot of stuff that tells you about Maru's life at the Y. And the cover has an amateur stick drawing of a ghost and a masked figure holding a knife – very exciting and very juvenile. You must read it."

"Like I have time," I said, and helped myself to the last of the bowl of pilav before going to my text books.

"Here's something to lighten your mood," Stephen said, pushing a yellowed newspaper cutting. I glanced at it and since it was short, I read it. It was from *The Deccan Herald* and the date had been written down but not the year: December 23.

The Fate of the Fair

It was one of those social evenings which end up in inspired spurts of oratory.

"Equality", said a lady, "equality of men and women... woman emerging out of ages of down-trodden existence to take her place" blah blah.

The young man in the red checkered shirt waxed equally eloquent. Equality, he grunted, you women under cover of equality fleece us of everything. You want equality in jobs but concessions when it comes to a seat in the bus that we have to vacate for you. He dramatically raised his hand to call down heavenly justice and lowered it promptly, remembering that months of strap hanging in buses had ended in the sleeve seam bursting that evening.

"What they are after is superiority", said a mournful looking man who had evidently long lost the battle on home grounds, "and I guess they've got it."

The young man impatient at such display of weakness continued, "You have special seats in the bus, carriages in the train, queues at the ticket counter and whole classes in the back rows of the main floor in cinema theatres," and so on and so forth.

But I know what men are after; why they give special seats for the women and children specifically in the cinema - so that they can enjoy the film untroubled by squealing children who are left to the womenfolk to manage. All noble actions are prompted by selfish motives, I've heard it said, and a visit to the cinema more than confirms the motive behind this act of generosity that reserves the backmost rows of theatres for ladies.

Accompanied by a friend, I went for the matinee today and here is the picture fresh from the oven.

We were a little early but the seats were fast filling and we got only the middle row. The benches in the ladies' class are hard and narrow, usually brought from the scrap heap to serve us.

TIK 20 they say, whispered my friend, gets rid of bugs; she scratched herself very discreetly in a ladylike manner. By the end of the film we had shed off all attempts at ladylikeness on this score.

Ramu Oh Ramu, engeda irukke nee? It was the woman in front looking for her offspring. She pulled him in by the ear, gave him two sound slaps and seated him next to herself. The yell he set was a cue for every youngster to join in, which they wholeheartedly did; his infant brother who contributed greatly to the din was vigorously rocked into a daze. As soon as the lights went out, the youngsters stood on the bench the better to see the screen and after being clouted by those behind, they cried themselves to sleep.

The story went its usual way. The hero chased the heroine round trees under a bursting moon and static clouds; at this the woman to my left took my hand and gripped it in suspense whether he'd make it; a raw picture-goer evidently for who doesn't know he'd catch her under the palm tree?

It was then a death scene which continued interminably. I wriggled impatiently in my seat. I felt something under my feet. Shoo, I said thinking it was a dog. But it was a baby belonging to the woman behind who was too busy blowing her nose to heed her straying infant. I pitied the poor mite most probably licking its dirty hands while toddling around. But soon enough my pity vapourised as I felt a warm stream washing my feet!

The old woman was dead when I looked up and the hero was carrying out her last wish, garlanding the wrong girl, while the right one sang a mournful song under a mournful sky. The whole place was now suffocating with sniffles; the woman behind was crying heart-brokenly and a general chorus of "Ayyaiyo pavam" drowned the actors' words. The woman to my left started telling me of a similar case in actual life and the woman to her left, a veteran film fan drew parallels, complete with details of dialogue, star cast and playbacks from other films. My companion asked her to lower her voice. That did it. Followed another half hour of tirade against us. Was it her *sasural* that she should keep quiet? Was the theatre owned by our grandfather? Just like college girls to dress finely and think only they can understand films she'd have us know she was not uneducated either, she had studied up to the fourth class before her father got her married and sent her to this wretched city where people were steeped in pride just because they went to colleges. And didn't she know what happened in colleges? All the evils and iniquity of city life....

Suddenly from out of the dark came two figures who insisted on sitting on top of us. Somehow they squeezed their by-no-means-light bodies between the two of us. The strong smell of cheap hair oil and unwashed clothes, added to coughs of all kinds of clearing throats.... the atmosphere was slow-poisoning us.

The film showed signs of ending; so we thought we'd stick it to the bitter end. The wife was dying and we thought she'd join the hero's hands to the heroine's and breathe her last and relieve us of our suffering, But no. She recovered and we knew it would take another three reels for the grand reunion. We stumbled our way over feet and babies, earning some voluble curses.

The queue had formed for the next show and we cut our way through the snake-like line. Making way for us, a man said to his neighbour "Women are lucky, they have reduced rates.

~

Uncle Siv called me a few days after that.   We've been calling each other more frequently of late. Before he could say anything, I asked the question I wanted to.   "Who is Lakshmi?"

"Lakshmi? I don't know any Lakshmi except for Mrs.Vishnu."

"Who?"

"Vishnu who rests on Adisesha on the sea of milk, you know."

"Oh please Uncle Siv, get serious. Some Lakshmi whose daughter got married there in Winnipeg. There is some mention of something taking place soon after Lakshmi's daughter's wedding and it even says you were away at some conference at the time."

"My priti maid, there probably never was a Lakshmi. It is probably just a lead-in for some point she wanted to make. Or if there was, the least she'd have done is change the name. What is the context?"

"I don't care who she is, was or will be. I just need to know what year the wedding took place."

"But why? what are you doing with all the stuff?"

"I have to arrange the stories chronologically, that's why."

"My priti maid,"

"And don't call me that."

"Oh dear what can the matter be, my Johnny's so long at the fair.
My lady is jumping mad, frustrated, breathing fire through nostrils.
Okay okay, I'll try to find out."

"So why are you so happy?"

"Thanks for asking. Called to tell you what a close call I had.
Some buyer actually made an offer on the house. He was ready to give
my asking price, can you believe that? for this old house. And so I had
to go through the papers with a microscope to see how I could nail him
and get him off my back. Whew, that was close. I am never going to
place it with any agent again."

"Uncle Siv, you are incorrigible. Why do you want to live in that
old house? Just sell it while it's still standing."

"Can you see me raring to my full height? Yes sir ma'am. Never
again trust an agent with the house. He'll find a buyer. Whew, what a
close call."

"So when are you coming to see me?"

"Why, is something going right or very wrong?"

"Can't I just want to see you?"

"Okay, that's two points being punched in this very minute into
my organizer – One, who is Lakshmi? Two, look for a freebie
conference in Ottawa."

"Uncle Siv, you have tons of funds and can get consultations with
the NRC any time you want."

"Not to mention I can always spend my own money to visit my
favourite priti maid."

"I have to go, now."

"Me first," and he hung up.

The phone call helped. It was good to know Uncle Siv was in
such good spirits. I often worried about him, usually during my lunch
break and resolved to phone him in the evening, but invariably forgot.
What with Stephen at home many evenings, and nights though he
always leaves in the wee hours of the morning so he can get three hours
in his own bed. Living just a block away helps, or may be that is the
problem.

Stephen. He is getting a little more insistent each time. Wants us
to get engaged, proper ring, party and all, before he takes off for Nigeria
and World Vision. I am not ready. So we had a flare up yesterday that
gave me an awful headache. Why would I want to bind myself when
you are going to be away for months, I asked, and he didn't have an
answer. Next you'd want me to wear a chastity belt, I goaded him.
You know damn well we are meant for each other, he said.

He went away in a huff and I wasn't sorry to see him go. He was getting to be a steady fixture, even getting a nice dinner ready if his shifts permitted him to finish work early, and I wasn't ready for that. So I was getting to be the b word. Any little thing set me off. But he usually keeps his cool. Which makes me madder. The other day he came straight from the gym and I said his taste in outfits was getting worse by the day, and all he said was, "Shabbiness is the privilege of the rich, Maru has said so. Did you know she has a whole booklet of aphorisms and we need to figure out what are hers and what are borrowed. Like 'Eccentricity is the privilege only of the old.' It sounds familiar doesn't it?" But today he hasn't kept his cool.

I looked into his tray to read what he had referred to, and I found the notes and sayings. "We live on momentary gleams of pleasure and satisfaction," said the cover of the booklet, and inside were a great many sayings and proverbs – looks like she started on some translation of her great aunt's sayings, which she marginally notes were often quite vile jokes on body parts. Also interesting were the Xeroxed sheets from a book that Maru had copied. There is no title but she has written "African Proverbs" on top of the first sheet, which has a story called "He who shits on the road will meet flies on his return." Maru and scatological jokes. May be I could tell some of them to Stephen when he cools off. Like the one where the constipated man walking under the railway overpass had a stream of yellow shit pour down on him and was lost in admiration – What an arse, what a great arse! Every time she came up with something like that, she would say they don't sound funny in English and she would laugh that wonderful laugh of hers. Laughter is one of the first things we lose when we come to a new land, she has said somewhere but it wasn't true of her, that's for sure. May be she got it back after the first few years for I remember her laughter most of all.

~

There is so much from the 1970s, what am I going to do with all this stuff? More dreams, either Maru had a lot of dreams in 1970, or she had a lot of time to write down the dreams.

Today I came across a huge envelope of stuff that has scribbles and scrawls from god-knows-when. And newspapers too. Why has she stored this tabloid-size paper from July 1968? *International Consumers' Magazine.* Good Lord, it is subtitled King of Kings' Magazine and is just a trashy proselytizing mag with great and glorious

jesus christ things in big block letters; it advertises itself as: Tourists,
Use this magazine as your travel and shopping guide on your holidays.
I can't believe it – there is a picture of the Queen with a caption: Queen
Elizabeth II, First Universal Ruler of the Fifth Universal Stone
Kingdom. What is this? Stephen would know what to make of it. Why
hasn't he called? It couldn't be a legit mag, could it? But there seem to
be regular ads in it – for Fort Rouge Motel on Pembina – must check if
such a place really existed in 1968. And for Esso Service at some place
in Blackfalds, Alberta! Is this for real? Stephen would know.

This must be from 1968 too, for it is a sheet tucked in the tabloid.

"How can you stand it?" most of my friends say when they come
to the daycare to pick me for tea or a shopping spree after I have
finished my volunteer shift that ends at noon.

"By enjoying it," I reply, and they shake their heads in an "I
should have guessed she is a barmy kind of person," way.

I really do enjoy it. Sure it can be tedious and tiring to
handle twenty odd children, one or other of whom is pinching
his neighbours or needing a Kleenex or has to go in a hurry to the
bathroom, but at the end of the morning, I remember only the
delightful freshness of a vocation in which each day brings a
fresh experience or incident. I wonder if parents would send
their children to the nursery if they knew what vivid pictures of
life at home the kids sketched during their matter-of-fact
narration of what happened at home.

Helen shares my feelings, and we swap stories. This is her
story for today. She had a little accident over the weekend and
came to work with a collar to support her neck. She figured she
would use her accident as a learning tool and talked about the
importance of seat belts and how she would have been a lot more
hurt if she had not kept her seat belt fastened. The children were
duly impressed and would no doubt carry the message home.
Close to noon, she took the collar off because it was chafing.

One of the children was very disappointed – Oh gee, you
still have your neck," he said.

Here is another newspaper, this time a real one, for I can't believe the
other is for real – The Hindu dated March 27, 1966. Holy kamoli, a

wonder these papers haven't fallen apart, though they are pretty yellowed. The lead story is about the ex-ruler of Bastar being found dead along with seven tribals, after a clash with the police. Tucked within the folded paper is a sheet titled,

For the Bastar story:
Vir Deo (the hero) is Danteshwari's high priest. The Gonds are his followers. The Bhumiyas, though his subjects, are somewhat different in background. (See *Tales of Gondwana*). Put in a sub plot of Gond-Bhumiya interaction – a bhumiya medicine man or soothsayer. Bhumiyas, though disinclined towards cultivation and other work-taxing occupations, are thinkers and muse on natural phenomena and know the movement of the planets etc.

There is another sheet as well:

Colorado Rural Electric News will pay 3 cents a word for a 750 word story. Could I write about electricity coming to Chinnarpet, a village in India? An old man foretells all kinds of gloomy happenings should electricity come. When it does, and the only village lamp post springs with light, he changes his mind and sees a vision of prosperity. Or, it could be, "I do not see the glow-worms any more, my son." And the next morning, there are mounds of moths lying dead under the lamp post.

I am sure this doesn't belong here in this newspaper, but certainly belongs in this 1960s pile. Wonder why she has this Bastar story. I quickly perused the news story. Pravir Chandra Bhanjdeo, the deposed ruler of Bastar, and seven tribals were found dead by the police in the Bastar palace, after a clash between the police and a large number of tribals. A large group of tribal Adivasis had protested the locking up of nineteen Adivasis who were under trial and attacked the police with their bows and arrows. "The police party fired some tear-gas shells," but since the crowds still refused to disperse, the police used "ten grenades, forty two shells of tear-gas and 61 rifle cartridges," in self-defense. The Adivasis sought refuge by running into the palace. Next morning the police, the report went on to say, found the king and his followers lying dead within the palace.

    In self-defense – it enraged me – imagine firing grenades into a crowd who had bows and arrows! and the crock about the police happening to find them dead, it was so obvious they had gone in and murdered the king and some others.

~

Stephen hadn't phoned me since the spat. It was time to offer the olive branch, as he had so often done in past spats. I phoned him at lunch hour that Friday. I got his answering machine. I said I would treat him to dinner if he was free to come.

I thought there would be a message for me but there wasn't. However, Stephen was at the door a half hour after I came home. He hugged me in a long quiet way, and said, "Thank you for calling me over. It's been a terrible week. Watson seems to have the energy of a volcano, but boy am I exhausted, operated on an abdominal tumour the size of a grapefruit – it had been there for decades, it seemed like, and Dr. Watson turned it over to me. With him looking over my shoulder, and me snipping at it and snipping at it, holy christo, I am so relieved it turned out okay." We sat on the sofa, and I stroked his hair and felt a great wave of tenderness when he lay on my breast. He fell asleep in two minutes, and I sat for another ten minutes thinking about this sudden wave of tenderness. I could feel a slight fever on him; I eased him onto the sofa, covered him with a quilt, went to the kitchen, and made some hot soup.

He slept all night on the sofa. He wanted to go back to his apartment so he wouldn't pass on the bug to me, and more important, to my patients – but I insisted. I fussed over him and babied him all Saturday, feeling all warm and fuzzy that I was actually enjoying fussing over him.

I told him about what I had been reading, and gave him the super-large envelope, even though I had read only the newspapers so far. He didn't think it was worthwhile digging up details about The International Consumers' Magazine. Even oddball churches had thousands of dollars to spread their word, and advertisers didn't care, especially if the rag were placed for free in motels and high-traffic areas. But he was greatly intrigued by the police killing of the minor raja. "1966, and the rulers were still around?" he asked. I was glad I could actually provide him with some info. I knew that part of India's history – granted much of it was from Malgonkar's novels that Maru had insisted I read. I told him of how the British, during the Raj, had promised all the native rulers that they would continue to rule forever and how after Independence, the new government had sent royalty packing, with a monthly allowance, which too was discontinued a few years later, but even in the 1970s rajas still had a lot of standing even if only in their little fealties.

"Poor blighters," he said. "Wonder when that's going to happen to the First Universal Ruler of the Fifth Universal Stone Kingdom."

"Don't be so disrespectful, I bet your grandpa would have stood up any time *God Save the Queen* was played," I said.

"I wish I could have been in India at the time of all those kings and kingdoms," Stephen said.

I remembered one of Maru's stories from her teens, and I told it to Stephen. When Maru's dad retired, (people retired at age fifty five in those days, I explained,) and went elsewhere on a two-year contract, the family stayed on in the city so the kids' college routine wasn't interrupted. But since the assigned government-owned residence stopped with his retirement, they rented a house in Civil Lines (the hoity-toity part of any city, I explained.) It was actually only half of a house, because the other part was kept locked, and only used whenever the owner came into town. It wasn't even a half-house, more like one-third. It was a single large room, about twenty by forty feet, which had been the audience chamber by day or party-hall by evening, in the days when rajas were rajas. The raja, by now no longer a raja, had walled off this room from the rest of the house, and had enclosed the front veranda into a kitchen-cum-dining room, as also the back verandah, and had rented out the one-third-house. Maru's family had arranged the furniture in four quadrants, so that there still was a living room with its comfortable cane-woven chairs, and a study with desks and chairs and bookshelves for all the siblings, and almirahs and shelves for clothes, and all the beds were lined up in two rows in one of the quadrants, and they lived happily ever after.

Stephen sat up. "Whoa, go on. What else? I can see you have something more to tell."

I waited just long enough for him to get impatient and then I told him the tiger story.

The owner of the house was a raja of one of those little principalities in Madhya Pradesh, and his mother, more often than he, would come into the city to do her shopping. But one Sunday, the raja came by, after a shikar, in which he had killed a tiger, and his men skinned the huge tiger in the backyard, and it took them all afternoon, and they stretched and cleaned the skin, and the raja was so proud of his marksmanship for he had shot the royal tiger through the eye so clean that the skin was blemishless when it lay stretched in the back yard. And the whole house stank of meat which they cooked in huge cauldrons in the backyard and fed to a huge retinue of people. And, here comes the best part, or the saddest, I paused and waited till Stephen was about to throw a cushion at me. Maru was just so mad because her siblings had let her sleep through the whole afternoon and so she did not see them skinning the tiger, and had only woken up when the strong cooking stinks hit her.

"You never miss a chance to insert your vegan prejudices, do you?" Stephen said.

"I am simply relaying Maru's biases, not mine," I said.

"You've made me a vegan, I suppose you know that," he said.

"Vegetarian, lacto-ovo vegetarian," I said, "vegans don't take milk products."

I was so glad to get one over him; he was always so disgustingly knowledgeable about the definitions and etymology of words. Etymology – I got that from him.

I wanted him to get off the sofa since he seemed well enough, and to clean up and make himself presentable so we could go out for a drive, but he was totally into Maru's stuff. What made her so interested in this tribal chief that she hoarded this for thirty years, he said. I said, "Isn't it obvious? She was always for the underdog. I knew for a fact she would befriend abused women, much to the disapproval of other women in the community who thought such things should not be talked about. Even I got mad just reading how the police riddled the tribals who had just bows and arrows, and I can imagine she'd have got all upset."

Seeing Stephen was not about to budge, I pushed the carton of folders closer to the sofa and went to take a shower. As soon as he heard me come out of the bathroom, he shouted for me to come over. He was at the computer. "Hey, sweetums, you'll love what I found, an outline for a whole novel on the Bastar drama." Still with the towel around my hair, I took the sheets he was holding out. "Read this first," he shoved an inside page of the newspaper that I had not seen. He had folded up the paper for me to read what he had focused on –

"When Raja Rudra Pratap Deo died without a male issue, the Adivasis rose as one man in rebellion and made the British forces yield to their unprecedented demand of recognizing the only daughter of their king as the heir-apparent. They argued to the finish that when a woman could rule over the British Empire, why could not the tiny state of Bastar have a woman ruler? They won and Maharani Prafulla Kumari was installed as their Ruler. Though the Maharani was married to a prince of another big State, Mayurbhanj, the people of Bastar would not give the royal consort a position superior to their Maharani. The Adivasis, it is said, refused to pull the *rath* when the royal consort took a seat near his wife, the Maharani of Bastar."

No wonder, Maru was valorizing this ruler – the Adivasis considered him their god, and they had their heads screwed on right in the way they saw women, and so this Pravir guy was a hero of her story.

Stephen had left the computer open on a Google page. On the screen was an entry on Pravir Chandra. He was her eldest son, born in 1929. Stephen was rummaging through the contents of the envelope while I was reading. Seeing I was finished, he held a sheaf of foolscap sheets. "Here, read this."

Pravir Chandra Bhanjdeo of Bastar: A Quasi-Historical Romance.

Inspiration: Pravir Chandra Bhanjdeo was found dead in his palace on March 26, 1966. There had been a police-tribals tussle the previous evening. Obviously, the police (perhaps under Congress orders) killed him. Our newspapers are intolerably stupid to dole out only what the PTI sends and PTI sends only the government version. *The Hindu* coverage claims to be from its correspondent. Obvious that the correspondent has picked up his news from PTI Bhopal instead of rushing to Jagdalpur to get a first-hand report of this heinous act.

I can see Pravir Chandra as a hero. I remember his deposition, his fight and his defeat – the *Hitavada* carried all of it in much detail at the time.

I know nothing about him except that he was educated in England, that he wanted his throne back, that he was popular with his subjects, and that now he is dead.

I might have to make his capital closer to some railway junction so I can open the story with him returning from England unannounced on hearing that his father has ceded away his kingdom. Real history might make the bottom fall off my plot, but we'll see how and what is to be done.

March 27, 1966

I called out to Stephen. "She must have really been inspired – look she's started writing the very next day."

"I'd say she had been thinking about the story and the newspaper item was the trigger that set her actually to start writing," he said.

Pravir Chandra stood on the platform, suitcase in hand; he waved off porters who came running towards him. "If sahibs carry their own bags, what is to become of us?" a porter mumbled angrily as he rushed off in the hope of getting another passenger with luggage. Pravir Chandra smiled. The station had not changed much in the last five years, nor had the impudence of porters.

He walked to the telephone booth. It was occupied. He stood by impatiently. A young porter approached him. "Sahib needs a porter. Sahib's servant will take sahib to the hotel in a tonga," he said, smiling ingratiatingly. Pravir laughed. "Take care of my suitcase while I make a phone call," he said, entering the booth from which a businessman with his brief case and dark glasses had just hastened out.

He gave the operator the number.

"Palace," he heard.

"This is Pravir."

"Your Highness?" gasped the voice at the other end.

"Yes, is my father home?"

"Yes, Yuvraj, shall I call him?"

"No, just send the car to the station."

"Welcome home, Yuvraj."

"Thank you, I am glad to be home. Is that Ram Babu?"

"Yes, yes, Yuvraj!" he sounded abjectly happy at being recognized.

"How are you, Ram Babu? I was very sorry to hear of your brother's death."

Ram Babu was about to reply but Pravir Chandra, not wanting his humble thanks, continued, "Tell the Maharajah I shall be with him soon. And hurry with the car, will you?" He placed back the receiver with impatient violence. He would have to wait for another hour before the car arrived.

The omelet he had for breakfast made him thirsty. He looked around. There was a stall at the far end. He looked at the rows of cheap coloured drinks which the vendor, for effect, had placed one on top of the other, forming a cone of red, blue, green and yellow rows. He shrugged his shoulders and turned away. One part of him smiled at the memory of those coloured drinks that tasted like sweetened hair-oil because of their cheap flavour and excessive syrup; another and nearer-to-the-surface part of him was repulsed by the sight of the bottles and the dirty, thick glass tumblers and the flies on the sweetmeat shelf. A third part of him looked at these two and wondered why he had changed and to what degree.

~

"Here's another of Aunt Maru's attempts at an opening chapter," Stephen said, seeing that I had finished reading.

The Howrah Mail slowed down. Pravir looked at his watch. 1:36. He looked at the telegraph wires running alongside the track, sagging between the telegraph poles, on each of which was a white tin plate marked with numerals indicating the number of miles the train had come from Bombay. Pravir wondered how many miles more there were, and that the little plates could not say. He would know, Pravir thought, looking at his co-passenger's head that was craning to peer from between the horizontal bars of the window, he is sure to know these stupid details. Just then the other man pulled in his head saying brightly, "The signal is not yet down. Only a wayside station, not for Mail and Express trains, but we have to wait for the signal." He looked at Pravir who was looking out his window as though neither of them existed, and suddenly seemed to remember that the young man had been uncommunicative all along. He was sorry to have forgotten the fact for the umpteenth time in those nine hours since his boarding at Bhusaval. He opened the door and stood with his back to Pravir.

Pravir stared at the man's profile and watched him biting his lower lip, pulling thin shreds of skin from his parched, dark lips. He realized that he had hurt this man. I am sorry, stranger, he thought, but I don't know what to talk about. I am not interested in anything you might have to say. I am rushing home from England because my father has gifted away my kingdom. I have fights ahead of me and within me. And even if you were my dearest and only friend, I wouldn't know what to tell you. I stand alone. Yes, alone. Do you know what my crest is? A man walking up a snowcapped mountain. And my motto? Aham

Ekaha. I stand alone. There is my father's crest too, of course, the arms of the house of Bhanjdeo. It has a lion, have you noticed how indispensable lions seem to be for royal arms? But this lion does not bear aloft a crown for GVI, or a flag, it just sits majestically while two deer drink from the pond at its feet. Rather good, don't you think? Mine is better. I was not born just to be king among beasts. I was born to be a god among men. I, Pravir, God of the Adivasis.

The other man shut the door and came back to his seat as the train crept forward. He was still sullen.

Pravir made a great effort and managed to say aloud, "I hope you get some good company at Raipur, where I get off." The other smiled spontaneously, the happy smile of an easily-pleased being. "Oh, I do want company," he said, "as long as it isn't a family with half a dozen squealing children. I remember once I had to ..." and he went on in his annoyingly cheerful manner to relate the incident.

Beyond the range of hills covered with sal trees and giant jackfruit and peepals was a hill that stood alone. It was rocky and had only small shrubs, mainly a type of berry that hung in green clusters when raw and turned bright purple when ripe, and had orange flowers clustered flat on the head of the stalk. There were also wild flowers, tiny violet flowers that could hardly be seen in the green; yellow flowers that were bright and short-lived; balsams of different colours that bloomed in the winter months and had burrs that withered yellow and pricked the unwary walker; and several types of trees that flamed red in April around the time of Holi festival. The top of the hill was monolithic and flat. It was bare except for moss that grew in occasional niches on the rocky surface. That, Pravir thought, is indeed a hill that cries out for a temple. And he, Pravir Chandra Bhanjdeo, was going to build it, he the high priest of goddess Danteshwari, would raise an edifice in her honour that would shame Bhubaneshwar and Belagola.

Pravir looked out again. The green landscape of miles and miles of uncultivated virgin land that had thrilled him a few minutes ago was now infuriatingly monotonous. The telegraph wires kept bogging up and down. 604/4, 604/5, 604/6. The train was running late. It should have reached Raipur an hour ago. But that should not matter. It will reach soon. Very soon.

"She even has a page of the railway timetable stuck on the next page," I said, "she was doing her homework. Two different openings. Which one do you like better?"

"The first gets into the action right away but the second gives an effective panoramic view of the geography of the place, what do you think? May be you should read the outline first."

I picked up the sheet he was holding.

Chapter 1 - Pravir's return in early 1948 from Cambridge. Anger, disappointment that his father had signed away the kingdom.

Chapter 2 - Father-son estrangement and reconciliation. Meeting between Pravir and Chief Priest who inspires him (diabolically?) to be the High Priest of Danteshwari Devi even when his father was still alive.

Chapter 3 - Pravir tries to rejoin the old order, but having been away and his new sense of mission make him impatient of the life of opulence and debauchery.

Chapter 4 - Pravir and the princess. Passionate, poetic love which shows his childishness, his child-like naiveté, and infinite ego. Her reaction – greatly impressed by his presence but unsure of herself when alone.

Chapter 5 - The wedding. Pomp and pageantry...

Chapter 6 - Death of the king. Coronation. The Adivasis worship him, Vijaya dissuades him from taking on godly power. Rift in the lute between him and the princess.

Chapter 7 - Pravir lives among his devotees. Ideals of reform. Chief Priest and Adivasis persuade him to disregard Govt of India officials who are tightening their hold on the affairs of the state.

Chapter 8 - Princess leaves him after her son dies of exposure at the feet of Danteshwari.

Chapter 9 - Underground activities against Union now changed to campaigning to win a seat in the Congress. Fails to win, and so goes to the side of the dacoits and adivasis. Prohibits adivasis from accepting government handouts. Purposely retards progress to insulate Bastar from rest of the country. Subhadra, a devadasi older and experienced in both love and war, advises him.

Chapter 10 - At Subhadra's prompting, encourages dacoits to murder Congressmen. They are caught. She induces him to betray their trust. They die. Pravir suffers great remorse but S has grandiose plans of an insulated but powerful kingdom. Raises price of timber.

Chapter 11 - Congress refuses nomination. New alliance with dacoits. Loyal and gallant this time. Some adivasis are killed by police who think they are dacoits. Massacre and sacrifice to Danteshwari of innocent villagers to teach Congress a lesson. Becomes immensely popular with adivasis because he revives old rituals for the goddess. Yearns for heir.

Chapter 12 - Wins election as an independent. Urges government to help adivasis, but Congress uncooperative. Meets Princess again. Begs her to return. She is induced by Congress to bait him and returns. He flies into a rage on finding that out, goes to the point of making love to her and then throws her out. But she has fallen in love with him and begs him to let her stay, even is she has to share him with Subhadra. He rejects her.

Chapter 13 - Incident of chopping off of hand. High Command on this pretext imprisons him. Escape bid fails. On parole for Danteshwari's festival. Popularity increased multifold; adivasis hail him as god incarnate. Police open fire without provocation and take him back to prison for a longer term this time. Vijayachandra made prince. In prison, completes his book: I-Pravir, God of the Adivasis. Subhadra has aged, past childbearing, jealous, they drift apart.

Chapter 14 - (1964) Underground training. Protest against rice procurement. Matters come to a head; arrested again. Indo-Pakistan conflict in the background.

Chapter 15 - Urmila Yadav enters the scene. Romance of no mean intensity. She is beautiful, young; new dreams.

Second last chapter - Urmila in Raipur refused bribery cheque from Indian government. Palace old and dilapidated, now a fortress. Vijay taken into rebellion. Police atrocities.

Last chapter: Police-adivasi fight; police atrocities; Urmila waits to be called to the palace to be queen. Brutal murder by police.

I said, "Aunty Maru seems to have done her research, don't you think? She must have been quite serious about this novel. I am pretty sure all those incidents did happen, and we can find out easily enough if there was a real Urmila Yadav or someone like her. And did you notice the detail about the baby dying at the goddess' feet? Must have been some legend she was basing it on."

"Or Yul Brynner in *The Ten Commandments*," Stephen said.

"No way," I said, "this was written long before that."

Stephen had already looked for the information. "1956," he said. "Cecil B deMille's classic starring Yul Brynner, Charlton Heston, Anne Baxter."

"Why did I think it was Elizabeth Taylor? 1956, eh? So you think she used the child scene from here?"

"Not necessarily, but could have. But, as you say, she probably took the main events from real life. Historical novels need a lot of background information to work well. Perhaps a lot more work than other genres. Would be fun to write that novel for Aunt Maru. I'd be happy to give up what I am doing and turn to my first love if my second love would marry me and love me forever more."

"You never told me that writing was your first love!"

"You always pretend not to have heard what you don't want to hear, my second and to-my-death love. My grandfather's library did it for me. I read a lot of what he called classical stuff that every kid should know; Walter Scott – I could use my Walter Scott to complete this novel. And now with all these search engines, holy christo it would be fun."

"You actually read all of Scott? No way, Aunt Maru had half a dozen books by him, and even when she rented the old Ivanhoe movie because she had to see it again after the new one, I couldn't get through the novel. Must be the Scot in you that you could enjoy Scott. Ivanhoe for sure had Elizabeth Taylor, right?"

"Yes, she was Rebecca in the 1952 Ivanhoe. And I don't have any Scottish blood in me, to my knowledge."

"Why don't you Google? You might find out you do have not just Scottish blood but even some royal blood. That would account for some of these fascinations of yours."

"Before I act out one of my fantasies, I do want to tell you that Aunt Maru was off-base about the father scenario, as you can see," he pointed to the computer screen. "Remember that his mother was the queen, not his father. Also, she died in 1936, and he became Ruler when he was still a minor. He was born in 1929, and here is an entry that also thinks as Aunt Maru did, that he was ambushed and killed by the police."

He continued, "I think I would have enjoyed living in those days, not sure about being this prince but I always fantasized about being Robin Hood. I think I would really have loved to have been Robin Hood. Wouldn't you have loved to be Maid Marian, Preetums?"

I had to think back to a time I had long forgotten to remember what he was talking about. To go back to age twelve, that seemed another life altogether, one buried when I got to Frantz Fanon, and Gilbert and Gubar, and Chomsky, and then on to the world of Gray's Anatomy and what comes after. But Stephen had that wonderful capacity instantly to revive and live his ten-year old self. A kind of innocence that completely captivated me.

"Or I could have been an Indian prince," Stephen said.

"I think even the best of them was a jerk of sorts," I said remembering another sheet I had read, about Chittammai's friend the maharani. "None of them seemed to have been a faithful husband, and there was at least one who was no husband at all though married for donkey's years." It was one of the stories I had put in the Stephen box – a carton in which I dropped stuff I wanted him to read. I gave it to him.

I wonder if I can make a story of this story that Chittammai told me:

He was a saint, a reformer, a devout Hindu, an enlightened ruler. He lived a simple life, hating the ostentatiousness of royalty. He dismissed his personal bodyguards and went about unattended. Often he could be seen at dawn, driving his motor car around the city. His life was exemplary except for one side of it. He did not live with his wedded wife, a Rajput princess. His Dewan had advised him to bring royal Rajput blood to improve the plebeian blood of his dynasty. With pomp and pageantry, he had been married to her. Every household in his kingdom, every little shop, had a framed photograph of the king and his queen taken at the wedding.

Then, how soon after the wedding I do not know, the rajah shunned his queen. He put wealth, servants, comforts at her service, but he told her never more to show her face. She was banished from his presence. Probably it was his mother (or was it his sister?) who induced him to do so, saying their dynasty will not prosper with mixed blood. He lived a celibate life. So did the queen. She lived alone, separated from her husband, walled away from the subjects, cut off by sheer distance from her father's land and people. Years later a cousin came to serve the king, sent by her father, so C thinks, to see that she was at least put to no hardship. Whenever C visited her, she begged her to come more often....

Once the maharaja went on a pilgrimage to Badrinath. When he returned, the queen begged him to grant her audience that she might touch the feet that had touched the sacred temple of Badri, but he refused.

(The story of Sada's trip to Alakananda and our maid servant's attitude towards his walking sticks comes to mind - the way our maid complained one day about the old walking sticks piled behind one of the almirahs which made sweeping so difficult and then when she came to know those staffs had been used to climb up sacred mountains, she made it a point to wipe them clean and touch her head to them everyday.)

Another story is about another uncle of the maharaja who, so the story goes, went on a tour of India. In Calcutta, he eyed with lust a young woman who stood on the balcony overlooking the road he walked on. He sent her a message. He received a reply asking him to come to a particular place for an assignation. He did. There four hired ruffians awaited him, butchered him to death, buried him and raised a stone over his grave overnight. The price of lusting after a Bengali landowner's daughter does not differ from beggar to prince.

The celibate raja was succeeded by his nephew. The father of this nephew was a rake, a sensualist, a gambler. He had been banished from his brother's presence. He spent his life outside the kingdom, dying in Bombay. (Was he the same as the one mentioned just above?) The nephew was married to the sister of a Rajput raja. She was beautiful, queenly, proud. She was a good hunter and a fine horsewoman, a lover of games and parties. She was highly westernised. She galloped cross country in riding breeches.

One night, the new king rushed to the British Resident, held hurried consultations, motored back to his palace, had his wife's possessions packed off in several trainloads, and so with the Resident's permission packed off his wife bag and baggage back to her father's kingdom. No one knows why. The queen had conceived several times but as often had a miscarriage. The story goes that she had bribed her European lady-doctor to induce abortion every time. Or was it that someone who did not like her had fed her something each time?

Later he married one of his relatives. He had many children. Still later, he lost his kingdom to independent India. And the curse on his dynasty still holds that says no king of this kingdom shall be succeeded by his son. Never before had there been a son. Now there is no kingdom.

I went to the kitchen to brew some fresh coffee. Stephen handed me a sheet of paper, which he said was next to it. I quickly perused it. It had nothing to do with Chittammai and I said as much but he said it might help me date the other piece.

This is the fourth typewriter I have owned. The first was an Olivetti bought in Italy by V on her way back in 1961. It had a beautiful Elite typeface. It was light blue and small and neat, with a matching vinyl case that had a black band running from top to bottom.

My second typewriter was a small Olympia bought in 1963 when I was at Bloomington, for $61.50. It too had Elite type but the type somehow was not as embossed as the Olivetti's. I had to buy a belt because the lock could not bear the weight of the machine. It was perhaps the prettiest looking of my typewriters. I gave it to S. when I left the United States.

My third typewriter was given to me by my better half. It was by far the swankiest typewriter I have ever had – an Electra 110, bought literally on the eve of our departure for home in June

1965. It had a bold Presidential Pica typeface, and many symbols and Greek alphabets. It was an electric machine, 220 volts, with mathematical symbols, vertical and horizontal half-space and all. We paid about a hundred and eighty dollars for it and then two hundred rupees customs duty. I left it with B when we set out for Canada.

This is the fourth typewriter. It is a Smith-Corona Super Sterling, bought at Eaton's today, the 9th of February 1967 for $99.50. It smells of paint and newness. I like the typeface but I am not sure that I will be as happy with this as with the others. I expect to keep this for a long time, for years and years, unless I get a windfall through my writing, in which case I shall go for the swankiest typewriter of all times whatever that is at the time.

Stephen thought there was something wrong with the dates and the information, which just didn't tally with other dates and other data. I made a note of it and put it away.

Here was something with an exact date on it. Good. I marked it top right corner and put it back in the carton. Then I noticed that this too had been on a foolscap sheet. Drat, so the other might not be pre-Canada either. Stephen had gone into the kitchen to brew some coffee, and I too had to get back to my books. There was something about the dates that bothered me but I would look into that later.

Why was she using Indian foolscap sheets? Drat, everything has to be looked at again. As I was putting sheets away, I noticed a single foolscap sheet with the words "For Chittammai's maharaja story." It must have got separated from the other sheets. Even though my text books were calling me, I read it since it was only a page long:

Today I came up here for some reference books. The library assistant said I would find authors' names in the The Times of India directory. Next to these volumes were the Indian Year Books of old. I happened to pick out the 1947 volume and happened to open a page titled "Indian Princes and Ruling Chiefs." From each page looked out a prince, turbans, jewels, moustaches and all, and each page mentioned the dozen or so titles of the prince, his biography, rule etc.

I was thrilled, pageantry and splendour flashed out from those yellow-browned pages. I looked up under Bhopal and Jaipur and Hyderabad and Mysore. By the way, the commentary usually follows a pattern that includes "Born, Educated, Married..."

I looked up the kingdom in Chittammai's stories. In the 1941-42 volume there was a reference that blew me away. It said the Maharaja was married on 15th May 1938 to Princess Satya Premkumari Devi, sister of H.H. the Maharajah of Charkhari (a State that is not listed anywhere in the volume). But the 1945 volume (the 1943 and 1944 volumes were not on the shelf) had no mention at all of the wedding. Ah ha! says I, here is the story of how history gets rewritten, here is the princess who was sent away in secret (with the compliance of the British Resident.)

Then I went on to look for the author I had come to check but got caught up with this – Travancore is an anglicized form of Sri-Vazhum-Kodu (place where Sri dwells). Parasurama, having destroyed all the kings and kingdoms, gave the land away to Brahmins in expiation of his sin. He could not stay on the land since he had given all of it away, and so he went to the Western Ghats to meditate. Varuna and Bhooma appeared and said he could get land out of the water from Gokarnam (where he was at the time) to the distance he could throw his axe. He threw it from Gokarnam to Kanya Kumari, and that was Keralam.

There was a "note to myself" at the end:
Must look for the other 1939, 1940 etc. Year Books next time I am at the Library.

I made a note: So why was she interested in Travancore or Kerala? Must ask Uncle Siv. But Stephen had a lot more to say about the other piece when he read it.

"What a life, this makes me sure I wouldn't want to have been an Indian prince, Gee, imagine having to get a Brit's permission for personal problems!" We argued as usual, I saying Canada still has a Brit ruling over us and he saying it was not the same at all, the Queen was just a figurehead and I saying, So why not get rid of the figurehead like so many other countries have done and he saying Canada was not the same as India, and I said Anyway that's not the main point of the story. It is that the British can so easily doctor history through Year

Books. That's the point. Stephen whistled. "I might have to rethink about wishing to be an Indian prince, butchered and buried just for ogling, hmm. Let me see if there are more such stories." He went to one of the cartons and started rummaging.

"Hey, wait," I said, "you are not authorized to touch my cartons."

"Okay," he said, moving to the sofa with a handful of sheets. "I really should get back to the report I have to write for Watson," and he started reading Maru's sheets.

"Listen, looks like Maru loved Lewis Carroll."

"I would assume so," I said, "everyone loves Lewis Carroll."

"You mean you've actually read him?" he asked in an innocent voice just to make me mad.

I threw a cushion at him. I grabbed the sheets off his hand. "A foolscap sheet," I said, this means it is pre-Canada probably. I quickly read the piece.

"These cards just refuse to come right," Usha said, flinging the pack on the table. Most of the cards fell to the floor.

"You are right," said a voice next to her, "we won't."

Usha looked around but saw no one. There was a cough from the Jack of Clubs on the table.

"Well, I never," Usha exclaimed, looking at the Jack of Clubs who was as quiet and sad-looking as ever.

"No, we don't like being cursed and flung about," Jack continued. "We have feelings, you know. We don't like to be hurt any more than you do. That's why we haven't been coming out right."

"You awful mean things, I've been playing for an hour and a half! How could you set out to spoil my games?"

"Our game, if you please," said the Ten of Diamonds.

"Why?"

"You were playing with us, weren't you?"

"No, I wasn't."

"Which means," said the Ten, as though closing a case in a court of law, "if you are not playing with us, you were playing against us, and why wouldn't we try to avoid falling in line as much as you would try to get us into line?" He looked around triumphantly, and all the other cards smiled approval and clapped.

Usha had a feeling that the cards were laughing at her. Pricked into maintaining her point, she haughtily said, "If I were playing with you, it wouldn't be called 'Solitaire,' so there!"

"Excuse me," said Ten ostentatiously, "just a private word with Nine, if you don't mind," and then turned to Nine with a loud stage whisper, "Have you noticed, Nine, how impolite some folks become when they are losing?" Usha was looking at him as he spoke. "If you don't mind my saying so, my dear," Jack nudged her, "it is bad manners to overhear other people's talk."

"I feel like bonking him on his head," Usha said, crossly gritting her teeth.

"Bad manners, my dear," Jack said mildly, and rolled his eyes in a highly disapproving fashion."

"Why do you have to assume it is Lewis Carroll's influence?" I said, "she was forever playing solitaire as though her life depended on it."

"May be she started loving cards because of Lewis Carroll," he said. "If you say this is pre-Canada, that must be it, no one plays solitaire when they are kids unless they have a kink of some kind, a Lewis Carroll spill over."

We talked about the maharaja stories again. I couldn't get over the fact that the Year Books had simply erased a piece of information. Like erasing real Native culture from Canadian history books for the first hundred years because all books were written from the Brit angle. Stephen agreed, and since that precluded further debate, I went to my books.

~~~~~

FIVE

Uncle Siv left a phone message to say he had a meeting on Monday and if I were free the weekend he'd come early. I phoned him back that evening, and had to phone again at his office because he was not at home. "I'd be delighted to clear the weekend for you," I said, "we'll take you for dinner to a new restaurant that has just opened up on the strip mall down the road."

"We?" he said, "so at last there is a "we" in the landscape, eh?"

I was annoyed with myself. Sure I wanted him to meet Stephen, but I hadn't wanted him to be prepared. "No, Uncle Siv, it is just a manner of speaking, there's nothing happening."

"Hmm, WE," he said, "so what's his name?"

"Okay, I am seeing someone but it isn't serious."

"Hmm," he said.

"Okay, his name is Stephen Woodhouse."

"As in Leacock?" he said, "I trust he lives up to his names and has a sense of humour."

"Yes," I said, "but he spells it with two o's, or rather three."

"O O O," he said. "I am delighted."

"Wait, I want you to bring some photo albums," I said, "the early ones, they are in the glass-doored bookshelf in the family room. The ones with pics from your early days in Winnipeg."

"O O O," he said, "will do."

~

I phoned Stephen and asked if he was free Saturday evening to meet Uncle Siv who was coming by. His elation came clearly over the wire. When Ma came for a conference a few months ago, I had instructed him to disappear and not even phone. I wasn't ready for her. But Uncle Siv was okay; as a kid he had been my confidant, my surrogate parent along with Uncle Sharad. Nothing I had ever told him ever reached anyone else, except Maru of course. If Stephen and I spent a lot of time together, it drove me crazy, and if we didn't, it drove me crazier. I needed a second opinion, and looked forward to seeing them together.

I went straight from work to the airport and brought Uncle Siv home, intending for us to go out for dinner. I told him just enough about Stephen, that he was a Resident same as me but two years older because he had done the teenage trips - worked a year after High School and then travelled in Europe and all that for a year before joining University.

Stephen had a surprise waiting. He was home, and dinner was almost ready. He had even taken out the good china and got out a tablecloth and got the wine all chilled in the ice-bucket. I almost wished Dad was here – he would have appreciated those elegant touches. Uncle Siv was more slapdash about matters of elegance and probably wouldn't notice these finer points. Stephen formally shook hands, and asked Uncle Siv to join him in the kitchen while he tossed the salad. "Whoa," Uncle Siv said, looking at the pots on the stove. "Regular Indian food, by the smell of it. Why do you bother with salads?"

"A bit of this and a bit of that," Stephen said, "just in case my *palak paneer* and *pilav* haven't turned out right, there will always be salad and garlic bread. Hope you are okay with garlic."

"I think this calls for a shower and dress clothes," Uncle Siv said, "do you think I could do that?" He held up his suit-bag.

I got out a new towel and showed him the bathroom. Then I hugged Stephen because he was looking just so handsome and the table was set just so right, and he had even made a *raita* to go with the pilav, and I was just so happy to have Uncle Siv at my own place. I guess we went on a little longer than we realized, for Uncle Siv cleared his throat from the open bathroom door, and pretended to be combing his hair.

We went to the living room and Stephen brought out the wine, and we raised our glasses to each other. I rose to get the food to the table.

Uncle Siv asked, "So, how long have you been in Canada?" It was a private joke for him, to ask white people the question we were so often asked. I think Stephen was taken aback, but when Uncle Siv followed it up with "So, where are you from?" he caught on and grinned. "We come from simple stock," he said, not to be outdone, "can't claim we are descended from any Peshwa."

"Correction. Priti's father's forebears were ministers to Peshwas. In the caste hierarchy, that is a notch higher than royalty."

"More brahmin than the Boston B's, I get it," Stephen nodded. "I do believe my mother's great aunt was married into a Boston family, does that count?"

"Not if from the mother's side," Uncle Siv said seriously, looking at me for my reaction.

I pretended not to have heard, and called them to the table. We sat down, and as he opened out his napkin, Stephen said, "Berkshire. Family legend goes back to early 18th century Berkshire and a Sir Charles Woodhouse whose wife Martha had seven children, only one of whom survived to adulthood; she died delivering the seventh and he married again and had another two. I had an aunt who was a family-tree fiend, but she couldn't find if we were from Martha's son or the other woman's children, whose name I have forgotten because I want to be Martha's descendant."

"Good idea, erase all but what you want to believe and it becomes the truth. But really, Sir Charles hnh? Anant will like that. He is top drawer, you know, lots of palace stories and scandals in his family."

"Whew, what a relief to know I just might qualify for the top drawer."

They laughed. "So, what is your specialization?"

"Just Resident in general Surgery as of now, but I'd like to go with Ophthalmology, I think. My grandfather started losing his sight in his forties and couldn't read by the time he was fifty-five. He was a scholar, a Medievalist, and taught me Latin without books, grammar mainly, endless learn-by-rote declensions. And I believe he died early because he saw no point in living if one couldn't read." Stephen had leaned forward, the way he leaned when he was really into something. "I think that was when I decided I would study eyes." Then, seeing he was being too serious, he leaned back and said, "But I have been waylaid by just one pair of eyes and don't know what to do next. I think I will drift into family practice instead."

"Don't talk of family practice as though it is not worth doing," I said. "The whole system sucks – not enough doctors who stick to keeping young people healthy, too many wanting to keep old terminal patients alive. I'd like to switch if I didn't have to go back of the line all over again for a residency."

"Sexism no no no; ageism okay I guess." Stephen smirked.

"Please, not when we are having delicious pilav and palak paneer with wine," Uncle Siv raised his glass. "To men who can conjure up a dinner for women who… I'll leave you to fill in the blank."

"To Doc Siv," Stephen said.

I would have come up with a quick repartee any other time, but was too intoxicated with the feeling of exhilaration that the two got along so swimmingly.

"I think you should go with eye-care," Uncle Siv said, "When you lose something suddenly, you do wonder about continuing to live; may be it is the same when you lose it over a period of years. I can sympathize with your grandfather, I too think that if you can't read, life might seem useless and not worth living."

Stephen missed the personal point and said, "But nowadays, even the blind can read with their ears; I volunteer at CNIB and read books into their recorders. And I am planning to go to Africa with World Vision; I hope to leave as soon as my term here is over. I'm working on getting the travel documents ready. I've been told I could do more good if I were to specialize first, but I am itching to go."

"Have you heard of the MSMF? Manjari Sankurathri Memorial Foundation, started by a civil servant from Ottawa who lost his entire family in the crash of Air India flight 182."

"Tell me more, the name rings a bell."

"He too must have gone through the phase of not wishing to live, but he picked himself up. He resigned his job, went to his native state in India, and set up an Eye-Care programme. His team of eye-surgeons take their medi-van to villages and set right patients with cataracts, which is the commonest problem and also perhaps the easiest to set right. He built an eye-hospital and one thing led to another. Now, the Foundation runs a dozen or more free eye-camps each year which go out to where the patients are, and a free hospital complex complete with amenities for overnight stays for more complex surgery, and residences for visiting doctors and paying patients. And what is more, there is a free school for children. It is a recognized Canadian charity, and so even if you don't want to go out as a volunteer doctor, do consider giving a donation to help the school."

Stephen said, "Now I remember. There was a CBC documentary on him. Yes, it was very impressive, but I remember thinking that the children were super-disciplined the way they sat in pin-drop silence at meals. I am not sure that is the way to go."

"Why not? In churches here, people sit in pin-drop silence. We don't, in our temples people are chattering all the time, and children run around, and I am sure that bothers white visitors as much as the funereal silence at marriage services in the churches bothers me. And let me tell you, that most of the great work, the innovations and research being done in Canada is by us who have come from elsewhere and been trained in that kind of classroom discipline of sitting upright and still, and having respect for learning and for teachers."

I had heard this many times before, but there was an edge of impatience, even of anger, in Uncle Siv's voice that I had never heard before. To change the topic somewhat, I asked what he thought of Stephen's plan to go to Africa for World Vision.

"India would be better considering you are from India but Africa is fine too. Shramdan," Uncle Siv said, "to give of one's labour, old Vinobha Bhave ideals. "

"Bhave? Isn't that your cousins' family, Priti?" Stephen asked.

"Not related, but would be proud to be," I said.

Stephen saw an opening and jumped for it. He said how miserable he was not to have met any of my family and how I refused to visit his parents and refused to invite him over to Winnipeg. He went on to say he was so happy to have met a member of my family at long last; and especially because he was meeting his competition who had been taking up more of my time than any other single person.

Uncle Siv told him he could come down to Winnipeg any time and stay with him, and he would do the needful re: intros. "We can make it look like pure coincidence that we bump into her parents, and that you are my friend, and we can leave Priti out altogether if you wish. I am sure Anant and Vee would enjoy meeting you."

"Only because thank god I am top drawer, Upper Canada and all, eh?" Stephen said.

"That helps, sure. I won't try to hide that bias on our part. Family background matters to us, I am quite unapologetic about that. However, out of sheer loyalty to my pretty maid, I would suggest that you say nothing of your relationship without her permission. You can have a beer with Anant and me at the Club or I could wangle so you get to see both of them, Vee and Anant, but as my friend, not Priti's, if you are okay with that deal."

"He is not getting anywhere near Winnipeg," I said.

~

After dinner, Uncle Siv said he had something for me in the car. He asked Stephen if he would be so kind as to go down to the car and bring back the large leather portfolio case from the trunk.

"I wondered if it was a gift for me, but since you didn't bring it in, I thought it was to do with your meeting," I said, as Stephen left with the car key.

"I think you should keep him, and not return him to the shop." That was a phrase from our childhood, how our parents wouldn't return us to the shop even when we had been naughty. We always got our punishment but I guess it was reassuring to know we would never be returned to the shop the way our mothers kept returning so many things to the stores.

"So you think he's okay?" I asked.

"More than okay. And that from one who never thinks anyone is good enough for one of his own."

"Whatever it is, it is heavy," Stephen said, coming in and placing the package against the recliner. "What is it?" I said. Uncle Siv first gave me two photo albums and then unwrapped the brown paper sheet around the top half. It was a jigsaw puzzle, one of those 1000 piece puzzles that Maru loved.   I said, "Stephen, I've got to tell you about this pastime of Maru's."

"Obsession," Doc Siv interrrupted.

"Every Christmas, because that is when they came on sale by the scores, she bought several, and did them the rest of the year. Any given day, you could see a puzzle spread on the formal dining table. She went about it very methodically. First she brought two 24x30 inch plywood bases, of which she had several, from the basement. Then she separated the edge tiles from the rest; and put together the frame with the edge-tiles on one of the plywood sheets. This would take several days. Then she would put it aside and on the other sheet place her bowls, six or seven fruit bowls from one of her first sets of melamine tableware, and start separating tiles that looked like they might belong to a section – one bowl for sky, one bowl for grass, one for the mountains, one for the house, and so on. All her puzzles were of landscapes with a little house, or manor houses and palaces with big gardens, and it was easy enough, so she maintained, to see to which bowl each tile belonged, more or less. This would take days and days. And then she would start on the main job. That would take her forever. If they had called guests for dinner, the bowls and plywood bases would be carefully moved to their bed in the morning, and put back on the dining table after the party stuff was put away. Once the puzzle was done, weeks or months later, Uncle Siv would glue the pieces from the back in some elaborate process during which time there were to be no parties, no visitors, and he would frame the whole thing so it could be hung on the wall. Of course, it never was – and to be honest, what looked so fantastic lying on the table looked rather plugugly on the wall. I don't know if they were ever hung, but I sure know there were a dozen just stacked up in a corner of the basement."

"While you are at it, you might as well relate how she got her obsession," Uncle Siv said.

"For that you have to go to the beginning of time," I said. "The year she left India she started taking courses in the English department, because that is what she had done her B.A. in – English and Philosophy and what?"

"History," Uncle Siv said.

"Two of the first things she bought for herself were a typewriter, an Italian one, I forget the name (Olympia, the Italian one was an earlier gift she got, said Uncle Siv) and a 500 piece jigsaw puzzle. Don't ask me why she bought the puzzle but she did. She spread it out on the dining table of their small apartment, and since it was also their study table, they could neither eat nor write properly until it was done, and so she spent all her time at it. But it was just impossible, and so she set it on the carpet on newspapers, and carried on for days; her assignments lay ignored, her term papers never got done on time, and she developed a backache arching over it on the carpet. She had to abandon it after three weeks so she could finish her courses. She was so disgusted with her incompetence that come Christmas break she bought herself half a dozen puzzles and of course each puzzle took less time than the one before because they were all cut in the same pattern, and the moral of the story is," I spread my hands just the way Maru always did, "once you get the hang of how to read literature, the way any text is put together is the same even though each picture is different."

"The typewriter I can see, but there must be a Freudian or some such reason for a 1000 piece jigsaw puzzle. Figure that out."

Uncle Siv said, "I am sure you can come up with a very imaginative reason, but the truth is usually rather mundane. She once spent a summer with her cousins who came from the States to spend some time in India, and they had a 750 piece puzzle. They would come in, look at it, pick a few tiles that fit exactly and then walk away. Maru couldn't get even one tile in place, not even by fluke during the entire two weeks she was there. And so, when she saw these 1000-piece puzzles stacked up at Eaton's, she just had to get them. To prove to herself she could."

"So what do you think this means?" Uncle Siv tore the other sheet of brown paper and held up the frame. It was the usual English garden landscape with flowers at the bottom and clouds at the top, but at the centre was a huge tiger, moving against the innocent flower beds towards the still blue lake.

We studied it in silence. Or rather, Uncle Siv studied us as we studied it. "It is stunning," I said.

Stephen said, "What did you say about getting the hang of how to read literature?"

Now that I was asked a question, I couldn't remember what had come so naturally when I was retelling the story. Uncle Siv said, "Once you get the hang of how to read literature, the way any text is put together is the same even though each picture is different. That is what Priti said, I don't know what Maru might have said. I am thinking the word 'hang' is atypical of her, but yes could be, she often used juvenile language with young people."

"I think what it means is that the tools of writing, like the structure of sentences, imagery, symbols, all have their own patterns and the writer fits them together neatly, like a puzzle. A good writer makes them fit tightly." Stephen mused aloud. "But why the tiger?"

Uncle Siv said, "Two puzzles cut by the same jig saw in the same pattern. That is what this is. A good metaphor lends itself to many interpretations. Like The Ancient Mariner, if you see him as a religious allegory of a lost soul, all the other events in the story get their meanings consistent with the main allegory. And then if you see him as a poet, a much richer story emerges – like the poet in Kubla, he is isolated in his world of imagination. Bring me the poem and I might be able to explain what I mean more clearly."

I said I didn't think I had a copy of *The Ancient Mariner*. Uncle Siv got quite angry about that. What was I doing with shelves and shelves of books if I didn't have the classics. How could I call myself an educated woman if I didn't have the classics. As a boy, he went to bed with Palgrave's *Golden Treasury* under his pillow. And here I was without a standard poetry anthology.

Stephen, a little stunned by this onslaught of derision, came to my defence by deflecting Uncle Siv back to the debate. "I understand your point about allegories, the many allegories that can come out of the same text, like Kafka's little parables about the policeman; if the policeman is an uncaring God, the church tower, the clock, the train station, each falls into place a certain way; but if he is the enemy that has taken over Czechoslovakia, the tiger has taken over the flowerbeds. Could that be it? In any case, allegories are passé nowadays. Rushdie has said he is tired of being read in India as an allegorist. He is quite adamantly against allegory."

"Rushdie is a bit of an ass when it comes to his essays. A fine novelist but a half-baked commentator – his pontifications are rather inane, especially considering all his novels are allegories, and by now he is getting rather repetitive. Forget Rushdie." I was amazed at the confidence with which he dismissed Rushdie, and I could see Stephen was quite amazed too.

Uncle Siv made a sweeping gesture with his hands. "Sorry, sorry. Mustn't lose my temper. Thing is, I have been looking at this longer than either of you, after all. When I was gluing and framing it some years ago, I never bothered to think about its strangeness – it was a job and I did it, and as Priti said, it was just stacked along with the rest. But when I tried to clean the basement the time I put the house up for sale, which thank God I had the good sense to retract, this puzzle just jumped at me, and I've been wondering about it ever since. And I brought it for you because it has to be relevant to your work. Got to be. It is just too oddly out of place with her other puzzles. I suppose she threw away the other pieces from both the puzzles that went into this."

Stephen turned the picture towards himself. "I think the tiger is our inner power, in full control of the world around. See how he is not destructive, the flowers are not trampled on, he is in control of the beauty of the world."

I said, "I think the tiger is our inner fear. I think Maru has written about it somewhere, tigers, I am sure she has written about tigers. I will get it or I will at least remember it as I go through her papers. I am sure I will."

"I will leave it with you, and it is time for me to go to my hotel."

"Why don't you stay here tonight? Tomorrow you'll have time enough to sleep and prepare for your weekly seminar."

"Thanks, Preet, but I'd better get going; I'll call for a cab. I have a full slate tomorrow, meeting friends. Been rather incommunicado for a long time. I would have continued that way but one of my friends from my student days at IIT is in the seminar too, and once he knew I was coming, you bet the rest of the old Indian crowd knew it too. I owe it to him to resurface as it were."

"You mean I don't get to see you again, that's it? when are you leaving for home? What are you doing Monday night after the meeting?"

He put his hand on the left side of my face, how long his fingers were and how soft, and said, "I will come again, as often as you want me to come, and that is a deal." Then he added, because I guess my tears were showing, "How about tomorrow, high tea at my hotel? About 4 or 5? Are you both free?"

I smiled. "In that case, you can sleep at your hotel. We'll drive you back."

"May be you could drop me on the way," Stephen said. I am sure he said that to tell Uncle Siv we had our own separate places.

"I need you here," I said. "To clean up," I added.

"Of course," Uncle Siv said, smiling.

~

Next morning, after a rather heady night of love-making which made us get up quite late, I pulled the cartons to the living room, and opened them to look for the tigers. Stephen, who had stayed over and not left for his apartment as he usually did, said I was being rather maniacal, riffling through everything, mussing up any order Maru night have had in mind, and undoing my own work of the last few weeks. "I've pencil-marked the possible date on everything I've read so far," I said, and continued to search. "At least tell me what you are looking for," he said, "I can help."

"It is one of the scripts that Aunty Maru wrote for her weekly television shows back in the 80s."

"TV host in the 80s eh? Interesting. Innovative."

"It was called PALI."

"As in the language? meaning what East Indians in Canada are doing is like what Pali is to Sanskrit, kind of popularising the classical?"

That is what I loved and hated about Stephen – how quick he was to grasp the essence and how this one-upmanship frustrated me. Because that is exactly how Maru had explained - how the acronym for Performing Arts and Literatures of India so well expressed the commonising of the pure original for public accessibility. I did not want to expand the acronym to Stephen and now he had hit the nail on the head.

"Oh she was way ahead of her times, my Aunty Maru. So involved with inspiring young Indo-Canadians to stand tall, as she would say, telling them about India and having guests born in India who were super-fine at their profession, whatever it was, just to show we were everywhere and doing a fine job at whatever we did. She would write her scripts on 5x8 cue cards, and put the date on top. That is what I am looking for, 5x8 cue cards with a script called The Language of Dance or something like it. It came to me early morning. I dreamt I was watching it all over again as I did when I was a kid and she had this clunky video player that most others were still only renting for the weekend along with Indian movies. It was about *mudras*, hand gestures in dance, and she used posters from an Air India calendar, or maybe it was an Indian Airlines calendar. She collected calendars.

I got off the floor and took a dance pose, and showed Stephen some *mudras*. Though it was a good twelve years since I was last on stage, the movements came easily, and I remembered as though it was yesterday those first days of my dance career when as girls of seven to sixteen, I the youngest, ten of us lined up in Maru's basement, and were taught by a motherly lady from Montreal our first steps of Bharata Natyam.

I said, "Indian classical dance is very set in its rules; like you said about Latin declensions. We can't get to real dance until we have the hand and foot movements coming out of our ears. Mudras especially, hand gestures. There are twenty-eight one hand gestures and twenty-four two-hand gestures." With my hands, I went through them in sequence as though I was once again seven years old and Mrs. R. was standing in front of us, cymbals in hand. "Pataka, Tripataka, Ardha-pataka, Kartari-mukha, Mayura, Ardha-chandra, Arala, Shukatundaka, Mushti, Shikhara, Kapittha, Katakamukha and so on... and then there are two-hand gestures – and combining these, you can tell any story there is in the world. Like, here is a bee buzzing around a flower while the deer runs lightly through the forest and the peacock dances and the birds in the trees chirp, and here is a woman getting ready for a tryst with her lover, and when he comes, here they are in their togetherness, two bherunda birds cooing and kissing." And I flung my hands around Stephen's neck and kissed him because of the joy of dancing love-stories through my early teens on the stages of the city, long before boys and sex were anywhere in our lives.

"You are good, sweetheart, oh my, are you good? I didn't know anything about this part of you at all? Why did you give it up?"

"At one time I thought I was going to be a dancer, Canada's best dancer ever, but that was just a phase, like phases we all go through until we figure out what we really want to do. When you find out about all the poverty and AIDS and pesticides in the world, dancing sequences about love-sick young women seems juvenile, irresponsible....Now back to finding what we are looking for, that script. Tigers, our inner fears, and the mother figure, Maru was always into mother-daughter vignettes may be because she had three sons but never got the daughter she always wanted." And even as I said it, I thought of all the girls she had mentored, and that she had chosen me to be in charge of all this.

After a few minutes during which I had totally disarranged everything, Stephen held up a sheaf of lined paper on which it was xeroxed, two cards to a page – Imagination and the Language of Dance, August 29, 1981. I started reading it aloud. He lay on the carpet, his hands under his head, and listened.

The language of dance is very like any other language. It communicates through generally accepted symbols. As in reading, the more familiar you are with the nuances of the language, and the wider your vocabulary, the more enjoyable is the experience. As in reading, the initial steps are the same – you have to learn the letters of the alphabet, going through a routine that has a lot of repetition, and little rhyme or reason. Then the letters are put together into words – R-A-T rat, M-A-T mat, S-A-T sat. Then comes the thrilling part for an imaginative child – when the words are strung together in a sentence that conveys action or feelings – Pat's rat sat on the cat's mat. At this point many things come together, generating a variety of responses. First there is the sound. Children enjoy the *sound* of words long before they know their sense. Dr. Seuss's books are so popular because they *sound* so good. One of my young friends used to say she was born at the WinnipegGenerationHospital, which you must grant, sounds so much better than Winnipeg General Hospital, and has its own serendipitous meaning. My daughter, when she was two or three, used to string along words whose sounds she loved; one of her favourites was "what a fantastic, automatic, bombastic bumble bee fiasco" and if it weren't for the "bumble-bee" one would have thought she knew the meaning of the words he was uttering.

Sound, then, is a basic tool in the language of dance just as it is in the language of speech. All of us have a sense of rhythm, and since one always dances to music, all of us can enjoy dancing and watching dance. It always increases one's pleasure if one knows about other aspects as well. In dance, the other basic tools are facial expressions and body movements. The fourth tool is what we are going to talk about today – they are called mudras, or hand gestures. Most of them are quite mimetic and you can figure out the basic meaning rightaway. Here are some pictures from this year's calendar issued by Indian Airlines. Take this picture, for instance: A woman holding a mirror in one hand and putting the red dot on her forehead with the other. The basic meaning is clear enough – she is putting on her make-up so to say. But in dance, this gesture means a whole lot of other related things as well. It means that the woman is young, and that she is in love because she is decking herself with care, and that the associative meaning is that she is about to go out to meet her lover. So that, when a dancer makes this gesture, you know she is saying something about love and lovers. The gesture builds up anticipation and atmosphere in the minds of the audience.

Take this one. You can see from her face that she is looking at or looking for something, but the hands don't tell you anything unless you know the language of dance. It is like coming across a new word; you need a dictionary or a teacher, to give you the exact meaning. Once you know the meaning, you remember and recognize it next time. This mudra signifies that the girl is standing under a tree in the forest. It says a lot more, if you know the words of the language of dance.

Back to plain words. Take the word "tremble." The dictionary will tell you it is "to have a slight irregular vibratory motion, as from some jarring force." But trembling means a lot more than that. The word communicates a whole lot of feelings of fear, anxiety, helplessness.

So also in dance. Your associations will build up the whole scene. The sky is getting dark, the chirping of birds has died down, there are soft rustles on the grass; she is afraid, she is disappointed, and yet she is still hoping he will come. All that is packed in this gesture when it is accompanied by small movements of feet and eyes and face.

Let me first explain the mudras shown on these posters. Then I shall make up three different stories with the same pictures to show you how you can use these mudras to say a great many different things. The most challenging and satisfying aspect of any educational experience is to use knowledge imaginatively. For language, whether of dance or literature or science, is a medium for flights of imagination, and imagination is the most wonderful gift given to humankind.

(Cameraman to move through sketches of mudras with my voice-over of names and descriptions.)

Now let us make up three different stories with these posters. (Remember to give cameraman copy of script.) The first could be a Bharata Natyam piece, where Radha calls to Krishna.

Come to me, my lord Giridhar. You, who in boundless compassion raised the mountain aloft to shield your friends from Indra's rainstorm, have compassion on me, your devotee.

Come, my lord, I want to see you with your flute at your lips, peacock feather crowning your brow.

Come to me with your lovely earrings and your garland of *Vyjayanthi* flowers.

My friends tease me because I am always parting my veil to see if you are anywhere near.

I have been waiting so long, Giridhar, my limbs are tired, my eyes heavy with disappointment; why do you delay?

Was it in vain I decked myself, bordering my hands and feet with red henna, smiling into the mirror thinking of the pleasures to come?

The twilight is deepening, Giridhar, and a peahen is eagerly looking at the dark sky for the rainclouds that will make her lover spread his turquoise fan.

It is getting dark, Giridhar, and still you have not come. The Bherunda birds, nestling in their love, mock at me.

The shades of night have fallen, my lord, and still I wait for you under the forest tree for the sound of your flute.

O Giridhar, who lifted the mountain on a single finger to shield your friends from rain, have pity on one who is dying under the shower of love's darts. I wait for you Giridhar, I shall always wait for you.

Next, let us take up the same mudras on the posters and write a script for a Kuchupidi sequence. One of the differences between Bharata Natyam and Kuchupidi is the attitude of the dancer, and the body and facial movements that go with that attitude. Whereas in many Bharata Natyam sequences, a woman begs and implores her lover to come to her, in Kuchupidi she is more aggressive, confident of her beauty and her power to attract. With the same posters imagine the movement of hands and eyes that go with this story:

You are always bragging and teasing, Giridhar; you who lifted a mountain, can you sustain my love, Giridhar?

Your flute and your crown of peacock feathers are open for all to see. You flaunt your gold-orbed earrings as you come tripping across the fields. But my nymphlike beauty I keep behind my veil which I shall part only for the one I choose. Are you he?

I am not like these others, pining for lovers who keep them waiting.

My mirror tells me I am surpassingly fair; I wear these rings and bracelets, this henna and kohl paste only to conceal my natural beauty that is saved for the one I shall choose; would you be he?

Now, let us put to use the same mudras and posters for another kind of story. This poster of a Kathakali dancer with his hands in the Urnanabha mudra signifies a tiger and its ferocity, and the long claw-like nails and red eyes again signify the tiger. I love this other poster where the dancer is showing a two-hand mudra of gentleness; I make this dancer a mother because the veins on her hands seem so right for a mother-figure. Along with the other posters, I will use over and over again the posters of the mother and the Kathakali dancer, and the music of the drumbeat will dominate whenever the tiger is mentioned.

My mother was always by me, her soft voice caressing me as I lay in the warmth of her dark-bodiced bosom.

But there was always the other too, silently pacing the forest floor.

My mother's veil was of fine silk, and she breathed the fragrance of her jasmine love.

And the tiger's yellow stripes bound fast my tongue.

Be happy, my child, my mother sang, the world is a lovely place. You who lay like a lotusbud in my waters and are now cradled in life, open yourself to the sun.

I fear the sting of the bee, mother. Mother! I called. But the tiger's stripes bound fast my tongue.

And so it has always been since then; my mother's lulling voice and my own strangled silence as the tiger stalked the forest floor.

Hear the happy chirping in the forest, she said, oh look at those Bherunda birds nestling and basking in their love. And see the peahen eagerly watching for the rainclouds that will make her lover spread his fan in dance.

With steady heavy quiet steps he walked the forest floor.

Mother, the girls deck themselves for their twilight tryst under the forest tree. Red henna on their hands and feet, kohl paste lining their black eyes, flowers of many colours adorning their hair. How beautiful they are, Mother, there is such breathtaking beauty in everything they do, in every mood they have. See my sister's farway look as she draws her veil modestly over her head with her right hand and then shyly parts it with her left to see if he is come. And my bold cousin does exactly the same thing but oh so seductively. I see all my friends, so breathtakingly beautiful because each fancies her lover is none other than divine Krishna, his lovely earrings swaying as he teases her. Each sees her love with Krishna's flute and his crown of peacock feathers. Seeing them I forget all else, Mother.

Be happy like them, my child, she said, placing holy vermilion on my forehead and embracing me to her jasmine heart.

The night is dark, sisters, don't you hear the silent feet on forest grass? Sisters, so breathtaking in your love, do I alone hear the tiger padding across the forest floor? Mother, oh Mother, though my voice is bound by his black stripes, hear me!

And my gentle mother, her veined arms ageing before their time, was by my side. My daughter, who like a lotus-bud lay in my waters, you are now grown to lovely womanhood. What ails you, my darling, whose happy songs filled our home with light, tell me, what ails you, my little one?

The tiger quietly walked the forest floor, wrapping my tongue in flames.

Tell me soon, my little one, for I must go. My lovely lotus flower, why do you turn away from the sun who is lord of all life? She looked sadly at me, and receded, her white skirt a speck in the enclosing night.

And the tiger came on, padding silently across the forest floor.

"Sends shivers down my spine," Stephen said. "You read beautifully, and I could hear the drumbeats. Whew."

"Let me finish," I said, and continued.

As a writer, that is the ending I would have. However, in the context of dance and its elevating power, the ending I feel should be more reassuring, and so I have this alternate ending:

My daughter, who like a lotus bud lay in my waters, you are now grown to lovely womanhood. What ails you, my darling, whose happy songs filled our home with light, tell me what ails you, my little one, that you turn away from the sun who is the lord of all life?

And then I was struck by a deeper fear and fancied her white skirt was already receding in the enclosing night while the tiger came on, quietly padding across the forest floor. But she placed her gentle hands above my head and said, "Do not be afraid, my darling child; it is the law of nature that we always stand beside you, he and I, always. I the other now as he was once.

Stephen said, "Powerful, but know what? There is some disjunction about the audience she has in mind – she starts off in language suited to children almost, and then the last story is like wow, sex, fear of sexuality."

I did not say anything, for it struck too close to home. There was that phase I went through when sex and boys were wrong, very wrong, but girl-bonding was okay. Togetherness, why can't we just be the bherunda birds cooing and basking in their love forever and a day, instead of wrestling with our bodies and minds? The arguments I always seem to have, god the arguments we have over nothing.

We didn't get to meet Uncle Siv again after all. He phoned to say he was still at the lunch party. Just about everyone they had known during their Ottawa stay had turned up. It must be awful, I said. No, no, he said, it is okay, they mean well, and one just has to put on a face to meet the faces that one meets. But he would come again, now that he was back he would be hopping in, to Toronto, Montreal, Ottawa, once every month or two.

~~~~~

SIX

I had the weekend to myself. Stephen was visiting his parents. My long rotation was over, and I wanted to stay in bed for three days at a stretch. I gave the apartment a long overdue vacuum cleaning and even completed my laundry that had accumulated over three weeks.

I found a stack of typewritten sheets. By now I had figured out that Maru had a new printer early in the 1990s and did not use the endless-ream but single sheets. This was on single sheets – post 1990s, I jotted down on the right hand top corner. And then I realized from the number VIII that I need not have taken such a roundabout way to date it – It was numbered VIII – part of the saga she had started in 1993 surely? It was set in Ottawa. That's easy enough to check, but she could have written it later, who knows? I remember reading some of this already.

VIII Chikkamma comes for a visit.

I wrote about my community work experiences - the time Folklorama was first started and my work for the India Pavilion, the time I started all those dance courses in the late seventies, Spring 1978 to be exact, the time I had a weekly television show "helping Indo-Canadians stand tall" sort of thing, and then the heady days of my work with the Immigrant Women's Association which took me to Ottawa and all that, and then wow, the headiest perhaps of them all in that it gave me the most humungous headache ever - the time I was President of the local writers' guild. I wrote all these and more, with just the right mix of satire and fun, and then came December, and that month has a way of cutting into everything else.

Preempting everything, every single thing, including my voice. Gone, all gone. A year has gone by, just like that. But something else has come up, something I never believed could happen. Chikkamma has come back into my life.

~

Maru sat up and fluffed the cushions on the couch where she had been having a catnap. The room echoed with sounds of Christmas, carols sung at the bay party two days before Christmas, glasses clinking with christmas toasts, and the laughter of voices as family and friends had filled in the year's news to each other.

The snow fell softly on the lawn outside. From her house elevation she could see the entry signs to Route 417, Queen Elizabeth Way, shining luminescently against the green metal.

She heard the mailman at the door, or so she thought. When she opened the door, she let out a squeal at the small lithe figure that entered. "Chikkamma! what a surprise! come in, come in. " She opened her arms but then shied away as her visitor raised her right hand in admonishment. "How is one supposed to greet you, Chikkamma, maybe I should fall on my knees and touch your feet ....? I mean this is such a surprise! I have thought of you so often over the years, and now to see you face to face, I never imagined...."

"I see you are stumped for words. Not a good omen, one might say, to be losing your vocabulary. Writing your memoirs, I hear, but only about your life since you came here, from what I can see. What else can I expect? For twenty years we feed you and teach you and tend you through mumps and measles and diarrhea and whatnot, and bang slam, you shut the door and write only about curling and Ottawa and your feminist friends."

"I mean, it isn't like that. I do plan to write about my whole life, honest, not just about Canada."

"I'll believe it when I see it," she snorted, seating herself on the rocker as though she had been there all her life.

"How did you know I was writing? Oh, it must be Aunt Meena; I did show her some of it when she came for a couple of days from Frisco after visiting her son."

Chikkamma placed her large cloth bag next to her chair and gestured she wanted it to stay right there.

"Of course, of course, no problem," Maru hastened to her hosting duties. "Can I get you some coffee? may be tea would be a good idea? "

"What I would really like is some hot chukku vellam to clear my throat, but I don't expect you'd have any. So no thanks, I am fine. Sit down, and don't pace in circles like a cat that has just littered."

I sat on the couch, next to the rocker. It was incredible. Chikkamma had not changed one wee bit. She sat ramrod straight as always, stretching her five foot one frame to an intimidating height; her grey hair was curly and tightly knotted into a little bun at the back; and she wore the generic Conjeevaram silk sari that she had always worn, very small checks of white and some non-descript colour that changed with each sari; she must have owned a dozen of these checkered saris but I had always thought of them as one generic sari. And she was here! Chikkamma was here, in my living room in Ottawa this December afternoon. Incredible.

"Meena got your annual letter just as I was leaving for here, and so I know all about what everyone in your family has done this past year. So let's not waste time over formalities. Coming straight to the point, it was news of your daughter-in-law's pregnancy that sent you scurrying to your typewriter, right?"

I gasped. I had not made the connection, but yes, Arvind and Kathy could not come for Labour Day and so they had come for Thanksgiving, and yes Kathy was just beginning to show, rather early yes, she was hardly three months gone, and yes, she did look so beautiful, fragile and hardy at the same time, and yes, I had started my memoirs the day they left. The dishwasher had not been cleared of the previous day's dinner plates et cetera and so I had stacked the lunch things on the counters and wiped the table clean (an old habit from the old country - if you want to show that you want the guests to visit again you should clear their plates from the table and wipe it clean before they leave, a sign that they are always welcome to another meal there, and may it be in the near future) and then I had done something quite uncharacteristic - I had taken out my kumkum box (? what does one call a kumkum chimizh?) and placed a red dot on Kathy's forehead - a long and happy married life blessed with children - before hugging them goodbye. And then I had gone to the computer and had typed the title - Maru and the Maple Leaf. I couldn't remember if I had typed much else, but Chikkamma was right - I had started my Memoirs the day Kathy, her figure just beginning to curve with pregnancy, had left with Arvind.

"You are probably right, Chikkamma. I doubt I will have as much to show for it at the end of nine months, but I guess there is something about a pregnant body that sends writers on the birthing path."

Chikkamma laughed, a small snorty kind of laugh that reminded me of Chittammai, Chittammai of biting tongue and colourful adages. Chittammai would never miss a chance for a nastily pertinent retort, like "Yes, especially menopausal women."

But Chikkamma was not given to such hard-hitting retorts. She said, "Don't worry. Gandhari carried for two years."

"Oh no! don't talk of her! considering what she came up with at the end of it!"

"Sh, don't say inauspicious things. Everything will go well. If you would just write about the right thing, instead of getting stuck in elevators."

How did she know that? How could she ever know that I had written about getting stuck in the elevator in my Ottawa story, how? because I had very definitely edited it out as slowing the pace, so how could she have known?

"And not the first time either. How many stories have you started on in your life and left halfway? At least Gandhari delivered her foetus, even if she did hack it into a hundred pieces. And Duryodhan was not all that bad as he is made out to be, you know. You really should write about him, the way you wrote about Karna."

I brightened. "You're absolutely right, Chikkamma, I've always wanted to know more about Duryodhan, I think he was rather okay, fighting great odds, you know, the way everyone was always praising his cousins no end, yes considering the cards he drew, I think he played really well though it might be difficult to ignore his machinations."

Chikkamma smiled.

I continued, "I am so happy to see you, after all these years of me thinking and thinking about you, Chikkamma, this is just so incredible!!!!!!"

"Ramrama, don't go on and on. For everything there's a selfish motive. I have come to stake my claim, what else? If you are really going to start writing, well, you have to write my story, and don't you forget that."

"But of course you know why I haven't been able to. You've been buzzing around in my head for years but how can I write when you haven't told me anything."

"Oh come, Maru, excuses excuses."

"One teeny weeny bit of info is all I have."

"Isn't that enough?"

"How can it be? I can't even to begin to understand why you did such a thing."

"There are enough people still around who remember me. That is what biographers are supposed to do. Dig around, ask people."

"But why have you never told me anything? Why can't you be like Chittammai, now she was such a wonderful storyteller, and she's given me so much information."

"Chittammai this Chittammai that. The way you hung around her, like a toddler clinging around one's knees."

"Jealous, are you?" Maru tried to goad her.

"Not that you've done anything with all that material either."

"I will, I most certainly will, so help me god."

"I'll believe it when I see it." Chikkamma snorted, louder this time.

Then she said with sudden passion, "It has to be written down, her story, my story, not to boost our vanity, ah, what need of any name or fame do we have? But for the future, so young girls will know and remember the way things were. Do you think I haven't seen the way older women are treated, yes, even by the likes of you. Yes, even here, yes even in those feminist gatherings and vigils you go to; I have seen them, the women of an earlier age ignored by the young women and patronized by your generation."

Maru gasped. Chikkamma had been around, unbeknownst to her. How could she know so much?

Then, as suddenly as she had appeared, Chikkamma decided to leave. "Just remember what I've told you. And note that I am watching."

"Please, Chikkamma, what's the hurry? I thought you'd stay with me a few days. Halfway around the world, and you still fly in and out the same way you used to forty years ago; I remember how you never stopped even for a cup of coffee, and how often you made Mother so exasperated trying to get you to stay for lunch or tiffin. In and out like lightning.

"So why should I change now, hnh?"

"So where are you going to stay? With Aunt Vidya, I suppose, your favourite always."

"Jealous are you?" Chikkamma laughed her short delighted snorty laugh and went away, leaving Maru just a little breathless.

There was some mixing up of "I" and "Maru," I noticed. Clearly she was trying out both ways and had forgotten to make all the corrections once she switched from I to Maru. I wonder what an editor does with that kind of problem. Nohow, I am not an editor, no way, I am just trying to sort the stuff.

I phoned DocSiv early morning to catch him before he scooted off to his lab.

"Who is Chikkamma," I asked. "There is a story about some aunt of hers called Chikkamma."

"What's the story about?"

"I'll ask the questions," I said.

"She was her aunt of sorts," he said, "born about the turn of the century, the last century."

"Can't be," I interrupted, since she had visited Maru in Ottawa.

He continued unflapped. Chikkamma was a cousin of one of Maru's uncles; she was one of five sisters, whose father was a well-known teacher and administrator at the government agricultural college; he had built a house for each of his daughters on a huge estate in Mylapore; he had sent all of them to college, and in those days when most girls stopped going to school at twelve and were married off at thirteen, this man was an oddball. Chikkamma had not only earned a college degree but had gone on to become a school principal, and stayed unmarried. At the age of twenty eight, she had fallen in love with a married man, and they had got married.

At this point I screamed, I guess, and he explained that bigamy was not illegal at the time. But, as always happens when I get into my feminist mode, I interrupted and said a great many things. And he hung up on me saying he had to get to work.

Well, that clarified Maru's story all right. I read it again. Yes, there was a story waiting to be written. It threw me for a loop, though, to try to imagine may be my grandmother in love with anyone, least of all a married man. I remembered the nine yard saree women of her generation wore, and the old lithographs in my grandfather's house back in Pune, men in oversized Peshwa turbans and women in nine yard saris, as in Ravi Varma paintings that were framed and hung all over the house. There was one of a young woman, leaning against a tall peck-table, as my grandfather called them, (to peck finger foods off at cocktail parties?) and as I recalled her slender, elegant grace, I figured yes may be they could have been in love after all, even when swathed in nine yards of material. And then I remembered women wearing the nine-yard sari in the South Indian way, and no, the whole thing was just so cumbersome, I couldn't imagine love and passion. And yet, this Chikkamma had loved a married man! Was that a dumb thing or was it something outrageous? I decided from the voice I'd heard in Maru's story that this was an outrageous thing to do, and Chikkamma had done it. Good for her.

The phone rang. It was DocSiv. "Listen, you obstinate mule," he said, "and don't dare interrupt me. Oh what the hell, I can't tell you Chikkamma's story in this foul mood." And he hung up.

So I called him but he wasn't home. I called his office and there he was. "What are you doing, at work so early?" I said. "It isn't yet seven in Winnipeg. Did you have breakfast? I worry about you, Uncle Siv." He thawed.

"I'm okay, my priti maid, how are you? don't you have to go work?"

And so we talked. Chikkamma had a child. In those days, men in the civil service were transferred every three years, and so when the children were at a certain age, the family set up two homes, a permanent one in Madras so that the children's education wouldn't be interrupted, and another wherever the man was stationed, and the family visited him during the summer holidays, while he came once a month for festivals and such the rest of the year. When the time came for Chikkamma's husband to set up his first family in Madras, Chikkamma signed over her house to him and his first family, and she moved out with her little son to a house nearby. And she never lived with him again.

"You're kidding," I said. "Why would anyone do that?"

"She was a fine charismatic woman, I remember her. Always on the go."

That clarified things even further. No wonder even Maru was left speechless. I loved her instantly - this old woman looking over Maru's shoulder, insisting that her story be written.

So this piece, Chikkamma's visit - is identified as VIII. I looked at the binders I now had for each decade. What exactly was I trying to do? To get the chronology. But of what? I thought I was getting a chronology of her writings. But perhaps that was not what she wanted. "It has to be written down, her story, my story." But may be that is what I had in mind. Her own story. Her life as written in her works. So the chronology of the writings per se was not important. But of course it was, that is the only way one can write a life story. Or is it?

The questions totally befuddled me. It seemed so much easier to diagnose diseases. I put away the papers and set about getting ready for work. May be I could go early today and make up for my long lunch breaks, even though no one checked.

~

After Stephen had read the story, I told him what Uncle Siv told me about Chikkamma.

"But you didn't ask him about Chittammai, I guess," he said.

"For Pete's sake, she is not important," I said, deflated that he was not as excited as I was about Chikkamma's unconventional life.

"Of course she is important. She must have been quite somebody, see how jealous Chikkamma is of her."

"Come on, she clearly says both their stories have to be heard. She is not jealous."

"You know what I mean," Stephen said, "not jealous like malicious about-to-kill kind of jealous, just jealous like I am jealous of Uncle Siv and Maru for being more part of your life than I am."

"Oh my poor destitute lover boy," I said, "I will make up for it."

Later in bed, I remembered Chittammai quite clearly. "Maru had a lot of stories about her," I told Stephen, "how Maru's father retired to Bangalore and how she continued to study in Central India but went home for the holidays, and how her parents occupied her great uncle's empty house when he, a well-known scientist, moved to be closer to his laboratory. Maru had a great many anecdotes and for some reason I remember the stories about the servants more than any others. I guess it is because the whole concept of servants seemed like another planet in my teens, though I did remember from my childhood visits how many people there seemed to be in grandpa's house who seemed to do nothing all day except line up for their morning and afternoon tea in the back yard. But Maru's stories gave them faces and names and warmth and reality. Like Muthan. He used to take care of the cows. Chittammai had a farm some eight miles away in the countryside; even though they usually had only two cows in the city any given time, there were many more on the farm. Muthan would walk the eight miles to the farm, and walk back with one or two pregnant cows and take care of them for months and help in the calving process. He would walk the dry milch cows back to the farm and return the same day in time for the evening milking. Once, when a cow seemed to be dying, Chittammai had him grind all the tablets she had – penicillin and quinine and aspirin and what not and feed it to the cow, and the cow got better and could actually walk to the veterinarian's clinic. Cows were his life."

I lay back thinking of the story and laughed.

"Well, aren't you going to tell me his story?" Stephen said.

"I don't know if I can tell it well enough," I said. "Like once Maru wanted to visit someone who lived a few blocks away and she wasn't sure whether it was the fourth street from theirs or the fifth. So when she asked Muthan for directions, he said she should turn right at the street that had a water trough for cows, on the far side. So she went off and missed the water trough because it was so small, and had to retrace for the correct street, which had a public tap on the near side, the kind where you pump with a huge handle, with long lines of people waiting with their buckets and pots for their turn. That was Muthan. Had eyes only for cows' troughs and never thought of the faucet for humans which was so much more visible a landmark."

"I agree," Stephen said, "you don't know how to tell a story, but I like the guy. My mother's father had a farm, and she has stories of her childhood on the farm. Said pigs are really neat creatures which find a corner to do their daily dumps, and cows despite dropping their dump wherever they happened to be, never sat down on them."

"Haw haw," I laughed artificially. Even though the facts kind of fascinated me, for example why do we say dirty pig/pigsty etc., I wasn't going to let on they did. Weren't buffaloes supposed to love sitting in mud ponds? Somehow I distantly remember buffaloes at grandpa's little town walking around with mud caked on their behinds, and little boys giving their buffalo a bath at the lovely lake we had at one edge of grandpa's estate, but after my 'haw haw' I couldn't very well continue the topic.

~

By the sheerest of coincidences, I found three pieces relating to Chittammai's story the very next day. Two were in a folder and one was in a book that was in one of the cartons, *Close to the Heart*, a fund raiser for breast cancer research. Whoa! Did Maru have breast cancer? I thought. No way. She had a story in the volume though, and it was the cow story!

Cancer Simple as a Flower
"How can he say such a thing? 'cancer simple as a flower'? a flower, why a flower? Does he think cancer is beautiful? Or innocent? Or natural? What else does a flower mean to you? Maru, tell me. Cancer simple as a flower, yeah flowers die fast, I guess that is what it is huh? And he's supposed to be a great poet, huh." Lynne threw the book off her lap, and slid downwards on the hospital bed and pulled the sheet to her face. "So why do you think hospital beds are never placed along the wall? Isn't one supposed to turn away and face the wall just before one dies? Like cowboys are supposed to ride off into the sunset.?"

"You read far too much, Lynne," I said.

"Never has been a problem so far, so why now? I've been on the Dean's Honours list from day one, I was supposed to do my Master's in Cambridge, remember, Rhodes scholarship, all those references from professors you typed for me?"

Lynne was our best Honours student in the last ten years. As English department secretary, I had been typing references for students for a decade, and there had not been another Lynne MacAlister in my time – straight A+ in nineteen of the twenty courses. More important, I had known her for twenty years as my neighbours' kid. My little Giri and she had walked to school together Grade One to Six, at which time we had put Giri at SJR, a private school.

I picked up the anthology and flipped through the pages. "Karl Shapiro," Lynne said. I turned the pages. There it was, with Lynne's highlighter markings, "Auto Wreck." I read it.

"You know what he means, Lynne, 'suicide has cause, stillbirth logic,' but an auto accident makes no sense."

"That's what he says, but auto accidents happen because of bad drivers, drunken drivers, or mechanical defects which drivers are supposed to check for from time to time, all of which go right back to human volition. A human being DOES something, like drinking or not taking care of his car, and an accident is the deserved result. But cancer ? what have I done? how could I possibly have prevented it? I've never smoked, never afforded the luxury of tanning my skin on beaches, never had reason to use contraceptives. I've never even used tampons, for godssake. There's absolutely nothing I could have done to prevent it and nothing I can do to stop it. There's nothing I can do, period, except die soon and get out of this mess."

She was referring to various types of cancers but not her own. But she was right. She had not done anything wrong. I took Lynne's hand and stroked it, starting with the fingertips and gently working upwards. Lynne was angry. But that too was a defence mechanism, for the alternative was depression and loneliness. Everything had happened so suddenly. She had gone into the walk-in clinic with what appeared to be a minor problem and a week later was in hospital, diagnosed with cancer; now, six months later, she was back in hospital, awaiting surgery.

"My great-aunt Chittammai had breast cancer in those days when we didn't have all these cures."

"The aunt about whom you have so many stories?" Lynne got interested. "She died of cancer?"

"She died in time, as all of us must," I replied, "but she managed to do a great many things before that. Like saving the cow that had cancer. Want to hear that story?"

It was perhaps my voice that did it; I didn't speak in low tones or with fake joviality (we'll get you out of here in no time) as perhaps her other visitors had, but in my usual anecdote-voice, that she had heard over the years during the times I had been in a babysitting pool with neighbouring mothers.

"That's not a question but an Ancient Mariner grip, right? holding me with your glittering eye. I'll have to hear no matter what." Lynne was more relaxed already, and teasing me the way she usually did. I said, "You remember where Chittammai lived? in this big house on an acre of land right

in the middle of Bangalore? that had been built there before
the city had grown around it?"

"Yup, I remember, where you used to get monkeys
visiting every summer? remember the time a little monkey
died and all the monkeys kept a vigil over it all day? tell me
that story again."

"Some other time. Today it is about Gauri the Cow." It
was something about my motherly figure and voice that
almost made Lynne settle down, twirling her hair with her
left hand, the way she used to in her childhood days of
afternoon naps.

"Chittammai had hardly returned from the hospital after
her mastectomy before she fell near the steps and broke her
ribs."

"Oh no!!!"

"She took that too in stride, there she was in a wheel chair,
all bandaged up, and running the house at full throttle as
always."

"With all those domestics and gardeners and chauffeurs."

"But the only thing she couldn't do was laugh, because of
her ribs."

"She had a hearty laugh for her petite body, right?"

"A+ for your memory, Lynne. One day, Muthan, the man-
of-all-work, brought a cow from their estate - they had a country
cottage, you remember? just outside the city, where they had
fields and several cows and bullocks. The cow had a tumour that
had grown to the size of a pumpkin in the three months that
Chittammai had not gone to the estate, what with her surgery
and ribs and all. The farm hands had made the poor cow walk
all the way to the city because she was so ill. So there she was,
tottering into the yard, and before the vet could come, right
before our eyes, the poor thing flailed out her legs, each
outwards, and crumpled to the ground, right there under the
jackfruit tree.

"The vet came, took one look at the cow, and shook his
head. Bad news, he said, when a cow does that, falls that way, all
splayed out, there's nothing that can be done, as good as dead,
sorry ma'am, not a chance, no point doing anything either,

throwing away good money after bad, sorry ma'am. And away he went."

"Oh, what a jerk," Lynne said, now quite into the story.

"Aren't you glad your doctor isn't like that?"

"Sure am, but go on, what happened?"

"So Chittammai asked the chauffeur to go across town to bring another vet, he was chief of the Government Veterinary Hospital, way across town. She told Muthan to bring the stoutest, longest ropes he could find in the store room, and get four men from the cigarette shop across the street, where servants from nearby houses congregated. Then she wheeled herself to her room, and came back with her medicine chest. It was a large wicker basket, one of those things one used for picking flowers. She took out all her old penicillin and other vitamin pills – she was on B12 and A and C and D and what not – and had Muthan grind them all together, mixed it with molasses, and then had him shove the mush of vitamins and molasses into the cow's mouth. Two men had to pry Gauri's mouth open so he could place the mush ball against the cheek of her mouth.

"The cow was too weak even to swallow, and so she lay dribbling at the mouth. Then Chittammai had two men pull two ropes over a branch of the jackfruit tree near the cow, had them ease one end under the cow and make a knot so they could pulley the cow up and adjust her feet the way they should be under her, kind of standing but supported at the same time by the ropes. Chittammai went to the cow, stroked her and spoke to her. And after about twenty minutes, the cow started slowly moving its mouth, chewing the mush."

"You're kidding, right?"

"It happened right before my eyes, don't ask me what the story means or how it relates to your poem or you, but it did happen. The vet was not in town, but the cow turned for the better, and of course the tumour was duly operated on."

"Don't tell my doctor any of this," Lynne laughed. "He wouldn't let you come within reach of me. Just mushing all her own medication into a ball and stuffing it into Elsie's mouth, I can see it. Wow, I'd have liked this Chittammai of yours, what made her think of all these things? The ropes, what an idea!"

"I asked her that, and she said it was a Friday, and she wasn't going to have the poor cow die on a Friday, goddess Lakshmi's day."

"Maru, you've lost me. What's this superstition?"

"I guess it is no use trying to get anyone to understand, but had it been Tuesday, she'd have said she wasn't going to have the poor cow die on Hanuman's day, and if it were a Monday, that she wasn't going to have it die on Siva's day and so on, Devi's day, Krishna's day, Kartikeya's day.   We just have something special on every day of the week through the year to tell us we shouldn't let anything bad happen on any day without putting up one hell of a fight, simple logic, right?"

"You think you could come by again and tell me more of these oddball stories, Aunty Maru?"   She hadn't called me "Aunty" for at least six years, grown out of it as children do, and I felt tears choking me up. But I could also feel Chittammai at my shoulder, and I knew all would be well.

As it turned out to be.

There was a single sheet in the folder and I glanced at that one. Seemed like an outline of sorts because it was titled "For the Chittammai story." The "Note to Myself," read,

"Maybe our epics are about our own everyday experiences, to tell us the epic characters went through the same highs and lows as us, though we may not belong to the same *grand* domain as them."

1900s: And Rama placed his hand on the bow that few had dared touch and none had lifted. He rose, bow in hand, and strung the arrow with confidence, and TWANG, the great bow broke, sending a shiver of fear and admiration through the ranks of courtiers. And smiling, he received the victor's garland from Sita's tender hands.

1910s: And Rama called Sita and said, "My queen, often have I heard you say it would gladden your spirit to visit the sages we knew in the days of yore. Prepare to leave at dawn, dear lady, for you shall have your heart's desire." And Sita rejoiced, not knowing that her lord had told Lakshman to chariot her into the forest and to leave her there.

1920s: And Sita prayed, "I am old, Mother, though the world thinks me fair as I walk by his side, a queen. My lord thinks me fairer than all, Mother, but he is a newly anointed king who meets each day's challenge with firmness and dedication as fits a king, but he forgets he is also a man. Woman's youth is fleeting as the dawn. Therefore Bhoodevi, Mother Nature most divine, visit him that he may come unto me.

1930s: And Sita danced lightheartedly on the new spring grass around their hut. And she played with the bright-feathered birds and the gentle-eyed deer that ate out of her hand. And sages from all over Dandakaranya hailed Rama as their protector for Rama went forth, ever ready to challenge their enemies and returned ever victorious.

1960s: And Sita with drooping head and heavy heart sat under the weeping Asoka tree. The children who might have been mine are lost to me. How long have I to wait, Mother most divine? How long ere this dark night end and dawn break?

November 1970: And Dasaratha called his son to his bedside and said, "Bharata, take thou my crown and sit upon my throne. Here is my ring and here my royal robe. Take them and rule over this my empire."
And Bharata answered, "Nay Father, what of Rama thy first born, dearer to me than any other?"
And Dasaratha said, "Bharata, gladly would I give him my throne. Dearly would I love to hear his voice commanding these my people for he is the best of all my sons, foremost in courage, confidence, compassion and all that go to mould an ideal king, but I fear it is not to be. Take thou my crown and anoint thyself king."
And Bharata with deep reverence touched his father's feet and said, "Nay sire, his is the title and its claims; his is the realm and he shall have it. I swear to be a faithful regent, all my life if need be, but bless us that it may not be long."

And Kausalya, with tears in her eyes and a mixed joy in her heart that now dared to hope, closed her lord's eyes that he might sleep.

~

The other story was much longer. It was typed on the back of large posters – 11x17 sheets – that had been prepared for one of the dance concerts Maru had arranged, by our teacher's daughter, Kalpalatha. I looked at the dancer. How lovely she was, younger than I am now, and a superb dancer who was also such a charmer in real life. And when she was describing goddess Parvati in one of the dances, a little girl, two or three years younger to me, got up in the theatre and joined her arms in prayer shouting "Ummacchi, ummachi," the baby-language for goddess in Tamil. Yes, she indeed danced divinely, and we were duly impressed. Our dance teacher must be really good if she could teach her daughter to dance so well, we thought, and dreamed of the day we would be like her daughter.

Anyway, I chose the sheets, which because of their size were scrunched up against the side of the carton.   The typing was not as clean as in some of the sheets I had read. The size of the paper and the typing showed that this was before the age of computers, typed on a typewriter, with words xed out and retyped whenever a letter had been typed in the wrong order. But it must have been after 1979, because that was when, the poster clearly said, the concert had taken place.

The first page was there, with just a note, but the next page seemed to have jumped to the middle of the story.

Note to myself: Time to start sorting out my notes of the summer of 1972 and do something with all the wonderful stories Chittammai told me. When I look at the notes I have written, I am surprised, what with the baby crying and the number of telephone calls for Chittammai and the servants with their questions and the driver with his erratic schedule, it is a wonder I got so much done that summer. I guess I'll just type up some of my handwritten notes for now.

Chittammai's wedding story

Lakshmi's brother-in-law, however, had contacted the father already, and even as S came back from the post-box, he received a telegram from his father-in-law to stop all arrangements rightaway and that he was arriving by the evening train.

The older man was in a veritable Viswaroopam when he arrived with his wife and his younger children. How dare S take the final decision, how dare he write to him only at the eleventh hour as though inviting him to a distant relative's wedding, worse, as though announcing a wedding which he was not expected to attend. How dare he bring disrepute on the whole family by flouting convention? How dare he throw his daughter out of caste? Let him keep his progressive rot to himself without victimizing others. How dare he measure the depth of a well by throwing the neighbour's child into it? Let him experiment with his own children, not with others'.

S. touched to the quick, forgot all the diplomatic niceties he had rehearsed. He came out with equal vehemence. His daughter, indeed, and how father-like had be been? Ready to throw away the child to a widower of forty, if it hadn't been for S's intervention. He, S, had searched the matrimonial market with a sieve and picked the finest bachelor around, one earning no less than two hundred rupees a month. Not a widower, not a cripple, but a sprightly eighteen year old genius. And so he ranted on, saying things no one should say to anyone, least of all to one's father-in-law.

~

If Sunday had been mayhem, Monday proved to be total pandemonium. Cee arrived with his family from Waltair that morning. He too had not received the initial news directly from his sons. Cee had recently asked his cousin V to arrange for him to see several girls. But for a month after that, there had been no news. A close friend had written that Ceevee was keen to get married before leaving Madras for Calcutta. Then he received a letter from V that Ceevee had decided on a girl, sister-in-law of social reformer S, who had made a name in the city for his unconventional ideas. Cee waited to hear from his sons, meanwhile preparing to leave; the train journey itself would take two days, and of course he had to make arrangements at the college where he was Vice Principal. Then came a telegram that the wedding was set for the 28th. He got his family together and rushed down by the next train, arriving in Madras on Monday.

His elder son CeeS, his mother and sister, who were keeping house for the boys so they could study in Madras, received him in anxious silence, trying to gauge his stand. As long as he held his peace, no one dared broach the topic. He first instructed his younger children to have a bath; he himself had one and showed them the dirty black towel, full of coal dust from the train, and he and the children laughed.

The only other adult who was at ease was Ceevee. He sat at his table, busily writing up a report on his experiments, that he wanted to complete before taking up his new job. To his father's enquiry as to how he was, he said he was in fine fettle except that he was rushed for time. He did not know what facilities Calcutta could offer for his research and he knew he wouldn't have much time from work once he went there.

His father shrugged his shoulders and smiled. And this boy is to be married tomorrow, he murmured, and turned to his firstborn, questioning him.

Oh it is impossible to figure out which sheet comes next. Stephen has the patience for this kind of thing, not me. This doesn't seem the right one, but let me read it anyway.

His father was irate. Why was CeeS standing like a stone Ganesha? Was there a kuzhakkattai in his mouth? Had be been struck dumb? Why had he not headed off his younger brother from taking rash decisions? Didn't he know poor Ceevee was impractical and impetuous?

Am I my brother's keeper? Yes, yes, I am. I am my brother's keeper and my father's too, and I shall guard their honour and repay debts and suffer all their impositions for send not thy servant to ask for whom the bell tolls, it tolls for thee.

Poor Ceevee, he was busy with his studies, but you had more time to think of the consequences of his irrational acts.

Ceevee's studies, Father's future problems, did anyone care for his studies, his problems?

And why did you ever go to see a girl not from our subsect? That is where you should have put your foot down.

"Ah, Father, we have gone through this before – a man's fundamental right to meet the girl with whom he has to walk through life."

What about all those girls your uncle had arranged for Ceevee to see?

"One was squint-eyed, another was beautiful but obviously stupid, another was, I forget the details but yes, all of them were rich, stinking rich. One father promised a thousand rupees, another a gold water pot and so on ad infinitum. That was our uncle for you, a one-track mind going after money."

Father's rage was all spent. He rationally knew that the minor difference of sects was not at all important but his wife had nagged him into taking this stand.

Why did you allow all these arrangements to be made without consulting me?

Go ask my brother, he wanted to say. But he did not. Ceevee was a selfish, egocentric, spoilt brat but perhaps he was born to be king.

CeeS looked at his father. Softly and clearly he said, "Ceevee wished it, father, and I acted in good faith."

His father's eyes softened. He looked at his son, a spitting image of himself at that age. So handsome, so young, not yet twenty two. Why was he berating his son? All he had done was to have seen which way his brother's desire lay and helped him realize it. For which he had been arraigned, and sentenced even before that.

You did well, my son, he said, and rose from his chair. He moved as though to embrace his firstborn but demonstrativeness was not in his nature, perhaps not in brahmins' nature anywhere. The more fools we, he murmured, and picking up his *angavastram*, he went out for a walk.

Anna has gone out without having his meals, his sister said the moment he left the house. She was concerned about herself; until he had his lunch, the womenfolk could not eat. Grandmother said, Pray God he doesn't get the sun, going out at midday on an empty stomach.

His wife whispered, Did you hear what he said? You did well, my son. That's what he said. You did well, my son. And what does that mean except that he is going to agree to the marriage? Alas, the shame, the sorrow! She raised her voice and cried.

~

I tried to get the pages in sequence and then left it for Stephen to figure out. Stephen read the fragments that night while I slaved at my studies.

Next evening, I had my books spread out on my little desk in the bedroom. Stephen had his on the dining table. The phone rang. By the time I reached for the phone, that was by the bed, I heard Stephen say, "Hello DocSiv, I don't usually pick up the phone but I saw your name on the caller ID and thought I'd sneak a hello before Priti picks it up."

I didn't say anything. I figured I'd listen in first.

"You sound cheerful enough. So I needn't worry, I guess."

"Actually we are a bit stressed out, exams next week."

"Already?"

"We have them all the time. The underlying premise of the system is that if we get out of the torture with our sanity intact, we can be allowed to hang out our shingle. May be Priti has fallen asleep over her books. I'll check, at great personal risk I can tell you. She said she'd shoot me if I dared disturb her."

"Know what 'brahmacharya" means?

"Celibate? as I recall."

"The period of studentship in one's life, and celibacy is part of it because they had figured out that state is most conducive to studies."

"Right, and you can see that Priti strictly follows the old precepts, quite intent on shooting me etc."

"Touché. Are you taking good care of her?"

"Absolutely. Though she couldn't say the same about her taking care of me."

"Ssh, she may be on the extension."

"She probably is."

"Could be, she does have that sneaky streak in her."

I was not going to bite. I just kept listening.

"Hey Doc Siv, I have a question about one of the stories. There seem to be many unfinished narratives but this one about Chittammai is killing me with suspense."

"Oh, the biography of which she wrote about two hundred pages?"

"Two hundred? No, this is just on a few large pages and is about the wedding that didn't take place, I presume. Both fathers have come steaming mad to Madras from wherever they were, and one has said if at all the wedding takes place it will be over his dead body, and the other has just gone for a walk. How does it end?"

"You have to put two and two together, Stephen, wherever the twos might be hidden. This only assuming you know Chittammai's husband was a great scientist. If not, of course you couldn't find any of the twos to put together. The answer is yes, they got married and lived happily ever after. The wedding did not take place on the scheduled date but the progressive liberal leaders of the community prevailed on her father, to be a beacon light of reform etc., if you read any of S's orations. The other father was somewhat more reasonable as you may have gathered, and gave in much earlier. Actually, the event was reported in *The Hindu* of the sixth of June, 1907, or close to that date anyway. I went with Maru to the newspaper archives section to check on the details. She must have it somewhere. Rest assured, they got married and lived happily ever after. Chittammai was totally devoted to him, though listening to her colourful tales, one would think otherwise. One thing is for sure, he could not have done all he did in science without her. Indeed she was as great a woman as he was scientist. If you have any other questions, let me know, but it is past my bedtime. Say hello to Priti."

I replaced the receiver a second after I heard Stephen replace his. He came to the door but did not knock. He went back and I could hear him putting the kettle on. The more coffee we drink, the sleepier we get, but it keeps one awake during the making of the darned beverage.

~~~~~~

SEVEN

We had a huge argument over dinner. I walked off to the living room and spread my papers on the dining table. Stephen cleaned up the kitchen, and with newspaper and book in hand, he lay down on the sofa, sticking his bare feet over the arm of the sofa. He then got up and picked a sheaf off one of the cartons. I have to make sure he doesn't get to pick through the folders and stapled sheets at will. But if I said it now, it would be like I was taking revenge on our spat. Anyway, he seemed to be holding some clipped sheets from one of the Indian folders – Maru had a lot of those, old large file folders from another age, with their thin steel flaps to bend back and clip in place, for two-holed foolscap paper. Maru's pre-Canada writings, of which she seemed to have a carton. Many sheets were handwritten, and the rest were typed on a typewriter, often with a ribbon that badly needed changing, with the circles in 'o's and 'e's and 'a's all smudged and black.

I remember the day Dad and Ma came home from a garage-sale fundraiser of the Royal Winnipeg Ballet when I was may be thirteen. Ma had a battered leather suitcase that had been owned by some star ballerina of another age. It was beat up and shabby looking, but I guess I too would gladly pay three times the twenty dollars she paid then if I could get even a strapless tote bag once carried by Evelyn Hart. Dad had bought a Remington typewriter, a clunker that was heavy enough to cause a hernia if he didn't have one already. He was so pleased with it, he placed it on the formal dining table for a week so he could brag about it to friends. Maru dropped by soon after, and Dad and she drooled over it for half an hour, even changing the ribbon – four new spools of ribbon came with it but turned out to be as dry as the first one. Dad had typed the first line of one of his favourite Hindi film songs – I think it was the only one he knew – and both laughed and sang it together – *Chaudhvin ka chand ho, ya aftab ho, jo bhi ho tum khuda ki kasam, laajawab ho.* Because he sang it so often, I knew the lines and even the meaning – those olden days songs from India sure had romantic exaggeration oozing from the pores. And they laughed and laughed recalling old movies and stuff. How they used to laugh, Dad and his Indian friends, I don't think we ever laugh so much.

Now Stephen was laughing. Holy Christo, he said, your Aunt Maru was one sicko teenager. He held up some sheets of paper and repeated, Holy Christo, just read this. I just said "hnhn" and pretended to be too busy. I was still pretty mad about the argument. After reading the sports section of the newspaper, Stephen got up and said he was going to bed. The cheek of him, just like that, he went to bed and was asleep in a trice. On my bed! after a spat like the one we had! I couldn't believe it. When I was ready for bed, I found him sleeping the way he usually sleeps after we've made love, on his side, one knee more bent than the other, his right hand across and up, ready to reach out and touch me from time to time. But he didn't. He slept like a log.

He was still in bed when I woke up at seven. My waking woke him, and he got out of bed. He always slept in his briefs, no pajamas because that would mean carrying them back and forth, and he stood there stretching himself. He looked so handsome, his lank torso with thin golden hair around the nipples and nowhere else, I was ready to eat him up but not ready to make the first move. I wanted to run my hand over the golden curls on his thighs.

He brushed his teeth, got dressed and started getting breakfast ready. I went to the kitchen in my pajamas, and sat down groggily at the table. "For once I got enough sleep," he said. "See, we can have a good argument and still sleep in the same bed. The bed doesn't have to be only for sex, you know, there is the togetherness of *brunda* birds. I really think we are ready for the rings and all."

"Bherunda birds," I said, "why can't you get any Indian word right? Because you don't even try."

"Preethi," he said. "Not pretty, NOT PRETTY."

He was referring to how I hated it when anyone mispronounced my name. I knew I looked a sight. And I was too groggy to think of any repartee.

"I wonder about India," he said. "I wonder what life is like now. Maru's India seems so beautiful, so innocent."

"It has always been dirty, crowded, loud," I said, recalling all the times Ma dragged me there when I was a child because she wanted to visit family and there was always some handy excuse of one conference or other and I always fell sick on arrival and was passed on from one ayah to another, one aunt to another. When I got to age ten, I was spared all that because Ma went away for two years to live in India and I stayed back with Dad and Aunt Savitri and UncaShar and that was the best two years of my childhood. By the time she came back, I was old enough to say I was never going with her anymore, though I did go again once.

"It is where your parents were born," he said.

"So who cares? I was born here in North America, same as you. What does England mean to you?"

"But that was long ago. And England was never that different from here."

"So what? Why should you always think non-white people come from a planet of the apes? You are all such bigoted racists."

I knew I was crossing all fair limits, but I was in a foul mood, and I knew it was because I was sex-hungry and I was mad at myself for being so.

"As I recall, I could be wrong, in the planet of the apes the apes were rather superior to humans."

After he left, I read what he had thought so sicko, and it was.

Lesson in Etiquette:

Once there was a greedy boy. He carried plastic pouches in his pocket whenever he went visiting with his mother or to parties, and swiped a walloping lot of cakes and things. At home, at lunch and tea and dinner, he was the first to start and the last to leave the table, and when he did, it was with a longing look at the remaining food. As for breakfast, the glutton would rather forego an extra hour in bed than his milk and toast. It was no use Mother pointing out that there was plenty of everything and more in the kitchen. He *would* grab the bowls and ladles and heap his plate till the gravy oozed on to the table.

One day, one hot summer evening it was, they had fresh lime juice. Mother squeezed the limes, put in sugar and strained the juice into the glass tumbler so the seeds stayed back. Everyone came, and drank like genteel people should, leaving half an inch at the bottom. But this boy, did he do that? NO. He emptied half the sugar bowl into his glass, stirred it and quaffed it to the dregs.

As it so happened, the sugar had been bought just that morning. The grocer, tired of life and trying to make better his humble life in his own humble way, had mixed some sand with the sugar to increase the weight. He powdered the sand in his backyard. It was rather careless of him but it so happened that glass marbles had got mixed up and got pounded along with the sand.

Now, had this boy, like a gentleman, left a half inch at the bottom of the glass, the glass bits would have stayed there. But now the glass pieces went into his mouth, down his esophagus, stomach and small intestine. As they went down, they tore the walls of the said oesophagus, stomach and small intestine, and he collapsed in a pool of blood as he vomited and died. Floating in the blood he spit up were undigested bits of the afternoon meal. Amen.

~

Lesson in obeying Mother

Her mother had time and again told her to be back home before sundown, and that she was too young to go alone shopping or to the pictures. But she *would* go. One evening she went to the movie theatre. It was just two furlongs down the street and she knew a back door from the theatre that made it even shorter. And the show ends at 8:15 and she could be home by 8:30, which is not late is it? Besides it was a MUST picture, adults only and all that.

So she went and saw the story to its last embrace of a happy ending. She then went out the back door.

Now it so happened that three men were playing cards. What with the D.I.G. of Police out to suppress vice and such, these poor men could not sit under the street lamps. They had spotted this venue just within the cinema compound and yet not frequented, and safe from the prying long-nosed cops stationed every hundred steps.

Spirits were low. There wasn't much use playing high stakes because none of them had money anyway.

When this girl came along wending her happy homeward way, they ducked. But the step was too light for a cop's and the clinking of handcuffs too soft to be true. No wonder too! It is a girl by Jove, and with gold around her wrist and neck too! They sprang at her, two for the bangles, one for the necklace, for they believed in division of labour. And even a cat burglar of average intelligence knows that the best way to click a necklace off a neck is to approach from behind, twist the chain and pull. The gold gives way at some place or the other and the chain is in your hand. So this is what he did. But the chain happened to be a stout one and wouldn't break. So he tried to pull it right off but the neck happened to be in it, and the girl collapsed in a silent heap. Some girls are very cooperative. Each placed his loot in his shirt pocket and they left the premises.

Further ahead where the road trailed off into unlighted alleys and footpaths, they usually parted ways. For though they were friends and met often, each considered the others not quite good enough to introduce into his domestic circle.

"I feel a bit mean," said the tall one in the middle. "That was rather sad," he jerked his thumb backwards.

"Don't worry overmuch," said the short one to his left sympathetically, "all is excused in our struggle for existence."

"Your philosophy is always comforting," the tall one said gratefully throwing his hands over the other's shoulder and extracting the chain from his pocket as they neared the end of the road. "Jai Ram ji ki."

"Ram Ram bhaiya."

"Ram Ram."

~

Both of us were way too busy the rest of the week or we made ourselves so, and when Stephen phoned on Friday to ask if he could take me out to dinner, I said yes, and we resumed without either formally apologizing for the spat.

We had Chinese take-out instead, because to dress up and go out seemed a bore. I had placed, on the coffee table in the living room, a story I wanted Stephen to read. I remembered having read it in a book edited by P.Lal, one of the few stories that Maru had published, first in *The Illustrated Weekly* which I gather was the only national weekly at the time, and I remember crying over it because that was during my dance days and I was young, and I understood it so perfectly.

Panchali's Hour of Choice

His morning prayers over, his offerings accepted by Vishnu, his mind serene as the dawn that appeared in the east, Drupada stood on sacred Matsya Hill by the sanctified spot where a rock was carved into a giant fish out of whose mouth a river spouted and tumbled down the hill into the valley of perennial flowers. He looked with wonder and pride at the virgin river and the green slopes. And he called his chief architect, Visvadasa, and said, "Raise an amphitheatre here fit for the gods."

For three months they worked, under the blazing sun, by the light of the glimmering stars they worked, Visvadasa and his fleet of men. Visvadasa, who had been apprenticed to Visvakarma himself, spent three months building the amphi-theatre for the *swayamvara* of Panchala's beloved princess.

The tall grass on the slopes was mown down; little wild runners – blue and crimson, violet and blazing yellow – blossomed anew spreading a rich carpet for the populace who, like the never-ending breakers of the sea, would flow in to see their princess of matchless beauty choose her lord. Facing the sacred mount a hundred platforms were built in a semicircle for the earth's mighty warriors, and behind each dais were galleries for their retinue. In the centre was raised a hall with a marble floor, and sculptured pillars holding up gossamer canopies to deflect the sun off crowned brows. There were bejewelled thrones at the head of the hall for Panchala's royal line. And then Visvadasa prayed all day to his master, and from the brilliant red rays of the setting sun came the master's blessings. Then Visvadasa rose from his knees and set to work on the design of his dreams, a suspended balcony from where she of slender waist and broad hips, she of wavy hair and full dark lips, she who was like Sri descended from heaven, could watch the princes of the world compete for her hand.

Two ancient persimmons he uprooted from a virgin forest, and lopping off the branches, he implanted their ebony trunks twenty feet deep and thirty feet high; and from these ebony pillars he suspended a balcony with beams of beaten gold and stairs of silver. The structure was shaped like a fish, the insignia of the royal house of Yajnasena; its fins and tail were so finely set with rubies that pilgrims could see the glowing red from two yojanas away and say, "We have arrived at the city of our dreams."

On a dais below the balcony the celestial bow was placed unstrung; near the dais was a sapphire-walled tank two arms-length on each side in which the water stood still and serene like dew in lotuses. From the centre of the tank rose an ivory column on which a marble fish was stalked. Below its open mouth a punched gold disc revolved around an ivory axis. And he would win Panchali who, looking only at the reflection, could shoot an arrow through the hole in the revolving disc and cleave the ball in the mouth of the marble fish.

Prince after royal prince, heralded by the bard, came to the central dais. Head after crowned head went back, bowed, not in shame for it is no shame to fail in such a challenge, but in heavy disappointment that they no more could look at that face above them that had smiling eyes and scorn-touched lips.

And then came Duryodhana's voice, loud, arrogant. "Peers and princes, I present to you, Karna, of whom all have heard and whom few have seen, my friend, dear to me as my dearest brother."

In the silence that followed, a thousand eyes looked at Duryodhana, searched among the Kurus who sat beside and behind him, and waited, wondering why no one arose at Duryodhana's call.

But Panchali, who was not looking at Duryodhana whose name and notoriety she knew and disdained, Panchali whose bored eyes roved down the hall in search of some novelty to catch her passing fancy, Panchali who looked at all men with smiling eyes and scorn-tinged lips, saw now a youth at the far end of the hall rise from among the Kuru retinue like the sun rises from behind Matsya Hill. Panchali's heart leapt in wonder and joy like buds in the dawn, blood mounted to her face even as the river blushes at the coming sun, her fingers trembled as the sunflower trembles when its lord comes riding out of night, her scorn melted away like the dew from morning leaf, her maidenliness and modesty slipped from her and she felt a naked joy as she looked at the youth who walked up the marble hall.

Broad-chested and bold he was; the white silk cloth thrown over his shoulder hid nothing of his sinewy torso shining brown. Karna with unhurried steps walked between the sculptured pillars, his black eyes shining with Surya's fire, his long slender fingers itching for the touch of the bow, his thin unsmiling lips unmoved by the looks of envy and cheers of admiration that rocked the valley as he walked up the marble hall where sat a hundred princes and all their retinue.

Karna did not raise his eyes as all had to look at the fairest woman in the seven valleys.

Duryodhana spoke again, as his bard. "Gurus and princes! Behold a youth whose praises I could sing without cease; he can shoot a hundred arrows ere the first fall to the ground, he can blind a sparrow flying towards the sunset through clouds... but what need for words? See for yourselves his noble mien, his leonine strength, his indisputable bowmanship. Behold Karna, noblest of foes, truest of friends!"

Karna looked at Duryodhana. Panchali saw the look, saw his lips quiver with gratitude, saw a faint suffusion tan his face, saw, too, his eyes shining with a liquid lustre expressing adoration, love, gratitude by turn as he looked at his master who called him friend.

A strange jealousy tore through her breast and she wanted to kneel at Karna's feet and implore, Look at me thus, lord, and even if but once an eon, I shall be your handmaiden now and always. And resentment surged up swift against this man who could wake such longings in her, such naked passions, such jealousies as she had never felt before. And Panchali, with a sob in her throat and poison on her lips, spat out the words, "That you have been allowed to come thus far speaks for the gracious hospitality of the Panchalas. That you have chosen to exploit them by coming upright to the dais bespeaks your crude arrogance. O, you lowborn wretch, know this, a charioteer's son may become the Kuru's petted minion but never shall he sully the pristine glory of the Panchala court."

Five hundred nobles looked at the princess and quickly dropped their gaze, scorched by the anger and hatred that blazed like *homa* fire. Duryodhana sprang up.

"Listen, friends and gurus, listen! A Kshatriya is one who proves himself worthy by heroic deeds. Is there any who has not heard of Karna's feats? Is there any here who would dare challenge Karna to single combat with sword, mace or bow?

"A Kshatriya is one who protects the weak. Bards for centuries to come will sing of Karna's chivalry and valour.

"A Kshatriya is one who gives alms to the poor. It is not only the poor who beg alms from Karna. Do you not know that the jealous Indra himself craved of him the natural armour he was born with? Is there anyone in the three worlds who has been turned away from Karna's door? Alms flow from him as the Ganga in Sravana.

"Brahmanas and gurus! Do not our scriptures say a man may redeem his station by his deeds?"

The learned brahmins felt Panchali's flashing stare and refrained from answering.

Sarcastically Duryodhana continued, "Of course Karna is not your equal. He has too much of honesty and generosity and all manly virtues to be our equal. The princess judges well."

The very breeze caught its breath as it slid past Panchali.

Duryodhana unsheathed his sword and shouted, "Hear this. Duryodhana shall not stay where Karna is not honoured. Come, Karna," and Duryodhana walked out of the swayamvara hall and all the Kuru princes followed him.

Panchali looked at Karna, who with head unbowed, turned without a single look at her and marched unhurriedly down the marble hall, dragging her heart behind him. And she cried to herself, I shall run all the way and clasp his knees so he needs must stop and I shall say, "Karna, dearest Karna, I beg of you, take me as your handmaiden, yes, even if I be but one of many who shall feel the warmth of your arms, your loins, your passion," and surely he will not refuse me for he has refused none ever; should his bitterest foe ask him for his bow he will give it, yes even the mantra of invincibility granted by Indra he will part with if asked, yes even the punya of all his lives he will give away with a smile should any ask him. He will not refuse me if I ask, if I would but ask, if I could but ask."

Karna raised his eyes to the sun directly as no man but he could. And the sun went behind a sudden cloud, unable to bear the indignity heaped upon his seed. Between the sculptured pillars, down the marble hall Karna walked, dragging her heart behind him.

Prince after royal prince approached and retreated. The bards sang on.

"Sisupala, son of mighty Damaghosha, king of the Chedis..."

Panchali looked with unseeing eyes. What did it matter who came or who succeeded? "O Karna, Karna, come to me.

Come back. A hundred thousand gems I shall pile in front of you, to throw into the sea if you will."

"Jarasandha of invincible arms!"

Karna come back. I shall dance for you, with golden ghunghroos and bared belly I shall dance for you...

"Salya, king of Madra, unrivalled in horsemanship!"

Karna, my eyes thirst for you, my heart aches for you, my thighs grow moist with desire. Come to me, Karna, my lord and my love.

"Tamralipta, king of Patana..."

Karna, I shall leave my palace, my soft couches, my rose-strewn halls, and I shall follow you barefoot through wild woods; I shall cast away my jewels, my silks, my maids. Of what use are they if you are not with me, and what need for anything else if you are by my side? Karna, come to me.

"Srutayu, foremost of royal charioteers..."

I lit my lamp of life in a leaf cup and with flowers I placed it on the Ganga, with prayers that it may reach its shore. The waves rock it, brother, the winds threaten to turn it, the rain to sink it, O Govinda, save it! Balgopala, brother and defender, help me now!

"A Brahmin of lineage unknown, his name unrevealed..."

Panchali's eyes brightened, she rose from her seat, she leaned forward from her balcony, she raised her garland of full blown roses and cried, "He has come!"

He was nearer now, and Panchali saw that is was not Karna. Like Karna he seemed, but no, his eyes were larger, his lips full like a woman's, his form heavier. Panchali sank back.

But many saw her eager gesture, heard her cry of love, and in after time they said, "Ah! Her heart spoke even before her eyes beheld Arjuna. With what longing she greeted him, with what unashamed love! Truly, marriages are made in heaven.!"

~

While I was cleaning up, Stephen took his usual place, his bare toes sticking out on the arm of the sofa, head on a cushion, with newspaper and Maru's story in hand.

"So what do you think of the story?" I asked, sitting beside him on the sofa.

"Were you always like that?" he asked. "She's got you down to a T."

I threw a cushion on his face. He grabbed my hand and we kissed and made out a bit before I threw him off me. "I am serious," I said, "which are the ones I should be including in the final portfolio. Like those sicko stories. Clearly, I won't be doing her a favour if they are published."

"Why not," he said. "She wrote them, and so they are as much for publishing as anything else. It gives the reader a sense of her growth, from her teens to her prime. Of course you should include them, so what if they are pukey?"

I threw a cushion on him again. It fell to the floor.

"Like this one," I said, "would it make any sense to readers who don't know the story?"

"What story?"

I punched him. "The Mahabharata, of course, unless you know the original, you can't figure out what Maru has done with it, how she has Panchali talk about Karna's generosity some stories that happen only much later in the epic, how she has created a sub-plot that is sacrilegious to say the least."

"I know the epic in outline, thanks to all those Amar Chitra Kathas borrowed from my Grade Seven best friend, Dilip. So why is it necessary to know anything of it anyway? It is a story of a proud woman who falls uncontrollably in love with a guy. Isn't that the main point?"

"The main point is that she realizes that one can try to bribe with gems and seduction but finally we just have to pray to Krishna if we are to get anything."

"I don't know about that. Krishna seems to have given her only the second best."

"Arjuna was an okay guy. Point is that she got to play a part, a big role in something big, instead of being Karna's wife."

"Granted she got five men instead of the usual single, but they probably did not add up to one Karna."

"You don't know how to read a story," I said. "It is about the power of prayer."

"Oh come on, the main point is the poetry of the piece and the character of the proud princess, who is so like my own sweetheart princess," and that led to other things and we went to bed.

~

Stephen had something for me when I returned from work the next day, a hot dinner and also something he wanted me to read. He said Maru was interested not only in creating versions of Panchali's stories but other mythic women's too, like Eve and Mary and the woman at the well. Pretty neat, he said, though it wasn't very clear what was what. Who is Rina? he asked. This is written for Rina.

What he said rang a bell – Rina Singha had a series of dance-dramas on the Bible, and Maru was a friend of Rina's over the years. She had arranged dance concerts by Rina in Winnipeg. I told Stephen about the awesome experience of her concert at the School for the Deaf where the interpreter's actions were almost the same as the dancer's as she explained various dance gestures, for that is what Indian dance is – mimetic representation of nature and emotions. Rina had also taught the deaf children to hear the music through the vibrations felt by their bare feet on the wood floor of the school gym. She had worked on a Biblical series, I couldn't remember the name, geez, it will come to me, I told Stephen, something Katha.

Stephen was impressed, he always is when I talk about anything India, but also that Maru knew the dancer. He said he remembered reading about a project she had – Jesus Stories. Stephen never ceased to amaze me with the tidbits and trivia he knew about everything under the sun. It came to me. Yeshu Katha, I said, you are right about the title but in Hindi it is Yeshu Katha. Now Maru's fragments made sense, he said, they must have talked about it.

I must check with Rina if they ever collaborated, I told myself, I am sure she is still in Toronto. I read the fragments, and they were Maru's ideas and words. They must be, for this was a draft, words scratched out, sentences repeated. I remembered Maru talking about how brilliantly Rina had chosen her women and the exact episodes in their lives to recreate against a Rajasthani setting, with Eve believing like a simple Rajasthani peasant that Seth would literally take them back to Eden in their lifetime; Mary revelling in her trousseau, like any young woman anywhere; and the Woman at the Well moved to give up her flirtings. Maru was planning for a women's conference and had no time for me, and even as she talked about how Rina was coming to the conference, she shooed me off because she had so much to do and so many deadlines. I read the pages, which she had probably written for no reason other than that they came out of conversations with Rina.

Eve: Sleep and grow my baby, sleep and grow to manhood my son. He who cursed us has blessed you, Seth, and so I repeat this story, night after night, as I rock you to sleep. You must know the past so you can lead us beyond it back to Eden. Sleep now, with our story in your ears.

We did not know, my baby, that the serpent of shiny skin and sparkling eyes was not yet another creature of good and beauty in that lovely place where all was good and beautiful. Sweet sweet was the fruit, but all has been bitter since. We did not know such things could ever be, death and endless pain. My Abel dead, my Cain a wanderer, and a band of darkness shrouding our hearts, our souls. Grow soon to manhood, my son, for he who cursed us has promised that my seed shall crush the serpent's head. Oh my son, sleep well and grow soon and lead us back to lovely Eden.

Mary: Like the grape to bursting, my heart is full as I finger these bridal veils and shawl. He who sculpted our first mother from Adam's rib has moulded my youth and made me ready for love's red wine that Joseph is to bring me. How soft is this silk and how rich these bridal gifts!

Woman at the Well: (check John 4:7) I used to be happy once, exulting in my power to rouse men's passion with a single sweeping tinkle of my anklet bells, a sway of my hips, a glance from behind my veil.

How I dread this daily chore of going to the well. Women rebuke me with names and laugh with undisguised scorn. I don't know which is worse, their loud contempt or the men's silent lust as they eye me from afar. But their lust feeds me, clothes me, which is more than I can say for the women.

He looked at me, this stranger, not as other men look. He looked at me and I feel I am alive again. I feel this torrential emotion rising within me. I shall run to him and wash his feet with my tears and dry them with my hair and lie at his feet forever and forever. For he looked at me, this stranger, and smiled, asking for some water.

I took the sheets to the carton, asking Stephen just where he had found it. As it is pages were getting misplaced. But may be chronology wasn't the way to go, for Maru had already arranged some of these in some kind of theme classification as I saw when Stephen handed me a file folder that was marked Myth = Higher Truth, and there were a whole lot of other sheets. I told Stephen about Maru's very active involvement with dance from the mid-seventies to the mid-eighties, of how she laid the groundwork for the first organized dance instruction in Winnipeg and how she wrote that play *Sita's Promise* for our arangetram of sorts in 1981.

I had to explain to Stephen the difference between a real arangetram and the one we had. Stephen liked the way she had used the Ramayana episode of Rama's exile to get them to come to Canada so she could link up the two homelands with Sita promising the native-Canadian children that she would come again, that she through her children would surely come again and dance with all the children of this land who made Canada their home.

Stephen wanted to see the video of the stage performance, and was about to phone Uncle Siv but I distracted him. I didn't want him in direct contact with Uncle Siv, I didn't know why but I didn't want him stepping into the family. Not yet.

Next day, I looked through the file folder. There were other dance scripts, I realized.

There was one in an exam booklet whose first few sheets had been torn off. Maru had this odd obsession about saving paper. Every time paper is thrown away, she used to say, she could hear a tree fall in British Columbia. She once told me why she had so many of these final-exam booklets from which sheets had been torn off. Professors would bring to her office their years-old stacks of exam booklets that had to be shredded, and she would often go through some of them, picking out booklets that had hardly been used, usually the second or third booklet the student had probably asked for five minutes before closing time. She would tear and place the used sheets in the shredder-heap and keep the rest – they were like notebooks, and she used them to write her notes and storylines and such. She would offer them to her sons and to me for our notes but of course we had our own stack of freshly bought school supplies of three-hole paper and though we took the booklets to please her, we never used them. But she did.

I wonder how many cartons of these torn out booklets are stacked in poor Uncle Siv's basement.

The first page had a poem that I knew well, a poem she had written for the fifteenth anniversary of the Air India crash:

Come, Ambike, to where I stand,
Come, be seated, I pray.
Queen of beginnings,
Whose benediction brings worlds into Being
And in time dissolves them into Nothingness.
Goddess, lovely as the dawn
and frightening as moonless night,
Wide sea of compassion,
Wielder of sword incarnadine,
Giver of grief greater than any mother should ever have to
bear,
Sole comfort in my years of anguished despair.

Ambike! Creator of all past worlds,
and of those yet unborn.
Mother, in whom all opposites converge,
help me understand
why you struck down all that was mine,
Then raised me to dance exultantly by your side,
To sing in celebration that I am I, A woman,
born of woman, with woman power to feel
        joy at the sight of the rising sun,
        rage at my sisters' pitiable plight,
        hope for our children's future
        in this lovely land of endless skies.
May 2000

Yes, perhaps Stephen had a point about the crash being a watershed for the Indo-Canadian psyche. I remember how Maru stressed that point again and again in her talks, that Indo-Canadians had to build up a racial memory of key events that included historical details such as the Komagatamaru incident etc.

The second page had an outline:
Invocation Dance
This is a script for a multimedia-type presentation in which the poem gets written step by step, as it were, as the dancer

choreographs each scene over and over again trying out different options of steps and music. There is a recurring shot on the backdrop screen, of an airplane crashing downwards into the sea with the clap of cymbals followed by startling silence.

The scene is the basement of a large manor-like house. The large room where most of the action takes place is a dance studio, with wall-size mirrors, hand bars etc. for students' classes. There are large framed photographs of famous Indian classical dancers on one of the walls, and several wall hangings.
On one of the walls, is a large backdrop screen, behind which are framed paintings such as seen in any house. There is an empty alcove with Christmas lights strung around it in one of the corners of the backscreen wall. As and when required the backdrop screen lights up, and the scenes projected change to mirror the action described in the poem.
Modern technology with digital wizardry can surmount the problems of the back screen projector that we had with *Sita's Promise*, where the screen was a huge white blank for long stretches of time.... Photographs can be used to advantage, moving from one part of the screen to another, the same photo shown part by part, all kinds of tech-magic are available now. The big challenge however will be to ensure that the dancer is the focus and does not get lost in the collages of the backscreen, especially as the dancer will be small in comparison to the screen that has to be large to project the collages effectively.

There is a tape recorder which plays the same line over and over again several times to different paces of music until the dancer is ready for the next lines and goes to the tape-recorder to move it to the next section. The dancer is dressed in dance leotards, a beautiful top of Indian fabric with mirrors and tassels, and she is wearing ghunghroos.
There is a large brass lamp with several wicks, and the wispy smoke from the flame can be seen wafting upwards from time to time.
Come Ambike! to where I stand.
Come, be seated, I pray.

The dancer choreographs the lines of the poem over and over again, using different mudras and steps to welcome the goddess.

Queen of Beginnings, whose benediction brings worlds into Being.
Creation is danced into existence, as flowers grow and bees flit around and slender trees sway in the wind.

And in time dissolves them into Nothingness.
The dancer tries different ways to express this – first she dances to gentle music, a soft movement into stillness, then it is repeated in very harsh fast tempo and her movements reflect the trauma of dissolution. She tries variations again and again, each time differently.

The doorbell rings. The scene shifts to the front room upstairs. The dancer greets the two men who are at the door – a moving truck can be seen behind the open door. The men go back to the truck and return with a large crate. They bring it to the front landing and after some discussion, decide to open the crate on the front driveway.

Next scene: they bring in a thirty-inch high bronze statue of Parvati in a rare dance pose. It is a custom-made statue come all the way from the Artists' Colony near Madras. The men carefully manoeuvre it to the basement and set it up in the alcove. The dancer turns on a switch and the garland of small Christmas bulbs lights up.

The dancer gives them a generous tip, as can be seen by their appreciative reaction. The men leave and as they walk out, they converse about the weight of the statue, what it must have cost to be chiselled by professional artisans far away and shipped half way around the world. "And the house, whew, must cost a pretty penny," says one of the men. "Some people have all the luck, that is our world," says the other.

"And in time dissolves them into Nothingness," says the tape recorder to the sound of harsh music as of the crescendo of a

nightmare as the Air India airliner crashes downward.

Goddess, lovely as the dawn,
And frightening as moonless night,
Wide sea of compassion,
Wielder of sword incarnadine,
The dancer's movements are at an intimate but impersonal
level, and there is no semblance of anything personal as she
tries different variations to express the opposites being
described.   There has to be enough pauses between the
opposites for the music to change from soft to harsh.

Giver of grief greater than any mother should ever have to bear.
The line is repeated over and over again.
The backscreen projects images of mothers – Devaki in anguish
as her baby Krishna is carried away by Vasudev, Kausalya
grieving at Rama's exile, Subhadra wailing over her
Abhimanyu, Eve bemoaning the banishment of Cain, Mary
weeping at the Cross, Gotami on hearing Siddhartha has left the
palace intent on his search for the Light ... mothers during the
various wars... Meanwhile the dancer is overcome by personal
anguish as the backscreen projects her own life story -
photographs of her daughters at various everyday activities in
which there is a lot of hugging and laughing and the pictures
seem to fade and reappear on different parts of the screen.

Sole comfort in my years of anguished despair.   The camera
repeatedly focuses on the statue of the bronze goddess, on her
hands raised in benediction, her eyes, her face from different
angles... as the dancer weeps at her feet.

While she is still on the floor writhing in grief, the voice-over
reads:
Ambike! Creator of all past worlds
And of those yet unborn,
Mother in whom all opposites converge
Help me understand.

At this point, the dancer slowly rises only to fall again, and the
tape recorder keeps repeating in various levels of loudness the

same line: *Help me understand, help me understand*....followed
after some time by the repetition of *Why you struck down all that
was mine*...
During these few minutes she expresses her grief, anger,
helplessness, as she tries in vain to understand. On the
backscreen are projected collages of photographs, interrupted
by the scene of the plunging aircraft and clash of cymbals. The
photographs are from her wedding album followed by images
of her pregnancies, followed by images of her daughters growing
from toddlers in diapers to teenage, to various shots of herself
and her husband through the years.

The script ended there, obviously another of her incomplete projects.
Perhaps someone else can take it up, I thought, this fragment of an
outline, one of many such that lay in those three cartons of my
inheritance. Maru was so much into dance – she was the one who
brought Bharata Natyam dance instruction to Winnipeg back in 1978,
inviting Mrs. Sarasi Thiagarajan from Montreal after she interviewed
her daughter on the Friends of India TV show. The daughter,
Kalpalatha, came to Winnipeg with a dance group that was making
school visits all over Canada, and there was one Mr. Thawani who ran
a weekly television show in which Maru helped out once a month.
This was before she started her own PALI show. Ma and I were
invited to the dinner Maru gave for the group.
    I once asked her why she was smitten with dance and she said it
started after she saw Krishnaveni as Andal on one of her holidays in
Bangalore during her student days. At the time I didn't care to know
about this dancer but may be I should find out about her. I'll get
Stephen to do the research. Except that he'll come out of it knowing
more about dance than I ever did – he is so focused on anything he
puts his mind to. I wish I could be like that. But why bother when I
have him!
    I wonder if I'll find the story she said she started soon after that,
about a dancer. I forget the storyline but I remember thinking how she
would have been way ahead of her times the way she was modernizing
the old devadasi tradition of a singer's house being the meeting place
for music rasikas, by making her dancer the hostess at whose house all
kinds of social ideas were discussed. Just like her to have a novel that
discussed ideas! She told me all about the kind of ideas discussed but
it WAS a love story, she said. About this young dancer who loved a
guy but refused to marry him. A kind of reversal of her mother who
was true to the man who would not could not marry her, given social

customs. Or a reclaiming of sorts to give a new twist to an old tradition, putting the woman in control. Stephen will be interested in knowing more about that system where a particular set of people were custodians of the arts. Why is he so obsessed with volunteering in some faraway place? I wonder if I should make a commitment after all, and keep him here.

~~~~~

EIGHT

I thought I had taken a new set of writings to work but it turned out to be the same Chikkamma story. I read it again, and figured out that numbers V to VII must have been about her work with Immigrant Women, and that she had gone to Ottawa for some related work. But there's a separate zany bit that Stephen would love.

[This is one of the many stories that I started and never completed.
This story in the lighter vein goes on to tie up with the other story - Lloyd Robertson or some news anchor finding that at the evening broadcast of the news he can see into the room of a particular house, wherever there is a TV switched on, of which there are three - in the living room, the basement rec-room and the bedroom. He is focused enough on his job that he ignores them but his sub-conscious plays it back each evening, giving us various stories of everyday happenings in an everyday household across the country, and how the story takes a surprise turn.]

Flying Away
I don't like it. I am a simple straightforward kind of person and I like to know what is what, that's all I ask – to know what is happening. Which is why I don't like this – the way something in me keeps flying off god knows where. A weird feeling. I mean, here I am lying on the couch as I always do after giving lunch and waving the kids off to school and suddenly I feel myself breaking loose and flying away, except that I am still here, my body leastways. Not just my body because I can think and feel. I know I am here but as sure as today is Tuesday and *As the World Turns* will start in a few minutes, part of me wasn't here a few minutes ago. And this isn't the first time either.

It happened yesterday as well. But that was in the morning, about 6:30, and that's always a bad time for me; I know I have to get up but my eyes are glued shut and so I drift away again for a few minutes. That's quite normal, it has happened for years, ever since Satish was born. I am quite used to that kind of half sleep when I can hear the clock ticking or the baby about to wake up but some part of me is still asleep, enjoying the few minutes or seconds before the alarm rings or the baby bawls. That's okay. Everyone goes through that, everyone with a family leastways. But this was different. I could feel something leaving me and flying away. It's like when you fly a kite and tug at the string against the wind; you can hear the paper rustling way above you, and you can see the tug and then the wind drops and you don't feel the kite or the string though you can see them both. Yes, I see both – myself as I am, or so I think. I'm not sure though I was positive then. I can't recall if I could see my arms or leg or face. One gets so used to looking at oneself, one doesn't really see oneself. I mean, the other day I went out wearing only one earring. Mind you, I looked at myself before I left, I always do, in the mirror near the front closet, by the old hat-stand that I still keep like back at home when every house had a stand with a mirror where one could hang one's hat and raincoat and prop one's umbrella and leave one's shoes. But I didn't notice my earring, or rather the lack of it.

It happened again. This is really getting to me. All I want to know is what's happening. I don't know if I should say that though. When Neeta, my brother-in-law's niece was staying with us and I, feeling responsible, wanted to know where she was and what she did on her dates, and she told me, it would have been better if I hadn't known what was happening. The truth is sometimes worse than one's imagination. But not often. Yes, I'd like to know, that's all I ask, what's happening?

I read that again, that was me she is talking about. She was so easy to talk to, I had blabbed a lot that year I stayed with her. But she did not hold it against me, not Maru.

I'm still no wiser about what leaves me. If this is going to be a daily routine, I should give it a name. Names are important. I have this thing about names. Oscar Wilde might have had his laugh about the importance of being earnest, but I'm superstitious. I've heard Rohini say, she is from Poona or Pune as it is now called, that they have this custom of changing the bride's name to match her husband's name because that brings luck. Her husband's name is Chandra and so they changed hers to Rohini, even though she was Bhagya before that. And still is, in her parents' house. If I were from Poona, I'd have changed my name to Lakshmi, seeing his name is Narayan; only thing, my name was already Lakshmi. Very appropriate you know, and very lucky. I am superstitious. Everyone is, but few admit it.

So what shall I call it? This part of me that flies away. Heck, what's in a name: A rose by any other etc. I don't know about that. We had that maid called Gulab and she stank. I wonder why because she used to have a bath every single day. Used to sit by the well and scrub herself with soap – stolen from us – and draw water from the well and douse herself. But she stank. And named Gulab/Rose. The names poor kids are saddled with – like Kanya and Pavitra and such. How can anyone live up to these names?

What does it do when it's away? I mean, I've got to know. I'm responsible for it, ain't I? What if it smashes someone's window or shoves some kid off the 16th floor balcony? What if it, why do I call it "it"? it's me, ain't it? a living human being not just an it. I don't see how it can fly though, just fly away, since I see myself up there except that I darned well know I am still here. I can feel my arms between the knees as I lie on my side, as I always do. No, not in the fetal position; I am not sick in the head or insecure or anything. They say one who lies flat on his back has kingly qualities, self-confidence and all that. Yoga says the best way to fall asleep is to lie straight on your back and stretch your muscles one by one, fingers, toes, arms, shoulders, until the muscles are totally relaxed, and then you fall asleep like a shot. It is called "shavasana" corpse position. What a name! and they expect people to try it, knowing what it means. Thanks but no thanks. Yuk, as my baby Aravinda would say. My baby, already eight years old. She was born during a blizzard eleven months to the day since I arrived here. Narayan said she is lucky. He says the blizzard will work the same way quarrels between the parents of the bridal couple works during a wedding. If there's a lot of fighting over dowry and arrangements and what have you, the couple will be happy because their fated quota of unpleasantness has already been decreased by the time they start living together. I know he said it because he knows anything superstitious will reassure me, and it did. He knows me well, my Narayan, I wouldn't know what I'd have done if I'd married someone else, the usual type that expects the wife to stay home and cook and clean. I've taken evening courses all along, and he's always stayed home with the children. I can't bear to leave them alone, poor darlings, at some careless babysitter's or day care. I am so sure something disastrous will happen to them if one of us isn't home.

I wonder if I should tell someone about this. It would scare the children. And Narayan is too busy at work, god I wish his boss weren't such a slave driver. Of course I could tell Laura next door but she'll send me to a shrink, she goes for therapy herself. Why bother? It will go away by itself, or rather stop going away.

I was home by four o'clock. I phoned Uncle Siv at his office and asked about Maru's work with immigrant women. "Yes, of course she was heavily involved; I could name the organizations on my fingertips with which she was not involved," he said. "Have I caught you at a bad time?" I asked. "Any time is a bad time," he said, "it is NSERC grant-application time."

I asked him to tell me where I could get some information. He looked up and gave me the number for the organization. I phoned there, and a young voice answered. I asked about where I could get some history of the Association. She did not know. It must be somewhere, I said impatiently. She said they had a lot of cartons stacked up in one corner of the office, but ever since the office had moved to the University, they had only one staff member if at all and she was new and she was only acquainted with the Youth Mentorship programme which was the only thing they did.

What about women? Where do the women of the Immigrant Women's Association come in? She did not know. She explained that the Mentorship was a programme in which young first and second generation immigrants went to schools and talked about their experiences as kids of parents trying to settle in a new country, a kind of programme that helped immigrant kids stand tall, she said. It was started in 2001 by Maru, when the government cut off funding for the work the Association had been doing till then.

Stand tall, that was Maru's phrase, and so she would have been in it somewhere, I thought. 2001, she was doing new things to the very end, and a wave of depression came over me. I want her back. I want her back.

Two days later, I phoned Uncle Siv again and told him about the dead-end street he had sent me to. He thought for a minute and said he would phone me back with the number of someone who might know. He did, and gave me a Vancouver number for a name I knew well, mainly because both her daughters had been Pavilion Queens at Folklorama and as a girl of ten and thirteen I had of course adored them. The voice that answered thawed considerably on hearing my name. We talked about my parents and her daughters, and then I came down to business. I introduced the topic - that I was going through Aunty Maru's notes and was curious about some references to an Ottawa conference.

She laughed, again one of those hearty laughs of that other generation. Yes, it had been an eventful time, she said, and of course they never got even to first base, what with a strong eastern bloc that seemed to hate Manitoba members for disrupting the conference with their inclusionary stance of wanting to give white immigrant women equal space within the organization, but 'it was a famous victory.' The way she said it, it sounded like a quotation, and I hoped I would remember the line so I could ask Stephen. We talked some more, and she explained that at a nation-wide conference held in Winnipeg in 1986 before the national organization was formed, Manitoba members had taken a walloping because they insisted that they were in favour of a national Immigrant Women's organization with white immigrants as equal partners because many immigrants, no matter what colour, needed help in language and settlement challenges. But those from most other provinces thought the focus should be on a Visible Minority women's group because no matter how many generations they had been here, they were still discriminated against, and that was a more pressing problem than settlement issues of new white immigrants. Manitoba had nominated Maru for the post of National President a couple of years later, and she had ended her nomination speech with a poem that made even their bitterest opponents come embrace her at the end of it. It was the reference to Essequibo, she said, because so many of them were from the Caribbean. I could not quite follow the thread and was glad when she said she would take down my address and send me a copy of a Newsletter she still had about that meeting.

Her letter arrived in due time. The newsletter was dated December 1988. Maru had been with the group since their beginning in 1983, and was the editor of the Newsletter in my hand. I first read the shorter pieces to get a feel for what was happening. They consisted mostly of reports by different members of the Manitoba delegation on the workshops held at the conference in Ottawa. There was one short piece by a Manitoba member that clearly placed in context the Manitoba association's position. It read:

I attended the National Conference by chance and therefore had no expectations except to be able to see women work democratically for a common goal, that goal being "equality."
To my rude awakening, I saw and felt that ...many delegates lacked courtesy, understanding and direction. There seemed to be an exclusion of white immigrant women by a vocal visible-minority group.
In summation, as an immigrant woman not of a visible minority, I felt I could not and would not be part of such a discriminatory group.

Almost the whole issue was devoted to this fiery conference, with cartoons captioned by the person who had sent me the newsletter. One caption had two totally bandaged-up people on hospital beds, with a nurse or is it a visitor asking, "Sorry to bother you, but did Manitoba vote against the President's Report?"

Must have been quite a battle.

Maru's long piece that contained her nomination speech as well as the background for it brought back for me one of the Marus I knew, the activist who was forever swimming upstream. I reread paragraphs over again, wondering if things had changed at all in the fifteen years since she spoke those words:

If I wear a saree all the time, it is because Canada was a different place in 1966, a place my husband and I chose over the United States because we felt it was not racist and we would not be forced to fit any particular mould. The warm reception we got everywhere reinforced my strong sense of personhood, that I could wear my saree and be my own woman in the workplace. Long before multiculturalism was even a word, I realized that for our children to stand tall they must have pride in their roots and that cross-cultural dialogue was essential. I was involved in numerous community activities and for the last eight years have produced a weekly television programme that deals with women's issues, and women's education in such matters as Family Law, family violence etc.

Canada was a different place in 1966. Things have changed, and now racism is rampant, threatening the very fibres of our society. On racism, let me tell you where I stand and give you a new angle. We need to forge a new vocabulary that would reeducate ourselves and earlier immigrant groups. Take the word "mainstream" for example. We should never use the word for the white immigrants who preceded us, for that is to dig our own graves, to place ourselves perpetually in the periphery. Canada is multicultural and all of us are mainstream for we have as much right to be here as anyone who has come to this country in the last three hundred years. It is bad enough that the earlier immigrant groups should call only themselves mainstream, but it is far worse that we should call them and only them by that name and thus bury ourselves.

That is what is also wrong with the Free Trade agreement. It is bad enough that the United States has the power and propensity to dictate to us on tariffs and subsidies to the lumber industry but it is far worse that the present government seems to be begging the U.S. on bended knee to take over our fuel, our timber, our hydro, our water, our country in short. And we have had to listen, even at this conference, to politicians who spew out reams of statistics pulled out of thin air that our sisters in the garment factories will be better off if we sign the deal, when we, and they, damn well know that our sisters are going to be sucked dry and spat out like orange pips.

All this is not anti-Conservative propaganda but a matter of issues. Our organization is not a forum for promoting any party leanings or politicians. Any speakers I choose will not be politicians but women who have lighted the way for the rest of us, one of our own. We have to be political and politicized but always on ISSUES, not on parties or personalities, even if they are the ones who fund us.

We have the strength to ask for government funding without being obsequious. Let us hammer our way onto boards and decision-making bodies in full confidence of our strength; let us make the funders see that it is WE who are doing the giving – of our knowledge, our time, our cultural sensitivity – that they are the receivers and we the givers.

Lastly, I believe in developing our potential for art and celebration, for our artists are often our most eloquent spokeswomen. I would like to put a tongue in every wound, a song to every smile of our experience as immigrant and visible minority women of Canada. Let me conclude with some lines from one of my poems.

I remember the poem and I do remember Maru telling me how the construction of a poem depends on sound, and how because she had used Alps and the Andes, she wanted to pair the Ganges with a river in South America and looked up the map and chose Essequibo over Amazon and Orinico because of its sound.

I wonder what came of all these battles? There doesn't seem to be anything much going on the immigrant women front or women's front at all. But maybe I am out of touch. I will know more about her work with local women when I read more of this carton.

~

Outline
A story that is waiting to be written. An offshoot from what happened at IWAM today when a woman came in for counselling who had a burn she claimed to be from the radiator. I will make the victim from India of course. There are so many stories waiting to be written from the tidbits I hear about abused women, as we at IWAM try to set up a Counselling section.

A white doctor, female, Janice McKnight, recruited by an Indian woman to speak to her group. Battered women. One of them turns out to be the wife of a student from India she had loved. She is furious at first and shocked when she knows what has happened. Assumes he is the culprit but turns out that the woman has a lover who beats her up.

Has to be handled carefully. Is it Janice's story? Or Ranvir's or Nimmi's (rename her too since I have used the name Nimmi somewhere). Where does social worker fit into all this. (does Janice find out details from Nimmi or from social worker, shall I call her Pratima Kumar?)

He goes to India on hearing his mother is ill. Comes back married and they never see each other again. The propensity of Indian men to be under their mothers' thumbs....

Janice recalls their time together. Put in details.

~

Janice's peripheral vision took in the waiting room as she walked through the back door of the building to her private office. She was only twenty minutes late but already there seemed to be half a dozen patients. Her sandwich would have to remain uneaten, as usual.

Getting into her white coat, she glanced at the list of people to whom she had given an appointment over the telephone during the weekend. It was to have been during the hour she usually set aside for lunch but she was already late. Only on the last weekend of each month did she have a stand-by colleague who answered calls for her. The rest of the time, she let calls through to the answering machine and sorted out the urgent calls to answer rightaway. Only one of the calls had been urgent, and the baby had been duly delivered the previous day. The list was short, thank god. And one of them was not a patient. Pratima Kumar. She should not have given her an appointment, Janice thought. Mondays were always terribly rushed. But the accent had thrown her off-balance, and she had started on a friendly note instead of a professional one, and then it was too late for anything except to grant the five minutes that the woman had sought. Janice was annoyed with herself, for her weakness with Indian accents; no matter who it was, she still reacted with reflexive friendliness. Five years, already five years?

Her nurse, Doreen, came in and as per procedure, stuck the patient files on the two doors on either side of her office. "Mrs. Johnson said you'd see her," she said, "and Mrs. Dunn doesn't have an appointment but... you know how she is. Just popped in."

"Since I'm late already, as usual I'll start with the first two who have real appointments," Janice said, "but squeeze in the

other two after them, and I'll see Mrs. Kumar here now.   Let's
hope we can catch up by three o'clock."

Pratima Kumar was in her mid-thirties, average height for
an Indian, dressed in a simple but clearly expensive skirt and
sweater outfit. Her complexion was light brown, smooth,
unblemished; Janice always noticed women's complexion, her
own freckled cheeks having been her cross ever since she could
remember.

Janice motioned her visitor to the other chair as she took
hers. "Sorry to be running late," she said, "But one can't help
with delays in natural births."

Pratima gestured, Don't apologize. "That's fine. If I were
your patient, I would be glad to know you are not one of those
who'd rush me when I am in labour. I do greatly appreciate your
giving me an appointment during your lunch hour. I'll come
straight to the point. I need you to spare me an hour and a half
any morning you can, to talk to my group. I work with them,
kind of helping out in a wholly informal way."

"Talk about what?"

"Anything would do, like simple rules to follow, good
habits for good health. Anything at all."

Janice felt a trace of impatience. She should not be spending
office time on this; maybe she should postpone this meeting to
after-hours. That would have been easier had she been on time.

"Perhaps a volunteer from the Women's Resource centre
would be more suited," she said, "or maybe a Public Health
nurse.

"I need a doctor." Pratima's voice was soft but firm. "I beg
of you, Dr. McKnight, to spare just one hour. I need your
presence more than anything you might say. My women need
an open door, doctor, and it is my hope they will find their way
to yours."

Was she trying to bribe her with prospective patients? No
thanks, her list was already longer than she cared to have.

Her visitor sensed that the doctor was about to turn her
away. She leaned forward. Her voice trembled, not with
nervousness but with anger. "One hour, Doctor, just one hour
any time between nine and three. These women," she paused as
though she had trouble saying the next words, "are battered

women, and they need an open door. You cannot deny them that, please, How about Thursday morning? You're usually free Thursday mornings, she stated rather than questioned.

Janice was annoyed. The gall of the woman. She had snooped around and found Janice's schedule.

"You have done your homework, I see," she said, not without sarcasm.

"Yes, Dr. McKnight, I have, and I am begging you. Isn't it strange how readily one accepts being humiliated when we are working for our volunteer commitments?"

"I have a question. Why me? Who referred you to me?"

Pratima did not reply and Janice felt a tremor of nervousness. Was it…please god, no.

"Because you are a woman, and you work alone, perhaps the only one to do so."

That made sense. "But wouldn't they communicate better with someone who could speak their own language?"

"Come, doctor, you can't mean it? Battered women, and from India? They'd do their darndest to hide it even if it kills them. And besides, what makes you think they don't know English?"

Janice got flustered, though she didn't show it. She had not meant to sound patronizing. "Sorry, one shouldn't assume new immigrants don't speak English…" she said. She felt even more annoyed with herself for being so apologetic.

She said more brusquely than she meant to, "Look, I've never done anything like this before, and I haven't been interested either."

"May be it is time you did and were? Thursday morning then? I can pick you up if you wish, or this is the address. My phone number is on it too." She rose.

Janice said, "I think I've been had."

"You won't regret it, Doctor, and I do greatly appreciate your promise of help."

Janice had mixed feelings as she watched her visitor putting on the short fur jacket that she had carried on her arm and had place carefully on the back of the chair. There was something striking about her, though feature by feature she was not attractive except for her skin. She was large hipped and her eyes could have done with some mascara and eyeliner. But she was definitely attractive. His wife probably looked just so, Janice thought and as always wondered that their paths had not crossed in all these five years.

"They'd do their darndest to hide it even if it killed them." Not just your women, not just immigrants either, she thought, the old wound bleeding again. Five years, already five years?

~

I guess I really should spend some time on Maru's involvement with IWAM. Or should I? I don't know when the Counselling section was set up but I do know it was functioning until the big close-down of 2001 when the government cut off all funding and moved the section to some other agency because that was when Maru entered the fray again and fought for IWAM to survive.   I am not sure I know what I am doing!

~~~~~

NINE

Stephen did not come all week, and he phoned me on Thursday to say he was going away the weekend to see his parents. Now that he was free of everything, he was just lazing around, helping other guys, standing in for those who wanted to go cram or go on a date or whatever. He was just marking time, lucky guy, and getting ready for his stint with World Vision. He still wants us to get engaged before he leaves, and I am still saying the time had not come, but I did wonder if I should say yes. I mean, how long does one have to wait to be sure? I couldn't think of not having him near me any more than I could think of myself doing anything other than what I am doing. So why am I still so stubborn, as he says? May be because he is so stubborn.

I spent the weekend sorting out more stuff, looking for those missing sections V to VII. I found VII even though I don't any more know what papers were in which carton.

VII   Maru at the Crossroads.

If I sound all upset it's because I am. When I started on this memoir junket, that's what it was to be, a real junket trip, a home movie of all the fun things that happened to me on the way to the forum that would be so well put together that it didn't look like a home movie at all but a really hilarious narrative such as would pay tribute to those who shaped my childhood years, Stephen Leacock, Mark Twain, P.G.Wodehouse et al. Remember how I said I would take whatever thread I chose to? Never never say things like that. Remember what happened to Blanche in "A Streetcar" and the white woman whatshername in Flannery O Connor's "Everything that Rises…" ? Each said she knew who she was and bang slam, they didn't any more. Never tempt the evil eye; that's why infants are smeared with black all over their face in older cultures, and one's secret name is never given out. So that was an error as ever was. I should never have said I am in control of my narrative.

The other headache is behind me, my term at the Guild having ended last month. I thought I could finish up with my quilt and concentrate on these memoirs. But before I could do so,

Sergio Marchi made his announcement that he wanted taxpayers' input into immigration policies and Canadian multiculturalism, and I find I can't put away my quilt just yet. For of course, I have something to say about how Canada has always taken the cream of the crop immigrants, made sure taxpayers of some other country have paid for their education and then made them start at the bottom rung etc. The government's always done that, but now it looks as though the minister's office is trying to get what they want to come from the people themselves, to shut the door on sponsored parents and dependents, ensure that for every tax-paying immigrant, at most only one non-taxpaying immigrant is admitted etc., that is the formula they want us to tell them, and of course quite a few will say it, what with the Reform Party on an upswing. I now understand what Britain's "Divide and Rule" policy meant. Some of my fellow writers, like Himani Bannerji and Ashok Weerasinghe, have long been saying Multiculturalism is a ghettoizing ploy by the white power bloc. I wouldn't go so far, but I can see why one could see it that way. There is a pretty scary backlash that's gathering momentum, all the rednecks of the Keep Canada White concept surging forward and blaming all economic ills and recession on immigrants from Asia and Africa. So, of course, the quilt cannot be put away.

And then there are all these other rugs and shawls I've been working on, so there's plenty of hooks and threads all around me, and heh, I figured instead of cleaning up, I'd sit in the middle and pull a memory thread here, a Marchi thread there, and show Marchi some of the patches on my quilt.

But too many other things have started happening around me. Threads are flying at me from too many different spools, the patches on the quilt seem to be making themselves into faces that are making faces at me; the tapestry says, what about me you haven't told anyone what I am all about, and all those half-tatted doilies and what-nots are threatening to form a union because I haven't been working with them and they don't have benefits or Unemployment Insurance. One of these troublesome complainants is a needle point I started a couple of years ago; inspired by Manitoba's own Elijah Harper who singlehandedly slew the demon Meech, I started on this needlepoint of an Indian head, and then found out that if I really respected Elijah and the valiant

Mohawks of Oka, I shouldn't go ahead with my needlepoint. Cultural appropriation. So I stopped.

Well, that is not enough, he now says, this half completed head, I have to declare myself, he says, now that there is all this controversy over a closed conference for racial minority writers to be held in Vancouver later this summer. But I have more questions than answers, so how can I declare anything except that I do believe in solidarity. I'll go along in solidarity even if that's not what I would do, I said. I wouldn't refuse anyone entry, I said, I would just structure it so only those really concerned would turn up. We've had our exclusive get-together two years ago, and now it is time to dialogue across race and minority-majority lines. This is a national union, for heaven's sake, and you can't exclude members. There are a great many of them who are decent human beings and a great many who need to be educated but let us have them, both types, as long as we are the ones who decide on the schedule and speakers. But the others, sisters and brothers in our new parlance, voted to restrict admission, and I said, okay in solidarity I will go along. We will have a writers' conference just for racial minorities, whites to be excluded. But at the end of it, we must set a direction and start moving towards it and not have yet another start-from-scratch conference two years from now. I have been around community organizations too long not to know the tendency to have such conferences year after year; heritage workshops, multicultural education panels, immigrant women's conferences ... A marvellous sense of euphoria and togetherness for the space of a weekend, all adding up to having the same panels and same resolutions passed year after year.

About this particular issue there are all these lines and labels, more questions than answers that I have accumulated over my travels. Please tell me if you can make sense of my journal started about the time I stopped work on the needlepoint. I attended several conferences and seminars last year. Here it is.

~

Cultural Appropriation: Journal of an ongoing Journey
The baggage that has accreted around the terms "Voice Appropriation" and "Cultural Appropriation" has polarized people. To one constituency, the terms signify censorship and to the other they signify racial exploitation. During this year that commemorates five hundred years of resistance, I started my journey of questioning.

My journey, literal and figurative, started with a conference where we first sat in a circle and listened to native drummers. One of the organizers spoke about how it had been foretold that this land, Turtle Island as it was called in her cultural lore, would one day be home to people of different colours. She took four coloured threads and tied them to her sacred eagle feather: red for the First Nations, white for the Caucasians, yellow for the Chinese and black for the Africans. I was wearing a brown sari; I wanted to pull out a thread from my sari and hand it to her, to add to the other four. But I let it pass. Which was just as well because later it was clear that her cultural lore specifically mentioned only four colours.

She talked about Turtle Island, about the wealth of traditional wisdom they once had, about depredations suffered at the hands of early traders and settlers, about the loss of land, of identity, of dignity. She stopped speaking and she cried. And then she went on. This wrongful appropriation must stop and we will ensure that it stops by insisting that anyone engaged in literary exploration of any culture not one's own must seek permission. All who seek to write about the First Nations must first obtain permission from the elders with offerings of sweet grass and tobacco, and certain promises. She stopped, tear-choked, several times.

Audience response. I had heard almost the same speech from the same person twelve months earlier when it was given to a large hall of academics, most of whom were white and male. The tension in the air was palpable in that large auditorium but they sat in tightlipped silence, as white (mostly male) academics usually do. After the talk, a few voiced their objection to her position, with tightlipped precision as white (mostly male) academics are trained to speak. I found the situation hilarious - both, the speaker's perfect sense for the dramatic and academia's response. But here, at this meeting where native drummers had opened our discussions, the response was quite different. One after another, ten to twelve individuals, most of them non-white and non-academic and nonmale, stood up and thanked her - for crying, for her openness, for affirming that emotion had a place in our discourse. Yes, we would support her in her stand. We would draw our line of resistance.

At one of the many airports I passed through recently, I spoke to a stranger who was clearly headed for the same conference as I. We got to know each other a little more during the next two days. She was a researcher into native culture; during and after last year's panel on Voice Appropriation, she too had cried, but by herself under a tree outside the auditorium; she had decided she would abandon native studies because she was white. A native elder had recognized her and comforted her. I came to know she was married to a native and had several children by him. Is she or is she not eligible to do this research, I asked a first nations spokesperson. The answer was No, she was not. I could partially empathize with the spokesperson's concerns. In any struggle of resistance, one has to draw a line and defend it; else, little by little one is pushed into retreat.

~

At another conference, I presented a paper. It was on a novel about a nemesis casket, a metaphor for Canada, that contained all kinds of records which each character had put in, stored, edited, excised, rewritten over the years. We loved that writer, our comrade. He was a Canadian whose ancestry could be traced to at least three different bloodstreams, three different races. He had appropriated voices from the country's mosaic and given it to the main characters who were related in different ways as in a large family, another of his figurative devices. The writer's own life and novels moved towards synthesis, towards the concept of one culture, ultimately composite and Canadian however different and hybrid the roots; many-voiced, many-hued but composite and whole. When so many of us have so many bloodstreams in our veins, where does one draw the line for "appropriation," and why?

*****

Blood lineage, and only that, gives one admittance into the inner circle, was the activist's message. Even if it is only one-quarter, eighths, sixteenths, of one's bloodstream?

Also, can one assume blood will not misrepresent, distort?
Insider, outsider, where do we draw the line, and how?
To every issue there are at least two sides.

*****

That should give you an idea of where I'm at, and why I am
entangled in all these different threads. To fill you in on the Racial
Minority conference plans, someone in Parliament objected to public
funding for an "exclusionary" conference and the government in
panic pulled out from the promised support. So totally irresponsible. Of course public funds for the conference are perfectly
justified, though I'd rather have another kind of conference. I'll be
on my way there soon in my trusty van.

*****

Chikkamma gave me an earful. Not about that directly but in a
related context of who can speak for whom. She came by the other
day. "Just let Sergio Marchi try keeping me out, hnh," were her first
words as she entered.

"If you don't stop volunteering for committee work on writers'
organizations, you will never get any of your own writing
completed," she said, sinking into her favourite rocker. She is right,
of course, that's been the story of my life, spending all my time on
some cause or the other, but I wouldn't admit it in front of her.
"You've been reading my stuff," I said, taking the offensive.

"All that is thine is mine, fair is fair," she chortled, not the least
perturbed at my accusation. "About this Appropriation," she said,
"first why not call it Misappropriation for clarity? Also, it is not a
question of who is entitled to write what but how well they do it.
Just off with their head, if they don't do it well."

"Not so easy. Who defines 'well' and 'badly?' Those who think
all that is thine is mine?"

"Touché," she made the gesture of "surrender."

Having scored, I was prepared to be more conciliatory.
"Chikkamma, we are going through a rather marvellous phase here,
a Native Renaissance, and we just have to give them room, no
questions asked. In another fifty years, may be."

"We in India have had more than fifty years of affirmative
action regarding scheduled castes and tribes, and it hasn't been

enough. But what would you know or care about the Mandal
Commission riots?"

Without giving me a chance to show off my knowledge of what
was happening in India, she continued, "And why did you delete
your last sentence, 'All this kerfuffle about Rushdie but nobody
questions the ban on those who play down the Holocaust.'?"

"How did you know about that? How could you know about
that?"

"It was still on the large clipboard, how else? Think I'm
clairvoyant or something?"

"I've been here long enough to know one had better not talk
about Rushdie or the Holocaust."

"Political correctness," she chortled like a child who had found
a new toy. "Political correctness." She drew out each syllable. "I
didn't think you'd fall for it, tsk tsk. I wonder, though, is it PC or
plainandsimple ignorance and/or arrogance that makes some of
your sisters on the net say the things they do? You made a good
point there, insider, outsider, where do we draw the line? Can one
assume blood will not misrepresent, distort? Apply it to your sisters
on the net. Methinks there are too many bloody insiders playing
Judas. I am referring to the Ramayana and Gita debate that is going
on. What batty commentator of the Gita is she reading? that woman
who says the first chapter is about women being "not very intelligent
and therefore not trustworthy?" You and your net sisters. Bah. So
many politically correct Hindu women that think they have to berate
Rama and Hinduism, and uphold every other culture and religion in
the Ayodhya problem. Listen to any interfaith panel of speakers
and you will see that Christians, Jews and Muslims usually spend
most of their time talking about the merits of their religion but
Hindus elbow each other to get to the podium to talk of how women,
children, castes and classes were/are oppressed in Hinduism. Why
don't they try to understand Rama for a change, instead of endlessly
saying he drove his pregnant wife out. That story is in the Uttara
Kanda and most scholars agree it is a later addition. Would
Macaulay ever be pleased or what? Colonialized minds running riot
under the guise of progressiveness on one hand, and on the other
political correctness that stifles reason and courage in people like
you. Bah.

I cringed. I would think about responses, cutting responses culled in chiselled metaphors later; later I would think, Just wait, someone else always rebuts such arguments because the net I am on is full of thinking sensitive women, but now I cringed. Everything she said hit home. The only reason I don't advance these views is not because I am chicken but because I don't know how to cut and paste on the screen and so never write anything on the net. The backspace key on my Z-term doesn't work, is my excuse, and I just can't type anything without a backspace key to correct my typos. But I wasn't going to confess my computer illiteracy to Chikkamma.

I wanted to be aggressive but it came out as a whine. "You have got into my password and access codes, how could you?" What if she chose to use my internet group to spout off on her own? The group she had broken into was a South Asian women's group, sworn to confidentiality; not that we discussed anything the FBI could use, but how could she betray my trust in giving her free access to come and go as she pleased?

I knew the answer, of course. I had absolutely no control over her. She was Chikkamma, the holy terror Principal of a girls' school, and much else, but I won't tell you just yet.

~

When Stephen returned the following week, over the Thai take-out that he had brought, he said that he was thinking of going to India to work at the Sankurathri Eye Hospital. Better India than Africa, I thought, if at all he wanted to go. But I couldn't understand his need to go volunteer at the other end of the world. If at all one wants to change the world, why not start at home? But I guess it is not easy to baulk the system and work for free here. A free Eye Clinic in Canada, with not just diagnoses in medi-vans that come to your door but also surgeries at the hospital and overnight stays as well, that would be the day. He said he was happy with the decision. He had contacted the Ottawa office and it seemed like it was going to be easy to push the paper work through, as work-term volunteer.

That night, as I sat at the dining table poring over my books for the exam next week, Stephen started talking from his usual place on the sofa. "I had Dad drive me to Grandad's place," he said, "and I couldn't believe it, the old house was gone, and a sprawling new modern bungalow there instead, I couldn't believe it. They did it so fast, just razed it and built upon it so fast I can't believe it. We've had such great times in that house, with its gables and gargoyles, and now it is gone, absolutely nothing left of it." He sounded quite upset and I couldn't understand why. "Happens even more to people," I said, "think of it, a guy dies and that is that, he gets forgotten very quickly, and in a generation it is as though he had never been."

"Not the same," Stephen said, "as long as there is family one goes on, children and all that, the DNA is still around, a bit of us always floating around. But a house, pull a house down and it is gone, one generation to remember it and then pouff, nothing, it is not fair, the house was a good house, they had no business tearing it down. We should have kept it in the family, why are people in such a hurry to sell something just because they themselves have no use for it?"

He realized the impracticality of it himself and said, "Oh, well, guess one had better get used to the idea that it is gone, but still and all, that house deserved better."

May be that is why I was drawn to Stephen – he was so connected to the earth, this land, the way I have never been, can never be. I wanted to hug him tight as though by osmosis I could get that connection to a house, a place. Did I care for Winnipeg? About the city itself I couldn't care less, a pretty ugly city that, except for the sky, and I wouldn't have noticed the sky I am sure if Maru hadn't harped so much on the beauty of the endless blue skies. Of course, I sometimes felt nostalgic about our house in Winnipeg.

All this talk about houses reminded me of something I had briefly glanced at in Maru's writings, which I had thrown into the finished-reading carton. "Maru seemed to have the same hang-ups as you about houses," I said, "she has a whole folder called Houses." I got up, riffled through the "finished reading carton" and handed it to Stephen. "Here's something to keep you busy, just don't talk to me till I have reviewed the chapter I am on. Then you can tell me if I should throw it back into the reject carton or Read Again carton." I read the first paragraph before I gave it to Stephen and realized why I had thrown it in the reject carton – because the sheet I first picked up was not addressed to me but to that other person, that nameless faceless alien reader for whom Maru had written explanatory notes about India.

Houses.

Let me tell you about houses today, all the houses I have lived in.

We have always lived in big houses with extensive compounds. I was born in my grandfather's house in Madras – now, that is a custom followed by many in India and like many customs it is rooted in practicality – not just to farm off the wife and kids to someone else's care as one might think, but because a woman gets a lot more attention and tending in her mother's house than in her mother-in-law's. Not that my mother had a mother to go to though the house was there and my grandpa, but just that I have to place everything within the culture it is set in.

My grandfather's house was built by him when he was still working in the North. In those days, everyone built a house in the city that they planned to retire to, and for our family of course it was Madras. Just about everyone had left the ancestral village by 1920, and a great many of them were in "government service" as the civil service was called. They were usually in the Railways or Post & Telegraphs or some such pan-Indian job that transferred them to the four corners of the country. An aside, well you have to listen to my asides whether you like it or not, this was the British system which believed that if you never let officers stay put in a place for too long, they couldn't create any mischief or get corrupt with bribery etc. and so officers were never in any place for longer than three or four years even if they were posted again to that place four years down the road. My grandfather was in the Railways, in the Audits department, and in time became Auditor General. But the time we are talking of, the 1920s, Mylapore was the area which was the stronghold of the Brahmin elite, the leaders of the new age who had been schooled in English the whole way and now held high positions in the British government.

[Note to myself. Now, really, all this typing is getting to be a bore. And there are so many houses to write about. Here is what I have to say about Grandpa's house, written by me when I was a teenager and of course I treasure it because this copy is what he had typed up and sent back to me with his comments.]

And clipped to this was a foolscap sheet typed with what was obviously one of those clunker typewriters with an old ribbon. The sheet itself was a carbon copy – the lettering was purple.

There is a red road, a lane avenued by tall coconut palms. It is blissfully cool in the burning Madras afternoons and threateningly dark even on the brightest of nights. On either side, there are massive houses of the old type of architecture, sombrely looking at the palms. Each has a boundary wall, none has a good garden, big houses without sweeping driveways or velvet lawns – just massive, mostly belonging to retired gentlemen of the old world – the type of well-read scholars that was existing in the country, especially in the South, a type that is fast dying out, even in those just a bit younger.

A shady dark alley ending in a low white wall beyond which has sprung up a new and distasteful colony of modern flats and houses with new-fangled gadgets.

To the left of the road stands that to which two score persons and more converge as their Home – Chandra Vilas. Chandra Vilas, standing there as far back as memory can stretch, persons drifting in and out, breakfast being served all morning going on to lunch, merging into tiffin. Something is always being served to someone or the other – a late breakfast coinciding with an early lunch – no break except for an hour in the evening before the three hour dinner starts.

Chandra Vilas – built as though someone had taken a handful of passages, rooms, windows and verandahs, swung it round the head and flung it out, and they settled down anyhow – into Chandra Vilas.

There are some things, objects and actions, purely characteristic of Chandra Vilas – the huge easy-chair placed bang in the middle of the passage; the oonjal in the dining room with children hanging on to the chains, sitting on a plank and swinging right up to the wall with the regular *kiin kiin* of the iron rings; the balustrade down which children are forever sliding; the two huge white pillars on the front veranda with just enough space between them to lure the chubby leg of a toddler and to abstract the piercing cry of a healthy Chandra Vilasian, the place between the easy-chair and the dining room where people are forever clustered, where jokes innumerable have been shared, daily incidents related, all the sorrows of the housewives poured – the misdemeanour of the servants, the mischiefs of the children, the disorders of infants' stomachs, the remarks of their respective husbands, the programme for the evening, quarrels and misunderstandings evolved, created, cleared – all the most interesting juicy spicy things that happen to them or near them, of them or for them, everything is spoken there at the entrance of the door with its beaded arch, between the passage and the dining room.

At the sound of one voice, the slip-slip of a pair of slippers, the lolling youth bounds out of the chair, children scamper off the oonjal, gossipmongers scatter away, prospective picture-goers disperse, balustrade travellers rush out, and the wailing infant is hushed by a hurrying mother.

May the chubby leg be another's, the buttocks that slide down change, the youngsters on the oonjal mature into adolescents, the happy-go-lucky picture-goers partake in the discussions of housewifery, and may the bay room that has witnessed the arrival of twenty odd babies welcome the first cry of a new set of the latest models of Chandra Vilasians, but may the rich voice never break, may the slip-slip of the slippers ever be the same, and may their owner ever be present to guide and rule CHANDRA VILAS.

There was a handwritten comment by the grandfather:
"Alas, Chandra Vilas is a deserted Corner House today as the centre of gravity has shifted to the "back" house due to several causes which cannot be stated on paper, ever since the library has been gifted away by me. Again, the advent of great grandchildren is so far off – since my daughters' daughters have taken to intellectual professions and are resisting to keep up a home, this being another reason." Dated 8/12/56

There was also a copy of a letter, from Maru's famous uncle, on his University letterhead, in his neat bold handwriting, dated just a few weeks later:

I have received a copy of your piece. It is a beautifully written essay and it brought back memories long submerged by the weight of years.

I lived in Chandra Vilas during its first years – 1925-1930; and in my recollections of Chandra Vilas, I have always superimposed my impressions of those years on the present. And reading your sensitively transcribed impressions of the present, I felt embarrassed as one caught in the act of looking through the wrong end of a telescope...Yes! to you Chandra

Vilas stands "there as far as memory can stretch," but from my end of the telescope, Chandra Vilas has always appeared freshly built: the very building of it having been a novel adventure. Do you know... that when Chandra Vilas was built, we resided in the house next doors; and I kept the roll of the workers – charming carefree men and women whose joyous faces I can still recall – masons and helps who poured the concrete and laid the bricks.   I can even recall my first visit to the freshly broken ground when the foundations were being dug.   And certainly, you cannot recall ... the lovely centre of us all during those lovely long-gone days – your grandmother, my mother... Yes to you "the huge easy chair placed bang in the middle of the passage" is an incongruity.   But do you know that when we returned to Chandra Vilas, six years ago, after a lapse of fifteen years, I should have felt disconsolate if the Chair had not been there? There, on that Chair ... your grandmother used to rest during her long and painful illness; and I cannot recall Chandra Vilas without her lying in that Chair, with that anxious devotion for us all... And the beaded archway, you mention; that was a decoration... your grandmother beaded herself; and I can recall the joy that suffused her face as she first put that up.... Those days are beyond the stretches of your memory; but your portrayal of Chandra Vilas brought back nostalgic memories in me. The memory of the freshly built Chandra Vilas and the memory of my mother and I do want to thank you for your beautifully written essay on Chandra Vilas.
With best wishes,
Yours affectionately,
Ayya Maama

Stephen whistled and then hushed himself loudly.
"What?" I said.
"Nothing, nothing at all. Not a word till you finish the chapter."
"Might as well get it over now that you have distracted my attention," I said with mock annoyance. "Don't tell me you've read all of it already."
"Oh no, just the first one, about her grandfather's house. Grandad's house had pillars at the front, too, believe it? Also, you never told me Maru was niece of this great scientist, if the letterhead with the Chicago University crest is for real. Grandad's house had

gargoyles. Do you think this house had them too? I can't believe it is gone, not a stone or tree left; if I'd known that was happening, I could have gone one last time. It isn't fair."

"Oh please," I said, "think of your Grandad, not of some old house." But I was jealous of him, of Maru, of UncaShar talking about his place back in Poona of which Jayant once said, 'a shambles where you have to walk half a mile to get to the shithouse.' These people had something that I had never had, and never would, it wasn't fair.

~

I took the Houses folder and threw it into the Read Again carton. Next day, I took it out and started reading again. What struck me was the way Maru had these postscripts about possible story lines scribbled everywhere. On one of the back pages of her uncle's letter was a paragraph written in pencil.

Story-line: in 1936, when C returned from Cambridge, he searched out Ramanujan's widow. Traced her to her elder brother's house, illiterate, a poor relation, a drudge as many women and most widows of poor families were. For sixteen years she had lived with her brother, giving him her pension of Rs. 50 per month that the government had granted her. C spent some time with her, telling her about the genius of her husband. Had I but known all this, she lamented, I would have made something of my life, educated myself, been his widow instead of a nameless, illiterate dependent in the dark world of brahmin widowhood. Later on, C persuaded the government into raising the pension to Rs. 75.

My story: What if C's good deed was not a good turn after all? He might have introduced her to her husband's genius but had he not also taken her to her full realization of her wasted life and left her there? Develop her gratitude and his genuine interest but the reader should realize more than she does about the lot of women and widows more specifically. Is ignorance better than knowledge in that it helps alleviate one's resentment at a world lost for no fault of one's own? She had taken widowhood, loneliness, drudgery as her destiny but is now filled with vague undefined and indefinable longing and regrets. Note, did C style his hair the way he did in emulation of his hero?

Note: (Feb 1982) Pritish Nandy interviewed Mrs. R, at age 82, where she says, "I didn't understand his work, but I knew his worth." Will have to think how this info impacts on my proposed outline. Article also says her pension is now at Rs. 300.

~~~~~

TEN

Next time Stephen came, he brought a number of books from the library – beautifully illustrated books of tourists' India, which lay on the coffee table for two weeks and were then replaced with volumes on the History of India. But he was not there to read them. He dropped by for short visits, and spent his nights off with me, if I was free and amenable. I was very busy with my work and did not care either way. If my shift permitted, it was pleasant to spend the evenings by myself, watching TV, listening to music, reading Maru's stuff. But he was always back of my mind, reading the stuff with me as it were, and I imagined what he might say of this, that or the other. Sometimes I put some of the sheets in a blue tray for him to read. Whenever I finished reading something, I put a check mark on the top right hand corner, and the decade to which the item belonged. Sometimes they had the date mentioned somewhere, and if so, I wrote that down just below the check mark; otherwise, I wrote the year or decade and put a question mark beside it. I brought an empty carton from the convenience store, and put into it the sheets I had read. Now, Stephen could read anything he wanted from that carton and I need not be afraid of him reading anything I did not want him to read. I was not sure what it was that I wanted to keep from him, but I felt it was only right that I ensured he did not come across any family details that were personal, even though I hadn't seen anything personal so far. I was pleased with my organized approach.

But then I noticed themes, or clusters, jottings on the same subject that were written at different times. I wondered how I should organize them. Logically, they seemed like they should be together. So I have trays – again shallow empty cartons I brought in from the convenience store – for themes. I already have one for events or diary entries, one for dreams (I will have to read them before I pass them on to Stephen but it helps to sort as I go along, and I will read them at some point) and this one is for how writers write. I have to think up better names for these trays. Stephen can help with that, he is never at a loss for names and labels and identification markers.

The first is typed with a note that says it is being written by invitation for a magazine with a deadline of September 1999, and the others are dated and handwritten.

Tending a Bonsai: The Making of a Poem

Poetry-making is like tending a bonsai. It requires a great deal of effort and patience, and at the end of it, an unimaginative person might dismiss it as a stunted creation. One needs to be sensitive to the internal requisites – of denotation and connotation – and to be sensitive to the subtle effects of sound and metaphors.

The seed of a poem often comes easily, but to sow it, tend it, clear it of weeds, prune it with the care that it takes to tend to a bonsai – all that takes talent, craft and patience. By craft, I mean the work that goes into the conscious cultivation of artistic potential that results in a work of art.

Often a poem starts out with a line that repeats itself in one's head; it is a combination of sound and meaning that makes it lodge in one's head and periodically come out like a cuckoo in a clock, demanding attention.

Here is a fat note book where the first page says "August 26, 1970". But there is writing only on the first few pages.

August 26, 1970

Plots for short stories and novels strike me. At the sight of someone. At the sound of something. At the thought of some happening that has happened or might happen. To write them down as they come would be ideal. Or probably a waste of time, for ideas overrun their potential all too often. But discarding can be done later. One must write them down, those fleeting ideas and dreams. But no time. Writing takes long, far too much time. And my handwriting has been getting worse. Rush, rush, rush. Condense. But write. That's the point. Put them down on paper. Paper is the only thing that will last, not memories.

But when it comes to jotting down names and real people and incidents, one hesitates. Because often even the core of the story that one creates is imaginary though suggested by something actual. Actual, that is the word, not real. For who knows what is real. Semantic hairsplitting? No. Risky, apt to be misconstrued should someone else come across it. But write down. That is the only way of retaining sparks, ideas.

But if they are so soon forgotten, are they worth keeping. Yes, yes, yes.

~

I read through some sheets from a stack titled "Stories waiting to be written." Most are in her handwriting but I saw that some were typed and so I picked one of them up for easy reading. She had notes to herself as in many of these sheets. This one had more detailed description of people than elsewhere and I would have guessed it was an early piece even if she had not noted it down. I was pleased with myself – I was discerning stuff I would never have recognized earlier.

Theme sources. This is handwritten on foolscap size paper so probably written in Trivandrum in 1965-66.

On the 27th of April we were travelling towards Palghat in the Cochin Express. There were two others in the first class compartment – a short balding short-sighted man in white half-pants, a half-sleeved shirt, knee length socks and black polished shoes; and a woman, slim, fair, young.

The man was probably in the navy – who else would wear white shorts and speak fluent English with a terrific accent, the accent heard in guys who pass out of Anglo-Indian schools and join slick careers like the services or lower-executive positions in the railways. He spoke fluently and without stopping almost all the time he was sitting. For a couple of hours in the afternoon, he went up and slept. His face and figure were quite unattractive; he had scanty hair receding rapidly; his eyes were small, and looked round and large through his soda-beedi glasses. His eyebrows had little hair but when he raised his eyebrows as he often did, they formed two distinct little lines which would have met somewhere at the middle of the forehead if extended upwards. His nose was small and had no bridge. His mouth was large. He was thick-lipped and his teeth were sparkling white, so even, so beautiful I felt they were false, indeed I got a feeling of certainty that they were dentures. Feature by feature he was very plain, yet there was a kind of sex appeal in him, in his confidence, in his fund of information facilely meted out, in his knight-errantly conduct that might pall with time but is invariably attractive for a change. So there he

was, his curly short thigh hair showing under his shorts, his
eyebrows and fingers eloquently reinforcing his speech, his
right shoulder very close to the girl's, his mouth rather comic,
talking nineteen to the dozen.

The girl was between 22 and 25, so it seemed to me. She
was fair, the whitish kind of fairness one sees in Poona-
Maharashtrians; her eyes were beautiful, mild-looking most of
the time; her nose was enviable as were her curved lips which
were pink and thin. Her teeth were not small or even and they
seldom showed when she smiled. She had many many pimples
on her face. She wore a pink-mauve sari and a darker coloured
blouse. Her hands were beautiful. She wore no ring. She had a
gold chain around her neck. There she was, an ideal companion
for him, smiling, with that encouraging expression that seems to
say with an occasional smile - I am listening attentively, though
I seem absent-minded.

Who were they? That they were lovers seemed obvious, that
he loved her more than she loved him was obvious too. Were
they married? I overheard her say she did have a ring such as
married women wear and he said something I could not hear.
It was surprising that he could talk in such a soft voice that I,
sitting just four or five feet away, could not hear him. I could
hear her, women's voices always carry, however low. He was a
Roman Catholic, for suddenly he whisked out a rosary, joined
his palms and prayed for a while. I was pleased with myself,
that I had pigeonholed him just right as soon as I heard his
accent. She was a Hindu, judging by her appearance and the
sindoor on her forehead. They carried a suitcase between them;
he had an attaché case such as businessmen carry nowadays
and graduate students carry out in America.

~

Story-line: And he made the milk to flow. I have the synopsis
somewhere else, but just so I remember, it is a story of baby
Krishna, who made the milk to flow in a barren woman? A
devadasi? A virgin? No not a virgin – keep that for christianity
lore.

Must translate Meera Bhajans. Also, write a story with Bhoj at the centre. It is Meera's story but Bhoj has to be centre stage. How can that be done? Must use lines from the bhajans. M.S.'s rendering is so powerful, the overwhelming sensuousness of *"Aadhi raat mey darsan dehai prem nadi ke teera,"* and the exhilarating spiritual abandon of *"Vish ka pyala Ranaji ne bheja, peevat Meera naachi re,"* the utter truth of *"Loga kahe Meera bhayee re baavari, nyaat kahe kulnasi re…"*

Bhoj is frustrated that his wife resists him. He is too honourable, perhaps too proud, to take her without her consent. One day, she sees a peacock fan over their bed and gives in. Bhoj happy but later realizes she wasn't really there for him, that she was elsewhere fantasizing. Have Bhoj listen to her songs. He wishes he could have such passion for God but all he knows is his passion for his wife, who resists him or is not really there. He sets out on a long, heartbreaking but determined courtship, ignoring all other wives.

Once he tells her, When I am Rana, I shall decree that Krishna be worshipped everywhere, but even as he says it, he feels ashamed, knowing Meera is thinking Love cannot be ordered. He suggests they go on a pilgrimage to Vrindavan, half hoping that would rid her of her obsession, half hoping that he too would be wholly converted, to be as single-minded in his devotion to Krishna as she was.

Or it could be Meera's story after all. Bhoj could still be the heroic victim.

"I gave him all I could, which was not much. He died a warrior's death, and left his father and his people grieving."

~

There is a stapled set of papers in the same book with the translations of Meera bhajans as sung by M.S. Subbalakshmi, clearly identified. I wonder if the translation could be made into a little book.

This fat note book has jottings – not on every page, there are a lot of blank pages between pages that have been written on. I get it! the blanks are for episodes that came sequentially but never got written down. Couldn't be. Look at the years it spans!

The other day, waited long for the bus at the Bay. A young couple, the girl about 16, obviously pregnant; carrying bags of baby things, full of verve and vitality. Boy only a little older, tired, unsmiling.

Reminds me of the couple at Assiniboine Park, the other way around, the girl on her knees, with hand stretched out and crying, the man half turning away from her.

~

September 25, 1987

Working on the premise that there is a short story waiting to be written in just about everything that happens or doesn't happen, let's start on a notebook a la Henry J.

The sparrow episode. About two weeks ago, after one of those early-frost nights, probably the Monday of the long weekend when the garage door-opener was fixed, why else would S and G have been outside? I saw a sparrow sitting on the grass just at the edge of the patio stones, sitting rather dazed, dead I thought with irrational panic – Bird in the House? – I bent down and shooed it away. It flapped away to the vegetable patch. Thank goodness it is alive, I thought, and went about my work.

Next morning, it lay dead at precisely the same spot at the edge of the patio stones. I walked around it leaving it there because I was driving Arvind to school because he had to carry not only his saxophone but some other boards for his art project, and it was late already. When I returned, the cat had carried it away and there was blood on the sidewalk. A couple of days later, the wings and head reappeared, again at exactly the same spot. I felt queasy. S and A got rid of it, in a plastic bag.

Last night, as I was turning into Stafford off Harrow after my television show where I had interviewed K and V on women's studies, I saw a sparrow on my rear window, passenger side. When I accelerated, it fluttered against the window, desperately trying to stay instead of flying away and I

It ends there, just like that.

The next sheaf I picked up was also from 1987; so good to see something clearly dated. It is the script for one of her TV shows, on the large cue sheets, secured with a large clip.

I labelled it with a check mark and date, and quickly glanced at it. Too long and explanatory, but I knew Stephen would like it. He is cramming everything he can find on India as though there is no tomorrow. I leave this on the blue tray for him.

Pooja Vidhana – August 1, 1987

Today, we have the third part of this series on "The Meaning of Pooja."

Sankalpa is the declaration of intent to do pooja to a particular deity for a particular reason. The Sankalpa starts with a Meditation mantra that is followed by Pranayama and the Sankalpa mantra. The Sankalpa mantra states the time and space coordinates with meticulous exactitude to exemplify the need for total concentration and precision in the performance of every step of the pooja.

I would like to comment that though scholars might argue about such details as the actual length of each period of time mentioned in Hindu Cosmogony, what is remarkable is that ancient Hindu philosophy had already formulated concepts of time and space that are now being revalidated by modern research; that Hindu scientists of old had realized the astronomical magnitude to the numerical figures involved in the life and motion of planets, and had realized too that the process of creation and of dissolution into latency, of srishti and sthithi, goes on in cycles.

The ability to conceptualize such abstractions is considered the yardstick of civilization, and Hinduism emerges as the most advanced and continuous of all world cultures.

Let us quickly go through some of these concepts mentioned in the Sankalpa mantra.

Brahman, the eternal transcendental spirit called forth Brahma to create the universe.

A Brahma epoch equals 3×10^{14} human years. We are in the Sveta Varaha Kalpa.

Each kalpa has 14 successive periods. Each period has a Progenitor called Manu.

Each such period is called Manvantra. We are in Vaivasvata Manvantra.

Each kalpa has one thousand chaturyugas. We are in the 28th chaturyuga of the second half of Brahma epoch.

Each chaturyuga cycle consists of four yugas called Satyayuga, Tretayuga, Dvapanayuga and Kaliyuga. We are in the first quarter of Kaliyuga.

There are countless galaxies in Space. Each galaxy has various Dvipams or islands. We are in Jambudvipam. Bharata is the ruler of Jambu.

There are seven khandas or continents on Jambu. India is in Bharatakhanda. Canada is in Amerikakhanda.

On Jambu, there is a sacred mountain called Meru. We are south of Meru. Lokmanya Tilak locates Meru at North Pole. So all continents are south of Meru.

A cycle of historical time is called Shakabta. One shakabta equals 60 human years. We are in the first year of one such cycle. Our present year, mid-April 1987 to mid-April 1988 is called Prabhava.

The other details mentioned in the Sankalpa mantra are familiar enough. Let us hear the mantra, which is preceded by Dhyanam or Meditation, and Pranayama, the meaning of which we talked about in the last show. The English translation precedes the Sanskrit:

At this auspicious time in the second half of Brahma's Epoch,

> on the day of Brahma that is called Sveta Varaha Kalpa,
> during the time of Vaivasvata Manavantra,
> in the twenty eighth chaturyuga,
> in the first quarter of Kaliyuga,
> on the island of Jambu,
> in the land ruled by Bharata,
> in the continent of America,
> on the south side of Mount Meru,
> in the year named Prabhava,
> during the southern sojourn of the sun,
> which is the season of summer,
> in the month of August,
> on the eighth day of the waning moon,

this Sunday when the Moon is near the star Rohini,
on this day which is specially good with respect to Yoga,
karana, and all other aspects,
for the benefit of my family and myself in respect to
well-being,
stability,
vitality,
longevity,
health and wealth,
for the fulfilment of desires and longings,
for the realization of the four-fold human goals of
Righteousness, wealth, desires and Liberation.
For the obtaining of good progeny by the grace of Sri
Krishna,
On this holy day of Janmashtami,
I resolve to perform to the best of my ability,
The worship of Sri Krishna
With the sequence of sixteen services
As prescribed in the Kalpasutra,
Having started with Meditation and Pranayama,
I shall now do the Kalasa Puja.
Having thus resolved, I cleanse my hands with water.
      O Sri Vignesvara, for our benefit and well-being,
and in order that you come again when we invoke you,
I prayerfully reestablish you from this turmeric image to
your eternal abode.

(The kalasa [pot] is filled with water, and decorated with
scented paste, turmeric-coated rice, leaves and flowers.)
The face of this kalasa is Vishnu,
Siva is established in its neck,
At its base is Brahma,
In the middle is the Divine Mother,
In the abdomen are the oceans,
The earth with its seven islands,
The four Vedas and their various parts,
Are in the water inside this pot.

UMA PARAMESWARAN

All these Divine Beings are IMMANENT in the kalasa. May they, who are capable of destroying all sins MANIFEST themselves for the purpose of this worship.

I call on the seven holy rivers, Ganga, Yamuna, Godavari, Saraswati, Narmada, Sindhu, and Kaveri, please come, please reside in these waters.

Water taken from the kalasa is then sprinkled on the pooja material and also on the worshippers. The next step is the most important – and is called Prana Pratishta. God is immanent everywhere; in order for God to manifest in an image, we need the help of the Prana Pratishta mantra. There is a protocol prescribed for the use of the Mantra text. If this protocol is not followed, the recitation is simply a chanting of a hymn with possibly no effect. For the effective use of the mantra, we need to mention the author of the text, the metre to which the text is set, the Deity to whom it is addressed, and the purpose to which it is directed. This mantra is like an entry code which must be entered into the computer programme before the words that specify the programme are typed, and the programme itself comes to life.

The use of the mantra is to bind the divinity that transcends earth, space and the heavens. Once we make these declarations and meditate upon the goddess Prana Shakti, she manifests Herself before us. In her presence we pray that the image in front of us be invested with life and limbs. The image then comes to life. Until the end of this pooja, this image is to be treated as the personhood of the deity to whom this pooja is addressed.

For this Prana Pratishta mantra, the rishis are Brahma, Vishnu, Siva.

The metres are those of the Vedas – Rg, Yajur, Sama and Atarva.

The deity is the Supreme Goddess, Prana Shakti.

The sound codes are Aam Hreem Krom.

We use the prescribed hand gestures in order to bind the divinity that transcends earth, space and heavens.

May the Supreme Prana Shakti

Who is seated in the lustrous red lotus floating in the ocean
of lac-coloured water,
Who holds in her lotus-like hands the noose to draw souls,
The bow to punish the wicked,
The sugarcane stick,
Five arrows,
And the bowl with which she feeds the entire universe,
O Prana Shakti of shining eyes and full breasts, who has the
colour of the rising sun,
Bestow felicity upon us.
I utter the holy sounds, the syllables prescribed.

May life forces enter this image,
May life be established in this image,
May this image be endowed with mind, skin, eyes, ears,
tongue, nose, voice, hands, feet, orifices,
With the five vital airs of Prana, Apana, Vyana, Udana and
Samana.

Thus is this image now endowed with life.
Be invoked,
Be established,
Be in close proximity,
Be in front of us,
Be covered by this image,
Be friendly,
Be benign,
Be pleasant,
Be beautiful,
Be pleased with us.

O Lord of the Universe, for the duration of this pooja, please
reside in this image.

(This concludes Prana Pratishta – the goddess has now
invested the image of Krishna with life. Next we have the
Pradhana Pooja, the Main worship, of Sri Krishna. Each verse is
a step of the Sodasopachara, the sixteen services to the Deity.

Each name of Krishna has a significance that is of relevance to the
act being performed.)

I meditate upon the Divine Child, Krishna, who nurses at
his mother's breasts, who has the dark mark of SriVatsa on his
chest, who is beautiful, and who has the hue of the blue lily. I
meditate on you, Balagopala.

I invoke the Supreme Lord, who was born to Devaki, who
took the form of a child, who is indeed the embodiment of
existence, consciousness, and bliss. I invoke you, Balagopala.

O son of Vasudev, who resides in the minds of the sages, I
offer you this throne decorated with gems. May you find this
acceptable. Salutations, Balagopalakrishna, I offer you a seat.

Divine Lord who is worshipped by Indra, I offer you water
to wash your feet. O Lord who has purified the whole world by
letting the river Ganga flow out of your toes, salutations.

Supreme Lord, I bring you water to wash your palms. You
who vanquished the demon Agha and are served constantly by
sinless sages, accept my poor offering.

O delight of Yasoda, from this golden vessel I offer you the
waters of the holy Ganga to rinse your mouth. O Achyuta, who
art forever firm, accept my offering.

O Madhava, ocean of virtues, Slayer of demon Madhu,
please accept this madhuparka made of honey, curds and ghee.

To You who destroys those guilty of the five great sins of
Brahminicide, Drunkenness, Theft, Fornication, and Evil
Company, I offer this panchamritam, mixture of five nectars of
milk, curds, ghee, sugar and honey.

Lord, whose lotus feet are worshipped by Indra, who art
worshipped by Kamadhenu the divine cow, receive this pure
water for your holy bath. At the end of your bath, I offer you
water for ceremonial rinsing.

Gopala, who stole the gopis' garments, Ananta, who made
Draupadi's sari endless and thus saved her from dishonour,
Krishna, who wears raiments of yellow silk, I bring you my
offering of clothes.

Son of Vasudeva, Merciful Lord, Protector of incomparable
glory, receive this sacred thread and protect me; bind me to
Yourself.

O Purshottama, supreme being who is bedecked with garlands, anklets, bracelets, bangles and other jewellery, to you I offer this ornament.

Salutations to you, who blessed the girl named Kubja, receive this scented powder made of kumkum, musk and camphor.

O Slayer of Sakatasura, O compassionate Lord who showers inexhaustible benefits, accept these rice grains coated with sacred turmeric.

I worship you with jaji, champaka, punnaka, malati, mallika, and other flowers. I worship you who is adored by Arjun, son of Kunti.

(Next, we worship every part of the Lord's body.)

Salutations to you, Govinda, I worship your feet.
Gopala, I worship your ankles.
Uncreated One, I worship your knee.
Destroyer of Putana, I worship your thighs.
Destroyer of Sakatasura, I worship your waist.
The One who is fond of butter, I worship your navel.
Damodara, I worship your abdomen that was bound by Yasoda's churning cord.
Your chest on which rests the tulsi garland,
O four-armed one, I worship your hands.
Destroyer of Kamsa, I worship your neck.
Muchikunda's Lord, I worship your face.
Kuchela's friend who bestowed immense wealth on him, I worship your cheeks.
Your lotus eyes,
Your ears, ocean of compassion,
Your forehead, you of graceful form,
I worship your head, Lord whom sage Suka praised,
I worship your curls, dark-haired Lord,
O Supreme Lord of all, I worship all your limbs and pray for your Grace.

Next week, we shall have the concluding section of this special series on the Meaning of Pooja.

Sure enough, Stephen wanted to know where the rest of the script was. I told him I'd keep it for him if I came across it, but he wanted it NOW. He said he could help me find the other scripts if I weren't so possessive of the cartons. What is mine is mine and will never be thine, I said. He was quite taken up with Hindu cosmogony, and went to the computer to read up on whatever he could find.

"Are you checking up on Aunt Maru's facts?" I asked, somewhat accusingly.

"That too," he said. "You would like that checked, wouldn't you? You can't think of publishing any of this without some careful editing."

"Aargh, I don't see how we can take that liberty of changing her words around. I won't change a thing, not one single thing."

"Not even obvious typos and misplaced commas and incomplete sentences?"

"Of course those, but nothing else. Not even those run-on sentences that Maru seems to have loved, that go on and on forever. That is her style, we can't touch that."

"How about annotations? Don't you think a few annotations would help readers? Like she says here, Each name of Krishna has a significance that is of relevance to the act being performed. Don't you think we need the entry code, as she herself says? Each name means something. What do they mean? How are we to know?"

I snatched the sheets from the desk. "Ananta, who made Draupadi's sari endless, just think for a moment and you will see – Ananta means endless, and connects to the story of how Krishna by making her sari endless intervened when the Kurus tried to disrobe her at court; Putana laid him on her lap to nurse him at her poisoned breasts and so the thighs; "son of Vasudeva" is offered a gem-studded throne because Vasudeva was a prince whose throne was taken away from him; Kubja was a hunchback who ground sandal paste for the tyrant Kamsa and Krishna greeted her as 'the beautiful one' when she offered him the sandal paste she had just ground, putting her devotion to him above all else, and when she looked at herself in the mirror, she had indeed become beautiful. And our souls too will be made beautiful when we offer worship to Krishna, turning away from our worldly masters. In short, not rendering anything unto Caesar but all to God."

"When did you learn all this? I am impressed." Stephen said. "Oh look," he said pointing to the computer screen, "Sakatasura was a demon who wanted to destroy child Krishna. When Yasoda placed the sleeping baby in the shade of a cart one day, Sakatasura entered the cart in his invisible form and was about to overturn the cart on the baby, when Krishna started crying, kicking his legs up and out with such force that the demon was killed. Neat, very neat, but one needs to know the stories in order to get the point, don't you think?"

"And someone said the other day that all there is to the Panchali story is that she fell uncontrollably in love with a guy," I said, triumphantly.

Stephen, always trying for the last word, said, "One has to be given the key, a hint somewhere. Aunt Maru, I admit, has given the key, but even a couple more specific examples would help dimwitted readers like me. Really, this is neat, I want to read more of these simple intros to Hindu rituals. Really, more people need to know these basics of Hinduism. Let us look for the other parts of this series. Oh darn, I just remembered, I told Jim I'd meet him at eight."

I did not find the preceding or succeeding TV scripts, but I did find a book Maru had written for one of our Youth Camps. The sight of the blue cover with the Om written in a spirograph circle, and with little earthen lamps running along the edges took me back to the years the Hindu Society organized a week-long camp at Riding Mountain in July or August.

We had the whole camp to ourselves. We were may be thirty or forty kids between eight and eighteen, and many of our parents were there too. Not Dad and Ma of course, they've never been temple-going people, but Maru was there and Aunt Savitri, and of course all the Hindu kids I was growing up with. It was a lot of work, a boot camp almost, getting up at 5:30 and being at morning prayer assembly by 6:00, and having to listen to an earful of history and geography and politics and philosophy and arts of India, and Hindu concepts; but it was a lot of fun too, with Uncle Mohan who was both our taskmaster and fun-leader, making us play Frisbee and basketball and volleyball and some Indian games as well, like gilli danda and kabaddi. And we had that lovely dancer from India, Shubha Sridhar, who was living in Winnipeg at the time, who taught us how to do the Surya Namaskar and why we do it first thing in the morning.

But the book did not have the pages I remembered. There were only the prefatory notes and translations of the Sanskrit texts that were yet to be integrated so as to make the whole text. I remember well the colourful series she had on her TV show, her twenty-inch black Krishna dancing on the serpent Kaliya, she and two others, men, one of whom enunciated the Sanskrit words with such resonance, and the other explaining the meaning, while she read the literal English translation after each line. I was staying with Aunty Savitri at the time, Ma having gone off to India, and Aunty Savitri saw Maru's show every week, sat all the way through the half hour even if it was a repeat show, as it often was. I watched one of the repeats, for she aired it every August for several years, in time for Janmashtami. Aunty Savitri had a way of making people do what they should be doing without ever sounding a nag. When I stayed those two years with her, I went with her to the temple too, and I was happy to do so because that gave me some friends my own age among the Indian community, and I got to get into dance which I never would have if it hadn't been for Aunt Savitri being such a close friend of Maru. And so Stephen thinks I still have some of the dancer in me. May be some day, someday I will get back to it.

The Meaning of Pooja:

Pooja is the formal ceremony of worship that is performed in a prescribed manner and in a prescribed sequence. There are sixteen steps in all, starting with an Invocation in which we request God to enter the image in the sanctum, and ending with a prayer for Shanti – peace and well-being of all creation.

The pooja ceremony moves at two levels – the external, and the *manasic* or internal symbolic level. At the external level, we greet God as we would an honoured guest or king, offering Him/Her a throne to sit upon, washing His/Her feet, anointing Him/Her with sandal paste, offering flowers and songs, laying incense and gifts at His/Her feet. Each of these acts has a symbolic meaning.

God, as we know and as Prahlad showed his father, is everywhere. But we can concentrate on God more fully if we have an object in front of us, and therefore we have an image or picture. Because God is everywhere, we could take a pillar or stone, and concentrate on God through it. In our temples, we have pictures or statues that show God's qualities, such as strength, beauty, love, serenity, compassion.... We try to make the pictures as beautiful and perfect as we can, though we know we can never make them as beautiful or perfect as God actually is.

God manifests in different forms. The form or appearance that God takes is like a dress. You can wear a hundred different dresses, but the person inside is always the same – you. Similarly, God wears the form of Shankar or Parvati, Saraswati, Rama, Lakshmi… but it is always the same Essence.

Just as each of us has a favourite dress, each of us has a favourite form of God. You can pray to God as Krishna, or Lakshmi, or Kartikeya, or any of the many forms of God. When you want your father and mother to play with you in the snow, they wear their winter coats and gloves. In the same way, when you want to be good at your studies, you pray to the form of God that is Ganesha or Saraswati.

Remember, when you read the rest of this book, that the words in **square brackets** are my own poetic interpretation of that step of the pooja; the words in English are the literal translations of the Sanskrit verse that follows; and the Sanskrit words are repeated in the English script so that you can try to pronounce the words.

Remember too: as Hindus we should be careful not to perpetuate the usage of certain words that have been distorted by translators and their negative associations. Two of the words that should be avoided because of their misleading connotations are "idol" and "mythology." Both have very strong negative connotations of "false gods" and "false or made-up stories." Let us say "moorti" never "idol." Let us say "Hindu-scripture stories" never "mythological stories."

There are certain words that should not be translated but retained because translations are inadequate. Some of these words are "avatar", "dharma", "karma."

One more point: We must insist on pronouncing Hindu names correctly. To distort your own name is the equivalent of saying you are ashamed of it. It is easy enough to learn the right pronunciation, whether it is McMahon or Ngugi or Dostoevsky or Parameswaran. Pronounce your name correctly and insist that others do the same.

All the songs and slokas below are taken from the Pushpanjali book of our temple.

There are sixteen steps to a pooja. In sequence they are:

Ganesh Pooja – we start every pooja, and indeed we should start
the day, with a prayer to Ganesha, who removes obstacles and is
the god of wisdom.
  Om! Elephant-headed Lord of Bhutas and Ganas,
  Who has the essence of kapittha and jambu fruits,
  Son of Uma, Remover of sorrow,
  Vigneshwara, we salute your lotus feet.

Saraswati Pooja – Saraswati is the goddess of learning.
  Saraswati,
  Who is beautiful, like the kunda flower,
  With strings of white pearls and dressed in white,
  Who has in her hands the sacred veena,
  Who is seated on the white lotus,
  Who is adored by Brahma, Vishnu and Shankara,
  O goddess of knowledge,
  Remove Ignorance from my mind.

Avahana: Invoking the Deity
  [O Formless One, take form
  that we may concentrate on you.
  O Unmanifest One, manifest yourself
  that we might come close to you.
  Infinite One, whom our finite perceptions
  can never fully comprehend,
  enter these images that our senses may link
  us to You who contain all and are above all.

  O Brahman, transcendental Light,
  that dwells within us as Atman, our soul,
  Enter this lamp we have lit
  And be our guiding flame.]

  [We call on you, God,
  Who appeared to Arjun saying:]
  Whenever there is decay of Dharma and rise of Adharma,
then I embody Myself, O Arjuna. For the protection of the good,

for the destruction of evil-doers, for the establishment of Dharma, I am born from age to age.

Asana: Offering of Seat
Vishnu, all pervading spirit!
Vishnu, who contains the cosmos,
The sun, the pole star, all stellar bodies,
You are everywhere, lord of all that is here,
Anywhere, everywhere.

Lord Vishnu, come with your consort, Mahalakshmi.
Please come here, be seated.
Please accept my pooja, I pray.
[These slokas are often used for Avahana, but I have used them for Asana.]

Padya: Washing of feet
[We wash your feet, O lord,
With offerings of water and of prayers
We wash your feet.]

I salute Lord Krishna, Guru of the Universe, son of Vasudeva, the destroyer of Kamsa and Chanura, and the supreme bliss of Devaki.

I salute Madhava, who is the source of supreme bliss, and whose compassion makes the mute eloquent and the cripple cross mountains.

Abhisheka: Ceremonial Bath
[Pour your grace on us, Effulgent Spirit,
even as we pour this water on these images,
which you have sanctified with your presence at our humble request.]

The Gayatri Mantra

Upaveeda: Offering of Sacred Thread
Chandana: Offering of sandal paste

Pushpa: Offering of flowers

[May this sacred thread we place on You bind us to You in faith and devotion, Lord, now and forever. As this sandal paste spreads fragrance, Your glory spreads all over the worlds.

O Lord of my whole being, I offer you these flowers from Nature's bountiful garden and from the garden of my mind, my soul; accept these flowers, Lord, accept the garland of your many names that I string and lay at your feet with devotion.]

[The garland of names below are of Krishna]

Dhoopa: Burning of Incense
Deepa: Lamp

[As the flame burns this incense and turns it into fragrance, Lord,
Burn away my sinfulness and purify my soul.
As I weave a circle with this lamp,
Weave your circle of protection around me.
Even as the beacon lights lost ships to shore
May your Light ever guide me through samsara.]

Naivedya: Offering of food
[Accept this offering of food, Lord,
that I bring to you with faith and devotion.
All my efforts, all that is good in me,
I lay at your feet. Bless them, Lord,
that they may always be at your service.]

Come bless this food and taste of it, pyare Mohan,
As you tasted with pleasure Bhilani's fruit
And Sudama's rice, so also taste our offering.
You who humbled proud Duryodhana,
come taste of our offering, pyare Mohan.
May whoever makes you this offering any time
Be blessed with joy and prosperity, pyare Mohan.
And may all who partake of this blessed food
Become yours forever, pyare Mohan.

Neerajana (Arati): Offering of Lighted Camphor

Partial translation:
Jai Jagadeesa Hare, Swami Jai Jagadeesa Hare!
Salutations to the Lord of the Universe,
Who removes his devotees' woes in an instant!
You are my mother, my father,
I have no other refuge.
You are the ocean of compassion, my Protector.
I am foolish and sinful, but please have compassion.
Take away my worldly desires,
Increase my shraddha (conscientiousness) and bhakti,
And help me to serve others.

Svarna-Pushpa: Offering of gold, gifts...
[All the material possessions that I have come from you, Lord. I lay them at your feet. Bless them that I may use them well.]

[This offering is often repeated at the time of visarjana, when we place a coin on the plate and take the sacred flame into ourselves by placing our hands above the flame first and then touching our eyes with our fingers.]

O, my Lord, You are verily the Mother and the Father, the Relative and the Friend. You are the knowledge and the wealth, indeed, You are Everything.

Swasti Vachana – Auspicious words and prayers for the well-being of all.
(Shanti)

Lead me from untruth to truth,
From darkness to Light,
From death to immortality.

Om,
May there be peace in the heavens, peace on earth;
May the atmosphere be peaceful and the waters calm;

May the herbs and plants bring health and peace;
May the Vedas be a source of peace;
May enlightened persons spread this peace;
May all things be at peace;
May Peace bring peacefulness to us, Lord.
Om Shanti.

Visarjana: Touching the sacred camphor flame to one's eyes-head-inner being, before reinstating the personhood of God that is within the image to its abstract Essence.

Divine Essence!
We thank you for making yourself manifest in these images and in this lighted lamp.
Return, if you will, to your eternal formlessness, to your infinite, invisible omnipresence.

Prasada: Distribution of sanctified food.

"Interesting," Stephen said. "But we must find the rest of it, the Sanskrit text and English transliteration. That would make it more self-contained and useful."

"I am trying to put together Maru's writings, not writing a Hinduism primer for you," I said, "let the author of Pi do that kind of cheap stuff."

"Hmm," Stephen said, "he did it well, so the world thinks, and so many readers can't be wrong, could they? More to the point, I think you are an obstinate mule."

I looked at him. That was Uncle Siv's favourite name for me, where did he get it? Has he been phoning Uncle Siv on his own?

"Look, Preetums, you have something good going for you in this inheritance you've received. If you'd just let me help you, we can really honour your Aunt Maru's memory."

"I am not going to be baited into getting together some evangelical proselytizing primer for pseudo-scholars and critics to misconstrue and misquote," I said, and took away everything he had on the table.

"I love it when you start breathing fire through your nostrils, I absolutely adore you when you do that," Stephen got up from his chair and kissed me on the back of my neck. By now he knows my erogenous zones, and of course I can't resist.

"I hope you know I am being nice only because you are going away and all," I said.

"I promise to go away every little while when we are married, skiing, mountain climbing, deep-sea diving, anything to get out of your hair," he said, "I'll sign on the dotted line of the prenups right now, if you wish."

He knew that would make me breathe more fire. We've had that discussion often enough, even though we were both on the same side. We would stay together as long as we both wanted it, and if we ever separated, god forbid, we would let go without expecting anything material from each other. We said that whenever all the sleazy details of prenups and break-ups came on the gossip channel.

I pulled him back into bed, and rode out my fire.

~

In the same carton, I found a whole lot of scripts written for her television shows. They were on a great many different topics – community services, Family Law, Immigration rules, India's music, architecture, and of course a whole sheaf of stuff on India's dance forms, her favourite. But there were also a great many shows on Hinduism, with children retelling stories, dances with children, and shows like the one on the meaning of pooja. I got these together and put them in a binder along with the two earlier ones for Stephen to look at. He seemed more drawn to religions than I ever had been.

Sure enough, he read them all and that weekend, he shoved sheets of stapled paper and told me to read it. "All these old religions studied the stars and planets, isn't that fascinating? And thought about the significance of force fields – Stonehenge, the Aztec calendar, I must look into what the Egyptians had found."

I glanced at the sheaf he had thrown at me. It was handwritten and suddenly I felt nostalgic seeing the neat straight handwriting.

Sandhya Vandanam: Prayers at the Crossing of Lights.

Today we shall introduce, recite and translate Samdhya-vandanam, the personal prayer performed in the Hindu tradition at sunrise, noon and sunset. With me are Prof. R. Venkataraman who will give an introduction and Prof. K. Ramanatha who will recite the mantras.

Sandhya is a goddess, the visibly manifested power of the Sun-God. Sandhya literally means holding together, junction, juncture. The root work Saam denotes synthesis, the meeting point of pairs of so called opposites such as day and night, light and darkness, God and creature.

The concept of meeting point is a profound concept. Prayer, in its essence, is a striving towards that meeting point of human being and God, a reaching out towards that linking that would raise the human being to a level of consciousness where one can say I am Brahman – aham brahmasmi.

The natural divisions of a day - sunrise, noon and sunset – become symbolic nodes of contact between human and divine, and so sandhyavandanam is performed at the samdhya, the junction of the crossing of lights.

Sandhyavandanam is a time tested prayer that encapsulates the essence of Hinduism and at the same time is so universal that it can be practised by everyone. We are providing the translation so that one can understand the meaning of the words but it is important to note that the original Sanskrit mantras have a power of their own, linking us to a tradition that is part of us, deep inside; they not only communicate heights and depths of philosophical meaning but, like music, can take us to heights and depths of spiritual experience.

In addition to the words, there are specific gestures and actions for each part, and these are for making the worshippers constantly aware of the act of worship in which they are engaged.

~

First I shall give a paraphrase of the first part of Sandhyavandanam. This will be followed by Prof. Ramanatha's recitation of the whole prayer and then we shall go through the steps with explanation and literal translation.

~

We could speculate as to why exactitude, sanctity and secrecy were made so essential. Among the possible answers, one is that the timing, actions and words had to be precise because there is an intrinsic power in the combination of these three components, some force field that is activated, knowledge of the causes and effects of which have been lost. Since the power is there, we have to hold on to these precise prescribed details until such time as we collectively repossess that knowledge or individually experience it in personal revelation.

Another reason could be that at a time when knowledge had to be transmitted over generations through the oral tradition, it was necessary to standardize the Sandhya and to hold it as a treasured secret so that it would survive intact no matter what changes took place in society.

There are many ways in which the accumulated wealth of a culture could be lost: through the depredation of invaders, onslaught from barbaric cultures, through emigration and loss of contact, or through sheer carelessness and neglect. It could be that knowing of these dangers, old cultures evolved towards hereditary professions, making each group custodians of their particular art, craft or science. Thus Brahmins were made custodians of intellectual knowledge. With time, extraneous restrictive layers of class hierarchy and gender distinctions were probably framed so that Sandhyavandanam became the exclusive privilege of males of a certain caste instead of an all-encompassing and universal ceremony of reaching out for God at the crossing of the lights, the time period symbolic of the momentary union of divinity and human being. Also making a mantra accessible to all brings with it the danger of desecration at the hands of barbarians both within and outside the faith.

We have to hold Sandhya and Gayatri in sacred trust especially as we live in a time when sunrise, noon and sunset are mere hours on the face of our watches and not the mystic experience of the crossing of the lights on the face of the sky.

~

By the time I finished reading the rest of it, Stephen had gone off to his books and I could not ask him about the parallels he mentioned about Stonehenge and the Aztecs. I would miss these discussions, I thought, when he left for India. Uncle Siv was to blame, I thought, for putting the idea of India into his head.

~~~~~

ELEVEN

I was not happy with the thought that Stephen was leaving soon. Things were happening to me. Perhaps it was Maru's stuff. Perhaps I was hooked into Maru's writing only because I found Stephen's responses triggering all kinds of creative processes in me of which I had not thought myself capable. Perhaps it was the tiger that was pushing awake some latent aspirations, those fantasies I had as a teenager about doing something creative with my dance and sketching-art experience. I used to sketch once, and my Fine Arts professor at the University thought I should continue, but I went into medicine instead. He said the same thing that Maru has said about me, that I would do well in whatever I took up. I don't know about that. I would like to sketch Panchali's balcony, an ethereal surrealistic kind of pencil sketch of something hanging without any support. Or dance the Panchali story. I liked it that Stephen thought I was like Panchali. I had always felt only anger at her story but reading Maru's take on her was interesting. I could use both the anger and the woman-power.

I found one of the missing sections of the long story today. Section V and this one is definitely addressed to me. I am pleased about that. Have to check back on just where it starts.

I sure hope you liked that story. It may even have some fodder for social anthropologists. When we first come, we keep remembering where we came from but we also love the new world around us and can't wait to experience it, all of it, rocks and all.

Since I got drawn into making that sociological/ anthropological statement above about how the immigrant heart and mind work, I figured I'd continue with that thread. I can hear your quiet groan, why can't she go on with those first days now that she'd got me hooked? I'll tell you why. I am into all kinds of woman things - crochet, knitting, macramé, quilting, as you will know when you see me in my work area in my home. There are any number of threads and yarns and strings, skeins and skeins of them. Take your pick I'd like to say, but I won't because this is my work area and any trespasser is likely to end up strangulating herself on the many threads around this place. So just sit back and let me pick up any thread I want. That is the deal, take it or leave it.

On this wall is the tapestry I am weaving, and on this wall this mega quilt. Well, I've been working on the quilt for a long time and the other day I said to myself that now that I am into memoirs, I really should stop sewing more and more patches, bring it to some kind of final shape and put it away so I can concentrate on all the fun memories of Maru in the land of the maple leaf. But along came another huge skein of tangled wool and I am still spending every minute of my time trying to untangle it. These brief forays into my memoirs sure is helping me keep my sanity. What skein you ask, well I can't go into it now, didn't I just tell you I am trying to get some respite from it?

All that comes with the territory, but what I set out to say was that I was going to work on that immigrant-phase thread for a moment. Like I was saying, first we keep looking back and then we are too busy getting our place in the rat race to do anything else, and then we turn to our civic duties just as Manu the lawgivers have set out, that all responsible citizens should get involved in community activities. So I did, through the seventies and eighties, I was into every kind of community activity you can think of, including several national women's organizations in the eighties.

But you are tired after all the dissection of cadavers and cramming of Gray's Anatomy, and don't want any serious stuff. Okay, let me tell you the Volvo story.

We have always had a Volvo

How long it had been going on I don't know but it was towards the end of winter that I noticed the car was using up a lot more gas than it should. So I took it into Bernie's Service Centre, the place I'd patronized all the ten years I've been here. He asked me how many miles a gallon it was giving now and, of course, I had no answer. I am not the type that enters figures in log books kept neatly in the glove compartment or pinned back of the sun visor. I never used credit cards either. And the only time I looked at the odometer was when the numbers were about to move to the next hundred, or better still to the next thousand. There is something magical about the way the numbers change all at the same time.

I didn't have an answer. But I knew I wasn't getting the usual mileage. Instead of filling up once in ten days as I used to, I knew I was filling up more often, certainly once every six days. In a tone of long-suffering patience one hears said of husbands, he suggested that I keep tab of the mileage for at least a week. As I was about to drive away, he asked me if I had taken the car to any other service station since the Fall lube and tire change. I wouldn't do that, I said, any more than I'd drive any car but a Volvo.

~

Ever since I had returned from India, leaving Manda and Brinda with my parents, I had felt quite lost. Maybe I had been more disorganized than usual with my housekeeping. Maybe going to the Co-op twice or three times a week didn't help any. There was always a forgotten soup can or bread loaf or butter to pick up, and driving three miles and back from the Co-op on a matter of principle had its price. It was Linda who had talked me into joining the Co-op, telling me how morally necessary it was for consumers to band together to beat nefarious profiteers responsible for this runaway inflation etc. Duly impressed, I had taken to doing all my shopping at the Co-op south of the perimeter. I liked it, especially because the floodway had been a recent discovery for me. The newspapers and Uncle Bob on Channel 7 had talked about the floodway every Spring of my stay here but I had discovered it for myself only last Fall and I can spend hours watching any expanse or non-expanse of water.

But floodway or not, six or seven miles even twice a week couldn't possibly call for so much gas. No, I was positive I hadn't been driving any more than usual. If anything, much less. With the girls away, I had little to do, and because there was so little to do, I did even less. I spent my time worrying about them.

I also took to keeping a log. Now that I had walked out in a huff from Bernie's, I had to find another service station, and I knew better than to go without any data. Which is how I discovered the car was giving the usual twenty-two miles per gallon it should. Nothing was wrong with the car. Except that it was being driven long distances by someone other than myself.

Recently Sivaram had been working later than usual. Up at seven in the morning, out by eight, back at five for dinner and out again, to return long after midnight. It had been the same every summer.

Except that this summer the car was guzzling gas. Or rather, it wasn't.

For three days I worked out all kinds of sums with the figures in the little blue book, took the average for the month past, for each week, for each fill-up, each dollar. No matter which way I worked it, the mileage was always around twenty-two, which is as it should be for a five-year-old Volvo. On the fourth morning the odometer had jumped thirty miles instead of the three that it takes for a trip to and from the university.

It was the fifteenth of May when the thirty-mile jump showed I couldn't but accept what was happening. I sat at the living room window all morning. The lawn was a lush unkempt green with a few bald spots where I'd let the snow moulds lie too long. All my neighbours had raked and mowed at least once. There were tulips along the walls of the house across the street. On my yard, the last of the crabapples from the Fall were being eaten by robins. The lilac was showing green heads. The beautifully curving poplar tree outside the bedroom window was still bare. It had lost its leaves very early last Fall. Perhaps it was dead. The mock-orange cutting gifted and planted by friends two summers ago was sprouting leaves. But the friends were far away though they lived just a mile down the road. I brooded a while on when and where we had taken the fork in the road that we were now so distant though living where we had always lived. I was never more conscious of my inability to read the writing on the wall, my inability to realize facts until I had been hit over the head with them.

The Volvo had hit me over the head all right.

Balaram would soon be home for lunch. But he could make do with a cheese sandwich and milkshake. Were there any social engagements for the weekend? Friday and Sunday. Damn. What had been the menu the last time we had them over?

Anything to avoid facing the issue.

But one had to face it. Not one. I had to face it. Sivaram was having an affair. What a word, affair. Relationship? liaison? adultery? fornication? Was there a difference between the two or was the last just Biblical lingo for the other? I looked up the dictionary. Just another hairsplitting activity to avoid the issue. I was thirty six years stupid and my husband was having an affair. All those words seemed obsolete anyway. Nobody was a harlot or adulterer. Or everyone was. Everything had to be redefined.

Next morning, as I was at my perfunctory make-up in front of the mirror, the full meaning of it came over me. There were wrinkles on my neck, my skin was beginning to sag, there was no doubt about it, I was getting old. I who had scornfully laughed at the fallen breasts of women hardly out of their teens as they walked about the change rooms at the swimming pool, I who had pitied my white neighbours who came back from Bermuda and Hawaii with tanned skins that were duly praised by envious friends but seen by me as wrinkled and pathetic, I who year after year had brought skin-softening turmeric and sandal paste hand-pound from homegrown herbs back in India, I was growing old. My husband couldn't get turned on by me anymore. It was as simple as that. 'For this is the way the world ends, this is the way the world ends, not with a bang but a whimper.'

Oh darn, some pages are missing or not in order. Stephen can sort them out. What looks like the last page is here though.

So what happened, you ask. Where does the story end, I know what you are thinking. Thinking now you know the answer to why Sivaram is away so much, why not one of my children lives in this city etc. etc.

The reason I don't have an ending for my story is that I do, but it is so simple, so mind-boggling that you won't believe it. You'll think I am copping out.

Well that summer, we decided we'd fly down to Acapulco for a holiday, especially since Sivaram had a convention in Mexico City. We returned on a Sunday afternoon. As always, Sivaram had to go to his department, it is an obsession with him, to run to his department the moment he returns from anywhere. This time, he came right back from the garage, with a very strange look on his face, totally at a loss and yet totally relaxed, like something a chiropractor might do, break your spine and suddenly you feel great? You know the feeling?

My God, he said, someone's been driving our Volvo. The odometer has chalked up seven hundred kilometres in our absence !!!!!

And then it hit me! Do you know what I am getting at? Just think, just figure out what had been going on in his mind all these months that I'd been imagining curvaceous blondes and black-haired young men in his office !!!!!

So, nice story ? Of course it is my story. Oh you mean, did it really happen?   It could be someone else's real story, have you thought about it? Of course I am making it up, that is what story-tellers do, you know. You mean you've been assuming all those early anecdotes are real? about me looking for my mother's birth date and all that and being so dumb about curling? You know what I think? cutting up all those frogs and cats and humans, and answering those moronic multiple choice questions on names of bones and muscles is making you a bit, what shall I say, clinically dead as regards storytelling cornerstones? Well, I guess I have to be thankful you are not putting me on a couch and psychoanalyzing me.

I note the possible date on the first page as usual, except that it is a question (When was Maru age 36?), and then paste a note: "Stephen, remind me to ask you another question."

I am so sure too that this tailpiece she had added to this Volvo story is crock. May be there is a reason why those pages are missing. I found a couple more pages but not all. Of course, it happened to her. She's changed the stuff about her kids, the daughters, but I mean everything in it is so Maru and Siv. Gee, I can see her typing that whole crock paragraph and laughing aloud – she had that habit, of laughing aloud even when she was reading alone in a room. Wodehouse was her favourite. What did she see in Wodehouse? Stephen loves him too, and Uncle Siv. I guess it is the British education they all had. I can't half understand the words on BBC, let alone all that word-play.

~

"So what is the question you want to ask me?" Stephen said, taking his usual place on the sofa with his bare toes sticking out from the arm.

"Read it first," I said.

"If I knew your question, I could keep it back of my mind as I read."

"Maru always wanted me to read first and discuss afterwards. Said a reader's first reading should be without any preconceptions."

"One is never without preconceptions," Stephen said. "Like, the moment you see the title, *We have always had a Volvo*, you think of Shirley Jackson's *We have always lived in the Castle*, and so right away you know something weird is going to happen, something pretty terrible going on under a perfectly normal surface."

"What if the writer had never known anything about that Shirley Jackson?"

"A remote possibility but hardly probable, if I know anything of what I've gathered so far about Aunt Maru."

"So, if you know so much about her, how come she always told me to read the text first before I read or heard anything anyone had to say about it, including the author, she would repeat that several times, 'including the author'."

"So where were we? What is your question again? Oh yes, read the text first. Of course, yes, I grant one must read the text first, unlike the imams who cried for Rushdie's blood before ever reading a word of his novel."

"Speaking of Rushdie, what did you think of Uncle Siv's verdict on him?"

"I thought he and Aunt Maru must have argued about Rushdie many times."

"Oh shucks, you are just so good at deflecting everything, and I fall for it every time. I might as well ask my question. You know whatever little Maru got published were written under her pseudonym, right? Like 'How we Won Olympic Gold.' You've read it, right?"

"Yup, you should sneak it into your collection too, whether it is in these cartons or not."

"Listen. Olympic Gold was published several times, and in the last republication, she changed the names of the characters to her own name and Uncle Siv's!! And that is what she has done in this Volvo story too. So what do you make of it? Olympic Gold is absolutely not real-life at all – none of her kids were toddlers in 1988. But this one – it is for real, I think it screams real-life, and she keeps the real names! Totally weird."

"Shirley Jackson." Stephen said, starting to read the first page.

"Back of your mind, try to figure out the year or at least the decade in which it was written," I said. "And why would she use Uncle Siv's name?

He looked up within a minute. "I guess she would have changed the names if she had ever got around to looking for a market," he said. "Which means you should too, if publication is your aim – which means it becomes a responsibility, a commitment on your part to edit edit edit. But then, you say she has stories with her own name as a character."

After he had read it, he called to me. I was folding the laundry, and I brought the basket from the bedroom to the living room.

"I bet you think this is real life and happened when Aunt Maru was about 36 years old, right?"

"Yeah, it screams real-life," I said.

"I don't know when she might have been 36, but I think internal evidence is more important, like she speaks about 22 miles to the gallon, seems to me, and when did we go metric? And is she right about a Volvo giving 22 miles to a gallon?"

I threw a cushion at Stephen. "This is fiction, for pete's sake."

"I know, I know, but these are the details that have to be right. I am sure she'd have made sure they were right before she marketed them, but now all that is up to you. You could also find out when Salisbury House at that corner she mentions was pulled down. And Gulf, heavens, Gulf gas stations were from the middle ages."

"Forget it." I said, remembering the amount of time I had spent finding out about Jo Paquette or Ouellet or whoever and not getting anywhere. "As to miles per gallon, she mentions kilometres at the end, so there. May be she was writing with some American magazine in view and forgot to be consistent!"

"I thought you've always held she was Canadian all the way. Would you move down South any time? Have you thought about it for us?" He knew that would make me mad, the way doctors moved south of the border all the time, and we went through the whole argument again.

~

Next day was my off day but Stephen was on his long rotation. After doing a long overdue vacuuming, I curled up with Maru. Oddly enough this was computer-typed but printed on lined paper. I guess she figured she might as well use some of the reams she bought at school-reopening sales. This seems to be part of the Memoirs. Why couldn't she have put them together with the rest, Sheesh.

Headache from Hell.

Yes, it is already February 1994, and here I am only thirty pages into my memoirs. So what happened these last few weeks? I told you I had done a whole lot of social work of sorts over the years. Each comes with a headache but this was a mega headache, I assure you. As head of a writers' organization, I got all knotted up in trying to unravel a messy piece of knitting that someone else had started but had dumped on to my lap; there were only two employees in the writers' organization I headed at the time, and they couldn't get along with each other; seemed one didn't like the other's bossy ways even though she **was** the boss; and the other didn't like the first's choice of a live-in partner, and at one point did what no one, even if a boss, should be allowed to do in our human-rights conscious society. Let's give both sides a fair hearing, I said. But everyone was screaming at everyone else and the world around me was a pretty big mess; this was when I started writing these memoirs, remember, to get a respite? When I found some solace, as so many others including Will Wordsworth have before me, in a timely utterance to give that thought relief, some guy thought I was calling him old Will (why would I do that when I like Will and don't like this geezer the least little bit?) and he told everyone and his dog that I was some sort of leprechaun and they set out to hound me out of what they considered their territory. And after a quarter of a century in this place, I walked through alleys that I didn't even know existed, and discovered that the artistic fraternity-sorority is about as class conscious as the frat houses that lined any American university campus in my days back in the U.S. of A.

At home, this had its repercussions. Sivaram, back for a stint from his research leave, heard my story and wanted me to resign from the whole rotten environment. But since that is just what my colleagues on the Board wanted me to do, I naturally wouldn't do it. I asked Chikkamma for advice, and she laughed. Anyone who works at a cesspool is likely to get shit on his shirt, she said. You do know, don't you, she said, that there is no way you are going to be able to clean any of this muck? So, I said, does that mean you are on Sivaram's side, that I should just wash my hands off this sordid affair? I wanted her to say yes, maybe I was praying she'd say yes and then it would have been two to one, simple democratic process of being forced into decisions that I did not concur with, same as on the Board. I didn't say that, she said, I doubt you can do it being as you are your mother's daughter and my niece once removed etcetera etcetera. You will finish your term of office because we, of Maitreyi Nivas, always finish what we undertake, that is the cross or curse we bear. But I don't finish anything, I said, look at the tons of half-finished stories and poems under my bed and now in my computer. I don't have to finish this crummy business.

Your writing is not a public undertaking. Also, remember what you did last night? she asked.

Shitbowl. Yes, as one who used horse sense to solve practical problems, several months ago when the toilet tank was not filling up to the level it should, I had placed plastic tabs, the ones used for bagging bread, to jack up the lever of the toilet tank, instead of calling in the plumber to replace the entire thingummy jig that controls the stopper. Last evening, they had fallen off and flushed into the bowl. I could see them - a little pink head and a little blue head - sticking out of the hole in front of the bowl. Was it a sign? Was Kathy perhaps carrying twins, a wee boy and a wee girl? Toilet bowl brushes and all the six kinds of liquid, powder and gel cleansers in the house couldn't dislodge them from their place. Even though they peeked out every time the tank was being flushed, they tucked themselves back at the end of it. So at eleven o'clock, I taped down the seat, told Sivaram to keep away from that bathroom and we went to bed. At what should have been a private moment of togetherness, much to Sivaram's frustration, I got an inspiration - a coat hanger, of course, that women's handy foetus-murder weapon could be the answer. And it was; the straightened end held the plastic tabs captive so they couldn't retreat and I tugged them out with my bare fingers. Yuck, you may say, but Chikkamma knew it for what it was - we women of Maitreyi Nivas never walk out on a job.

That was my oracle. When my esteemed colleagues on the Board asked me for my resignation, I said, No thanks, I owe it to those who elected me to finish my term. Which made everyone mad all over again on both home and MWG fronts. Anyway, a good twenty five years after our life on Wellington Crescent, I realized the clout "class" has even in this country. When one leaves a class-conscious homeland, one usually assumes it is behind for good. But oh no, it is alive and well in Canada, and let no one say otherwise; and when anyone talks about class and gender oppression in other countries, I hope you'll have the courage to show them around our own city.

That is all for now. Am too busy still with all the shit flying around.

~

How many such fights had Maru been in, I wondered. Always for the underdog, always writing long letters to people, even though she knew problems were always plotted and resolved over a draft at a pub by the men she worked with. Maru was a fighter but seldom a successful one. May be I should put all the different fights she fought together in a folder. No time, no time, these long rotations are killing me.

~~~~~

TWELVE

I cannot focus on my work. I cannot let anyone know I am on the edge. I have to go on. Michael John was a team effort but this was mine, all mine. I so thought she was okay but during the nanosecond that the cord had choked her, something had gone terribly wrong and she was gone a few hours after we had delivered her. I had done everything right, my finger could feel the cord and I had loosened it, clamped it on either side, cut it, delivered the baby and I could swear she was not bluish black but pink when they rushed her to the neo-natologist. I can't handle this. I must handle it. I ran to Maru for help to get out of the slough of despondency. What is this early piece doing in the third carton?

5th March 1967

I had two dreams last night.
The first was about Sip. She looked exactly as when I last saw her. We stood at the door of the Jaipur Palace. I was ahead, I stepped into the loggia and hastily stepped back seeing a regular sentry, bearded, burly and turbaned, standing in front of a regular palace door, massive with huge knobs. Sip said, Come in. I was acutely aware of wearing some awful footwear. I followed her past the sentry. We were together for some time. I got the distinct feeling that Sip was caged – sentries, palace and all. She spoke in low tones as though in hiding. I said, It is as well you called me, else I'd never have got past that guard. A few minutes later I invited her to something, my nephew's cradle ceremony probably, and I invited her sister-in-law too. And her sister-in-law very polite in a steely way, pointed out to Sip that they could not go because of some flimsy excuse, and I now knew for sure that Sip was in a prison. A phone call came for her but her sister-in-law took it, said Sip was not there and hung up. Heavens, I said, thank god you phoned me, I'd never have got through to you.

We wandered around, Sip in tension, looking for privacy as it were. And in a large hall, we found it. Hastily, as though time was running out, she said, "You've got to do this for me," and I said, "Anything I can I'll gladly do." I felt very sorry for her, very very sorry that gone was the laughter and brightness and light on her face.

Just then Claudette came in, "Claudette?" I gasped. For though unmistakably it was Claudette, she was an ageing, thin, plain woman; she had become what many Bhawanis become by thirty, flat chested, sickly, sallow, old. Gone was the bloom, the attractiveness. We were in a room filled with people and I was trying to tell a joke about how just the other day I was looking at an old album with class groups, and I was so surprised to see Claudette's innocent face and small built frame looking back at me from the small snapshot because I always remembered her as a smooth-talking flirt. I was interrupted time and again but I kept on trying to finish my story even though I knew it wasn't worth telling even in itself and now certainly not with Claudette so flat chested and plain.

And then Sip and I were again alone. Feverishly she sought a word in private. By then I knew she was surely caged and dying. She said hurriedly, as though to finish before the guard or her sister-in-law came in, "My children, you know I have two, a son and a daughter, you must help them after I go," and I said, "I'll adopt them this minute if possible, but how can I get them past your palace walls?" and I thought of the sentry and the phone and the cage. "I'd gladly take them away and take good care of them."

And she said, "Both have some trouble. Piles. Both have had surgery. They can't exist without surgery. You must take care of them."

Something else happened but I don't remember. But I told myself in the dream or outside I don't know, "God, what an anticlimax! Why should there be this talk of haemorrhoids? Of all things, piles. And Claudette so old and straggly."

March 12. Darned if I can remember what that nightmare two days ago was all about. But last night's dreams are still fresh.

The second dream was scary.

She was reading a letter she had received or written. "As Appa and our late Amma used to say," she said, and I said, "What do you mean, our late Amma?" and she said, "Don't you know?" and I was cold and scared and parched all over, and I said, "What?" and she said, "Don't you know that..." "When?" "March. 16th March." And I was cold and stunned and inside and outside the dream. I said, it is not yet the sixteenth. Does it mean....

This was no help, the first was so weirdly anticlimactic and the second was scary. It made me think of my own Ma. I haven't spoken to her in ages, of course we call each other every week but our talks are so superficial. Maru must have had a great relationship with her mother. Was it a premonition? Why am I envying her all the time – and Stephen too, for his closeness to his grandad and family. May be I should cry more often, cry for Michael John and this poor nameless little thing strangling herself. See how I am distancing myself the only way I know how, as though it was her fault that she got strangled. Death is everywhere. Well, at least I am not the one dreaming weird stuff. I read the Sip dream again and started laughing at the ridiculous ending. Really, did Maru give the ending as part of a story? One of her juvenilia pieces transposed to 1967?

I threw it into the Dreams tray, and picked out a piece that stuck out because it was folded, unlike most others that were full sheets, usually clipped together. On the blank half that was on top, there was a handwritten note:

This is a real story and so a reminder to change things around if I ever use it. It was amazing to meet someone here who was our neighbour back in India, (I remember her, a few years older to us who were teenagers, living across the street and cycling in and out of her house) and even more amazing that I didn't know then she had the pluck to do all this. The postscript, as always, is how women work against great odds but are seldom recognized for their work. Or should it be that sometimes stories have happy endings?

This intrigued me, naturally.

P's story
These details were given to me when P was 47. On Tuesday
April 4, 1978 (my notes have only the day and date, and I found
the year should/would have been 1978)

Born 1930-31, I suppose.

Siblings – they were seven in all, she the second oldest.
They lived in Seoni, in a large house with a large compound.
Her father was a well-to-do lawyer. But he got severe diabetes
and his practice fell; they became poor and life became hard.

In 1947 or 1948 father's diabetes reached a crisis and he had
to come to Nagpur for an amputation. He and her mother went
to Nagpur, leaving the children in the older girls' care. The baby
was ten months old and still nursing and she cried all day and
night, refusing food. So P. took the baby and left for Nagpur.

She already had her school certificate and was taking
correspondence courses towards a college degree. Her mother
was at the hospital most of the day. So she took the baby and
went from school to school, looking for a job. Everywhere it was
assumed the baby was hers and no one gave her a job. The
family duly returned to Seoni. Soon she had her Intermediate
certificate. Her brother, two years her junior, passed Matric with
distinction and wanted to go to college. Their father refused;
money was needed; he asked the boy to take up a clerkship
somewhere. P fought the decision. She vowed she would put
her brothers through college. She wouldn't get married until they
got their degrees. She went to Nagpur and stayed with an uncle.
She went from school to school, and got a job at Moti Bagh
School in Mahal, several miles away. Her uncle's was a joint
family of sorts; four sons lived with their families but each paid
twenty-five rupees for the main meals. Breakfast and tea they
had separately. They'd rather she found a rooming place of her
own; she said she'd keep looking but would have to stay till she
found one. She stayed there a school year.

She had to leave early every morning so she could walk the
distance. Each family made and had their own breakfast around

their Primus stove; eggs, milk, tea and parathas, but no one offered her so much as a cup of tea. Only rice was ready by the time she left every morning, and sometimes not even that. No one offered or suggested that she take a lunch box. By the time she returned home after school everyone else had finished dinner and only rice and yoghurt remained. She seldom got to eat chapattis or vegetables during the week.

Two other teachers, Christians, found out she was practically fasting all day and they offered to share their lunch. But their lunch was always non-vegetarian. She decided to try it, and soon they made it a habit to bring extra lunch. She learnt to eat all kinds of meat.

The year after that, she brought her older sister to Nagpur. There was parental opposition but she was adamant that it was time girls started supporting themselves. Her sister came to Nagpur. The uncle and family did not like it at all. But P stayed on, saying they'd move out as soon as they found a room. At last they fixed a room, with a woman who had a half-wit son. They agreed on the rent and paid a deposit. S kept saying she was afraid the woman would change her mind. And sure enough she did. When they reached with their trunks and belongings, she wouldn't let them in. P stood her ground. Boldly and firmly she said a deal was a deal and she would stay until she found another place. They had left their uncle's and could not go back. There was nowhere to go. They wouldn't budge, and so they got to stay.

P rushed around before and after school, trying to get her sister a job. S, shy and nervous, never went anywhere. In her job hunt, P went to Saraswati Vidyalaya. Mr. Bharadwaj was impressed by her boldness and confidence and suggested she could get a job at his school. She declined. She wanted a job for her sister. Next day, she took S to Saraswati Vidyalaya to meet Mr. B. and then went on to her school. S met Mr. B. He said she should give a practice lesson in Hindi and told her where the classroom was. He said he would drop in to check on her teaching, and he went back to his work. S, nervous and sweating at the thought of teaching in front of the headmaster, bolted from the school without telling anyone. In the evening, P heard what had happened. Undeterred, she went to Saraswati Vidyalaya next morning and explained to Mr. B that S would do very well as a teacher on her own but was nervous in the presence of other teachers. Mr. B. gave her the job, and sure enough S turned out to be an excellent teacher.

Mr. B again offered to take P, and so at the end of the school year, P left Moti Bagh School and joined Saraswati Vidyalaya. At Moti Bagh, she had taught English, Hindi, Drawing, Math and Needlework. Here she taught only Hindi and needlework.

They took a house in Dharampeth and the rent was eight-five rupees, which was more than they could afford. By then her brother had come to join college and they decided to start cooking instead of buying dabba meals from the hotel. The house was large, and they shared it with Bharadwajs' eldest daughter, whose husband was in Telephones. They shared it for some months, but because they had to share the latrine, the other family moved out to a bigger place. Now   there   were   two brothers and two sisters in Nagpur. Money was always short. P had been giving tuitions. Now she spent all day working. An hour's tuition, six days a week, brought in twenty-five rupees per month, or thirty if she went to the student's house. She now had a bicycle and raced from house to house for tuition. By night she was exhausted, but there was enough money to run the house.

For nine years she lived in Nagpur; her social life was zip but she didn't mind. The brothers had got their degrees. She was well past the usual age of marriage. She was twenty-six.

She got married a couple of years later, to a distinguished professor, and lived happily ever after, but that is another story.

I read it again, trying to digest the fact that this P was just seventeen when she was running from place to place with a baby sister on her hip looking for a job. At seventeen what was I doing?

I tried to figure out who P. was. That should be easy enough, I thought, but did it matter? All that mattered was that she was a gutsy woman and Maru always gave gutsy women their due.

Stephen would have another viewpoint, I am sure. He would probably say the details of what cost how much and stuff like that was the reason if at all it is to be included in the final, whatever it is that I am trying to compile.

~

At dinner the next day, Stephen gave me an earful that I was going about it the wrong way. The job Maru had entrusted me with was not about her writings at all, he said, but about her life. He showed me a binder that was titled "Battles fought, and usually lost." Read this, he thrust a sheet in front of me, "Looks like she was co-opted into a committee just because they wanted a female. This was in the early 1990s when gender issues were hot potatoes, and you can see the fight she puts up. That's what she wants you to see, not the silly little vignettes and dreams you've been so busy sorting out."

I read it.

January 14, 1991
Dear Department Colleagues,
It is both uncomfortable and impolitic to speak up on issues in which one's own space and place are directly involved. But as a woman member, I feel I have to speak up. At the meeting of last Friday, the only item on the agenda was to discuss the fact that the present Hiring Committee does not have a woman. We were told that the President had issued directives that she be kept informed of gender-based statistics on committees, number of applications and number of candidates interviewed.

What we need is to cultivate sensitivity and sensibility about women's role and status in everything we do and teach. Merely having a female-gendered body on every committee is no answer any more than having women's writings in every course will ensure feminist readings. I know many men who are sensitive to women's issues and I know many women who are not sensitive to them. What is in our MIND is important, not whether we have breasts or not.

A motion was passed which in effect directed the Hiring Committee to co-opt a woman. A subsequent motion proposed by me that the coopted member be given voting rights was defeated seven to six with five abstentions. It was interesting to note that the vote of the department's newest member, who has been on board for all of twenty days including the Christmas break and who used his prerogative to vote, broke what would have been a tie. In short a vote is a vote. That is what the suffragette movement was all about and that is what the present issue is all about.

If I am asked to be on the interview panel, I think I might (I am not 100% sure as of now) decline for the following reason:

Women through the centuries have been persuaded to pitch in their expertise, time and energy for the "common good." Certain service roles have been traditionally women's – volunteers doing all the leg work on church-school-community committees, secretaries correcting syntax and spelling errors on articles in correspondence of male bosses...In the present context, the situation is similarly exploitative. I paraphrase the comment by a male colleague who was telling me why I should accept such an invitation, "I don't know enough about the field, and you do, to ask the right questions of the candidate but I can listen to the questions and answers and make the proper judgement." That is precisely what women have been told in male-run societies and it is time to stand up and say NO. So my brief response would be, No thanks, either make me an equal partner in the deliberations or count me out. A vote is the only real expression of equal partnership, even if one vote may not go far.

The majority of the department have made it clear that that they do not wish to entrust me with equal rights. It is not farfetched to infer that if I am invited to be on the committee, it is only to build a façade of gender representation through a back door; backdoors are convenient and the result would look good on paper and the President's directives would SEEM to have been followed. This ploy has been used in just about every employment sector ever since women and minorities started fighting for equity.

To summarize, logic says the majority in the department have expressed a wish to use my expertise without giving me a vote. Expediency says I would do well to accept an unequal partnership and try to exert some influence on the decisions to be made. Consistency to my principles dictates that I would be foreswearing my principles about rectification of gender inequality if I permit myself to be used to boost appearances of fair gender representation.

I could see Stephen's point – perhaps that is what she wanted me to do, highlight her activism but I was not ready to accept my lack of direction and admit to Stephen that he had a point. Or that I personally was interested in what she wrote and not what she had done in her workplace. So I took the easy way out. We are just going through the stuff, I said, just trying to figure out how to categorise the different pieces in some logical way – that is why I had these trays, I said, different envelopes and cartons and trays. I went on to talk about the problems, how one could be chronological or thematic or by genre, look at all the half-complete poems – not to mention all the talks she gave at meetings big and small etc. etc. "You are just being pigheaded," Stephen said very succinctly and went off to wash the dishes.

~~~~~

THIRTEEN

It was crazy at work. One of the residents had gone to his father's death-bed and another had fallen seriously ill. We had to fill in with extra shifts, there was no other option. Stephen was leaving in three weeks and I was by turn frantic that he was leaving and excited that I would be on my own. I wanted him with me till he left and I didn't like it that he left at four every morning. I even started cooking regularly knowing that soon he would not get the good food he was used to.

I came across this story one morning when I was looking for the Olympic Gold story, which I wanted to read again. Instead, I came across this Pinto story. It was one of the many versions it had gone through. I knew, for I had read it when Maru was still working on it. From my hasty perusal, it looks like one of the early versions with a great many gaps that she must have filled later. I will read it again but I wanted Stephen's response to it and so I put it in Stephen's tray. I really should jot down the points he makes because they are so pertinent and might come in handy sometime down the road, but there was never enough time. He, however, was done with his job here and had all the time in the world.

Pinto sees the light

When Nagappa planned the job, he was rather complacent. Abducting someone is no big deal really. He ironed his purple pants that a kindly foreigner had given him, donned it, took his ironing table on wheels and set off for the Ashram. He had been one of the Ashram's *istriwalas* for several years, ironing clothes on his mobile table. The table had a cabinet at the base, in which he stored his iron, coal for the iron, blanket and bedsheet on which he laid out the clothes to be ironed, and his cache of tobacco, matches and beedis.

~

And so Pinto had to be the one. Nagappa's dossier on him was as comprehensive as could be (fill in details about Pinto's qualifications, how he came from the U.S. to volunteer at the ashram, the ashram routine etc.)

~

So Nagappa had no problem abducting Pinto that Friday evening as he walked under the casuarina trees. "My wife is ill, doctor ayya," he said, beseeching him with joined palms. "I need you, please please do come." He was being totally truthful. His wife was ill, very ill, and Nagappa loved her dearly. Once outside the ashram gates and near the village, it was easy enough to gag the doctor, tie him up to the ironing table, cover him with the blanket, and take him to the abandoned hut that he had already stocked up with all the basic necessities that he had carefully stolen, including two of the pallets that the good doctor had donated on his first visit, and two chairs.

Nagappa tied Pinto's feet before setting him on the bed. Pinto shrugged. "Let us get on with it," he said, "what do you want from me?"

Nagappa came to the point. He wanted Pinto to transplant a kidney into his wife. But that can be done without all this violence, Pinto said, he was a transplant surgeon and all Nagappa had to do was to ask him at the clinic or hospital and follow due process. The hospital was well equipped, and free for the poor, by the grace of the swami. Nagappa, rocked on his haunches, and sucked at the reed between his lips.

The doctor was relieved. Nagappa meant well, and of course yes, he Pinto would help his wife get a transplant. The doctor rose to his feet thankful he had solved the problem, forgetting that his feet were tied. He promptly fell on his face.

"Doctorayya," Nagappa said as he helped Pinto get back on his feet, "are you putting me on or are you really as naive as a suckling babe? You surely know what happens at your hospital or at any hospital for that matter. The rich get everything, the poor nothing. Last year they swore my wife was next in line and then they gave the kidney to a doddering politician; they swore again she would definitely get the next one that matched, and last month they gave it to a business tycoon who gave them five hundred thousand rupees. It isn't going to happen again, Doctorayya; thanks to you, she will get it next week."

"Don't be crazy," Pinto said, "nothing is as easy as that. You can't sew a kidney into a person the way you would sew a sack of coconuts in this hut. Nagappa spat out the reed and took a fresh one."

There was an operation theatre in Section C, did Doctorayya know about it?   the old building that was now used as a warehouse was once the main hospital, and the OR was still kept shipshape for you know what.

What are you talking about? Pinto asked. There's nothing in that shambles.

Nagappa looked closely at the doctor. He lifted the lantern and peered at him. Unbelievable, but yes, this man really did not know what happened those nights between the time a terminal patient was taken to intensive care where the family could not enter, and the time his body was brought out and handed with great gentleness to the family. Ba Ram, Ba Krishna, the ashram took good care of all their peasant patients. The bereaved family was given every help possible, sympathy and often a generous amount of money for the cremation or burial arrangements and rites. They didn't have to be believers. Hindu, Muslim, Christian or whatever their creed, there was no discrimination whatsoever in the largesse the management bestowed on the poor family. A soul is valuable, no matter what religion they practised or didn't, they said. They did not think it necessary to say that, more importantly, a body is valuable, especially the organs that can be salvaged.

The next morning, Pinto woke up, astounded that he could have slept so soundly despite his tied-up hands and feet. Nagappa came in. He had a jug of water in one hand, a neem twig in the other. He untied Pinto's hands and let him brush his teeth. He then poured hot coffee into a brass tumbler and offered it to Pinto. Pinto took the tumbler and drank the coffee. It was good.

"This is very kind of you," Pinto said.

"I am sorry I can't leave you unattended," Nagappa replied apologetically.   "May be in a day or two when we know each other better, all things will be possible."

"That was very decent of you," Pinto said, handing back the tumbler.

"I wouldn't want to lose you the way the Ashram almost did on your first visit. Small service indeed for the service you are about to render me," Nagappa replied, equally formally.

"I can't render you anything," Pinto said, "I would need surgical instruments, trays and trays of them, and nurses and assistants ...."

"It is a fully equipped place, doctor, don't worry."

Nagappa loosely tied his hands, feet and mouth, just enough to restrain him, and left.

Pinto meditated. He meditated on the Swami. But his mind constantly flitted off to Nagappa's comment, I wouldn't want to lose you the way the swami almost did. By early afternoon, hungry and thirsty, Pinto digressed into wondering if Nagappa also had powers. Or could it be that all this was Ba-Lila, that the Swami had come in Nagappa's shape to tease him? Of course that is what it was. That is why Nagappa was so unconcerned about the surgery. May be the Swami wanted him to conduct some special surgery.

Nagappa came back early as promised, and laden with hot coffee and dosas, and a tiffin carrier with the night meal.

Nagappa untied him, and they had tiffin. Nagappa's knife case protruded out from under his waist cloth.

~

"But from where are you to get a matching donor? Do you have any idea of the machines and instruments we need to figure that out?" Pinto asked.

"The boy is dying. It won't be long." Nagappa said, with a tremor in his voice. "We have a strong sense of family, sir, we do, and the lad would tear it out himself if he knew it was for his aunt."

"His aunt? Your wife?"

"Yes, sir, Kichu is her brother's son. That is why I feel it will match."

"Kichu? I think I know him, he was in Ward G some time ago."

"He has been moved to T," Nagappa said, wiping his eyes. T was the terminal ward. "You must sleep well, doctorayya.

May be tomorrow I can leave your hands free?" It was a beseeching question rather than a cold statement.
(put in details of the next few days, conversations, actions etc.)

~

Four days later, Nagappa untied his hands and feet. Thank you sir, he said, that makes me feel much better. He cracked all his joints as though his own arms had been tied.

"How can you trust me?" Pinto asked.

"You are a good man, ayya," Nagappa said, touching his fingertips to the doctor's feet and raising his fingers to his heart. "You have to be, considering you don't know what happens in Section C."

That action of obeisance both agitated and relieved Pinto. The Swami would never do that, even in pretence. He knew his Swami. Which meant Nagappa was really Nagappa, the istriwala.

"So tell me. What happens in Section C?"

And Nagappa did. Pinto did not want to let on how shocked he was.

"You are talking through your hat," he said. But he knew Nagappa was not lying, not totally anyway. It could happen. Images and overheard conversations surfaced to his subconscious. The Trust secretary, the Director of the hospital, the Swami's personal aide and right hand man, all three top men in the ashram were tightlipped people who never volunteered to serve at the dining hall, who often did not appear for days at the general assembly though they were always there by the Swami's side on his morning walk to the prayer hall.

Pinto should have been devastated and he could not figure out why he wasn't. He felt something had been set rolling, destiny, some destiny involving him and Nagappa. Nagappa tied him up again before leaving.

~

(put in more details)

In those early days, when Pinto was filled with missionary zeal, as he lay in bed every night, he would remember that darshan. The Swami's hands were soft and his touch light, and as he leaned over him, his herb-scented breath on his neck, Pinto felt a tingle shooting through his body, up into the nape of the neck and into his skull. The rising of the kundalini, he told himself every night, and felt it anew. A tingle, an explosion in his brain, an experience of levitation, of being carried away. He was here on a sacred mission. The world was good. With time, as he settled down to the ashram and hospital routine, the kundalini did not rise because it did not need to. He consoled himself thus.

~

(I had better leave all the details and write the outline now before the Muse leaves me)

They came for him an hour after Nagappa had left. There was the sound of a motorcycle with a silencer, and then the door opened and two men came in. They were dressed in orderlies' hospital uniform. They seemed just a little surprised at seeing the doctor in bed. "Time to go," one said, "Doctor Sahib, everything is ready."

"Where is Nagappa?" Pinto asked.

"All taken care of," the other said. "Time to go."

They whipped out a roll of hospital bandage and came to bind Pinto's mouth. "Come on, you guys," Pinto said, breaking into English after a long time, "Nagappa trusts me as I am. What's with you?"

They smiled grimly. "Orders are orders, sahib." They gave an inflection to "sahib" that Pinto did not like. Like an afterthought.

Mouth and hands tied, Pinto sat on the pillion between the two and they rode back to the hospital. Things moved like clockwork. Pinto was got into surgical scrubs and was led into the operating theatre. Kichu was there, a peaceful look on his face, his body covered to the neck. When all the lights went on, Pinto saw he was in a state of the art theatre. His heart leaped with excitement. He felt he was back in Ames, at the Medical Centre, all lights GO. Assistants whom Pinto did not recognize materialized from the anterooms. A senior administrator, in OR scrubs, shook hands with him.

They led Pinto to an anteroom that seemed dark after the brightness of the theatre. Nagappa, brought in by the orderlies, was totally broken. They had to hold him up. He joined his palms in salutation and whimpered inaudibly, garbling his words.

"I will do my best, Nagappa," Pinto said, "take heart."

The team went to work. Hours later, Pinto smiled, hummed the line he always did when he was satisfied that all had gone well - "Hum oos desh ke vasi hein jis desh mey Ganga behti hai."

The team disappeared as quietly as they had come in. The orderlies remained, and their boss. "Time to go, Doctor Sahib," the orderlies said in unison.

Pinto took off his gloves and cap and ran his hand through his hair. He looked around, slowly and appreciatively taking in the room and the machines and the equipment. And then he suddenly realized what had been in front of him all along but he had not noticed, just as Nagappa had said, he had been focusing on the job. The woman into whom he had transplanted Kichu's kidney was no peasant; she had smooth fair skin and patrician features, and her chart had said she was forty nine years old, whereas Nagappa's wife was in her early thirties. He had seen the chart but had registered only the details relevant for the operation. But now he remembered. They had not even bothered to hide anything from him! What were they up to?

"Time to go, sahib," the voices, still in unison, were more insistent, an edge of rudeness hidden with sullen care.

What were they up to? Pinto suddenly came all alert.

"It is my custom, a custom suggested and blessed by the Swami, that I spend a few minutes in meditation after each surgery," he said, looking straight at the boss, who had not yet taken off his mask and cap. The man nodded.

Pinto went to the recipient's side. He looked at the face and knew for sure this was no peasant woman. He closed his eyes and mumbled a prayer that clearly began with words that rang many times through the ashram from many lips, "Master, by whose infinite grace my hands do their allotted work...." He turned to the boy's body and started another prayer.

(Pinto realizes what they have done with Kichu....)

He felt his knees buckling under him, but he controlled himself. And then he knew why Nagappa was in the state he was in. They had probably pulled out his tongue.

Pinto was taken back to his hut. Next day, a passing peasant heard Pinto jabbering inside the cabinet of Nagappa's portable table, among the blanket and iron and ashes, smiling and stark naked, except for his gold chain.

Pinto smiled and nodded to some unheard music but said nary a word. His wife took him away to Ames with her.

Then the story started among the faithful, repeated across the world at their weekly prayer meetings; how Pinto had been beaten black and blue by thugs but when they tried to snatch away his chain, given by the Master himself, an invisible superhuman force had thrown them to the ground, had pummelled the shit out of them, and they had fled.

~

When I came home that evening, Stephen was asleep on the couch, both hands folded across his chest and the story under them. He woke up at the sound of the door. "I made a pot of tea for you but it will be cold by now," he said. "Let me make you a fresh pot." He got up and went to the kitchen. I went for a quick shower. The tea was ready and the samosas he had warmed earlier were hard in the oven, but I wanted them anyway. I told him what had kept me so long and he rubbed my shoulder.

"I have my work in India cut out for me," Stephen said, "the story has given me an idea – I just have to figure out a few details and then I can set up a transplant health tourism clinic there for patients from here."

I punched his arm.

"She has noted somewhere on the back of one of the pages about an appointment she had with someone at 4 p.m. of 8/11/88. The plot would have been sensational then," he said.

"I told you Maru was ahead of her times," I said. "This version is much shorter than the version I remember. She probably started it in the late 80s and kept adding all the time because I remember long conversations between Nagappa and Pinto about very current events at the time she was revising."

"Mind you, the bit about what actually happens in a transplant needs to be rewritten, she has got the harvesting and transplanting of the organ all in one place and we know that is not the way it works. Yes, but she should have published it then. The 80s would have made it a hit. Now, I wouldn't be surprised if there are novels and movies in the making already about the racket. A lot of what I've read so far would have made a lot more impact then than now."

"I guess she never pushed herself as a writer. No ambition, I guess."

"Wish I had met her. Sounds like me."

"Don't say it as though it is a virtue not to be ambitious. I wish you wouldn't waste your talents."

"Like going to India?"

"That's okay, a debt of sorts to the whole concept of volunteerism, but I mean in long term planning – you don't have a clue, do you, as to where you want to be ten years from now."

"No sweetums, I don't. But that's me. I'll never be the kind of achiever you are or your parents or DocSiv, and I know that's what is keeping you from taking the plunge. I am just not good enough for your expectations. Even though pedigree-wise I pass with DocSiv."

I knew he added that to lighten the atmosphere. He really was serious about my reluctance to commit myself. It had been bothering me too, this ambivalence, and one side of me said I'd find peace only if I could resolve the division in myself. It was time to say what one side of me had been thinking of saying for some time now.

"Listen, lover boy, and listen carefully. Take good care not to propose again because next time you do, I am going to say yes."

"Christo," he said, "let me grab the moment with open arms."

"Wait," I shouted, "wait. That would mean no India. That would mean perpetual nagging about your shilly-shally waffling about what you want to do with your life. So think first before you act on the bended-knee scenario. You know what happened to Kunti? As a twelve year old girl she had pleased a visiting sage serving him the equivalent of samosas and tea, and he blessed her with a boon, that any god she called upon would instantly appear and give her a son. She was delighted and wanted to test it rightaway and so she went to her garden and called on the sun-god, who appeared pronto and Karna was born. Of course she had to hide the baby and do the Moses thing, and a charioteer found Karna in a basket on the riverbank and brought him up as his own son. In short, don't test anything out without due thought."

"Hey, really? That's who Karna was? I didn't pick up that detail in my scroll-type reading of the epic, I guess. That's neat, gives a whole new dimension to Maru's story. I guess I'll have a lot of time to read the epics and a lot more about Hinduism in India. The way the MSMF programme is run, I think there will be plenty of time though I am not sure there will be plenty of books nearby. Who can tell me about Public Libraries in that neck of the woods? "

He was so excited about what he would do, how much he would travel, the people and places he would see, including an ashram like the one that Maru's story talks about. His little notebook was getting crammed with addresses, to-do-lists, questions he wanted to ask.

~~~~~

FOURTEEN

Stephen had dinner almost ready. Now that he has nothing to do except laze around, he is always home by the time I return, and most days he has dinner ready. Instead of me leaving Maru's stuff in the blue tray for him to read, he now has some for me. He gave me a cup of hot tea and one of the Maru's pieces. He said, "It has always been clear Maru was fond of P.G. Wodehouse, but you've never told me Maru was teaching in India before she came here."

"No, she wasn't. Haven't we read a hundred different times about the henna scarce dried on her hands when she came here with Uncle Siv?"

I looked at the sheets in my hand. "My First Examinership," read the title.

My First Examinership

We were in the Staff Room, having our afternoon tea and samosas. Virender was saying how keen he was to be appointed an examiner for the Pre-University exams. He really could do with some extra cash, he said, all this daily eating out at restaurants was draining his bank balance. And he strongly disapproved of the college canteen's recent decision to increase the price of samosas. Everyone was out to make him broke. An examinership would help somewhat.

"No correction work for me," I said. "Isn't it bad enough that we have to teach them through the year and correct their mid-term tests? I won't accept any examinership, not even on a silver platter with watercress around it." I said it plain and I said it loud. I would have thumped the table for effect if it weren't that the head of the department appeared too engrossed in his journal not to be listening to us.

"The difference is that you get money for this," one of our other colleagues said.

"And anyway, you needn't worry," another drawled, "papers are given only to those with five years' teaching experience," this in a tone that implied he had completed that span in the profession, and not so long ago either.

"Money," I said scornfully, "half one's summer vacation wasted for a mangy two hundred rupees!"

I hate to begin my story in this conventional way, for now you know the offer came the next day, but as someone has said before me, I am no orator as Brutus is... and anyway this goes to prove the old saying that truth is more monotonous than fiction. Something looks wrong in that sentence, but then what can you expect from one just out of the nightmare of reading through answer papers where "Death is better than cure" and "A bad workman quarrels with his stools"?

Next evening as I was indulging in a saline gargle to ease my teacher's croak, a peon cycled up to my door and handed me an impressive looking envelope which had 'Urgent', and 'Confidential' and 'On University Service' rubberstamped all over its face.

What could it be? True I had sent the judge's son out of class last week for playing on the harmonica and a cheap tune at that, but surely action could not be taken against me for that!

Or was it about that occasion when...

Or perhaps...

It was about an examinership, of course. Due to the unexpected number of students entering the university this year, said the covering letter, this offer was going out to etc. etc. and it ended that I was "requested to reply immediately...." I looked around for the bearer of the letter, but with an alacrity rare in office peons, he had vanished.

It was only a quarter past four. I knew I could reach the University office by five o'clock if I hurried. I panted up into the Registrar's office and waved the envelope importantly, but the Registrar's peon would not let me in. "Assistant Registrar," he muttered and glared me into another room. The Assistant Registrar was more accessible – to all evidently – for heads kept bobbing up from every corner. He was very efficiently nodding persons off the room after listening with profound concentration to what each had to say. I waited for the crowd to thin. Mine was a confidential matter. I knew the University Administration is labyrinthine in its red-tape. All possibility of contact between examiner and student is scrupulously eliminated. The students are given roll numbers, and the Admin. substitutes each roll number with a secret number before sending the exam booklets to the examiner. The examiner, moreover, is required to solemnly affirm not to reveal to anyone that he/she is an examiner.

So I waited for the people to go away, and leave me alone with the Asst. Registrar's confidential ear. It seemed I might not get my turn before the office closed for the day, and so I leaned forward and whispered, "It is about the Pre-University English paper, I..." He extracted a cotton wad from his ears and I repeated my words. "Oh, valuation work? I see. Gangu Ram," he roared, "take this lady to Lalaji. Tell him it is Pre-University English I. And also ask if Professor Sen has accepted the B.A. Economics II."

I crept out, shrunk in my insignificance.

A few weeks later, my spirits elated as I ripped open the bundle delivered to my door. The answer-books come in huge cloth bundles, heavily insured and bearing the University seal all along the seams as required by postal regulations. I tore the wrappings and placed the high pile on my study table. I counted the books twice over and checked each against the list of numbers that came in its own special envelope. I read the question sheet and long Instruction Sheet for Examiners. I then took out a new red pencil and sharpened it. Then, with an Om Ganesaya Namaha, I opened the first answer book. The first question was "Write a character sketch of about 200 words on one of the following characters: Antony, Portia, Juliet, Macbeth." Juliet Caesar was leading actor in Shakespeare play, English," I read. I sat back and laughed. I got up, told my parents that and laughed. I laughed long and heartily.

I laughed even after the first week of correction. I laughed my way through Romeo being in love with a "capulet daughter" asking "farash" to make them "man and woman"; Duncan "agreeing to come to Sir Macbeth's house as a ghost" and "Mrs. Macbeth sending two goondas"; Shylock living in "Varuna," sometimes asking for a "pound of fresh," sometimes for a "pound of mass (Hindi *maans*?)

By the beginning of the second week, my smile disappeared and emotionlessly I dragged myself through the re-written biographies of the poets in Question 2. Wordsworth loved a cuckold and called it a ghost because it had only a voice; he had a sweetness called Lucy but she died after growing three years in sun and shower; he transformed himself into a cloud in order to see the daffies; once he came upon West Mister Bridge and saw London that wears a garment only in the morning. Keats left alone with a night in gale wished to die so he could hear a funeral song. And poor Davies cried because his life was so full of care he could not stand and stare at cows.

My only consolation was that I grew more adept at addition, and took decimals in my stride as I totalled the marks. That reminds me, one of the questions required the student to use "addition" and "edition" in sentences. One answer read, "Edition was a scientist." If the same fellow had written that Addition was an essayist, I might have given him half a mark for knowing that there was an essayist with a name that would sound so to a Bengali. For the words "nun" and "none", one student had a sentence that totally blew me away – "None was in the forest where a nun, opposite gender of a monkey, was sitting on a tree." Usually, with the use of several vernaculars, one could figure out the intended meaning, but this made me realize I didn't know all that many languages after all.

By the third week, a perpetual scowl had camped between my brows. Urchins scampered off the road on my evening walks. My mood grew black and blacker as I wandered along interminable gutters of English usage. Not only did I overlook 'recieve' and 'ecomodate' but grew so utterly confused about spellings that I looked for 'erstwhile' under U in the dictionary. Dictionaries don't help really. Once I had advised a student, whose essay was riddled with spelling errors, to consult the dictionary when in doubt, and he with disarming sincerity replied, "But madam, I am never in doubt."

Most of them had laboriously learnt to spell William Shakespeare and Percy Bysshe Shelley in their entirety, but they took more familiar names for granted. And there in the Stygian darkness I heard about the 'massage of Gandhiji.'

Question six required them to write a letter to a bookseller. 'Stoodent' after 'satoodent' ended his letter to 'Dear Bookseller' with an 'OK then' or 'yours lovely' after their 'leest' of books that contained drab titles such as *Physics made Easy* and *One Day Botany handbook*. I was tempted to give half a mark to one who wanted a book that was not on the course or a handbook – he wanted *Tale of Two Cities* by *Scott*. That he should have heard of these two names pleasantly surprised me. Such was my heightened fury that even *New Tails from Shakespeare* and *English Prose and Worse* did not elicit a semblance of mirth.

From amusement to apathy to downright despair, the last three days were sheer nightmare.

"Have you posted it?" I asked, "really posted it?"

"Yes, mem sahib." Pyarelal was aggrieved that I should doubt his veracity. He hastily took out the five rupees and change left over from the registration charges. I almost embraced him in my relief. "Keep it," I said, and tottered down into my chair, my hand sweeping red ink, pen and pencils off the table.

When I came to, old Pyarelal was still in a standing swoon, staring unbelievingly at the large tip in his hand.

I tossed the papers aside. "I think this must have happened to her sister," I said. "Her sister was an English prof. somewhere in India, and Maru stole a lot of her stories, I guess, because she has dedicated one of her books to her acknowledging as much."

"You mean your hero Aunty Maru was just a cheating plagiarist?" Stephen tossed the salad so high little pieces of grated carrot flew out. He picked them up and threw them into the garbage pail. "Garbage can Open Sesame."

"Ditto for this piece," I said. "It is such ridiculous exaggeration, no student could have been anywhere near as bad as this."

"I don't know about that," Stephen said, "Seriously, the errors are so bad I think they are for real. As such, it is a priceless record of an age gone by. You should keep it. And maybe she was teaching in India before she got married. You need to check on that."

~

I found a huge envelope marked Contests. It was full of contest announcements with the department stamp on them. It was one of the secretary's jobs to tack announcements and posters on the department bulletin board, and sure enough Maru being what she was, had hoarded many of the posters instead of trashing them in due time. I flipped through them and handed the envelope to Stephen, asking him to throw them out after a quick look.

Next day, when I came home after work, I felt like resting a bit before starting dinner. So I lay on the sofa for a while. Stephen came in with some take-out Chinese food and started laughing as soon as he saw me. "You won't believe it, remember those pieces that I thought was a sicko phase in Maru's life? That streak seems never to have left her. I found that altogether different facet of her personality even in her recent writings. Had she ever talked to you about her writing contests?" I told him about her job of tacking posters on the Creative Writing section's bulletin board. No, no, Stephen said, I mean did you know she entered writing contests? I told him of one contest to which she had referred often enough in our inclusion-exclusion feminist debates.

Once she had written a story for the "First Great Canadian Lesbian Short Story Contest" and the manuscript had been sent back to her unread because she was not a lesbian. This was at the very beginning of the gay revolution, and though she recognized their need for their own space, it bothered her anyway to be excluded. She had another story about being excluded from a gay workshop at a Desh Pardes conference in Toronto event though she was there as a sympathizer wanting to know more about the movement of those times, the eighties.

"Do you remember the title of her lesbian story?" Stephen asked. I had to think about that. I know she was thinking about using the pseudonym Shikhandi as in the Arjun episode but couldn't remember the title and then it came to me. "Come in, Chris," of course that's what it was, playing on the gender-neutral name. "No, that is not the story I have here," said Stephen, "did you ever talk about an erotica contest? It seems to be a recent one, not at the beginning of any revolution."

"Read this while I set the table," he said and gave me several pages that had a headnote about an erotica contest. It was dated Dec. 19, 1998 : "So is it possible to write for the erotica contest for which Susan Musgrave is the judge and which has to be less than 3500 words and has to be in by the end of the month?"

The Feel of Silk at my Fingertips

"So why isn't Tessie in yet? Come on, come on you guys." Jenn hustled us out of our rooms, yelling from the foot of the stairs. I would gladly have hidden in the closet but since my room itself must have been a walk-in closet before the landlord renovated it with students in mind, there was no place to hide. No place to hide, what a great title, I thought, if someone else hadn't taken it already.

We sat in a circle at our usual places. Jenn had the recliner; Lisa preferred sitting cross-legged on the floor, being a yoga freak. Evelyn and I sat on the sofa. Jenn switched off the light. The street lamp shone a splotched orange through the drapes. The radio was on; the volume was too low to figure out whether it was an opera or news that was playing but the hum provided the right atmosphere.

Lisa and I drew lots. "Lisa first, Vicky second," Jenn announced. I cringed. No place to hide.

The front door opened and Tessie rushed in. "Sorry guys, I almost never made it, thanks to my antediluvian tank; it stalled on McPhillips. But I managed to get it off to a side street. I was lucky a tow truck happened to be around the corner for a battery boost. Got to tell you about my same-sex heaven. My first time, guys, wow."

"Ssh," Jenn silenced her; "You'll get your turn. Lisa start."

This was really neat, Lisa gushed. Eleven inches bow to stern. Ooh, moaned Jenn. Aah said Tess. Evelyn moved forward on the sofa. Lisa started on her narration. She has this silky voice that snakes over and makes one gooseflesh at all the right moments. But I tensed up. I was next. No place to hide.

~

When Beth and I came to the city in the summer from our native Altbach, Manitoba, looking for a place, we were sure we would share. We started with River and Stradbrook, of course, because John Reimer, who had been a student for ten years and was the undisputed mentor for all of Altbach High, said near the Village was the place to be. But the rents were high. Nassau, Roslyn, no dice. Beth was sold on the Village and wouldn't even consider any place else. She was going to the U of M and it made sense for her to be on the 60/62 bus route. So we parted ways, promising to phone each other if we found a good place. She was staying with her Uncle Fred, and I with my Aunt Mildred.

I walked a lot during that week, from noon to late night, but Aunt Mildred was nice about it; she didn't complain that I was using her house as a hotel. I was at her phone half the morning and then back only in time to crash for the night.

I hit the jackpot on the sixth day; it was a one and a half storey house on a street just three blocks from the U of Winnipeg. There were three students in it already and they were looking for two more. I left fourteen messages at Beth's parents' number during the next two days; I knew her family was on their annual holiday but I figured she'd be in there some time or other. But she never called back. Turned out she'd found a place and a part time job and so had joined her folk on their trip before starting her life in the city.

I had dinner once with the girls before I committed myself. They seemed really nice and the food was good, and Jenn told me how the system worked, the allocation of duties, who could have parties when etc. etc. I liked the way they were up front with all the details. Best of all, the rent was oh so reasonable. Okay, the room was rather small and the ceiling was low and sloping, and I was given it only because I was shorter than Evelyn, the other new girl, who got the other room upstairs. Which seemed fair enough. I could live with a low ceiling at that rent. I hooked up with them.

Jenn turned out to be the commander in chief. I wrote home about Jenn the Viking. She is really efficient the way she manages our common responsibilities. Like, she makes the weekly grocery list and first thing Monday she puts it on the fridge under a magnet that reads I AM BOSS, and we could add our personal list to it. Every Monday evening we drew lots as to who would go with her to Safeway that Saturday and buy all the dinner stuff with our pooled money, and other stuff on separate bills.

The carport was hers, as was the best bedroom, on the main floor, and she always took most of the Werther's chocolates with which we filled the candy bowl on the living room table, and never the end slices of loaves, but no one seemed to mind. She was a good cook, and so she was on kitchen duty Thursdays and made twice the usual amount. The leftovers were still tasty on Saturday, which is something I can't say of my own cooking. No one cooked on Friday because it was assumed everyone would be away on dates.

Jenn did a lot of the organizational work and she did it well. But was she ever bossy. We didn't take to each other. Evelyn thought it was just my country-girl complex. During the first week or two I got a lot of phone calls. Jenn might have thought well of me but I made the mistake of telling her that the seven of us from Altbach High were looking out for each other because we had never before lived in the city. She figured that gave her the authority to rib me every time she could. When talking to me she always had to say something like, "That yokel Bill called," or "one of your country bumpkins needs a shoulder to cry on, by the sound of her voice," or "in the city we...."

It was the third Tuesday of October that Jenn got the idea. The first weeks of orientation parties and hooplas were behind us; now we were into deadlines every day for midterm assignments for each course. That day, Jenn clanged the dinner gong soon after we'd had dinner. We duly came out of our rooms. She stated the plan. We needed a break from the grindstone or our brains would get stewed. For the next month, every Tuesday we would sit in a circle and share our weekend experiences. No cheating. It was show and tell time. Evelyn and I were getting ready to back to the library but we had to stay back.

Jenn took all of that first Tuesday to show and tell. Clearly, her own weekend experience had given her the idea. She had a long saga of foreplay to tell and a lot to show; love bites, wow his incisors must be quite something, with which he had tattooed their initials on her right thigh, just above her knees. It was just as well his name was Ian and not something that started with a B or G or some curlicue letter. The plus sign between the I and J looked like a Ku Klux cross but we duly oohed and aahed. It took an hour of biting, she said, between three great penetrations, but foreplay was his real forte. She passed on to us stuff she had learnt while he stroked her to find her erogenous zones. Did we know that eunuchs in Egypt carried a straw tucked behind their ear which they used when they had to pee? And that they knew how to satisfy women even without their tool? All because they made an art of studying erogenous zones. Like so, she laid me on my stomach and pressed my tail bone and oh did it feel good, though I'd have died rather than give her the satisfaction of hearing me say so.

Evelyn had questions. Egyptian eunuchs, she remembered reading somewhere, only had their balls removed and so why the straw? Eunuchs, as she recalled from her readings, were big strapping guys who were bodyguards in harems, and her second question was if they didn't have balls, would they have the necessary hormones to build muscle? Jenn said muscles had to do with exercise and not hormones; the point about castration was discussed at some length and tabled since no one seemed to know for sure about where balls and the tool stood in castration.

The next Tuesday, there was time only for Evelyn because Jenn had to go to the Library for a bibliographical reference she absolutely needed for the next day.

Evelyn had been at a long boring party at which one couldn't get to the bathroom because of all the puking that was going on; they blamed it on food poisoning and thought of suing the pizza place, but to be fair figured it could have been the heady home-made brew that someone had brought and everyone had guzzled fast and furiously. At some point in the narration, Jenn told Evelyn to wake up and do something worth talking about; we didn't want a ringside seat to her puking parties; we wanted sexual encounters related graphically and truthfully, and so she'd better charge her batteries before her turn came up again. While she said it, she looked at me.

Which was a warning to me too, I guess. I had better do something. Next day I called Hank, who was in Education at the U of M; he was three years my senior at old Altbach High but he had been my neighbour since I was yea high. He didn't have time to take me any place but invited me for dinner at the university cafeteria. "Chris wants me to go over rightaway, on a weekday, imagine!" I said as I hung up before handing the phone to Jenn who was waiting.

I was becoming a habitual liar with Jenn around; but there was no way out. If I had said it was Hank, she would have snorted because she had come in when Hank was once visiting and he had this huge glass of milk in front of him, instead of coffee. I still drink my three glasses of milk each day but I do so when she isn't around.

I took the first bus that came – it was #62 instead of the usual #60 and it went around to so many places in and out of Waverley Heights and Richmond West, I felt I was getting lost three times over. But then I noticed that the guy in the seat diagonally in front of me was gently masturbating under the raincoat on his lap, and time passed quickly as I imagined how comforting and easy it is for the guys. Someone said in Psychology class that according to Freud, male infants don't think of it as part of their own bodies, which is why they use it as a security blanket when they are little. And some don't grow up, like this one.

It must be great to feel it growing within one's own hands instead of someone else's. But could he really get his hand in while riding a bus (pun?). May be he didn't have his briefs on. No, that was a bit much. Assuming he did, what would he do with the wet briefs? Carry around a second one in his backpack?

At last the bus swung back on to familiar terrain and I got off at the terminus and walked to the university cafeteria. I hadn't met Hank for three weeks, and I thought something would ignite. But he was the same shaggy dog he'd been all the years we grew up together; we discussed the grain border crossing issue; about loaded trucks being shooed off by local farmers south of the border. What a bum deal our dads had with the border-crossing deal, we fumed. Running for office and raising shit in the legislature was the only way we could get a break for us farmers. Just then, we were joined by one of Hank's new friends, who seemed kind of nice but different. Turned out he was from south Africa and has loads of money and an apartment down on Pembina all to himself. He seemed to dig politics, and Hank and he got on famously.

~

By now Lisa was describing the bed. It had that nubbly chenille bedspread that was popular back in the seventies she figured, since they had a few of those in her parents' basement. With her knowledge of yoga and Kama Sutra, she taught him a thing or two, and wow, was he a quick learner! Like when the woman is on the top and twists a quarter circle the guy has to turn just so, and even the book says it is a tricky act that needs some practice but he caught on just like that.

I looked at Tessie, lying on her stomach, elbows on cushion propping her head. How flushed she had looked when she entered late! Had she spent the whole afternoon in same-sex heaven? Was it the name of a place? Somewhere off Osborne Street, I'd heard, there was a bathhouse where men did their thing. So there must be a place for women too.

I could see Tessie's cleavage as she rearranged her cushion. But I had seen her breasts all too often. Evelyn, Tessie and I shared the upstairs; they had the bedrooms and I the smaller closet-turned-bedroom. Early in September it had been hot as hell in our rooms which had no attic space between ceiling and roof, and Tessie seldom wore anything except her panties once we went up for the night. Tessie's nipples were like dried prunes, always stubbly erect. But she had lovely hands, long fingers. I could see her lying next to that other woman who had beautiful breasts. They were full and firm; the nipples were soft, each nuzzling in the pink areola which were two concentric circles, the outer one just a wee bit lighter than the other and fading imperceptibly into the rest of the breast. The nipples were soft and had to be coaxed awake. I could see Tessie's fingers and lips moving slowly over the mounds, the right mound to be precise, and the nipple jumping into her waiting mouth.

It was question time. Lisa sat back and viewed us smugly. It had no doubt been a good story. I latched on to the only detail I had registered before slipping into my thoughts. Eleven inches from bow to stern? Wasn't that stretching it a bit? I asked.

There was some discussion as to the average tool's limp and erect measurements, and my word-play was totally overlooked.

And then it was my turn. I slipped on to the carpet, leaning against the sofa.

"I didn't expect anything, you know," I said. "I thought he's just one of those foreign students with an accent and a lot of dough; dresses something awful, baggy pants from another age, but super polite you know, the kind you feel rather sorry for. From South Africa. So we go to his apartment after dinner at

Friends, and it is a bed-sitter, a huge one but the bed is right there, king size, no less. And he already had a champagne bottle sitting in an ice bucket; that pissed me off, you know what I mean, all set to go, like I was an easy pick-up. Anyway, try everything once, I thought; he was my first foreign student. As long as the champagne was good, and was it ever!

"So he dims the light and comes on to me. A real artist I swear. He runs his fingers over my hairline and down the nape of my neck and undoes my bra all in one continuous stroke. It is all so incredibly expert, I am more ready than I have ever been and I've been there many times believe you me, but he freaks me out by drawing back and having a sip of champagne. Sure doesn't know about timing, I say to myself, unwinding myself. And then he starts massaging me and I am ready to fall asleep, it is so soothing. Then he slips out of his pants. Is this weird or what?"

Evelyn and Tess say, Weird, and Lisa says Or what?

"So then I see he has boxer shorts."

"Oh yuk," Lisa says.

"No way," I say, "these were silk shorts, and he steers my hand over the silk and thigh, and I can feel the little curls on his thighs and the silk again and the curls and the silk again; it is so incredibly sensuous I could have come right then and there, but he turns and has another sip of champagne and lets me taste it with my tongue on his. And then he brings it out. I've never seen anything like it, anything so beootiful, and I don't think I can do it again with anyone else any more. It is just too incredible."

What? Why? What happened? they ask, caught up in my excitement.

"It is uncircumcised," I say, drawing out each syllable. Un-cir-cum-cised. The foreskin is all there, just as Nature made it, incredible. So soft all the way to the tip, I could touch it all the way to the tip..ooh..and there at the very tip it puckers up like a fish mouth."

I sink back, with the sheer delirium of living the moment. So what if it never happened.

"Is he black?" Tessie asks

"How far in is the real tip?" Lisa wants to know.

"No, couldn't be," Evelyn says, "if he were black he'd probably be a Muslim and Muslims are like Jewish guys, circumcision is a religious given for them."

"Balls," Lisa says, "he could be just a plain old white Christian."

"Lucky you," Jenn says.

And that makes my week.

"Disgusting," I said, "I don't believe Aunty Maru wrote this tripe."

"Imagine her writing all that stuff about Pooja one day and all this soft porn a little later, Hnh?" Stephen said. "But as erotica I doubt it would have made even the first cut. Too too soft."

"Nothing to suggest she wrote it, nothing at all, no typo correction, nothing in her own handwriting. It is someone else's rubbish." But even as I said it, I knew her style her signature was all over it, the colloquial tone was unmistakable.

"As you wish," Stephen said, "but I think it shows she was game for anything. A writer just has to place herself in a certain space and write from there."

"I might as well trash it rightaway," I said, and did.

After dinner, I started on the report that was due the next day. But it was such a bore. All I had to write was one page but it took me a long time. I needed some distraction and fished out a folded foolscap sheet. But I stopped myself. I had to finish that damn report.

~~~~~

FIFTEEN

Stephen called from the MSMF Guest House. As with his call from Mumbai, this was a short call just to say all was well. He seems to love the place already – he said the flowers are beautiful and the whole place is neatly laid out and the people he's met so far are great. I am leery when anything starts so euphorically, hope the trip goes well.

I told Ginny I couldn't come to her party. I had some lame excuse. Real reason is I don't want to be meeting the same old crowd in a social setting where one was expected to talk about something other than work. I wish I had friends outside the workplace. It was so comfortable, when I first came, to have a familiar crowd with whom one could spend time at ease that I never bothered to look elsewhere for company. And now, with Stephen away, somehow I wish I had another kind of group to fall back to. Perhaps I should join some gym or tennis group. Next time Uncle Siv comes, I should ask him to take me to where the East Indian crowd meets.

But there's always Maru's cartons to keep me company. I came across a wad of letters in a ZipLoc bag yesterday. I thought they might be from Uncle Siv to Maru, but they were not. Most of them were aerogrammes from India, old girl friends looked like. The aerogrammes are so small, with so little writing space on them, no wonder the handwriting is all squished up.

If Maru has placed them in these cartons, I guess they are mine to read. One way to spend a Friday evening, why not?

~

I can't believe I have solved one of the many puzzles in all this stuff. The people Maru mentions in the juvenilia section of her poetry collection – they are here! VESPURS. I think I have unscrambled the names too. One would assume that each letter is the first letter of a name. Looks like she used the second letter of each name. Devious, the way she worked it all out, changing names and events and facts in her published work, and some of these unpublished works that seem like they were in the final draft. Always using a part of the name but not the first letter. I don't know about the rest, but I know who E and S are. Maru used to talk of them often enough – the fun they had at their years at the Y. Their letters are here, written over five or six years, starting soon after they left the Y and tapering off two or three years after they all got married. I should tell Stephen about my finding. He is not the only one who can unscramble codes I'll have him know.

The reason I am dwelling on cracking the code is because the letters themselves are so sad, and I've got enough sadness in my life right now. That Maru wrote hugely funny letters is clear from their references to her letter-writing skills that made one of them respond: "The letter in which you referred to it kept me laughing for a whole hour and hubby came to the conclusion I have now lost my marbles." The other wrote: "The sick cannibal jokes were terrific. I rolled on the bed and laughed and laughed. Worse-half thinks I'm bats." "Believe it or not, skunk, I actually miss you at times."

But they are sad for so many reasons. How happy and carefree are the first few letters, about silly pranks they played on others with their girlfriends, like premeditatedly staring and giggling at the waiter at some ritzy restaurant,

"But it was the waiter who had the last laugh – he filled our sandwiches with rotten eggs."

Or:

"On the way to the cinema we (about 7 of us) decided we'd drop dead if we didn't get a sip of water. But our purse did not permit a cold drink. We entered a restaurant and sat down and importantly said, Waiter, water first for everybody. I pretended to scan the menu eagerly. No sooner had we gulped the water down, we rushed out of the place roaring with laughter. You should try it some time. Be sure not to miss the look on the manager's face.

Or the long narration about their flirting with the New Zealand hockey team:

"We were completely surrounded by Kiwis...You can imagine how furious our boys were – their college show and we, who weren't even remotely concerned with the college, in the limelight. We thought the players wouldn't be staying for dinner, so after saying good bye to them we went upstairs for dinner. What a shock it was when we had barely entered the room and the New Zealanders started yelling for us. The college folks had no other alternative but to seat us between the players....The kiwis are nice but very boisterous and very free.

UMA PARAMESWARAN

The outcome was that we also turned terribly boisterous, and received ferocious glares from the Principal and staff of the College."

Maru seems to have been at the Y still while they are back with their parents, teaching in their local college but having a great life. "I revel in the picture in which... you will figure prominently. The place – the YWCA dining room, the time – 7:30 p.m. You stare dolefully at the gloomy pans of the other inmates across the moth-eaten tablecloth, on which are delicately placed the insect-infested brinjals and the stone-adorned rice, while everyone makes a supreme effort to stomach the raw chapattis which show that the cook is in bad need of some hair-care to prevent the loss of his silvery hair."

I read the letters again and again, marvelling at the incidents and language that sound like capers one would have in one's tween years. Once I would have called it ignorance or crass immaturity. May be it is a kind of innocence, may be girls grow up slower in India, or did in those days.

Then they get married and there's some excitement about the pleasures of the bed and of housekeeping. "Pa-in-law visited us last week. He seemed pleased as punch to see the way I'm running the house. It's quite a job supervising fourteen servants."

But the first excitement of wedded bliss vapours away. They feel trapped.
"Air India have announced that they are going to enrol fifty air hostesses who must be unmarried. I'm applying for it.... I'm fed up of married life. It's always budget, budget, budget! Ugh! I wish I had shoved off to America or some such place. You're real lucky."
The other writes,
"Everyone talks only about rising prices these days; and they are rising like billy-o! Milk, potatoes, wheat, all 8 annas a seer last year are now selling for one rupee four annas. Life is one bloody (sorry) mess here."
One mentions a brother's death.

"He had done five rounds of take-off from the deck of *Vikrant*. On the sixth round the engine failed and the jet came crashing on to the sea. Ashok died instantaneously. The plane and Ashok were not located. They had searched with submarines, helicopters, deep sea divers but with no result.

Can you believe we'll never be able to see his laughing face and twinkling eyes?"

And a year later he is mentioned again. She is living in Bombay now.
"These flats are dreadful, kids yelling all over .... And then there is the sea and Ashok. Everywhere there's the sea and everywhere the face of Ashok smiling, laughing. Plenty of plane casualties. What is happening I wonder. The sooner we have a war and the complete extermination of the human race, the better."

The other writes:
"I expect nothing from life, it has nothing to offer me, so we're kind of quits."

Gone is the joie de vivre, life seems to have weighed them down even before it started. I mean, the letters span just a short five years, and it's already all over? But one thing is clear – I was not wrong in resisting the wedding shenanigan after all. I need not feel guilty. It is enough that I worry and think about Stephen all the time, and at times it feels just as though we are married till death do us part and all that, but we ARE free, I have to see it that way, we are free.

If I were to take the trouble to read only the happy parts of this stack of letters instead of the bleak ones, wouldn't we get another picture altogether? The tiger and the English landscape. Always the tiger by one's side.

If Stephen were here, we could talk about it. Or better still, we need not talk about anything. I should perhaps go to Ginny's after all.

~~~~~

SIXTEEN

It has been a long day. A premie delivery, barely 25 weeks. It was a privilege to be seeing Dr. Jenner at work. He is a legend. We hung on to his every word even though much of the time he would go through what we had read up already. "At 24 weeks, the chances are 50%" he said as he put on his gloves, and at 25 it becomes 80%. Since we can never be sure of exact dates, we must assume it is closer to 24, and hope it is a day or two past 25.

Then he went to work, speaking softly to the patient. When he held the baby in his large hands for he is a tall man, it was so small one could see his hand all around it. "Small, may be a little over 500 grams, but he has a good sturdy chest, a good sign." He tweaked the baby's tightly closed left fist before handing it over to the nurse. "Once upon a time," he said, and we waited in anticipation for he was known to end each delivery with an anecdote or joke. "Once upon a time, New York's pickpocket number one married Chicago's pickpocket number one and they eagerly looked forward to their baby, hoping he would become all America's pickpocket number one. Alas, the baby seemed born with a deformity, a tightly closed right fist. When the mother touched the closed fist with a sigh, the hand opened and the midwife's ring rolled out."

~

Stephen's e-mail is long and jumps around as he describes his first impressions. I printed it so I could get the feel of a real letter in my hands, and lay on the couch to read it so I can imagine him by my side. He still hasn't gotten over his jetlag, and has a bit of dysentery. I replied rightaway, warning him – for the nth time – to drink only boiled or bottled water during his entire stay and to keep away from restaurant food until his body gets used to the many changes of climate and time and food. I don't want to sound a clucking mother hen but I know India.

I confess I have been messing up the contents of the cartons. What I have read is neatly labelled but what I have not read is getting more and more mixed up. Every day I take a handful of sheets to work. I pick them up for no reason in particular – sometimes the title intrigues me, sometimes the colour of the paper, sometimes the size, sometimes the handwriting. If it is handwritten, I usually don't take it to work. It is hard enough to get anything read fully at any of the breaks, and typewritten stuff is easier to read when you have a sandwich in one hand. But the handwritten notes are more interesting to read. I wish Maru had kept a journal note book like everyone else who is into journalling. But not her, she's just written her notes on half sheets of paper, back of envelopes, those ridiculous list-pads with one's name on it that charity organisations send three times a year hoping to shame you into sending a cheque. I wonder if she kept this carton just for that over the years – to throw in her observations, reminders to herself, what not, anything that might be fodder for a story some day, like these two half sheets of paper, as though we have a paper shortage for Pete's sake:

Storyline – the vindictive ants. I had two anthills on the front lawn sprayed. What if the ants come in through some crevice in the basement? Must somehow include the story of that summer long ago when we used to sleep on the lawn on steel cots and I woke up from a bite and saw swarms of ants on the bed sheet with which I usually covered myself. How I always covered myself though others never did except early mornings when the breeze had a nip.
Storyline – the hollyhocks outside the bedroom window that give me the heeby jeebies when the wind blows.

Things like that. But today I came across a piece of writing on an envelope which was postmarked July 1976.

Funeral service – Mrs G. She looked like death, kind of painted up and ashen drawn. Do they place something at the sides of the head so it will stay straight? There was a fly buzzing over the open casket. I did not hear a word of the eulogies, my eyes the whole time on the fly that alighted on Mrs. G's hands, flew away, came back and circled above her head, and then came to touch someone on the front row, flew away, came back to the casket.... Once it came to my row and I thought it would sit on my arm. I almost screamed.
If I am destined to die in this country, I absolutely forbid an open casket. That thing lying there won't be me, and I don't want people gawping at not-me. And at flies, eek. Another Donne might pen a great poem on the fly flying from dead arm to living arm, breathing new life into dead passion, but no thanks. I

absolutely forbid an open casket. So I have said, so let it be written, so let it be done. Herewith sealed and stamped this seventh day of August, nineteen hundred and seventy six, add, in the year of the Lord just to make sure this is legal.

So like Maru, half funny half deadly serious, pun intended, as she would say. More than that, of course it made me remember my own mad behaviour screaming that I wanted to see her, I had to see her, I had a right to see her. I had come to the funeral chapel straight from the airport, having missed the connection in Toronto. When I saw the closed casket, I went berserk and Arvind took my arm, murmuring it was her wish to have it so, and seated me in his chair, at Uncle Siv's right hand, and Uncle Siv, who was sitting with his hands clasped in his lap, put his right arm around my shoulder and kept it there the whole time while everyone babbled forever about Maru.

More than all that, I was in a panic, because why should I come across this stray note written on an envelope now and not when Stephen was here safely with me?

I didn't sleep well at all. At about two in the morning, I switched on the light, and took a sheaf of papers from deep inside one of Maru's early-work cartons. It sure didn't lull me to sleep, I can tell you. Do I want to dream about Maru? No way. Why does she keep dreaming about dead people? Stephen would say we have no control over our dreams. I think we do. We dream only about what bothers us. May be yoga would help. They say there is a yoga exercise that makes you fall asleep in a moment. Lie on your back, Relax. Stretch your toes, relax, arms by your side, relax. That's all there is to it – if only someone can tell me how one relaxes.

May12-13, 1970
Lots of dreams.

S was at the stove making uppuma, and Siv was at the table, shaking his head as though to say, leave S to do something by way of cooking and you have a huge mess.

I went out, on to the veranda of the big house in Jabalpur. It was a summer evening and Appa was on the black low chair and V and B on the low cane chairs, and one of them had a pack of cards – I could see the geometric pattern on a pink background –

and Amma was in a blue sari with an inch wide gold border. She was looking reflectively at Appa across the rosewood topped cane table. I thought, She is wondering how he is coping with his bereavement and then I thought, What bereavement? And I replied, About losing Amma, his wife. But she is here, I said, and moved to her chair. She wasn't there. But I touched her left shoulder and of course she was there. Not dead but alive. It was wonderful to know that. I looked at her, and she slowly faded. Right before my eyes, she vanished. And then still in my dream, I awoke and knew all this was a dream but I was so grateful for it. But I was grateful that I had seen her. I thanked God that I had seen her.

And then I went up steps, up the elevator. The elevator stopped, the door opened and I could see construction in progress. Up more floors and I got off at a floor. I was looking for something, I didn't know what, but a kind of explanation for my gratitude, looking for Amma, looking for Krishna. Not in any frenzied search but abstractedly, sure with a kind of calmness that I would find something good, satisfactory, fulfilling. I walked down concrete floors of unfinished halls. Behind glass doors, in a somewhat dark room, there were many people moving around, some behind tables with tape recorders or microscopes or something.

I couldn't figure it out at all. She seems to be talking and also responding to herself. What did memories of her mother's death have to do with searching for Krishna at a construction site. Stephen would make some connections – some other story where someone looks for God somewhere up in the mountains. Stephen. I miss him, God I miss him so much. Please God, make everything turn out okay.

~

I picked up another sheet to get away from obsessing about Stephen.

Maru must have been pretty hung up on Panchali. No way to date this one but it could be the same period as the dream. Looks like she wanted to write a long play? Or is it a poem? Or what? on Panchali..

A comic interlude on the Keechaka episode. (note to myself: check on who swears-in witness – the court clerk?)

Do you, Draupadi, swear to tell the truth, the whole truth and nothing but the truth, so help you God?

Draupadi: No comment.

Prosecutor: State your name.

Draupadi: Yajnaseni.

Prosecutor: Did you call yourself Sairandhi when you were in Queen Sudeshna's court?

Draupadi: Why should I call myself? Names are used by others to call one.

Prosecutor: Did Lord Keechaka ask you to be his wife?

Draupadi: Yes, fools are known to ask for the moon.

Prosecutor: Did you tell him that you had five gandharva husbands?

Draupadi: Yes.

Pros: The Queen sent you to get some wine from Lord Keechaka's palace one day. Did you go there?

Draupadi: Yes.

Prosecutor: Did Keechaka kick you at that time?

Draupadi: Your much-loved royal historian herself says so.

Prosecutor: Did you tell any of your gandharva husbands about this?

Draupadi: What happens between a woman and her husband is no one else's business.

Prosecutor: Were any of your husbands present at the Court Hall of King Virata?

Draupadi: No comment.

Prosecutor: We know now that Kanka, the counsellor, is your husband Dharmaputra. What did he say to you at the Court?

Draupadi: That I should not cry so much.

Prosecutor: Did he say that as a reprimand or as consolation?

Draupadi: No comment.

Prosecutor: Did you meet your husband Bheema the night of the day you complained in the Court Hall?

Draupadi: What happens between a woman and her husband is no one else's business.

Prosecutor: Did you ask Bheema to kill Keechaka?

Draupadi: Ditto.
Prosecutor: Did Bheema tell you he would kill Keechaka?
Draupadi: Ditto.
Prosecutor: Is there anything you would like to say?
Draupadi: Any judge who knows his books would know
                that a woman cannot be asked to testify about
                her husband.

Ever noticed how nobody names their daughter Panchali or
Draupadi or for that matter any of her many names. Wonder
why? I like her, strong woman, knew what she wanted though
she didn't always get what she wanted. I think I shall give the
name to my daughter, when I have one. I should say IF, not
when. How can we take that for granted – what if I have a
hundred sons, as the blessing goes and nary a daughter; really,
what if? I'd rather have one daughter than a hundred sons, but I
am not going to say so. I am superstitious about saying what I
want. Some evil fairy might be overhearing and they are
spiteful. But if push comes to shove, I guess a son is better than
no child at all. What if it never happens, neither son nor
daughter; well, if it doesn't it doesn't.

I read it again. What if? So this must have been written even
before Arvind! I missed Stephen terribly whenever I read any of
Maru's stuff; I missed his comments and responses to her pieces; why
kid myself? I miss him; his arms, the golden hairs on his thighs, his
little laughs and his encyclopedic knowledge that so maddens me into
stomping on him. I miss him. He would have all kinds of questions,
who was Keechaka, where in the Mahabharata does Bheema kill
Keechaka, do I have any copy of a retelling of the epic, and he would go
right ahead and find the answers. What if? What if we never have any
children? My biological clock is ticking, ticking.

It was time to go to work. Two night shifts in a row. I grabbed
several of the India-style school notebooks – those 7x7 notebooks with
a god-picture on the cover which Maru seems to have used before the
days of notebooks made of old exam booklets. Each seems to be for a
story she never completed. All of them seem to start with an outline or
notes and some of them have some sections written out, but not one of
them is anywhere near complete.

Some nights are crazy at work, but these two days have been quite
uneventful. I got to read some of Maru's outlines. I just scanned over

them, scrolled through in computer lingo. There are some that stick in my mind. There is one about a nun who runs away from a convent to an ashram near Rishikesh. I remember how fondly Maru used to recall her visit to Hardwar and Rishikesh, the sight of an old woman bathing in the ice-cold Ganga and saying, *Sukh hee sukh, Anand hee anand* – this is Bliss, this is Joy, the faith that kept the place pure in spite of the crooked ways of *pundas* who kept exploiting pilgrims...

There is a story about one of the teachers at her school, the Note to Myself says, who had a lovely daughter that gossips held, was illegitimate. The father was an army man, who meets up with the daughter when she is a teenager. And at the end of the notes, Maru wonders if the mother and the Major should marry and live happily ever after or not.

There is another, and I am sure it belongs to the same cluster, about a young woman whose husband was dying of a terminal disease gently seducing his brother so she would have a child before she became a widow.

And another about the same theme except that the husband doesn't die!

And another about a young woman being seduced by her brother-in-law and years later she finds out her husband had suspected all along about the ongoing affair that ignites every time his brother come to visit. The husband is introvert and the brother a party-person extrovert who makes any room he enters come alive.

And another about a woman who is working in a city, goes home to get married and comes back a widow except that no one in the city knows about it. Comes out only when a young man proposes to her.

There is one that is kind of interesting – about a young man who jumps off the cliff so he could die at the peak of his happiness, and the second-hand of his Rolex watch keeps ticking away even if the minute-hand has stopped, which is weird, but, and this is neat that she was early aware of the sad plight of widows, the time-piece that he had given his wife for her birthday stops exactly at the moment he died, according to the autopsy. For some reason, she has written "J.B.Priestley's Time Plays" on that sheet, Stephen would know him I guess. I miss him, oh how I miss him. Daily e-mails are not enough.

Teenage stuff, Stephen would say, but that is important, that she started scribbling her stories so early – I should read them again at a slower pace and not the way I am reading now – they are all handwritten and though her writing is neat, who has the patience to read anything that is not typed? Also, it is so clear she is playing around a few core ideas from different angles all through her writings, early to her most recent.

~

    I am going to sleep all day. Last night there were two preemies. One was almost term, 35 weeks, and all is well, I guess, hope, assume. A week at Neonatal Intensive Care Unit may be. The other was a twenty-eight-weeker. The mother was admitted because she reported a fever. What struck me about her was that she was humming a song to her baby while she was in labour, in Ukrainian said one of the nurses. And she had a name all picked out and the moment he appeared, she called out to him – Vazeehl, my little Vazeehl. Yes, said Dr. Kelekis who was the attending doctor, "he is a little king indeed." Turns out it is spelt Vasyl, and means Basil, which is not the herb but "kingly."

    I spent some time with Marika this morning. She was born in Odessa and she spoke about how she once got lost in the Catacombs when she was about five years old. Her parents came to Canada when she was seven, but her husband Mikhail came only ten years ago and he still does not speak English all that well. She said this proudly and followed it up with how he spoke and acted just like her parents. And he dances divinely and was part of the Rozmai dance company, but now except during Folklorama he did not have much time for dancing. She had been working as a waitress and wanted to quit but then he got laid off and it was a while before he got another job, in Ottawa. I marvelled at how easily she talked about the hard times they had gone through but her parents had helped. Except that they had left Winnipeg last year and gone to British Columbia. where her dad was doing really well with a construction company.   So now she had no help but she would manage, she said, and hoped they too would one day go to B.C. to live.

    I came home exhausted. Night shifts in a row are terrible. Maru used to talk about low-income women who used to work night shifts so they could leave their sleeping children with the husband. They did it after working at home all day. I shouldn't complain.

    I wonder if Maru has written the life stories of any of those women she helped along. I know she published one but there must be stories about some of the others.

    I riffled through one of her binders. Seemed to be full of early stuff – but typed up. If I could figure out which typewriter was used, I could figure out the decade in which it was written – I should tell Stephen about this – but he didn't think chronology was the way to go.

I miss him. From our last phone conversation I gather he is enjoying himself. Talked about having lunch at the house of some kid with whom he is exchanging language-classes and how embarrassed he was that he could not sit cross-legged on the floor. I wouldn't be surprised if he comes back fluent in Telugu and with an Indian accent to his English! I remember that kid Raghu in Winnipeg who stayed a year in India and it took him another year to return to his Canadian accent. I remembered my own visits to India, the way we sat in a circle for lunch and dinner, all the five to ten children, and how children always had their meals before the grown-ups. We sat cross-legged on the floor, on a mat, with our stainless steel plates in front of us, each with our own stainless steel tumblers for water, and for diluted buttermilk with salt and kadipatha (curry) leaves. I wonder if I can still sit cross-legged on the floor, musn't give up that flexibility of body, must remember to start again on my workouts...

This poem of Maru's is intriguing, it is titled Apsara Love.

Come let us go you and I
Far from here where all ever is,
No yesterday nor morrow but always now,
Where your face is ever fresh,
Your body fragrant as the sky.

Come let us away to the vale of tears
That yonder lies girdled by the morning dew
Now bright, now dim, thro cyclic seasons swims,
Where love and sorrow spring each day anew.

O my love let us know the touch of sin,
So we may thrill at body mutual.
Let us undress our light celestial
So I may quiver at your touch
Your jealous hands running o'er my bare limbs
Stretched in dark dark night.

So I may kiss your tired creased face
So I may wait the livelong day for night,
And waking smell your manly sweat.
So we may yearn and cry, and work and fight...
And then sweet love, you will die one day

And I'll unplait my hair and spread it in despair,
And lay your body out in spotless white,
Weep and feel the pangs of broken bliss.
Then will I bury my beauty in your grave
And wait in agony of life without love,
So great my love, so deep so true,
I'll make this sacrifice for you, for you.

Rather nice handling of eternity. Undress our light celestial – I like that. Gives one a delicious erotic feeling. That is today's mantra to fall asleep, not that I need any mantra after two night shifts, but I have been sleeping badly for some time.

~

I fell asleep soon enough but instead of erotica, I had bad dreams and woke up in a sweat. A white shrouded body being carried on a bier and everyone chanting "*Ram naam satya hai.*" Stephen, Stephen, dammit, why aren't you here? I turned and lay on my side, clutching Stephen's pillow to my stomach. I tried to think of what Stephen would say of my panic: Instead of the first half of the poem, you thought of the second half, is all. Then I remembered something from long ago, on one of my visits to India. We were visiting an aunt, and Ma hustled me from the taxi into the gate just as a funeral group came up chanting *Ram naam satya hai, Ram naam satya hai.* Strange how childhood memories rise from the deep. But the explanation did not work to get me out of a weird sense of panic. I kept repeating, 'Undress our light celestial, undress our light celestial' as I tossed and turned. If I had more faith, I could have repeated Hare Krishna instead – may be that would help bring sleep easier than chanting a line of Maru's poem. I remembered the times I stayed with Maru when Ma was away at some conference or other and how she would take me to the temple on Sundays. Faith. Some real prayer songs instead of my simple prayers, Oh God, please make this a good day for all of us. Please God bring Stephen safely back home. Please God keep me from dreaming bad dreams. That is all the prayer I knew, though those chants from temple visits vaguely sounded at the back of my mind.

~

With Stephen away, and the dread of the final exam looming over me, I locked myself in my apartment any time I wasn't on duty. Maru had become my only companion whenever I wanted to run away from my books. I had gone past the emptiness, and I want her back, I want her back cries of grief and frustration. I felt comfortable talking to her, going over the day's work or notes as she played her solitaire, which is how we used to talk in those days, she forever with her cards which, she said, did not at all come in the way of talk.

On the computer I checked my mail. No news from Stephen. He had stopped phoning because he lived in a dormitory of sorts with no phone anywhere near and had to go to the public phone booth each time, and the waitline there was always long and he could never have relaxed conversations without feeling he was holding up the line. So we had decided we would live on e-mails. Ma had a note to ask if I could join her and Dad at their annual end of the year conference, which was going to be in Hawaii this time; she had made their bookings already to meet the registration deadline but she said it would be a nice vacation for me after my final exam and that I should join them.

In the second carton, there seemed to be a great many unfinished stories, and I read many of them to escape from the boredom of books and reports.

Ruksana carefully unwrapped the flat brown paper package, took out the linen tablecloth by a corner and swished it around herself as she pirouetted.

Grandma, for whom the show had been set up, smiled and took the tablecloth from the proud girl. She nodded approval as she turned over to see the wrong side of the embroidery stitches and saw that it was as neat as the upper side, no ugly crisscrossing of the cross stitch or chain stitch or stem stitch, no unnecessary knots and loops. "Beautiful, child, very beautifully done," she said, running her hands over the side of Ruksana's face and touching her fingertips to her own lips in a kiss.

"And now you are going to tell me how many embroidered bed covers you made for your own trousseau, and how you used gold thread for the veil," Ruksana said teasingly, sitting close to her grandmother, who drew her closer still and ran her fingers over the long black hair of her grandchild.

"Yes, Ruksi, we had ten large rooms in the old house, and in every room I had something that I myself had embroidered, cushions, divan-spread, bedcover, table cloth, and such colours and designs, dancing peacocks on my bedcover, but your grandfather, he liked only geometric designs and pastel shades.

"Tell me about the shawl you embroidered for Bapu," Ruksana said, cuddling closer, "tell me, tell me."

And Grandmother told her about 1929 and Gandhiji's visit to their town and how he accepted shawls that people had brought as gifts and how he piled them by his side, but hers he had chosen to use because, he said, it was the simplest of the lot, with just a row of leaves, in chain stitch Ruksana added, between two lines of cross stitch, in yellow Ruksana added, as excited now as Grandmother had been that day almost thirty years ago.

Most of Grandmother's stories were very sad, about the long trek from Sind, fleeing from the fanatical fratricidal fiends who overran their village and drove out the non-muslims, and how grandfather had shaven his beard and thrown away his muslim hat and passed off as a hindu because he believed India was home. That made him part of the Hindu exodus.

And how they, along with thousands of other refugees had lived in make-shift tents outside Delhi(check whether it should be Bombay), and how slowly they had regrouped and embroidered their way back to a livelihood.

And how the sufferings of those years had taught them never never to let religious beliefs dictate their actions because they had received so much love and support from the other refugees who had helped them as they fled towards the land they knew was theirs no matter what anyone else might say.

Grandmother used to have all the pictures - Hindu deities, Jesus, Guru Nanak, everyone

~

She was admitted last night. 22 years old. First pregnancy. Early miscarriage.

After the husband left, I drew up a chair and sat next to her. She lay with her eyes closed. I picked up one of the India books that Stephen had asked me to return to the library, and which I had been carrying around in my bag, never finding the time to drive to the library.

I sat for a long time but she did not move; it was as though she was waiting for me to go away, and yet I had thought from her earlier body movements that she needed emotional help – there was that tightness around the lips, that glaze in the eyes, as though she was holding it all in until the husband left.

"If you need us, we are here," I said, patting the call-switch pinned on to the bedsheet. I knew she was awake, her eyelids fluttered even though she was totally still.

"I would like some paper and a pen," she said. I told her I'd get them rightaway and went to my backpack. There was my cram-book as I called it, a spiral bound note book that I used to go over the data I needed to learn by rote for the next exam. I tore the sheets I had written on so far and gave her the rest of the note-book, and a pen. I could have told her she should rest, that rest was very important. But I didn't. Instead, seeing her feeling for the switch to work the bed, I helped pull the bed up, and propped an extra pillow behind her back. She smiled.

"I am okay," she said, "I will rest in a while. Thank you for the paper, I usually have lots of paper, I am a student, my finals are coming up next month."

"You have to get well first, don't worry about exams," I said.

Next morning, I took my rounds as usual, before leaving.

She stretched my book towards me. "I see you are a reader," she said, "I want you to read this in memory of him."

Him. I had never thought of it as him, but I realized my own insensitivity. I had better sit and read it quickly.

I opened the book – she had written eight or ten pages. I was about to draw up a chair when she said, "I don't need it," she said, "I just want someone other than the two of us to mourn him for a moment." Two of us, she said it as though her partner was present.

"I will see you later," I said, pressing her hand. We would soon know if she needed to stay. If not, I would not be seeing her again, but I did not think I needed to tell her that.

It had been a long night for me. Other than this miscarriage, there were two babies, both normal deliveries, a girl, a boy. The mothers were well, the babies were well. But I was tired. I would sleep as soon as I reached home, I thought.

But I didn't. I read the notebook instead.

It was our happiest month since our honeymoon three years ago. We are well settled, I, almost finished with my B.A., he just getting the job he'd always wanted. We had timed this so well. Knowing I would never bother with studies if we got pregnant, we waited till now. Every little thing called for an embrace. With ear and hand he would ask, Can I feel him now? And I would say, Soon, very soon. Days of convoluting motions within, and infinitesimal twistings, the pain of distending areoli and uncontrollable tracts, rancid taste in mouth, and joy, great joy.

I had a dream one day.

The trees were covered with leaves, green and flaming red, the grass was thick and green, the water edge like a bay, little ripples on the clean stretched glass reflecting grass and leaves and sky. And I caught my breath and said, "God how beautiful this is, and my little one will soon be here."

Did you laugh then, Fate? And did you laugh?

In the morning, there was blood. Just three or four drops of dark, muddy blood. It was like early in the first trimester, and I did not worry the way I had then. Early afternoon, along with urine was that dark muddy stain again, thick, spreading. I put away my books and went to bed.

I had a dream.

Something catastrophic had happened. It was not clear what. But it had to do with Mom. I want Mom, I said. I want her here and now. I told you long ago I wanted her here. If she had come, this wouldn't have happened. And the 'this' seemed to be connected with her, not with myself, something had happened to her. I wanted to cry. Deep sobs rose in my throat but the tears were swallowed by fear. Deep. Loud, rasping sobs but no tears.

It was five o'clock. I rose and went to the toilet. It was bright red now. I put on a pad and washed the soiled panty. I phoned the doctor. The clinic was closed. I called the other number on the message machine and left a message. Then I went back to bed. Don't use the phone, I told him when he returned from work, the doctor will call. But he didn't. He called only at 10:30.

It could be a miscarriage, the doctor said, is there anything but blood?

Such as?

Tissue.

Little clots, yes.

If there is tissue, put it in a bottle, a jar, and bring it with you if it gets worse.

How will I know it is getting worse?

If you have to change every hour or if you have cramps. Phone the hospital and check in. They will phone me.

How frighteningly frank doctors are. He was so even when I asked him during the last check up if we could fly to Vancouver during the February break to see Mom and Pa. If there is going to be a miscarriage, he said, it will come wherever you are. A short journey shouldn't normally matter at this stage.

At one o'clock, I went to pee. A big clot fell into the clear water. I flushed it away and then peed. A bigger clot fell out, and then more. My baby is going, I said. We scooped what we could and took the clots with us to the hospital, the pains coming in huge spasms. We waited. Like a sponge pressed against warm water, I felt the spurts. The nurse took me to a room, and gave me new pads. I lay down. He sat.

At about 2:30 my doctor came. Cool and spruce and fresh he looked. Did you bring the discharge? he asked.

"There's been so much more," I said, and the nurse nodded.

I was glad to see him. I told him I didn't think he'd come all the way in the middle of the night. "If it is bad enough that you had to come, I should be here too," he said. He closed the door. Then things started moving. He put in the metal jaws, put in his gloved hand and it came out all blood.

He mumbled something.

The nurse brought out a sterilized box of instruments. Hard metal distended me. His gloved hand was full of thick strands of blood that refused to drop. I think he put in the forceps though I could not feel it, and brought him out and plopped him into a jar of liquid.

Cotton.

He took swabs and wiped me. He took off his red gloves and dropped them into a can. We'll admit you for the night, he said.

He went out to talk to the father-not-to-be.

I raised myself on my elbow and looked at my child. Flesh of my flesh, blood of my blood, he floated in the jar. He is so grown, I thought, with tiny fingers and toes, but was I only seeing what the medical dictionary shows – pictures of little ones at ten weeks, fourteen weeks, twenty weeks, how they grow week by week? And yet this was his head, his long thin body, floating head down, my son.

The nurse picked him up.

It happens, she said. The baby would have died anyhow, she said.

Why does she say anyhow, I thought, does that mean he was not dead when they pulled him out? Does it mean he could have been saved? Why anyhow?

The father-not-to-be came in.

"Get well soon," he said, and held my hand. The nurse took away everything, even my son, swathed in my blood.

Did you see him? I asked. He was big, long as my hand.

Flesh of our flesh, blood of our blood, I thought.

All over in fifteen minutes, I thought, no pain, no feeling, so matter-of-factly they had drawn him out, tissue and all, over in fifteen minutes. But then, it did not take even fifteen seconds for him to take life. Not quite; eight hours the sperm takes to travel up the tube to the egg, I told myself, facts and figures bobbing on to my mental screen even as my blood that had swathed my son was being carried away. And I wondered if it was natural for one to be thinking of facts

and figures, and of beautiful words – flesh of my flesh blood of my blood – when one's little one has been carried away.
"Go home. Drive carefully, and get some sleep." I said.
"Yes," he said.

I got up. I should sleep, I told myself even as I got into my work-clothes. I had to go back and look her up. But she was already discharged. She wanted to go home, they told me, and the doctor said everything was okay, all dispelled totally, she was young, she'd be back here in no time with another pregnancy. Don't worry.

Did my face show so clearly, I thought. That would never do. One, we can't get emotionally involved in a case. Two, keep a poker face, no matter what. No matter what. No matter what.

I went home and wrote a long e-mail to Stephen about how I reacted to the whole experience.

~

This is a little spooky, that I should have picked this one today, not yesterday or tomorrow but today, the very evening of the day I spent brooding over that poor young woman.

I had picked it up because it was written back of one of the same posters about the dance concert way back in 1979. I looked at the young dancer with nostalgia again, and felt I was ancient, all the happy years behind me already.

The nurse at the emergency ward seemed overjoyed to see me. Needless to say, we were complete strangers. Her effusive reception reminded me of a cobbler who had taken over the shade of the peepal tree in my parents' house years ago by exercising squatters' rights, and who always greeted us with eloquent enthusiasm and insisted on driving a stitch or extracting a nail from our footwear. He invariably made a bad job of it, so we'd have to come to him shortly after with a genuine problem. He collected an inflated payment from our father for work done and undone.

Who knows what she's after, I told myself, smiling weakly in response.

The nurse touched my sari lovingly. "Beautiful, beautiful," she cooed. "The most feminine dress I've ever seen." And then, with sudden efficiency, she said, "While you are bleeding to death, my dear, do you mind if I see exactly how you wrap all this fabric around you?" She went on to strip me, carefully taking in the intricacies of sari-wrapping, while relating how this handsome young intern who was here two years ago (did I know him? His name was Ali?) had given her a blue sari, which she would wear for this weekend's party now that she knew how to handle it.

At this point, another equally cheery nurse took over while the first bustled off. This one had one look at my problem and dismissed it. "That's all right," she said, "happened to me last year. In my eleventh week I was, and what do I see when I wake up? Blood. So I wake up the hubby, phone the doc, pack my toothbrush and bed jacket and all that, and I go to the john. Before I even sit down, down plunkets the whole works, and I fish it out. Being a nurse, of course I know the whole thing is out, and I phone the doc and tell him so, and send the kids to school, Pete is eight and a monster in the morning, but my baby, she's a doll, she is, and I go about the day's work. But the bloody thing goes on for days, and I have to have a scraping after all. Happens sometimes," she shrugged. Then she went to the peanut-butter jar in which I had stored my findings, and dismissed it in a glance. "Durn small," she said, "Twelfth week did you say?" Yes, I said. Her contempt was withering. "I know you Asians are petite, but this one," she threw another look at the jar, "you must have miscalculated."

I felt I had to assert myself. I said I was positive about that, eleven weeks and a day since my last period, and to clinch the point I said my husband was away for three weeks before the next period was due.

"Ah ha," she said, and winked.

By now the nurse had hoisted me on a stretcher on wheels and had piled my clothes and shoes and handbag in a plastic bag on my feet, and covered me to the chin. Now she wheeled me to the Observation Room. "Say good bye to the hubby while I check your room number," she instructed and left.

My husband was only too glad to say good bye. He was not worried so much that we had left our toddler with our neighbour as about his work. He was in the middle of an experiment, and his insects had a habit of dying on him just as he was all set to draw the final data on that set of cultures or whatever he does in that lab of his. He said he would come back as soon as he could get one of our regular babysitters.

Then another nurse came over, and started ticking off what possessions I had come with. She was not in a good mood and made it clear she didn't like doing the job of a nurse's aide when she was a regular RN. She vented her temper on my sari because it floundered her. Was it to be listed under skirt, or slip, or what? Jewellery, what did I have?

"A gold chain," I said.

"And ring?"

"No, no ring."

She looked at me and I reassessed the contempt in the earlier nurse's look. That one wouldn't reach first base against this one.

"Is that anything valuable?" she asked, pointing to the red dot on my forehead.

"Oh, yes," I said, "Hindu women treasure it."

"Stone? What stone is it?"

"No," I started to explain, "it is just paste, sometimes a powder..."

But she had stopped listening.

"Pshaw," she said.

She thrust the pen into my hand and told me to sign. I signed without reading it. I had read the other statement I was asked to sign at the reception desk, and it had been far from reassuring. The sum and substance of it had been that I had of my own free will come for treatment, and that I would surrender myself to the good judgement of the doctors etc. etc. and that medical science was not infallible, and in short, if I was crippled, made insane, or killed while undergoing treatment, no one but myself was to be held responsible. What I mean is, when you have to sign statements like that, ignorance is bliss.

Then an orderly came up and started wheeling me. At the elevator door, I vaguely wondered about the phrase, "feet first." Was it the custom to wheel a live patient head first into a room and a dead one feet first out of it? or the other way around? I couldn't remember.

"We have company," said a voice, as I was wheeled in.

"They come and they go, but I am going to be here forever, oh," said another moaning voice.

"Company, I've had enough of company," snorted another peevish voice.

When the nurse downstairs had mentioned there was no private or semi-private room available, I could see my husband getting all het up, and I had soothingly said I loved company. A hospital, like a bus stop, was ideal for getting to know human responses. One could strike up an impersonal and enjoyable talk where the very quality of temporariness made the exchange spicy. But I had not bargained for three companions.

Another of those incomplete fragments.   This one had to be autobiographical, I thought, had to be.   That self-deprecating voice always gives away what is about herself and what is not, I thought.   In any case, I guess it helped me, if desensitizing is any help. Same story but the matter is laughed away.   But the poster made me wonder – was this really after 1979 since it was written back of the dance poster? Nothing could be taken for granted. The miscarriage could have happened years earlier or not at all.

I phoned Uncle Siv, and asked him if Maru had ever had a miscarriage. Doesn't everyone? he said, rather dismissively, and asked about Stephen.

~~~~~

SEVENTEEN

Stephen e-mailed me to say he could not write long e-mails the way he had thought he would because there was power outage a lot of times and even at night when he had the time. India, now he knows my India. But he was enjoying his work. That was good to know. I thought he'd get fed-up with all the usual delays.

All six preemies under my care are doing okay, except for baby Vasyl. Marika hadn't been tested for Group B Strep because the test is usually done closer to term. She has two other kids and so we didn't worry at the time but had routinely given her the usual antibiotics. Baby Vasyl was doing okay, gaining weight, he is 480 grams, but yesterday, he had trouble breathing. Today the blood test came out positive for GBS.

I want to know what Maru was like at my age. She was already here in Canada, and I am sure she had all three children by the time she was 30; maybe not all three, must look that up. Did she have any major problems, and if she did, will these cartons tell me anything of what they were and how she resolved them?

The third carton, the one marked P3 seems to have the early stuff as far as I can tell. So that is what I want to play my daily lucky-dip with.

I do wish she had included the year in these diary jottings. Why couldn't she use a regular diary? On the other hand, if she had, I bet she would have used a diary that was not of that year, but may be of ten years earlier, like the one I came across the other day – lovely pictures on the right and just an inch of space for each day of the week on the left. Hoarder, that is what she was, couldn't junk anything beautiful into the waste bin. So, there are a hundred large posters and a thousand postcards in the basement. Poor Uncle Siv, I wonder how he is going to cope with all those collections. If one of his three had been a girl, I am sure things would be different for Uncle Siv. But hey, he has me.

16th July

This afternoon at AssiniboinePark we met an interesting couple, or rather, an interesting woman, the husband said little.

We were walking in the English Garden when we met them
– a woman in a polka dot black on white dress, with a white hat
that had a streaming red band.

Shall I walk up and ask her why she is wearing a cake on
her head?

Probably it is a wedding cake. Must be their anniversary, I
said.

Must be a foreigner. She is the only one dressed up, heels
and hat and all.

Looks like a Mexican.

We lightly exchanged such thoughts and slowly walked
along. She came right up to us and said, "Oh, do you like our
Winnipeg flowers?"

"They are beautiful," I said.

"I suppose you have flowers that we don't have here."

"Some," I said, "and there are some here that we don't
have."

"You are an East Indian, aren't you?"

Several people had called me that, and I knew by now it was
their way of differentiating between someone from India and a
Native Canadian.

"We know an East Indian," she said, "he used to come to
our Church, and one day I said, If he crosses our path, we'll take
him out for pancakes and coffee. And do you know what? His
coat was right next to my husband's and I thought, Well, God
did want our paths to cross. And we went to the Pancake House
and he told us about life in his country. His name is Byron and
he teaches school. And what do you do?"

"I work at a University," I said.

"Oh, you people who come are so talented."

"He is from Trinidad," the husband said.

"And he told us so many things. And I told him to phone
us whenever he came to town. You see, people were so kind and
friendly when we went to Europe, and I told my husband, "It
happens that way because God knows that we try to help people
at home and so folks are friendly."

"I have an Indian boy too. See." She opened her pocketbook
and showed me a picture of a ten-year-old Native Canadian boy
sitting on Santa's lap. "He was burnt in a house fire waist down

and his mother, brother and sister died. He was in the hospital about four months, and now he comes into town once every few months to see the doctor. He came at Easter time for shoes."

"Oh, where does he live?"

"With a foster parent. Her husband was a minister but he died and so she took in two boys, this way she is paid and doesn't have to go out to work. He lives with her. And whenever he comes into town, he phones. Hi Bill, he says, always so cheerful. But I may not be there when he calls next. You see, I have cancer."

I flinched. She was so cheerful and talkative, I couldn't imagine she had cancer.

"It is spreading fast. I started treatment too late. I already have a breast out but it spread down my ribs and arms. I went for deep X-ray and responded well."

"Yes, rapid progress is being made," Siv said, "my father had cancer of the throat and he was cured."

"X-ray?" the man asked.

"Yes, Cobalt ray. Every year they are finding out so many new things about cancer."

"Yes, yes," she said, "but I was too late. I went Christmas before last and they said if it doesn't recur for five years, that would be good. I went again last Christmas and the doctor said some cells had got away. So you see, I am not well now. But then one mustn't think of it; live as long and happily as you can, do you have a family?"

"No, not yet," I said.

"God will bless you in good time. My daughter, she is 27, waited for years and then last August had a miscarriage. But she is expecting again, now. Oh, I am happy with my children. I myself had my first eleven months after we were married. And in the seventh month I tripped. I was always careful but that day I stepped on a loose piece of ice and went rolling down, and there was so much water, I wondered from where it came. I was very young, you see, just twenty. And the doctor said it was the water bag and that I might have a dry birth! Who would believe it in those days, just nine months married, and my mother-in-law said, You'd better carry another two months. No one will believe it otherwise. Fortunately, I did carry another six weeks! Who will believe it, yes? I read a lot. I like to know everything beforehand, you see. It is better that way. I spend a lot of time reading. Yesterday, I was reading about leukemia while my husband was painting."

"Is your father all right now?" her husband asked.

"Oh yes, he's fine."

"Oh, you paint, do you?" I asked.

"He was painting the room. And I said, I think I'll help you. And he said, With your muscles? You see my arm muscles have been removed. And even carrying a handbag is a strain. There is no muscle here."

I bent down and looked at her arm and made a sympathetic sound. I had furtively and wonderingly looked at her one full breast earlier.

"They had to remove it. Tie it off where they give the treatment. And the doctor said the lesions were healing well. Before X-ray, they had this mustard treatment. They give a large dose directly and so could hit the spot straight. Of course, it wasn't as sure a hit as deep X-ray. Even when it spread to my pelvic region, I wasn't worried. I thought it meant just the hip bones, but then I came to know it includes all the organs inside. But, as I say, it is always better to know. There are so many things we don't know. My sister's son, for instance, has to have his testicles operated. They are inverted. I never had a son, so I don't know. I don't talk of my illness to anyone. If neighbours know it, they will have pity." She looked around and lowered her voice. "But we don't need pity. We live as well as we can, God takes care. If anything happens to me, my husband will marry my sister, she is a widow with a son studying for engineering and it will be all right. You see, one must put one's house in order."

How come Maru seems to have met so many interesting people? I can't remember anyone just coming up to me and unloading their life story. And other people's too, a nephew's inverted testicles! The secrets one tells strangers, amazing. May be if I spent a little more time sitting with my patients, I could write reams of fiction.

~

I must scan for Stephen what I found the other day about Maru's meeting with two of her favourite authors. Also, she seems to have started publishing while in India itself, like, this is from a newspaper.

~

When the Time Comes

Chimneys spouting smoke all day long, blackening the aluminum-painted corrugated-iron-sheet roofs, blackening the sky, blackening the little town of Chinnur. The factory dominated over Chinnur and Chinnur's life was in the factory. From their small tenements that the factory had built over their heads years ago and which they now held there with repeated coats of mud plaster, the workers streamed out every morning. The sound of the sirens was their clock – it woke up everyone at five thirty, had them dressed and ready for work by seven and in the factory by eight. Ten, twelve, one, three, five, six, ten-thirty, it announced various shifts and breaks, and decreed Chinnur's routine. Babies were born to the siren, married to its sound and ruled by it. Chinnur had little to do with the outside world, except for the death of national figures, at which time the siren sounded mournfully at eleven.

Lakshman was the son of a factory worker whose family had worked there for three generations. He was an intelligent and meditative boy, qualities which Chinnur did not much care about. It had its schools, of course, and the founder of the township and factory had some idealistic plans. He had made his millions in the "beedi" trade and perhaps to atone for it, he had planned the factory to be an ideal place which treated its workers fairly. Child labour was prohibited, and schools for children were free, as was the library, which he had filled with all the books available at the time.

But that was years ago. With time idealism had fallen and so had the minimum age at which boys could enter as extra hands in the expanding factory. Now, boys born in Chinnur entered the factory as a matter of course, when they or their parents thought they were schooled enough.

Lakshman was different. He had a morbid dread of the factory. He himself could not understand it but it was there and would not be dislodged. From childhood on he had feared the huge chimney that towered over the rest – a massive chimney so black that it was silhouetted even in broad daylight. All day long it smoked, and to Lakshman it smoked away the lives of the workers. At night it was worse – a monstrous projection that silently brooded over Chinnur. Nights on end he had dreamed of it trying to swallow him. The crane lifted him high and there he stood at its mouth, painting it red, a bloody gory red, and then his foot slipped. He hung on to the rim with his hands and the chimney sucked in his hands pulling him up and then down, down, down, into the white heat. Often he had wakened in a sweat with a physical sensation of burning, and lain telling himself it was a dream, only a dream.

But it was a dream that held him.

The idea that the factory sucked in people was never dispelled. Everything suggested some fatal magnetic pull of the factory – the train with the raw material and fuel, the engine driver, a shining god of muscle, sucked in whole. The small doors with their standing-at-attention sentries sucked in the workers who were lost to the world till five – or sometimes forever when steel girders fell or the machines threw mangled corpses on their way or a pit caved in. Lakshman knew about the accidents, had seen the shrouded bodies brought out through iron gates, heard the women wailing, and the silence at the gates of the cremation grounds as the high officials drove in from their Gulbagh residences to offer their condolences.

As he grew older, the fears did not abate but the hatred increased. One day it would swallow him.

There was an escape route. The school. He would study, pass his high school examination, pass whatever else he had to, become a clerk in a bank – yes, that was his ambition – to be a bank cashier.

He worked hard at his studies. Lakshman's parents were proud of him but not unduly so for they did not think it man's work to study – to dig the ground and plant steel girders, to feed the furnace, to work machines – that was man's work, that was the goal for which the good gods had given them flesh and muscles.

It was a November evening. Lakshman was on his way
back from school and stopped by at the library, an apologetic
looking shack where an apologetic old man sat amid books and
magazines that were years old. Once or twice a year he went
from door to door at Gulbagh colony and collected magazines.
Sometimes officers transferred away would bring wooden crates
of books bought on train journeys, and text books their children
had used.

Lakshman had been reading Rajaji's *Vyasar Virundu* for two
weeks now. He had no intention of taking another book but he
liked to stand looking at the titles of the English volumes that
limply stared out of antiquated covers. One day he would read
them – when he mastered all the languages – Kalidasa and
Kamban, Tulsidas and Shakespeare.

Lakshman then entered the park and went to his favourite
peepal tree. He stretched his legs and leaned back. If I can't
finish this book by next week, he thought, I must put it away.
Then study, study, study for the exams – four months and
then....

He would go to Madras, oh the glory of it. He would have
to study some more, he had no idea how much, but he would do
it, and then he would start working in a bank. Every day he'd go
to the beach; perhaps someday he would even wear trousers and
a coat.

The three o'clock siren blared. Lakshman looked at the
chimney. No matter where one was, one could not escape the
chimney, snorting out smoke, waiting, sucking.

And his children would not know a factory chimney; he
would remove the shadow of the monster that hung over his life,
and to them it would be just one of the many projections that
studded a city skyline, not a living sucking monster to which so
many fathers had sacrificed so many sons. Young and strong his
brother had been and now.... He rose, he had to go home, his
mother would be waiting to go to the market so he could be
home with the younger children, two sisters who adored him.

He thought of the serious conversation he had with his
parents some weeks ago. He had told them how he wanted to
study further. They had naturally expected him to join the
factory. His mother immediately said as much. His father said,

"I understand your plans, my son. I have seen you hate the factory though I can't understand why, seeing as it is almost in our blood. We thought you'd join us, but let that not disturb you. Do not enter a job you hate merely because of a sense of duty. You have your life to live, son. We will miss you very much, but our blessings go with you wherever you go." While those words encouraged him, he marvelled at his father's unselfishness. "Not only my children," he told himself, "but my parents too I will move from the shadow of that hateful chimney."

When Lakshman reached home, it was half past three. His father was home already. Must have changed his shift hours, he thought. His sisters were playing hopscotch with the girls next door. His parents sat next to the kerosene stove, silent, waiting for the water to boil. When it did, his mother put in some tea dust and jaggery and milk and let them boil together. The silence surprised him. His mother usually related the day's happenings over their tea, and there was always some tidbits to relate.

Lakshman put away his books. His mother sighed. His father said, "The medical exam. The report came today. They have given me a month's pay."

His father unfit for work? He was so healthy, had never been ill, of course he coughed occasionally but everyone did that. One can't work in a coal-dust saturated factory without coughing occasionally.

"No work?" he said weakly.

"Not for now. If I improve, they will employ me as an outside hand somewhere may be, or maybe not. There are so many youngsters around." Lakshman choked to hear the dispiritedness in his father's voice.

"I have some work," he said, and left the house.

An hour later he returned. His parents were still sitting in the same place. He took off his shirt and hung it on a nail. He took an axe from the corner and went to the door.

"I'll chop some firewood before I go," he said. "I have been taken in the six o'clock shift. Muniyappa gave me a job."

"Work?" his sister asked, "what will your work be?"

"Feeding furnace 4 in C Block," said Lakshman, going out.

Didn't know newspapers published short stories, but this is a newspaper for sure, and under her maiden name. Then she comes to Canada and wins a prize for a story the very first year she was here. And then nothing happens for twenty years. What a pity. Caught up in family and volunteer work and all that, I suppose. But keeps writing some of the time at least, else I wouldn't have this awesome inheritance. What am I going to do with all this? I should keep this safely somewhere – perhaps her first publication? No, she has written somewhere that she won a writing award when she was twelve in an annual competition where she wrote about a boy visiting heaven, that he had called on God, and God appeared rightaway because nobody calls on Him anymore. Then in 2000 she wins the big award – best short story collection of the year, and then she leaves us, just like that.

~~~~~

EIGHTEEN

Baby Vasyl is getting worse. The brain bleed he had earlier was healing okay and we thought everything would work itself out. But yesterday I happened to be there when the nurse changed his diaper and even as she was wrapping the soiled diaper, I noticed a smear of blood. She should have noticed it – just as well I was there. I thought it might be just poop but the results came today, not good news, necrotizing enterocolitis. Poor baby, and poor Marika – she is there most of the day – I wonder if Mikhail is staying home taking care of the other two. Would be nice if her mother could come back and help out. I wonder how they manage – all the mothers of preemies. Our work is so much simpler, seems to me.

    I am exhausted. It is Friday night and I miss Stephen. I eat my Chinese takeout, eggplant-tofu-rice, and I turn to Maru.

    Why am I picking only depressing pieces? Because it is bad-luck phase. Maru used to make fun of that belief but she probably believed it, just as I am leaning that way. It is called Shani Dasai, when your stars are misaligned, with Saturn ruling the roost. Maru had a friend who believed in it totally, especially that with proper propitiation, Saturn could be appeased enough not to dole out total devastation, though a certain amount of bad luck was beyond appeasement. Since this friend had three daughters, none of whom was anywhere near getting married, she was perpetually propitiating Saturn, and saying how there were just five months left for one daughter, a whole year for another but the bad phase would end, had to end. Maru had to be there at every pooja, being a close friend.

    I usually peer into a carton, flick through the stapled stacks of sheets and pick one, anyone. Like dipping into a lucky-dip bag and drawing out a candy, hoping it is chocolate covered and not just one of those hard sucker-type candies. I am too depressed to be dealing with depressing stories. Where are those hilarious anecdotes she used to tell me? Her life at the Y, her early years in Winnipeg, her brief forays looking for work, her long years at the secretary's desks at the U? So today I didn't do my usual lucky-dip thing. I read the first pages of several sheaves and I found one – Off to Kathmandu. I recognized rightaway that this would help me. I loved the anecdote she had told me about her trip to Nepal, how she went with four friends, two of them Nepalis who were going home for the holidays, and visited dozens of temples with her hosts, and remembered only on her flight back that she had forgotten to look for the pornographic sculptures that were supposed to be found at every temple, and how she had totally missed out on seeing live sacrifices, that too were supposed to happen every day at some shrine or another.

The stapled sheets I came across start on page 5. I couldn't find the earlier pages. But this will do. The typing is pretty bad, with a lot of retyping after xing out words and lines. Obviously the trip took place centuries ago, as she said for everything, she had a tendency to exaggerate, and I can, I suppose, find out when she made the trip, and also when did she write it down? Isn't that also important to know? Stephen would give the right suggestion. Why hasn't he written? All those power outages he talked about, said he couldn't use his laptop any more, something wrong with it, and he has to use the office computer when the clerk could spare it.

Off to Kathmandu!

We reached Patna at about four next evening. B, our guide back at the college, had told us she always stayed at Janata Hotel because her father knew the proprietor and we would be safe. G, our Nepali friend, had no advice on hotels because she usually flew home directly from Delhi, and she was taking the train only because we were. We took a taxi and found that it was an awful hotel. It was on a narrow street; a big door with a threshold led us to a quadrangle. The rooms were around the open area. The proprietor gave us the key to our rooms, which we reached through extremely narrow verandahs, and found they were incredibly unlivable. The door was only four foot high and opened into a room that was about eight feet by nine feet. Beyond it was another room about five feet by nine feet. No bed, no shelf, no hanger. The rooms were dirty, with a dirty wall and a dirty window about a foot by two feet. We decided we could not possibly eat there, that we would have a bath to get rid of the train coal dust and then go in search of a good restaurant, somehow survive the night and take the first boat across the Ganga. There was a bathroom bang in the middle of a verandah overlooking the quadrangle. The door could not be latched from inside and the crack between the doors was wide enough to make us think we should drape a sari over the door. I bathed first, and the sari became wet and transparent. We took turns standing at the door so no one came near enough to peer. The water was cold, and we were not used to cold water.

Dressed and fresh, we left in search of a good restaurant. The main road was not far and we walked down. The alleys were filthy and so were all roads except for the main street. So this was our late President's birthplace, I thought, this was the capital of Bihar! God guard the people of this state!

We were quite hungry but we thought we should enquire about the steamer timings, and so we asked our way to Paleja Ghat.   Off the main street, through a patch of dark and frighteningly lonely alley, we reached the docks. It was crowded as could be. We stood in the wrong queue and then found the right one.   We were informed that there was a steamer at 8:30 that night and another only after nine next morning.   One thought of spending the night at Janata Hotel was enough to make us decide we'd take the 8:30 steamer even if it meant having to skip dinner. We bought second class tickets to Raxaul and hurried back. We found a good clean restaurant but as with good restaurants, our orders took forever to come; so that when we did get our orders, we were so scared we'd miss our steamer, we ate hurriedly and ran back. We took three rickshaws – they are really weird out there, low, with brakes way down below so the man had to bend all the way to the ground, and bells that he jangled constantly. The rickshawallahs cheated us but I don't remember to what degree.

Getting into the steamer, (it was called Jal-? Something, Jal-Azad?) was an ordeal, mainly because we had agreed to carry a trunk each for two other Nepali students who were taking a flight home.   The crowd was unbelievable and unbelievably dirty. At last we were on the steamer. Our luggage was safe and we had standing space! The third class was downstairs and jam-packed, with no benches at all.   Here in the second class deck, there were benches along the side of the boat but every seat was taken already; in any case, even if we had got a seat, our backs would have been to the river. We had comfortable standing space and watched a young woman bidding a heartbreaking farewell to a young man on the wharf.

The siren sounded, the anchor was drawn, and we were off! But from our position in the middle of the deck, we could not see the river. We tried to walk towards the side of the steamer but crying babies and sharp-cornered trunks drove us back. Then three of us, the non-Nepalis, to whom this was a rare experience, with great airs and confidence climbed up a flight of stairs to the first class. This was indeed a steamer. A huge hall with the top deck partly covered, and open all along the side. There were benches that faced the water, and with cushions to boot!

Our spirits soared. It thrilled me no end to think we'd cross the Ganga in a steamer, a real steaming steamer, and that any river could be so wide as to need a whole hour to cross it. It was a bit disappointing that we were here at night, but that was okay. The river lay around us, dark, foaming, roaring, the waves lashed the sides of the boat and circled back in wreathing white. The lights on the shore receded. It was beautiful – on the first class deck it sure was beautiful. Below was the smell of samosas and puri-aloo, and human sweat. But here we were on the beautiful deck, walking round and round, stopping, watching the roaring water. A chill wind sprang up. I went down to our suitcases and took out a sweater so as to fully enjoy the experience. Wishful thinking. Within minutes the lights on the other shore came into view. We scuttled back to our suitcases.

As I said, we were overloaded – though the three of us had only a light suitcase each, G and C, our Nepali friends, had heavy trunks, and there were the two trunks we were carrying for our other Nepali friends. We had to have porters. C went off to enlist one. The steamer drew alongside a huge floating wharf. There were no lights. There appeared to be a train on the track several hundred yards away. Soon C appeared with a porter, who heaved the luggage and sprinted away. We hurried behind him. The sand was so soft, so silken soft that I wished I could feel them under bare feet. Soon enough I did. My chappal slipped off and since the momentum had already carried me a few feet and since the wave of people behind enveloped me, I had a hard time going back and retrieving my errant chappal. I ran with both chappals in hand. The porter had vanished. I had visions of him slinking away in the dark with all our baggage. I looked back and there he was. Our feet sank into the sand and it was a job to take each step.

Halfway across the beach, I noticed that the train had vanished. We had missed our connection! But the porter assured us that was not our train. We unloaded ourselves of all the bags we had slung all over ourselves, and waited.

There were hundreds of people on the sand platform. Thousands, it seemed to me, when it came time to board the train. There was no raised platform; the floor of the carriage was four feet and more above the ground. Try climbing vertical train steps; try it with bags in hand. And the crowd.

There was only one second class carriage in sight. We elbowed our way into it; I think a man politely stood aside for one of us to board, but we tailed behind each other, which made him quite mad. We were literally standing on our own toes. But great is the power of travellers' will. Ours and others'. We edged and we were pushed, elbowed those in front of us and were elbowed by those behind us, and by degrees we wedged our way into the narrow aisle between the single seats and the long benches in a carriage meant for 30 people. And can you believe it? A man in khaki was stretched out on one of the six benches! Lying full length when there were fifty people and fifty steel trunks to be accommodated. He was sleeping, or pretending to. This is where the third class travellers are better. There, he would have been upped onto his own behind. Those who buy second class tickets are kind-of educated and quiet and in short cringing when it comes to putting folks in their place. They hesitate about heaving a sleeping man; they feel he has a right to occupy the place because he took the trouble to reach first. Huh! Never travel second class. At best, you find co-travellers who are distant and polite; at worst you find they are aloof and unhelpful. Not so the average third class passenger. He will curse you and the succeeding seven generations to eternal damnation when you enter the carriage, but will move up and make room for you; he will acknowledge your presence – which second-class folk seldom do.

Seeing young women, he pulled his knees up so one of us could sit. Three of us sat on our trunks, and after a while, he pulled his knees higher so one more could sit. The night passed. We even slept a little.

It was close to seven when the train arrived at Sugaoli. We were late. The connecting train to Raxaul was scheduled to leave at seven. We rushed about, unloading our luggage, hollering out to a coolie, and raced to the train. It was about to start. The guard was at its rear, waving a green flag. The last whistle was blown, and there we were, the first of us, a hundred feet from the rear end of the train. We yelled. The guard turned, saw us and lowered his green flag and raised the red flag. The noise of the engine working up steam decreased promptly. "Thank you, thank you, we won't hold you up more than a minute," I panted to the guard. I spoke too soon. Even as I looked back, one of the trunks flew off the coolie's head and split open on the platform. The guard's face hardened. I was getting ready to appeal to his sense of pity for the red flag was being perceptibly lowered and the green flag was being raised. But then I guess he saw the comic angle of the catastrophe, and held up the red flag clear and high. We shoved in all the embarrassing articles of clothing that had fallen out, and clambered into the train.

We were luckier this time. There were only three other passengers in the compartment. We settled ourselves down. In these narrow gauge trains, the benches run alongside the side of the train. If you want to look at the landscape, you have to turn sideways and crick your neck. But sometimes it is worthwhile. As now.

Dawn was breaking. Calm air, blue-pink sky, silent fields. Beautiful Nature is always so beautiful. But uncontrollable too. It was morning, and the body answers to Nature. Nature's call, I mean. I took a plastic tumbler and went to the toilet. No water, hadn't been any for quite some time judging by the stink and the remains. My first impulse was to rush out. But when Nature calls, it will not be denied. So a scrap of newspaper and I parted ways a few minutes later.

In a couple of hours, we reached Raxaul. Journey's end, for the time being anyway. We could take our time, no connecting trains to be caught, no guard to be placated. We could afford to let fall a trunk or two and pick up the contents at leisure. So I felt. But not G and C.

You know how it is; you tend to quicken your step on the last lap homeward, even if it is only an evening walk you had been to. I have noticed if often, especially the walk to the Y from the college. Analysis would probably show the motivating force to be hunger and allied needs. But no doubt the heart reacts in some people the way my stomach does. G and C wanted to reach home, home with a capital H. After almost a year away. I could sympathise.

So we decided to rush off to Birganj, the Nepali border town. C thought if we went fast, we could get one of the jeeps, of which there were never enough for those who came late. And if we got one of the Jeeps instead of the bus, we could be home by early evening. Their breaths choked with excitement – home by evening!

Okey dokey, we said, though the three of us would have loved a good breakfast. Raxaul is the Indian border town. The station was fairly imposing – a big, neat, empty platform. U said her dad knew a local big shot and she could phone him, but G and C felt that would take too much time, and we'd miss out on taxis at Birganj.

So we bundled into two tongas and left Raxaul station. Tell me when we cross the border, I said. What is it like? Are there sentries and border-lines? C said there wasn't anything on the Indian side, and that we just crossed a river.

No matter. I was still thrilled. A river. Over the bridge and farewell to my own my native land. Raxaul, brave little town on our border, farewell. India, I shall soon bid adieu. My homeland, I am going to leave you now. Across the river and I shall be in an alien land, in another kingdom, another government. Not India but Nepal! Not for long, dear old India, not for long. And if I should, not that it is likely but if, highly improbable I know but if I should die, dear land of the Vedas, land where the Ganga flows, lovely land of song and dance, remember I was proud to call you mine, proud I was thine. And now I am about to enter Nepal! Beautiful Nepal, tucked away in the Himalayas, land of temples and sacrifices, land of hills and valleys, beautiful little kingdom with a real live king!!! And pageants and processions! And cold and snow!

[All this melodramatic declamations might sound hokey but one, they are my usual tongue-in-cheek exaggerations and two, I honestly felt more sentimental then than when I stood on the S.S.

Orsova and watched the lights of Bombay twinkle themselves
into darkness.]

"We have to stop here at the sentry post," said the
tongawallah.
"I'll speak in Nepali and he will be pleased," H said.
"Nepali? Are we in Nepal already?" I asked.
We had just trundled across a wooden bridge over a sewer,
or what I thought was a sewer-canal. It was the river! The river
that separated India and Nepal.
It was a thudding blow to me. I felt cheated. I mean, I didn't
expect a board announcing 'You are leaving the Republic of
India' or any such thing. Heck, I didn't expect a welcome band
or a red carpet and buntings hanging across the road proclaiming
'Welcome to Nepal.' But I mean, a sewer, a wooden bridge, and
that's it? A rather ignominious exit from one's motherland, what?
A little something, a carved stone column from one of those
hundreds of excavations, or a little travellers' bench, a tree with a
placard nailed to its trunk, a flagpole with the tricolour....heck, at
least a sentry post with officious, pretentious rogues in uniform
plaguing the life out of you asking for name, authorisation,
contents of baggage.... I don't ask for much, just a little
something to help you feel the difference, so you won't feel
absolutely crushed when you notice, as you must, the appalling
sameness of landscape of the two countries.
Everything was the same. Same kind of trees, the same
bumpy road, the same kind of pigs grunting the same way as
they gurgled down the same kind of food. Cheer up, I told
myself. You are in Nepal. What if the pigs look alike? These are
Nepali pigs eating Nepali shit. A fact you cannot deny. Thrilling,
don't you think?

Birganj is about three miles from Raxaul station. It is a small
town, a dirty little town with mud houses built wall-to-wall on
narrow, dusty streets. It stinks. Of mud, of shops, of shit and
urine. The very sight of the streets, the very first breath of the
smells gave me a sinking feeling.
We proceeded to the shop where we were to be met by C's
family friend. He told us the Jeep-taxis for the day had all left

already and we would have to stay at Birganj till next morning but he had made all the arrangements. He was a tall, lean young man, good looking in a way. He took us to his house. The street was too narrow for the tonga to enter and so we got off and walked to the house while the men brought in the luggage. His mother and wife greeted us and we were given a room upstairs. We cheered up and loved them for being so cordial. We were given tea, the consistency of thin honey, and as sweet. There was no bathroom. Water was scarce, placed in buckets along the wall. The *lotas* they gave us were shining clean, but the buckets were dirty. I feared the inner sides of the buckets would be soft with that squishy something that forms on the walls of water-containers. I used as little as I could, knowing water was scarce. The latrine had a sack cloth for door. There were two latrines, both piled high, with flies. Flies buzzing around, huge ones with green backs, the usual small black ones, bigger ones with red eyes, who knows how many other kinds. Ugh.

It was past noon when we started out for lunch. When at Patna, I had told myself to tell everyone thinking of staying there, "Don't choose Janata Hotel," but I didn't even bother to remember the name of this restaurant, for my advice is, Don't ever stay in Birganj, period.

As we were nearing the restaurant, C's pains started. She held her side, gritted her teeth, and like a martyr walked on until we reached the restaurant. On the stone bench at its entrance, she collapsed.

This took me by surprise. I did not know what calamity had struck. G sat beside C, took her head into her lap and pressed her forehead, which had grown quite white. Her cheeks were white, and her lips were dark, quite black. "It is nothing," G said, "she gets cramps every month."

A natural phenomenon, one that was to plague us all through Project Kathmandu. But not in this way. Nothing like the suffering C was undergoing. She writhed, drew up her legs, stretched them again, lay limp for some time; then tense, hands and lips clenched, she writhed. Even her mouth could not be opened to pour some water. G sent our host to get some Aspirin. We stood around, worried, embarrassed. Someone told us a room was ready upstairs. We half carried her up and laid her on the mattress on the floor. I think she slept for half an hour after the episode that had taken a half hour. The whole thing shook us up, U and me for sure. We just did not know such things happened, that girls suffered such agonies. Our surprise was increased listening to the other two calmly relating experiences that girls they knew went through each month, sufferings that we had never imagined possible for so natural a thing. I distinctly remembered my own initiation, a no-event where Mother told me that just as boys started shaving, girls had this thing once a month for three days, and that I need not go to school that day. I even remember the panties I had on that morning – one of those we made twice a year in our sewing class and on which we were marked on the hemming and backstitch and the little embroidery with daisy stitch and chain stitch. That was it. I had not known anything about it till then and I wasn't any wiser about the hows and whats of it for years after. In those early years, I often wished the nuisance would stop and never come again, but one day I overheard a tidbit of conversation between Mother and her friend when an orange-seller had come and gone, that she was a hijra, and hijras often had beards and no breasts and no menstruation. Those five minutes of eavesdropping on adult conversation did me a world of good. I welcomed the monthly nuisance. Better four days of discomfort than a beard and no breasts.

It had always been a day or two of careful watching to avoid a disgraceful exhibition of stains, and occasionally feeling some discomfort. I could not imagine such torment and agony. I had heard of girls keeping away from class, seen them sitting out instead of joining in PhysEd, and heard from S. our student in charge of the medicine cabinet at college, saying a majority of girls suffer a lot every month. But I had never actually seen it. The aspirin took effect and C seemed okay.

Sometime later lunch was served. Served. Ha! Some service, some servers. Dirty plates loaded with half cooked rice with stones and husks, dirty bowls of dal and dirtier bowls of potatoes. And dirtiest of all was the serving boy. His face hadn't been touched by water for days, or his hair by a comb or scissors for years. His nose was chock filled with dirt. A boy of eleven or twelve, and his face all stained and dirty like a two-year-old's

that had a cold and had just come from a muddy playground.
Even as I write, I am getting nauseated. Ugh.

The food was quite inedible. As a special service, we were
given yogurt in dirty brass bowls, all green inside where the *kalai*
had worn off. And on top of it all, our host came in and
solicitously asked if we needed more of anything. Honest, I can
feel vomit in my throat even now as I write.

I am not fastidious about cleanliness. I have had meals at
wayside restaurants and enjoyed them – the kind of places where
the chapatti dough has a few mashed-in flies, where you have to
fan the sweetmeat tray to find out what delicacy lay hidden
under the flies. Picking ants from *dahi-badas* and eating the rest
without batting an eyelid is not a feat for me. I've done it many
times – on our badminton trips for instance – though I am not
sure I could do it in the future. But I draw the line at Birganj.
Even a toughened traveller like me couldn't stand the filth, the
stink, the plain dirt of the people and the place. Usually I wallow
in relating such experiences, but I cannot dwell on our Birganj
stay. Suffice it to say we had dinner that evening at a slightly
better place, slept in our host's house or rather lay tortured by
giant mosquitoes that left welts on our faces and limbs, and left
next morning from the dirtiest hole I've ever been burrowed in.

But now I must write about the fountainhead of our
problem that started spouting for C in Birganj that afternoon.
When C came to, she threw a bombshell. "Too bad, we can't go
to Pashupati Temple for another three days. In fact, I can't go to
any of the good places because we are not allowed to cross a
stream in this condition."

And details followed. Her family was very strict about it. A
woman having her period wasn't allowed to come into any of the
rooms in the house but stayed in a small room. She wasn't
permitted to eat with others; sitting far from the kitchen, she had
to eat off an iron plate. Any place she walked on, anything she
touched, had to be washed. Her touch desecrated. Holy water
was splashed on all parts of the house she used. And most
certainly, she could not enter any temple and Pashupati temple
was of course the holiest. May be she could not come within a
mile of it.

We listened in rapt attention. I did. I sure did. And I had good reason to. For I expected mine to start any day now. I hadn't given it a second thought. I knew all along of course that it would start during the week I was in Nepal. But what did it matter – I was stocked with pads and all I needed was some newspaper to wrap them in and throw them away. I could at a pinch shred and flush it down the toilet, though that was not a good idea. No trouble, no one need know, or if they did, what does it matter? Ha, what indeed.

I spoke about my problem to U in Tamil. We laughed. For of course it was a hilarious predicament. To tell or not to tell. That was the question. Whether it was nobler in the mind to hush it and desecrate the whole house or to confess and be slung out with an iron plate to eat from.

Oh, the advantage of having your own language! U and I could discuss it loud and long, without the others understanding a word of it, thanks to our mother tongue, however fragmentary our grasp of it, schooled as we had been only in other languages.

To tell or not to tell? Obviously NOT. But how to hide it? Oh, just flush it down.

What about going to the temples – almost every tourist place was a temple. Well, let us finish the main temple first day before it starts. Pashupati was the only real temple for me – the rest were for their architecture and gardens or whatever. As we spoke on, U held her head in her hand, "Oh no," she whispered, all this talking about it made her feel hers was getting ready to start even though it wasn't due for two weeks! And we laughed so loudly and long, the others were pretty miffed we were speaking in a language they didn't understand.

Off we were next morning, with our luggage and our mosquito welts and our fears. I don't know what happened to the Jeep-idea that had made G and C rush to Birganj without having what might have been our last clean breakfast for days, but we found ourselves in a bus that was far worse than the train ride from the beach. G and C had told us of how steep the road was and how nauseous the winding ascent. We started on an empty stomach so there would be less to throw up.

The bus was full. The front was first class, and had a little more leg space than the back of the bus. We were in high spirits once the bus moved. Sitting at the front, the human odours from those behind us were blown back by the moving bus, and we watched the scenery unfold as the bus climbed the hills. Half way in our journey, three hours from Birganj, was our lunch break. We were hungry, except for C who had started feeling ill again. We were half way up the mountains and our stomachs had held. No problem. We could eat now. And we did. Puris and potatoes and some bottled soda drink.

An hour after we left that place, we started feeling sick. First was C, G helping her clean up with her water bottle. Then it was G's turn. U closed her eyes and refused to feel sick by telling herself over and over again that she wouldn't. I closed my eyes and did likewise. The smell was awful – have you ever thought how one smells more acutely with eyes closed? It started raining and people by the windows drew down the canvas sheets to keep the rain out. This increased the stench. Of human clothes that had been there all along on the passengers at the back, unwashed or washed-but-not-fully dry; then of human sweat rising above the smell of *beedis*; everyone smoked, men, women, even the children, and almost submerging all else, the smell of food brought by the other passengers – garlic and onions and strong masalas. Ugh, ugh a thousand times. Any wonder we felt sick, even if there was no steep ascent, with the bus swerving now to the right now to the left?

I started to feel really really sick. It was coming up, and no doubt about it. Luckily, the bus stopped. One woman got out, squatted on the ground and threw up – a mountainous pile. A dog came and started licking at the pile. Everything in my stomach torrented upwards but I held my own. I should have turned away, of course. But the pile was fascinating. That a single stomach could hold so much! I felt myself losing control at both sides of my alimentary canal. I swallowed and sat tight. Fortunately the bus started and the fresh air revived me.

It was almost dark when we reached Kathmandu. We took a taxi (all taxis were Jeeps) and drove to C's place, through narrow, dimly lit streets. The jeep could not enter the narrow alley that led to her house, and so we got out and walked up. Servants ran out to get our luggage. Her folks were at the front of the house to greet us - C's mother, two sisters in law, both very sweet looking, and their chubby beautiful little children. Her mother smiled broadly and welcomed us in Nepali. The first thing C told them was about her condition and how she could not embrace them.

We went in. It was a huge house. There were four floors. It was typical of the aristocracy of thirty years ago. It was built of crudely made bricks, the floors were of mud, and the staircases of solid wood, polished to a sheen. The ground floor had a kitchen and a room for the servant and smaller stalls for the cows and fowls. The kitchen was large, about 250 square feet. One half was for the mud stoves and the other for dining. The staircase led up to our floor. There were three or four rooms on each floor. Our room was carpeted from mud wall to mud wall. There were numerous bolsters to lean against.

We were thrilled. We

It ends there, right in the middle of a sentence. Probably a baby woke up or the phone rang, and then she never got back to it, I guess. But the original must be somewhere, handwritten, in one of those Indian notebooks, seven inches by nine, with a very colourful god or goddess picture on the cover, they sure seem to love Ganesha pictures for note book covers, judging by the notebooks in which she has written her notes for the Chittammai biography. Or may be she wrote it up here in Canada, on those lined three hole reams she bought every summer at school opening sales in spite of knowing no one needed them.

But I wasn't going to look for it. Enough was enough. Why did she write about all this awful stuff? Stephen would say it is realism and to tell it like it is is commendable. Of course all this is real, I don't doubt it, but that doesn't mean one has to tell it like it is. We don't tell our babies' parents everything that happens. It is bad enough for us when we know the prognosis is not good, and it is not that we hide facts from them, just that we choose what to tell and what does no good being told. But in a piece of fictional writing, what are the rules, what the criteria of where one draws the line? I guess it is different for different people. That story Maru had once told me, for instance, about Kathmandu – about the round shining brass plate the maid brought to their room that first night and left in a corner. They found out it was for peeing into at night because the outhouse was a long way off and the air was cold at night. As they lay in bed, U and she laughed and laughed, imagining crawling in the dark looking for the right corner, crouching over, the tinkle of pee on the brass, and the idea of two people carrying the plate out in the morning, like how worshippers carefully carry an *arati* plate of yellow turmeric and kumkum water from the pooja place and sprinkle it just outside the front door with prayers. And how they laughed too because the pee-plate was so shiny and clean whereas the dinner plates had been of white enamel gloss with a blue rim, and everyone knows only dogs' plates and bedpans were made of metal with white enamel gloss and blue rims. And after all that laughing they felt their bladder bursting and then the question was 'To pee or not to pee,' and they decided that rather than use the brass plate, they would walk all the way in the dark to the outhouse and back. When one of the family got up on hearing them go downstairs, they sheepishly said they were going to the outhouse so as to keep the plate for the middle of the night visit, it being so cold and all, bladders had a tendency to distend middle of the night. That was U – she was a science student and though she was a chemistry major, she rather loved biology and kidney talk.

I think those stories are side-splittingly funny, but others might think they are sick, the way I do of this scatology. I wish Stephen were here so we could discuss it further.

~~~~~

NINETEEN

Stephen hasn't written or called. His last e-mail was short. His laptop was still at the shop being repaired. He was using the office computer and so did not write much. He described how the van had broken down on the way to the village and that when they arrived hours later, the fifty people who were scheduled to be seen that day were still patiently waiting.

My little Vasyl is struggling, and tomorrow we will be working on him, poor little guy. This morning we had a session on whether to go for laparotomy with bowel resection or peritoneal drainage. Dr. N. decided to go with laparotomy in this case. It will be a learning experience for me. Marika is tense and her milk is not flowing, bad news. I explained to her that her milk would help a lot, and I sure hope that did not increase her stress level. She said her mother was coming out next week, that is good news. I am glad for her. I was with her when her other kids came by this evening to see her – she is staying with Vasyl tonight. They are cute kids, a little thin and small for their age, but bright. "We'll be good, Mamma," they said; "You take care of Baby," the little guy said. Sad, so sad.

~

I think I will read one of these seven or eight notebooks with a university logo.   Each is from a different University bookstore. Looking at them, one would think she had studied at a dozen different universities. But that was Maru's habit – whenever she accompanied Uncle Siv to a conference, she would spend a little fortune at the Bookstore with the logo and name stamped on all the usual mementos – t-shirts for the boys, spoons for her collection, binders, coasters, pencils and pens. Poor Uncle Siv, I wonder how much of the cleaning up he's done. If I know him, nothing; I bet it's weeks since he even went to the basement except to do his laundry.

~

There must be a hand guiding my hand. I found the Nepal story in the very first book I picked up. It was all in the form of notes, all the main details, with notes about episodes in the pages that were missing in what I had read. But it was still incomplete, the handwriting trailing off in the middle of a sentence about how surprised they were to see that the women in the house smoked. The note book had a black cover –

maybe that's why I picked it up – for my mood. Michigan State University, it reads, founded 1855, 100 sheets, 65 cents. Wonder when she went to Michigan and for what. The price should help figure out when she bought it. Which doesn't mean it was when she wrote in it. Ha.

On the first page of the note books are these words:

In this I mean to write a great deal – everything I can on different autobiographical incidents that come to me. I hope I can get the privacy to write things down. If there is one thing I cannot do, it is to write any of my own creative stuff when others are around.

A couple of blank pages and then:

If I should die, let no one mourn me for long for I have held the joy of the world in my womb and in my arms. Yeats was such a nincompoop when he said, "What youthful mother... would think her son, did she but see that shape/ With sixty or more winters on its head,/ A compensation for the pang of his birth..." Who remembers the pangs once one holds one's newborn baby in one's arms. That first moment is compensation enough for the nine months past and ninety years to come, but what would he know, a mere man.

At least I have one answer – this Kathmandu chapter was written only after Arvind was born. I noted that down on the first page.

The note book has more entries – it has pen sketches of people she knew at the hostel – very interesting, except that it doesn't sound like the YWCA. I know about the Y. It was presided over by Lady B. a big bosomy woman who ran the place so stingily, she halved the debt in two years and cleared it in three. The Y residents were VESPURS and a few others. There were only two tables in the dining room, each to seat may be ten or maximum twelve. But in this place, there seem to be a lot of people, and a whole slew of teachers as well. Did Maru ever live in a bigger hostel? Even Uncle Siv may not know about all this.

~

Holy kamoli, what an interesting place, with episodes happening every day that could fill ten novels. And the details with which Maru has described each person, one of those sketchers who sketch for criminal court cases could draw them with eyes closed – so clear are the descriptions. I wish I could have such a clear picture of even one of the girls in VESPURS.

Quite an intricate plot could be made of all this, with several lead characters that weave in and out of the story.

I like S.

S was stout, not in an unbecoming way but in a way women in their thirties are stout. She always wore a white sari with a coloured border, like many Bengali women in their mid-thirties. Her hair was always well-oiled and neatly coiled into a tight, low bun back of her neck. She had a smooth, wheat-coloured skin, small eyes, a flattish nose and wide mouth. She had moles on her face, a large mole somewhere near her lips, a longish chin, teeth spaced out, fair smooth round arms, soft rather short fingers. She was serious and mature. She used no kumkum or ornaments, and that made me think she was a widow. But one day she told me her story, not as a confidence but matter-of-factly. Her parents had arranged her marriage despite her telling them often enough that she never intended to get married. The young man was rather nice in every way, good family background, a good job, good looks, good temperament. Three weeks before the wedding date, she threw a small bundle of clothes out through her window, told her mother she was going for a walk, picked up her bundle, and went to the station. She boarded the train to Calcutta, joined the Ramakrishna Mission and wrote to her parents of what she had done. She stayed there for several years and then came back, to continue her studies.

So she could have been younger than thirty, but she looked thirty five. I admired her courage, her straight clear execution of her decision. She was in charge of many things at the hostel, including the medicine cabinet to which she alone had a key, and girls obeyed her more readily than they did any of the resident teachers.

K. was head girl. She was a striking personality, the type girls would fear and admire, and authorities dislike and suspect as a troublemaker but cannot accuse of anything because her conduct and speech were so unimpeachable. She was short and had a good figure; she usually wore salwar-kameez, but looked lovely in a sari. On the hockey field, her fair smooth legs were whistled at by all who whistle at girls. She was called the Madhubala of the college, a tribute by loafers and roadside Romeos to her colour and looks. But the actress, as I recall, was sweet and damsel-in-distressy, whereas K irradiated hauteur and defiance. When she was not laughing, her expression was disdainful. She wore no make-up because her fair skin and pink lips needed none. She could have done with some oil on her brown unkempt hair, which she tied in a single braid, as was the fashion. She had smart outfits, but they, like her, had a "I-don't-care-a-hang" look.

She was not very good at English but she didn't care about that either. It was this air of hers that infuriated authorities, Miss B in particular. Even when she was perfectly polite she seemed impertinent. Her words were always correct but that air conveyed what they were meant to convey – I care a tittle for you and the likes of you. A confrontation between Miss B and her was a sight. Miss B would rage, her flat nostrils quivering and her breath short-drawn in anger, and K would stand at ease, her hands behind her back, her mouth and eyes in cool disdain but her words always polite. Miss B would accuse her of intentionally making herself the target of whistles, and of engineering happenstance meetings with boys when they went shopping, and K would say she had no such intentions and it was rather unfair of Miss B to make such allegations. Miss B would fume, "Don't talk to me in that impertinent voice," and K would say in a cool tone, "I am sorry, Miss, that you feel that way."

Did this iceberg ever feel emotion? Was she ever brought low from her proud heights? I rather admired her, for unlike my colleagues I was not a hostel "authority" in charge of anything.

It was during the Ki affair that I saw a chink in the armour and wrote a story around that.

Ki was a fragile, delicate creature. She was thin, her bones sticking out back of her neck. She had high cheekbones, thin pink lips, small but round eyes that appeared big, with the whites almost blue. Her nose was big and sharp, too big and parrotlike for the rest of her delicate face. Her hair was curly; her forehead was rather too wide to be beautiful but she was a beauty. She should have been called "Lata" for she was wispy like a vine, and needed to cling to somebody. Because such demands always get supplied, there were many who loved to spoil her with their help and attention. None more so than K, whose aura of superiority comfortably blanketed Ki from any problems she had with her late papers and frequent absenteeism.

Ki was called away home early in her third school year and came back after two months, married. She now wore beautiful saris, all new, all expensive and hand-embroidered. She dressed very elegantly in crisp cotton saris, and it was a pleasure to look at her. Soon it was clear she was pregnant. Everyone agreed it was no fun at all getting pregnant within ten weeks of being married. Ki was not happy either, and especially when K was around, had little good to say about her husband.

One day I came to the staff dining room to find Miss B furious. Ki had been rushed to the hospital the previous night and had been operated on to prevent a fatal haemorrhage. An emergency D&C had been performed. Her parents had been telegraphed, as also her husband. Her husband was expected that morning and the parents early afternoon. K wanted to visit her that morning, and Miss B. refused her permission – she wanted the family to have privacy. K went there anyway, and the story was that K had been there when the husband arrived; and that Ki had turned away from him, refusing to acknowledge him. And K had said, "You are a brute. You wanted only her body. Look what you have done to her."

The real story came out all too soon by putting two and two together. For the doctor had somehow got it out of Ki that she had taken more than one Codopyrin. Miss B checked with S about it. Soon it was established that Ki had asked S for Codopyrin for a headache three days running. Clearly she had stored all six tablets and taken them all at once to induce abortion. The emergency surgery took place on the fifth day. No wonder Miss B was purple at the gills. Whether the parents or husband ever found out all this is a moot question.

There she goes again. Maru. Can't figure out how much of this is true and how much fiction. She purposely misleads with little preambles such as "wrote a story around that." I think all her stories are true and she just wants to mislead me into thinking it is fiction. But I don't know what to make of the story that is on the next page to Ki's. Is it for/about what might have happened to Ki or is the subject someone like S? An alternate story – we know Maru had alternate endings to some of her poems.

Several months before their child was born, a change came over her. She was as one possessed with a secret joy. A glow radiated from her eyes; it was reflected in her movements that became light and swinging, as though she walked above the earth; it was there in the shine of her filled-out skin, a secret joy that separated her from the world, as though she was a world entire unto herself, a world that had no contact, needed no contact with anyone, anything. He felt her remoteness, jealously watched her secret pleasures at the movements within; he knew she was lost to him, as she lay with their child, talking endlessly to it with closed eyes, and hearing its answers with her hands. No one but he knew this because she was as always a part of the household life within the large extended family. But he knew, and he patiently waited for the day she would return to him with their newborn.

When the son was born, the son she had treasured in joy and fulfilment, so exclusively, so secretly, so engrossedly, when she handed over the tiny lustily-crying baby to her mother-in-law, after crossing the threshold of the house decorated with rangoli and an arati of turmeric and kumkum for their return, when she placed their son in the older woman's arms, it was as though she was giving him away, abdicating all connection, all claims over him, as though there was nothing at all between herself and the child, as though she was closing an account, paying back a debt and closing the account. She was, as before, as always, gentle and quiet. And as always, remote, silent. And he alone knew. She nursed their son, bathed him, crooned him to sleep, but he knew she was lost to both of them and to the world.

Here is another of those alternate angles. Is there a reason for this pattern of trying to figure out something? I suppose a photographer would do that – move to a different angle, different exposure, tilt the camera up, down, yes, I suppose that is it.

He and his father had always hit it off splendidly. Even before he was born, his father had only to place his hand upon my abdomen and he would jump up and around, reaching out with his arms and knees. But with me, he was always cold.

~

He had never responded to his father, never acknowledged his presence. Before he was born, I would talk to him and he would always respond, now with a kick, now with a nudge of his elbows, but whenever I placed his father's palm against him, he would never allow his father the pleasure of feeling him, but would lie still, or worse turn into a hard ball of stone as though holding himself away from his father's touch.

1960s. I found this in the early writings carton. Interesting to know newspapers published poetry!!!

The Girls' Dormitory   Sept. 1961 Hitavada

By day twelve neat beds in double row,
Twelve desks and chairs,
Trunks beside the cots.
Evening.
Tumult and songs, pillow fights,
Gossip, quarrels, hatched and reconciled.
And then comes the night.
Ten-thirty. Lights off.
And each to her bed retires.
Twelve girls each an island unto herself,
Alone, the loneliness stabbing all the more
Because the stretched hand can touch
The next figure, friend by day
Stranger now. Far away.
Each alone with her thoughts
That assume frightful magnitude by night.
Home, Father are you well?
Brother across the seven seas
Are you lonely, lonely like me?

Me straying far, or am I?
The pillow receives the silent tears,
Twelve pillows perhaps but each alone.
Each huddled figure alone with her thoughts,
Alone, all alone in the big black dorm,
The cold unfriendly dorm with beams from passing trucks
Throwing ghostly shadows and forms
On the bleak wall.

~

I found this scribbled on an envelope – an investment broker's
envelope, one of those with windows for the address. So certainly not
from the 60s or 70s, I doubt she had an investment broker till much
later. So why is it in this carton? This should be a good beginning to my
day:

I am stepping up on the social ladder. The dream of getting lost
on a hillside or in some underground labyrinthine hutments is
now getting upped to getting lost in a posh hotel – getting into an
elevator that goes only straight up to the top and down again. I
had a room on the second floor. You know how it is in tall
buildings – some elevators go straight to the penthouse level,
some only to floor nineteen and up etc. So I looked for an
elevator that stops on all floors and several of us got in and soon
I found, through a glass door on one side of the elevator, that we
were speeding along horizontally as in a train! Someone thought
of pushing the STOP button but I was afraid that if we stopped in
the middle of nowhere, uh oh! Better to keep going until we
reached some terminus where help will be available.
        At least in this dream there are people in the same boat as I
am. Or train, or elevator or whatever.

I've got to get a binder for just the dreams. I am sure if they are read all
at one time, they will tell me something. But that is silly, really, unless
some stuff appears again and again. May be they should be read in light
of something she wrote at that time – then they will give us a window
about what was going through her mind, what was worrying her at that
time. But that means, I do have to figure out what she wrote when. The
way Stephen and Uncle Siv kept poohpoohing that idea, I almost bought
it, and here is this dream-thing reinforcing what I was saying all along.

One has to figure out the chronology, I don't care what Uncle Siv or anyone says. Why hasn't Uncle Siv called so long? I have to return Ma's call, have to hear the message again, did she say she would be back home Monday or Tuesday?

Here is a date, but no year.

Today's (July 31) dream was even more weird than usual.
We are in Nagpur, walking down the Cement Road, marvelling how nothing has changed, except for the crowds. It is dark and already there are hundreds of people on the street. There seemed to be loose change on the ground. Looks like loonies to me. I go back and pick them up – loonies and quarters, more and more of them as we walk along. I am the only one picking them up. Soon the coins get bigger and heavier. I pick them and give a few to S. There are big houses on the other side of the road, and A says "Krishnaswamis', exactly the way it used to be." It is a house such as still stand on the way to the Music Academy in Madras, huge, with a large compound. We turn left at the corner – Saraswati Vidyalaya corner. The day is dawning. We sit on a low culvert – just a long curb really.
There is a guy in white who is looking at us, I notice. We turn around and sit with our back to the road; in the increasing light of dawn, there are people hurrying about carrying sacks of stuff for their shops that they are opening. We sit with our backs to the road, and I draw out the coins and S says the big ones are Spanish, see Franco Manigula he says of the head with streaming hair on the coin, and I say, but this is weird, maybe I should just throw them back on the road, may be they are accursed, why didn't anyone else pick them up, may be they are not real, do you see what I see – this is a loonie, isn't it? and this is a quarter, and A boredly says, yeah I don't know about the loonie, but this looks like a quarter or whatever you call it; and the quarter she says is a quarter is not a Canadian quarter or may be it is with one of those special designs of canoe or ship or whatever.
Then, speaking in Tamil, I insist that S tell me if he sees the same things I see, you know these may not be real, I say, may be each of us is seeing a different thing. The man in white – a small brown man – this is India and everyone is brown – edges closer to me. I turn to him and say in Tamil, "Do you speak Tamil? you

are Tamil, aren't you? we are discussing something and may be you could tell us..." and he smiles and sings or chants, like a hari-katha singer, some verses that seem to be Krishna speaking to Arjun and about people looking for something. However, he goes on and on in Tamil, explaining in a way that goes nowhere, in never ending circles of sentences.
End of dream.

Oddly enough, in the short dream before that, I am standing somewhere, and D – he is more like a little child really, in a pair of white shorts, and I can see that under the baseball cap he is bald, and so he is D, says, "I figured I'd mow the lawn. Just finished mowing the lawn." And when S is about to slap him on his back, he bends down, like a little baby goat may be, and S is about to carry him – puts his arm under its belly, and the dream ends.

Lewis Carroll. I wish Stephen were here so I could show off that I connected this to Lewis Carroll. Here's something that is not a dream but it is dated.

2nd March, 67
I opened a slab of Cadbury's Milk Chocolate after lunch and the silver wrapper with CADBURY written all over it reminded me that there was a time when I used to treasure those wrappers, tearing the slab very carefully, and then smoothening out the silver with my thumbnail till it shone evenly and square, and then pressing it between the pages of my composition book. The composition text book was the only one with pages wide enough to hold the Cadbury silver; it had a blue hard cover and was quite thin, with a poem or passage on the left side of each page, and exercises on the right side. There were passages from Eothen. [I can't figure out what this word could be, but it looks like Eothen and I can't think of any writer who comes close to this] and Dickens and Scott, there was "Mine be a cot beside the hill" and "The Brook." I needed a copy for something when I was in college, and so I went back to school one day and bought a used copy at the stationery, a little room under Sister Celine's care, and the copy turned out to be Sip's! I was so pleased and

sentimental about that for Sip was my first (and really only) school friend with whom I could share my jokes and arguments, Sip whom I shall long remember as the one who introduced me to P.G.Wodehouse, *Summer Lightning*, or was it *Money for Nothing?* and then to a whole host of P.G.'s books; Sip whom I met at PT class at the beginning of the school year in the seventh standard – she was a class below me but we had a common Physical Training hour for three classes V, VI, and VII at the same time – and her new shoes were too tight and mine were too loose (or maybe it was the other way around) and so we exchanged them; Sip whose wedding I went to, Sip, one of my lost friends, fare well wherever you are.

These I think of now as I write, but when I saw the silver wrapper of the chocolate, I thought there was a time when chocolates were rare, so rare and treasured, a slab cost twelve annas and once a month Amma would buy a slab and we would get a piece – there were eight pieces to a slab – and when our older siblings had left home to study elsewhere, the three of us would get to share the extra bits.

Once, when I was in the eighth or ninth standard, the nuns got a whole lot of crumbling slabs from somewhere and sold them at four or six annas each. Meera used to buy one often and that was a luxury – that whitish crumbling chocolate was nectar to us then.

When we went to Bombay one year, after our final exams which used to be in December, we went on a real splurge. Returning in the electric train to Kalyan, the three of us had a whole slab each, and the very idea of a whole slab was a long-dreamt-of luxury. Even after that, chocolates were a luxury, yes even though we were well-to-do, by then chocolates at fourteen annas a slab was still an extravagance.

Today I buy them by the dozens, a dozen at 86c the other day at the Bay, and I tear the wrapper without care and sweep the crumbs from the table without a second look.

Is it a long way I have come? I was never poor, and now I do not feel particularly rich. There is no nostalgia for those days and yet....

That wasn't a dream and so should not go into the dream binder. But it is the same time period. If Stephen were here he'd nag me into keeping the mess organized.

~

I woke up in a sweat. It was a horrible dream. Yes, I too have dreams but I never remember any of it when I wake up. But this one is different. There were children everywhere. There had been a fire, I think, in the Children's Hospital must have been, for a great many of them were in dire need of something or the other. But it was not here, but in India – the children were in knee-length khaki shorts and bare bodied, their black-brown hair sticking together as when it hasn't been washed in a while. There were women in saris, I am sure of that, nurses in Mother Teresa saris. And men on the veranda of a big house, and they seemed to be cooking and also drumming – yes there were huge clay stoves the kind built to make large meals for special occasions, and for sure I could hear drums as well, the kind of steady thud thud clang that one hears at protest processions in India. We were running from one to another and not able to focus on anyone for long because some one else needed us more urgently. It was terrible, and then someone blared from a megaphone that we should just leave everything as it was and run to save ourselves. May be it is another Chernobyl, I shouted, and the cry was taken up – Bhopal, Bhopal, and there was mayhem. We can't leave, I shouted, picking up a child that seemed to have no limbs, and he slipped away from my hands like an eel, a fish, and then there were more of them.

I got out of bed and put on my robe. I was shivering. Stephen, Stephen, where the hell are you? I then remembered where he was, in India, and shit, that was why I was dreaming all this. In the microwave, I warmed the half cup of coffee left over from the night, and after a sip poured it down the sink. Now I was shivering spasmodically. Idiot, I told myself, you can't be having such dreams, not if you are going to be surrounded by babies for the rest of your working life. But maybe that was the problem. Babies taking me over even in my dreams.

To distract myself, I picked one of Maru's binders. Nowadays, I have got into the habit of sorting each piece of writing the moment I pick it up. But as I read this, I really got the heebie-jeebies, as Maru would say. It was weird, totally weird. I was starting to dream Maru's dreams. That is the only way I can describe it, for honest to god, I don't remember having read this at all before tonight and yet I had just now dreamt it. It is my dream come back in more vivid detail, above the drums and cries I had just remembered.

March 10
One of those weird morning dreams.

A house somewhere in a tropical setting. Lots of people around but I had a room on the second floor.

I got up and went out; it was dark outside but there was a bulb at the corner of the house so that the yard was not totally dark. And then they came, little children with big eyes, bedraggled, and something was weird about them, and they came forward in a group, and there were some other girls with me – may be some of those who were at the Y years ago – and we fell back, but the kids advanced, and one of us, Suvarna from the Y, said "we've been told to go in, let us go in, we've got to go in." There was urgency in her tone, as if to say, these are gremlins, spirits, let us run in. "Won't they also follow us?" I said, thinking how can we run in when they are between us and the steps up the deck of the house? But we ran in and quickly shut the door. I wanted to go again to R, but she was in a part of a room that was behind a curtain, as in hospitals where there are curtains to divide one bed from another. U was sleeping there and muttering some kind of chant, very familiar but I kept wondering, "Why is she chanting these Palghat-Sanskrit chants," and R was on the far side of the bed. And someone at my elbow said, "We've been told to keep away from them," and I fell back, with U's chant in my ears. Then I went to another room, and cousin B was there, and he said, "These are spirits – in Indonesia" (or may be he gave some name of some island in the Pacific) "they are called" and he said some name, and he and I went outside again; and this time there were grown-ups, and they seemed to know him, and he introduced me to them, after shaking hands with a couple of them – they were all men. My cousin, he said, my cousin. And I kept saying, Are they real, can they be touched? "Are they real," and I stretched my hand, and quickly withdrew it and then stretched again, and I touched the hand of one of them but felt I didn't quite, for my fingers touched something hard, like his finger had a metal cap; thank god, I said to myself, that I didn't really touch them, but could be they aren't real, and can never be touched; are they real, I kept saying, can one touch them and hear them?

And then we returned to the house, but entered at a lower level, through the kitchen, and there were a great many men doing this and that, like cooks and servants, reaching out for a pot, a broom, putting pans back on pantry shelves, stirring a huge vat of something on wood-fed fire; and they were making loud sounds as they went about their work. We went upstairs, and there was our brother; everyone was in bed, but because of the noise from downstairs, he went down the stairs, and I went with him, and he asked the men to lower the noise level because people had to sleep. There were a great many men, all Indians, wearing *dhoti* and *jibba*, and they seemed to pay no heed to us, and then we came upstairs.

It was totally weird, and I thought to myself, what does this mean?

And those gremlins, so scary in their steadfast advance towards me, and me knowing they were not human but very much alive. One face I can see even now – brown but as though caked with dirt, and big eyes, not black but grey rimmed brown, and slowly advancing – in half pants, khaki I think, and eyes that for sure said he was not human, and there was a girl next to him, and a lot of children behind him. I was totally spooked, even if I had my folks around me.

Totally spooked, and I woke up and said, god it is eight o'clock and it is a tennis day and I have to be ready soon, and there won't be time at the computer now or at the U – too much work, but let me go through the scene again so I'll remember it in the evening and write it down, and I have.

I think I should stop reading Maru's stuff. Something is happening, something weird. Am I dreaming her dreams? Stephen would say these are dreams such as everyone has and that is why they are similar. But no, there's something happening between me and Maru's stuff. I think I had better stop reading.

~

I am more rational today. Reading Maru's stuff was an activity that was keeping me sane, I thought. But something is wrong there too. Work isn't going well. Baby Vasyl is getting worse. Marika is depressed and her milk is drying up. With Stephen away, I feel lost. I miss him, and now all I have are my work and Maru. And both are turning on me.

I suddenly wonder if I have been going up the wrong tree all along. Maru, now that I think of it, probably wanted me to focus on her life, not her writings. I have been reading only her writings but there's a lot of stuff in these cartons about various meetings and events, workplace colleagues and happenings, committees and Boards on which she worked over the years, all the social work she did and women's causes she worked for. I remember there was a whole big envelope of stuff on her activism for women in her workplace and that kind of stuff, which I have simply ignored. But that was her life, her real life, and I have been ignoring all that and reading only her writings, and that too mainly her early writings, juvenile stuff as Stephen would say. *Maru and the Maple Leaf* – she was so clear about it – when she started it, how she came and what happened after that, she is so clear about what she set out to do in her memoirs, everything is here in these cartons, oh bejesus, there has to be some psychological reason for my choice of reading material, maybe I wanted to fill in the gaps of what I don't know about her, those early years of her life before I was born, may be that is why I have glossed over her real life in Canada. It has been me all along, what interests me, not what her real life was all about. No wonder I am dreaming her dreams. At least that explains my dream if nothing else. Not as spooky as I thought may be.   Anyhow, all the cartons have been disarranged, if at all she had arranged the contents in any order. Do I know more about her early life, or her inner life than I did all these years? Not really I suppose. May be Uncle Siv was right, she never did write about herself, but Uncle Siv was wrong about her leaving me these cartons to sort out her writings, and I took his word for it and so have been going up the wrong path altogether.   She was cavalier about her writings. They did not matter as much as the other things. I've missed the bus, she used to say, and now I remember skimming over something that had just that – *Recurring Dreams: Missing the Bus* – I must find that again and read it more carefully. It is so clear now - she gave me all this to reconstruct her real life in Canada, the title makes it so clear – *Maru and the Maple Leaf* - how did I miss that? carried away by what Uncle Siv said?   Not that I've been doing what he said either. I've been looking for something else altogether, a companion, someone to give me emotional support, may be. The way I talk to her all the time, as though she is sitting on her recliner as always, playing solitaire while we debated and argued.

~~~~~

TWENTY

At last a letter from Stephen. I print it out as usual, and take it to the sofa as usual.

Dearest Priti,

My stomach cramped. Not the usual Sweetums my darling, or Preetums my sweetums, but Dearest Priti.

I am sorry to have been so delinquent. Yes, I got all your letters, obviously can't say all but quite a few, which makes me think all of them are coming through. When I am at work, I am totally focused and I love what I do. But when the day is done, I feel disembodied, like I have no connection to the living world. I am not the same person I was. I don't know in what way I have changed, or how or why, only that I am not the person you knew. So, I think it is only fair that I let go of you. I have read your letters over and over again, hoping they would make me the person I was, but everything seems far away, you, Ottawa, Pa and Mom, baseball, everything seems like it belonged to another life on another planet.

No, I am not going crazy or anything. Or may be I am. I am not trying to make excuses for cutting you off like this, but I have to let go of you. You have a life there; I don't know if my life is going to be here though I would love it to be; for once I am doing something excitingly useful; to give sight to the blind, and I have helped give that to scores of people already! It is absolutely amazingly fulfilling. But when the day is done, and I play my favourite music, I can't relate to it any more.

It is not as if I can relate to people here either. In this disembodied state, I can't relate to anyone. The sky is beautiful, though. I sit on a hill – there is a Hanuman shrine on top of it, a red flag flying on the tree under which is the monkey-god – and I sit on the parapet of what was once an outlook point of some minor chieftain perhaps, and the sky is beautiful. This shrine is far from a temple as such. Certainly not one of those temples whose architecture was so carefully explained by Maru in one of her PALI programmes. I miss reading her stuff, what fun we used to have, reading those 5x8 cards…It is just a crude stone carving, Hanuman's body smeared red by countless hands rubbing red paste on him.

Perhaps I should cut loose and come back. Or stay on and risk some total, perhaps catastrophic? transformation. I don't know anything any more. But one thing is clear – I can't drag you into this, into whatever it is that is happening to me.

I can't let go of you. I must let go of you.

Stephen.

What a bloody loser, what a goddamned bloody loser, I shouted, crumpling the sheet. I picked up a bowl of honey-roasted peanuts that was on the coffee table and threw it across the room at the kitchen cabinets. The damned thing didn't break; it just fell on the edge of the carpet of the living room and rolled into the kitchen. I raised my fist at the hand that guides my hand and shouted, "What the bloody hell are you trying to tell me?"

Then I uncrumpled the letter and read it again. It was very clear. I didn't need any external help to figure it out. He was cutting me off. And he had every right. We had talked about it often enough – or rather I had. That we would stay together as long as both wanted to but we were free at all times, free. He had taken his freedom and flown. As he had every right to.

It was time to leave for work. I shut down the computer, took my backpack, locked the door and rushed out.

Work, our saviour, our only saviour, that never lets us down. I am exhausted. Baby Vasyl. There must be something we can do for him.

~

I wrote a long weepy letter to Stephen and deleted the whole damn page. I'll wait and see what he says next.

~

I have come across a rather exciting piece of writing. It says something about her Pinto story. It must have been written in India, for it is on double foolscap paper folded to handle like a notebook. Maru seemed to have been doing that in India – folding six or seven sheets at a time, and starting to write in the "notebook." Often there is writing only on the first three or four pages, and of course the story is unfinished. Often the first page is full of notes, of what she plans to do with the idea, and then she starts writing and abandons it after five or six pages.

This one has a postie stuck on it, which means Maru had read it years later, here in Canada. The postie is stuck under the title, which is *"The Sholamari story* as told by Dr. B."

The postie notes:

This is what comes of using initials for people – bless me if I haven't forgotten who this Dr. B is. Who could he be? Or is it a she? I can't even think of any B names, leave alone names of people I might have known. A Bangalore or Nagpur telephone directory might help give me a long list of B names and as I go over them one might ring a bell. I remember the story now, but I can't remember any Dr. B! About my Pinto Swami in person! So he has been inside me all along and Pinto had to resuscitate him with his story, because, of course the Pinto story started with the ending, and the swami in that one, we know who he is, but his characterization comes from this – this story told me by some Dr. B. when I was probably a student!!!! B was a man, as I gather after reading the first page. Could it be the husband of a Mrs. B. who was teaching at our college when I had just joined the faculty?

This note is important, because it totally devalues the discovery I had made about the initials signifying the second letter of the name. But you never know with Maru. She is forever misleading me into wrong assumptions. These three cartons are for Priti. Did she put in all these puzzles and quizzes to keep me occupied for decades?

For example, the first paragraph mentions a salary for a job – it should be possible to figure out the time span with that! That is what Stephen would do.

Wanted Chief Administrator for a rural university project of Sholamari Ashram. Scale of pay 1000/ - 1800/ per month etc. etc. Who wouldn't be interested? Even the lower figure is a way lot more than my last paycheque was. I am too young to be a retiree. So I applied. And within four days of my application, I received a telegram that I was appointed and should join as soon as possible. I promptly packed up and left. My wife was not happy but this seemed too good an opportunity to pass. The train journey to Siliguri itself takes two days, and I had to board a bus for the final lap of the journey. I was given a royal welcome, with garlands and effusive greetings by one Dr. Das,

Secretary of the ashram, and his entourage. The entourage consisted of several gentlemen and soon it was apparent that each had held high offices in the government or some business before his retirement. I was taken to one of the cottages, of which there were several on the wide-spread land of the Ashram. We had a fine dinner and Dr. Das acquainted me with the wondrous plans they had for the immediate future. A nine-storey construction, with lifts and fans of course, was soon to start for what would be the administrative hub of the proposed university; my office would be on the second storey. A Women's Institute, they thought of calling it Sister Nivedita Institute, would come next, and at this point he asked about my wife's degrees and work experience.

Meals, I found soon, were always as festive as the one I had that evening. There was chicken and fish curry morning and night. I had carefully hidden a bottle of whiskey in my suitcase, but I soon found out no camouflage was needed. Liquor was not only admissible, it was a regular feature at and after dinner.

As I sat that first night listening to the hum of mosquitoes and eerie night sounds outside the screened windows, I could see why Dr. Das had replied what he had to my telegram about my bringing my car. "Only Jeeps here," he had said. Nothing but a Jeep, a tank might be even better, could be used for this terrain.

The Swami is a very great man shrouded in as great a mystery. He lives in a big cottage fenced all around. At the gate stand two pahlwans, with turban, moustache and lathi. No one can gain access to His Holiness except about fifteen persons. And even they had never looked at his august countenance. Mr. Das carried an incense holder and a cloth sachet of "dhoop" which he lit as he entered the Swami's room. Thus there was always a smoke screen between the Swami and whoever was getting darshan.

The Swami has never been seen by anyone, and yet he runs the ashram, overseeing the minutest detail. Nothing is ever done without his sanction and order. When I asked about my duties, Mr. Das, in his short checkered lungi and loose undervest, took some snuff, thought a minute, jumped up suddenly and taking the incense holder ran to the holy of holies. After a while, he was back and recited the Swami's message. I was to rest for two days and then get ready to interview students. Eighty students had been called from all over India. I was to prepare the exam questions for both a written test and an interview. I asked who would take charge of the list of materials, such as pen and paper, desks and supervision... At this, Mr. Das again sprinted to the sanctum and came back with the answer – I was to draw up a list of any and everything that might possibly be required.

The writing on that page ends there. But two pages seem to have been removed, for I see their jagged edges, and the story seems to continue after the blank.

We interviewed the boys, and made our questions tough so few could pass. But the High Command had already made the decision that all would pass. The boys were not happy on knowing they would be reimbursed for their journey only later. Two said they would sue. While Dr. Das shuttled between the Swami and us, I pointed out that no court would take up a case for so small an amount that was involved, and the boys felt defeated. News went to the Swami about how I had handled the case and Dr. Das told me the Swami was all praise.

The boys left, and I envied them for being able to go away. I was waking up to the farce. I wrote my letter of resignation before getting ready for bed. It was already eleven p.m. and I was tired. I now had some misgivings, for my son was in America and the extra money this job brought was much needed, for he wanted to come for a visit to see if he could find a good job here, and if he couldn't, he planned to go back to America. As I paced the room thinking, there was a knock on the door. Dr. Das was there, to tell me the Swami wanted to see me. They escorted me to him.

A rich voice from behind the smoke screen asked me why I was so worried. I told him I was worried about my wife and son. He told me that once anyone came to the ashram, everything would be taken care of. My wife would soon join me. She would be the administrator for the women's college that would start by the next academic year.

Would that suit you, he asked. I was nervous by now, and realized that things were getting beyond my control. I said I could work better once she was here.

She came within a fortnight. Mr. Das wanted her to be in charge of the kitchen, but I did not like that. The Swami, through the smoke screen, asked us if he might suggest something – they expected many foreigners to visit, and it would be useful if my wife could start teaching English to some of the local children and residents.

I go to the computer and look it up, which is what Stephen would do. Nothing, absolutely nothing resembling Sholamari, Shoulamari, Showlamari, that the search engine can locate for me. But Siliguri is for real – it is near Darjeeling, and even has a real engineering institute! I don't know how the story ended but its connection to the Pinto story is sure there.

So Maru has fooled me again, I suppose. The whole thing is a fabrication; yet she has said many times that quite a few of her stories are based on stories told to her.

I have to do something about Stephen's letter. I can't go on as though I never got it. I must tell him about baby Vasyl. He will understand why I have not replied.

~~~~~

TWENTY ONE

Baby Vasyl is holding steady. What a relief. Why am I like this? Why do I keep going to him every minute I can spare from my wards?

I have been like a zombie, rushing from hospital to home, home to hospital, which has been okay, any excuse not to face the fact that I have not replied to Stephen and he hasn't written either. I have not met anyone other than people at work since the letter. I spend the few hours at home glancing at sheets in Carton 2 and putting them back. It seems to be full of reports and stuff of the many committees she was on. Women this Women that. Just now I came across a binder with a whole lot of newspaper clippings. Whole newspapers too, I can't be bothered. I threw them back to the bottom of the carton. But there was a binder in a plastic shopping bag, all newspaper cuttings of reports she had written when she was a journalist.

She had told me all about her short stint at journalism. When she was doing her Diploma in Journalism, she had got her first job. She wrote for the local newspaper and she could look at the daily Events column and phone in what she wanted to cover and she always chose music and dance concerts or Rotary Club's college debates, something which she could enjoy. I remember how much she laughed as she said she earned three rupees per column, and you know how long a newspaper column is, and since they never gave her more than a third of a column to report any of these events, she barely broke even on her rickshaw fare, for the concerts were in the evening and she did not care to ride back on her bicycle late at night. All her pieces are here, yellowed with age, forty years my god, that is a long time. She had a story too about how facts are facts but they can be presented in a way that could manipulate the reader's reaction. We had a big discussion one day about television coverage and I argued that facts are facts and she argued that media manipulated facts through presentation ploys, and she gave this example – of how she had a piece of investigative journalism about garbage disposal in Nagpur, which is where she was studying at the time. The Corporation guy who gave her an interview was hopping mad when he read the report the next day. At the end of citing the facts and figures he had given, Maru had written – "the Corporation has six garbage lorries, for a population of 600,000 people." Facts but the juxtaposition made a thump.

I learnt a lot in those discussions, I must say, both from Uncle Siv's laconic interjections and Maru's stories with which she embellished her points.

One of the newspaper clippings was a story titled "Lie," 25th June 1961. She has written the date, but not the name of the newspaper. Must check with Uncle Siv.

Ayodhya was resplendent with colour and joy. It was the Coronation day of Ramachandra, beloved prince of many prayers. On the balcony of a rich house, on the street that ran into the forest, sat an old woman, a very old woman, a direct descendant of the royal house of the Suryas. Next to her stood a very young woman looking wistfully at the street below where colourfully dressed men and women festooned the roads with garlands of flowers and sang joyously to the sound of clarinets and drums.

The old woman turned her sightless eyes towards the street and said, "Ah if I could stand on my feet, I'd rush and kiss the feet of our darling Rama! Oh had I but eyes to see the purifying beauty of his divine form!"

The girl looked at the aged face, glowing with expectation. Her faint feeling of resentment at having to stay there instead of mingling with the crowd, vanished from her young heart. The old lady had taken her in, an orphaned mite, and had made her into a companion though sixty years separated the two. From her, she had heard about the glorious heritage of the Surya Vamsa, and tales of deeds and heroes; from her she had learnt the power and beauty of language, and hers was not an ungrateful heart. She gladly gave up the pleasure of going down to the street.

"You are here, my child, to be my eyes and ears. I have long waited for this day, this blessed morn that will see Rama crowned king of Ayodhya. And I shall see the pageant through you, lovely girl. Describe everything to me child, everything, from the deep imprint of the elephant's foot to the topmost gem of our prince's bejewelled crown. For from now on I shall live in this moment. To the end of my life, and there are not many dawns I shall wake to I know, I shall live in the memory of this glorious sight. Therefore, sweet child, tell me all, so that I can see with your eyes the sight that shall gladden my heart to my last breath."

The girl looked below. There was silence, a heavy silence, a pall-like silence as though a brahmin corpse was being carried along the way. The street was not deserted, people moved in throngs towards the city, but they whispered. Not the glad drumbeats that had announced the royal decree of coronation but silent whispers spread the news.

She leaned over. "What is it?"

"Rama is exiled," said a boy.

"Ah no, why?" But he was gone, racing to join the crowd. A young woman stopped a minute to give her the details of Kaikeyi's boons and demands.

"To whom are you talking?" asked the old woman.

"To the boy next door who has made a poem on Rama."

"Eons will sing the praise of the Surya Vamsa; poets for centuries to come will write of Raghava, glory be to him. But tell me child, I can hear only a confused noise for my hearing is weak. Come closer and tell me."

"It is the sound of festal music you hear," said the girl, "all the temple bells are ringing in sweet concord and the royal drummers are coming down our street. Behind them come holy brahmins calling the blessings of the Gods on our loved Lord. Their deep rich voices ascend skyward chanting sacred hymns. Then come the court musicians – of silver are their clarinets, and gold-stringed veenas burst into inspired melody for our Prince."

Up the road they came, a weeping Ayodhya clustered around the three noble figures. Men and women held Rama's feet, begging him not to proceed. And yet the crowd inched forward for Raghupati's steady feet ever moved onward.

"Has he come?" the old woman's voice quivered even more with excitement. "Can you see him? Child, child, tell me, describe him to me."

"Yes. He is here. Seated on a golden throne on the royal elephant that moves majestically is he, and the diamond on his crown outshines the sun. But even its brightness sinks beside the halo round his royal head. Gentle are his eyes and when he smiles the sparkling ripples of the Sarayu are put to shame."

"And Sita? Child, tell me," the old woman said in impatient excitement.

"Sita is seated by his side; woven in pure gold is her saree and you scarce can see her arms so full of bejewelled bangles are they, and the bells on her ankles tinkle music sweeter than all else. And they come near."

"And then?"

"Maidens are strewing flowers on the road, and camphor and perfume fill the air with fragrance. Dancers and singers open the way for the procession. And now, now the white cloud above opens and the Gods throw celestial showers of flowers on them and here comes Indradev and his heavenly train."

"It is but right that Gods should come. For our Rama is divine, our Raghurama, great scion of a great house."

"And now he is right here, and lady, he is looking at you! Our Prince has seen you and blessed you and yet so gentle is his mien as though he is asking for your blessing."

The old woman trembled. "Is it so child?"

"Yes, yes," she continued breathlessly, "In his eyes was divinity and he raised his joined palms and looked at you –so full of love and benediction is his look."

And now they passed below, Rama and Sita and Lakshmana, a little faster now, for they had half-persuaded the crowd to leave them. The girl's eyes followed them.

"This is indeed the greatest moment of my life," said the old woman. "I have given all my love and loyalty to Surya Vamsa and Ayodhya. And this is the happiest day for all. I have seen him riding in royal state to his coronation. Ayodhya is happy. Was there any tear or frown? Tell me there wasn't, for it will be a wretched death I die if I hear there was a frown on this happy day. But how can there be? Who in Ayodhya has not prayed for his birth? I have seen him and he is in my mind's eye. Thank you, child, for having been my eyes. God bless you."

The girl's eyes strained towards the distant figures which moved as though above the rest, on and on into the forest. Her voice came as though by itself, "For the greater glory of his royal race, for the eternal glory of humankind he goes – Ramachandra, beloved prince of many prayers." And the girl bowed her head and silently wept.

Is it okay to lie to spare someone pain? What if Stephen is trying to spare me by saying he is going off the deep end? The pain of the truth that he has found someone there? Easier to say he is going off his head than to say he is ditching me for another woman. Damn, damn.

I picked up another sheaf of foolscap paper folded to look like a notebook. The cover is gruesome in a juvenile way, with a ghost and a masked figure with knife in hand and blood dripping off the letters of the title: *Murder at the YWCA.*

As Stephen said, it is a good read, a story she wrote in her Y days where she kills off one of the hostel residents. Everyone is there, Lady B., VESPURS, and a few others not mentioned in anything I have read so far. But her humour keeps coming in the way of detective fiction. They don't mix, but how could she have known that at the time? I almost laughed as I read. But all I could think of was the line I remembered from that book she edited, *At the Gates*, where she says that walking on the edge comes naturally to young people.

Is that where Stephen is at? Walking on the edge, getting excited about godknowswhat? But he isn't young, for pete's sake. Maru was talking about teenage, not about thirty plus. And he isn't that kind at all. He is extremely responsible about everything. What could have got into him? I thought he'd follow up on that letter with another. But nothing so far, absolutely nothing. May be he is waiting for my response to his bombshell. How the bloody hell am I supposed to respond?

That is where all my thinking ends, how the bloody hell is one supposed to respond?

I write Stephen a page-long e-mail, making no mention of his crazy mail about calling us off. Let him think I never received it; let him start doubting he ever sent it; anything can happen with e-mail and on-line stuff anyway. I just wrote to him about my dreary, busy days; I wrote about my discoveries regarding Maru's stuff. I mentioned I hadn't cooked for days and was living on corner store muffins and cafeteria salads, same as you, I added, living on rice and dal day after day, or did his mess, as they called it in India, have any variety. I then wrote about Vasyl and how desperate I was, and how I knew I should not get so personally involved but I was, I was, I was. I said I missed him but then I deleted the line.

I punched the SEND key and sat for a while at the table. I picked up one of Maru's little Notebooks but put it away and went to bed.

Middle of the night I was wide awake. Why did I wake up? Is someone trying to tell me something? Baby Vasyl? Stephen? Ma, I must call her, didn't make my usual weekend call this time. I got out of bed, thinking I would make myself some coffee and review some stuff before meeting Dr. Rafter tomorrow – he likes to meet his team once a week to check on our progress.

But I went to the cartons instead. I chose Carton 3 because I had noted that it was a lot more organized than the others. There were a lot of clipped or stapled sheets as in the others but also a great many file folders of different colours, each labelled usually with a name rather than a theme. Each had loose sheets, mostly single, handwritten or printout, with notes. I picked up a purple folder labelled Lalli. Inside were two pages of notes and a printout. I read the printout.

October 28, 1974

I must get the Lalli story down. Facts: serious drift between husband and wife. Met them first on a Canada Day community picnic. Long phone conversations about her fears that he is going to divorce her. Though there is no basis as far as one can see, there is no doubt she believes what she says.

Who would have thought that I, Lalli, would sit out my evenings staring at the bleak prairie winter half way around the world from home, slowly going out of my mind? Lalli for laughter, the placards read, the year I stood for the student executive in college. I won, of course. I've never lost in any competition except this one called life. No, let me not be melodramatic. Except that some facts sound so melodramatic anyway. Murthy has gone back to his lab. He is a scientist, a good one, too. He's had his run of bad luck, what with a wife who should be in the loony bin but goes instead for shock treatment every few months, and what with being jobless for a year because he could not get his Ph.D. what with all the worry of having a loony wife. But now things are looking up. He has his degree and a position at the University, as they say, and I am really and truly going bonkers and he can easily get the separation or divorce or whatever it is one gets in this country. One can't on grounds of immaturity, which has always been his charge; your language patterns haven't changed any from your days at mission school slang, he says. But madness, ah that's indisputable. Unfit to be wife and mother, charge upheld, court dismissed. Except that it is years since I was wife or mother anyway. Suresh was his father's child for the first eight years and now he is on his own. I can hear him putting away his train set. He plays with it every night. May be he's bonkers too. How would I know? How can anyone know anything, except doctors who listen to everything Murthy says though they have nary an ear for me.

Storyline: Start with: He has gone to the lawyer, to set my house in order, he said. She assumes he has gone to finalize the start of the separation process. Part One to consist of long ramblings of her own life, childhood, post-partum problems in India – or should it be in another country where she doesn't know the language? somewhere in Europe? Part Two – two possibilities: Her stream of consciousness though incoherent tells us a lot about him, how he is trying to cope with her madness, tries various routes, overwork, counselling, doctors, gets into a cult prayer group.... How he wants to set his house in order; he persuades her to become a citizen to make sure she is okay no matter what happens. *We* get a feeling that he is lost but she never does; at the end when he commits suicide, we should be able to say, "Oh yes, there were clues all along" but she, focused on herself can never see or hear the overtures he makes. She thinks he has another woman.

Everyday when they drive past a friend's house she thinks, He is taking this road and not that just so we can pass their house.

Ends with his suicide.

Second option is to start with "I never thought it would end this way," go through the whole story as a flashback. That he is dead should be brought out only at the very end.

Perhaps the first option would work better.

For God's sake listen to me, he shouted last night. I wanted to point out that this was a variation from his usual God damn you, let me talk, but I didn't say anything. I knew what I had to do and I did it. I walked out of the living room and shut the door. My room. Each of us has a room of one's own, inviolable. We were agreed on that – our claims to a corner in this world that was entirely ours. The study is his. But since we have only three bedrooms, my room is not wholly mine. It is our bedroom.

Friend suggests she takes up citizenship, as he has. She tells him about it and he says it is a good idea. Why don't you? He said it casually but his mouth was drawn tight and yet so vulnerably, and his voice muted. That is how it was; whenever either of them wanted something very much, they dared not say it in so many words, and when they did, it was muted, tense under the casualness. He suggests it again, at the time he is setting his house in order, but she goes to her room.

Once, as I looked at the frozen Assiniboine I said, "Imagine the pioneers' boats going up and down this river, trying to beat the freeze with one more trip before winter...." And he prosaically said, the main traffic was always on the Red. Prosaic, cynical, and always so correct. (Irony to be brought out that though she repeatedly says he always knows the correct answers, we see he wasn't at all sure of answers, and that perhaps his answer of suicide was not correct.)

Freedom, she often thinks of the freedom she will have once the separation is legal and final. Now she has the freedom and still welcomes it, but we know now as we did then that she is not capable of handling that freedom.

I think I know the person around whom this story is built. She used to phone Maru when I lived with her and would talk for an hour each time. Uncle Siv once said Maru should just direct her to a psychiatric counsellor and Maru said the poor woman would heal herself if someone could just patiently listen to her – that was Maru, spending hours listening to women in trouble. But I remember the woman's husband – a quiet man with a perpetual worried, indeed harried, look on his face. But once I was waiting at the bus stop and cars were stopped at the intersection light. He was in the car right next to where I was standing, and he was chatting happily to the woman in the passenger seat. He was smiling – he had a nice smile – and he seemed so happy and carefree. It made me glad to see him so relaxed. I wondered about the woman, who had a briefcase on her lap and was probably just a co-worker, but I almost hoped he was having an affair, a respite from the crazy wife whom he was saddled with. One always thinks there is another woman – but it need not be that way. Something else is eating him. Stephen. I went to the computer and read his letter again. He says he misses Maru's writing but says nothing about missing me. Which show of hers is he talking about? I had stacked all her TV show scripts in an empty cereal box but it wasn't there as far as I could see.

~

I spent an hour, an hour I could not afford to spare, looking for that TV script on temples. No wonder it wasn't in the cereal box – it is dated 1994, way after her 1980s decade of hosting that show every single week. She did sporadic shows after that I guess.

Building a Hindu Temple

When I think of the architecture of Christian Europe, I see on my mental screen cathedrals such as Westminster Abbey and pleasure palaces such as Versailles; when I think of Islamic contributions to architecture I see mosques and tombs, magnificent mausoleums such as the Taj Mahal in Agra built by Emperor Shah Jehan for his wife Mumtaz Mahal (poster 1) and Shamsuddin's tomb in the Kutb Minar (poster 2) and Tipu Sultan's tomb in Seringapatam (poster 3). When I think of Hindu architecture (posters 4 and 5) I see temples, only temples.

In addition to places of worship, Christians built pleasure palaces and Muslims built mausoleums, both making a distinction between places for the body and the soul, but Hindus brought body and soul together in their places of worship and so built only temples. Temples were built to be the centres of Hindu culture (posters 6 and 7) to promote all the arts and crafts, all the physical, intellectual and spiritual pleasures of life, dedicating every aspect to the celebration of the sacred syllable Om (plaque on the table), the Eternal spirit that runs through all creation.

Today let us find out a little bit about what went into the building of Hindu temples. We have two sources to reconstruct the ideological and practical aspects of temple building. The ideological aspects are found in various texts because Hindu scholars recorded and codified everything they knew. Thus Vastu Sastra (poster 8) or the science of architecture, has been extensively codified in the Atharva Veda, one of the four Vedas which are the basic scriptural texts of Hinduism. For practical aspects of how temples were built, we have palm-leaf scrolls that recorded the day to day operations of temple building. For example, there is a palm-leaf manuscript from the thirteenth century related to the building of the Konarak temple (poster 9) in present day Orissa on the east coast of India. The manuscript lists in fascinating detail the number of the workmen, their salaries and duties. It also tells us the way craftsmen's guilds operated, how they helped widows and families of workers, how they had contractors and sub-contractors, how they trained and assessed the skills of their artisans etc. Just as kings maintained standing armies, Hindu kings also maintained an army of artisans, architects and priests whose sole and hereditary task was to build temples. From these two sources we can get some idea of the science and art of temple building in India.

Building a house for God is a sacred task and every step of the process is spelt out so that nothing should go wrong. Such sciences as physics, astronomy and mathematics evolved around raising temples for the glory of God. The Vastu Sastra lays down rules of mathematics that spell out such details as the ratio of the various parts of the pillar (poster 10) or the number of tiers that a shikara or gopuram should have, and how the stone beams have to be set for stability. Such crafts as sculpture and geometric designs developed because the house for God must be aesthetically pleasing (poster 11). Birds and animals were included because the house of God has to include all of creation (poster 12). Such arts as music, dance and love-making were included because the house for God must celebrate life holistically (poster 13.)

Rivers and ponds, caves and mountain peaks are considered favourite places of the gods. Take a look at this temple (poster 14) standing firmly on the earth but with its gopuram reaching into the sky, symbolizing the connection between earth and heaven, between human being and God. Here (poster 15 Khajuraho) is an even richer representation of the way temples mirror clusters of mountain peaks. Mountain peaks are favourite abodes of Gods.

Siva and Parvati live on Mount Kailas, Lakshmi and Vishnu on Vaikuntam mountain. As you come closer, you see another aspect of the journey – the total structure rising tier upon tier is symbolic of the soul's aspiration to merge with the divine Soul and the long steep path it has to climb (poster 16). The beauty of Hinduism is that you can stop at whichever of the many steps you want and commune with God. The journey will take longer or maybe you will never reach the peak but the climb is its own reward (poster 17, of Lingaraj). Now let us take another view (poster 18). A Hindu temple has a natural or manmade body of water, a river or a pond, in which the worshipper takes a dip, symbolic of bodily purification before undertaking a journey towards God. When you go to a temple, you usually take a plate of flowers and fruit as offering (poster 19).

The architecture of the temple is a representation of the different types of communing with God.   You enter the outer porch and you ring the temple bell in salutation; the porch is open to sunlight, and the world is around you; you can spend your life here if you so wish, hearing the sounds of the world and the sounds of prayer. Then there is the outer hall (poster 20). In larger temples, this hall has sculptured pillars of breathtaking artistry. Here music and dances are performed, and here learned teachers give their lectures and harikathas. You have stepped away from the world and entered the world of beauty and elevated thoughts.

If you go farther into the temple, the inner hall is behind you and the garbhagriha, or the sanctum sanctorum ahead of you (poster 21). Here you give your offerings to the priest. Then you enter the corridor that surrounds the sanctum. The path is narrowed and dark; on either side are walls with little niches that let in some light. Then you stand in front of the sanctum. The sanctum sanctorum is dark except for the oil lamps. The image of God is usually of black stone and the details are not visible. Your senses are still very active; you can hear the priest's chants and the sound of the bell in his hand, and you can smell the incense and flowers that are piled all over the sanctum but your senses take you to another emotional space, the space within the sanctum, the dark cave in the mountain where God is. You stand there for a time, the priest gives you back your offering, which has been blessed within the sanctum. You retrace your steps through the hall of pillars to the front porch; you sit awhile on the stone near the large bell, symbolizing your reluctance to leave the holy place. Then you ring the bell in salutation and farewell and return to your house, bearing the sanctified food and flowers that you share with your family.

Now let us consider the actual building of a temple as laid down in ancient texts. Every step was researched and carefully executed with religious ceremonies performed by priests. First was the choice of the site. The soil was tested in various ways to see if it was firm. The colour of the soil, its texture, its moistness etc. were factors. A simple test was to dig a hole, then fill it up, and then check it after a certain time as to how much of the soil settled or sunk. This told them how much more or less water, soil, etc were needed to make the ground firm.

Then the ground was levelled and cleansed. This was done through rituals that requested all residents, be they forms of life or spirits, to leave the site so that the site may be given over entirely to the deity. Then the ground was ploughed and cleaned of thorns, weeds etc. And planted with different types of seeds. Their germination time helped the architect figure out certain other details about the soil. Then the ground was ploughed and sown with different kinds of grain, which were harvested. After several such seasons of ploughing, sowing and harvesting, the ground was declared ready. The ground was again levelled, so that it was like the surface of a mirror says one of the texts. Then came the setting down of the mandala, or ground plan of the temple. As I said earlier, Hindu mathematics was developed long before the Christian era, and Hindu scholars had set down mathematical formulae long before the science of numbers was known to the rest of the world. The concept of zero, for instance, originated in India. Intellectual concepts of time were so advanced that Hindu mathematics has names for such large numbers as 10 raised to 34. Here is a random sampling of names for the large numbers (poster 22).

Mandalas are emblematic of the sense of order that exists in the movement of the planets and stellar bodies. A mandala is drawn on the ground plan of the temple taking into account various factors related to the planets, the solar journey, the exact location of the temple, the direction that the temple will face etc. (poster 23).

A square was drawn and this was further subdivided into 64 or 81 squares. These numbers are related to the period of the precession of the equinoxes. 64 and 81 are exact fractions of the number of solar years in the Pythagorean Great Year (poster 24).

Let us take a look at the ground plan. (poster 25). Here is the entrance, the outer open porch; the bell is usually located just outside the porch or in the inner hall. This is the inner hall, and here is the narrow corridor around the garbhagriha, and here is the garbhagriha or the sanctum sanctorum.

(Poster 26) Here is the vertical view of the temple, taken from the top. Notice that the topmost point of the gopuram is directly above the centre of the sanctum. When the temple is built, a Sri Chakra is placed below where the sanctum will be, the deity, and the temple itself, resting as it were on the Sri Chakra.

(Poster 27) The Sri Chakra is a sacred symbol for Sri, the Mother of the Universe. The outer square is the symbol of the order that encases the universe; each concentric circle represents a power, a power required to reach the divine; the triangles represent other needs, such as health and protection and prosperity; the innermost triangle is the spiritual energy that surrounds the locus, the bindu which is the symbol of sarvananda, eternal bliss.

Hindu architecture is very comprehensive in the way it connects mysticism to mathematical forms; underlying the connection is the basis of Hindu philosophy that there is order in the universe, and that God is the creator and sustainer of that order, and that justice and order will prevail over injustice and chaos. When the world gets corrupt, God will intervene. As Krishna says to Arjun in the Bhagavad Gita, "Whenever there is unrighteousness on earth, O Arjun, then I Myself shall come forth. For the protection of the good, for the destruction of evildoers, I am born from age to age."

Without the posters she refers to, all this made no impression on me. What did Stephen see in it, and when did he read it, without telling me? I tried to read it the way he reads. The way the inner sanctum is always dark, unlighted except for lamps that hardly lit the dark granite. I remembered my trip to Sri Rangam temple on one of those side trips Ma took from one of her conferences – Vishnu lying on His side, and the priest expecting me to bow down with folded hands, and me gaping at the sheer size of the statue.   Stephen would see something else, of how one has to enter the cave of darkness before one sees the light, but for me, I guess I am one of those satisfied to sit in the outer sanctum – near the bell, surrounded by the world. But Stephen, oh Stephen, are you in the cave of darkness? Remember how we used to read the 5x8 cards with me sitting on your lap on this couch that has not been lain upon since you left, the way your toes stuck out, oh Stephen.

I wish I had some faith of some kind, any kind. The simple kind would be best: God is.

I came across one of Maru's stories the other day.   I remember I put in the the PALI tray. I read it again:

The Man who Bathed in the Ganga Seven Times

Once there was a man who lived in the southernmost district of India. His children were all grown up and his wife was dead. One day, he called the whole family and said, "It is said in our Scriptures that everyone should bathe at least once in the Ganga before his death. A dip in the sacred river cleanses us of our sins and we will go straight to heaven. So, I have decided to go to the Ganga."

They said, "It is a long way, Father. Stay with us so we can look after you in your old age. When the time comes, we will pour Ganga water on your lips, and sprinkle Ganga water on you to speed your way to heaven."

But the old man had made up his mind that a full dip in the sacred river would earn him moksha. So he took a sturdy staff, telling his grandchildren it was so he could beat snakes and scorpions out of his way, even though everyone knew he was already so old that he needed the help of a staff.

He walked northward. He walked and walked. Every night, he slept where he could, ruined temples, under the trees, in abandoned huts. By and by he came to a river. Joyously, he ran to it, crying, "Oh sacred Ganga, I am so happy to have reached you. Cleanse me of impurities so I may go to heaven when my hour comes." He stepped into the river, and came out feeling cleansed and pure. A man was passing by and the old man said, "Brother, I feel so happy to have washed away my sins in the Ganga." The man laughed and said, "Brother, this is not the Ganga but river Kaveri. Ganga is farther north."

So the old man walked north. He walked and walked.

At last he came to a river. Joyously, he ran to it, crying, "Oh sacred Ganga, I am so happy to have reached you. Cleanse me of impurities so I may go to heaven when my hour comes." He stepped into the river, and came out feeling cleansed and pure. A man was passing by and the old man said, "Younger Brother, I feel so happy to have washed away my sins in the Ganga." The man laughed and said, "Elder Brother, this is not the Ganga but river Krishna. Ganga is farther north."

So he walked and walked northwards.

At last he came to a river. Joyously, he ran to it, crying, "Oh sacred Ganga, I am so happy to have reached you. Cleanse me of impurities so I may go to heaven when my hour comes." He stepped into the river, and came out feeling cleansed and pure. A man was passing by and the old man said, "Son, I feel so happy to have washed away my sins in the Ganga." The man laughed and said, "Father, this is not the Ganga but river Godavari. Ganga is farther north."

And so it went on. Tapti, Narmada, Soan, Yamuna.

Now he was very feeble. Even his staff, instead of helping him, felt too heavy in his hand. He fell ill. And he walked fewer and fewer miles each day, asking every passer-by for directions, for he could no more figure out which was east, west or north; daylight became a blur, night utter darkness for the stars were too far away for him to see. One day, the man he asked said, "Grandfather, you are very near the river Ganga. It is just there, may be another five hundred steps and you will be there."

"Thank you, child," said the old man. "I am here at last, to dip my body in the holy river and cleanse it of all sins." The man went his way. A few steps further, the old man fell down, and could not get up. He dragged himself – there was the river. He could see the sun shining on it and the ripples dancing all white and gleaming. "I will rest a while," he said and drooped his head, never to rise again.

And Hari received his spirit and said, This man I shall take directly to Vaikuntam, for he has bathed in the Ganga seven times, fully believing it will give him moksha.

What wouldn't I give to have that kind of simple faith, that I have only to believe and pray, and Stephen would be back here with me.

~

The closer I come to the final exam the more time I seem to spend with Maru's stuff.

I found the essay I was once looking for. Missing the Bus, published in a magazine called MIX in the Summer of 1999. I had to go through a whole carton of stuff I had already read to find it and I mixed up some stuff I had carefully labelled, and I don't know why I was so intent about finding it. I thought it would explain her obsession with dreams.

Recurring Dreams – most of us have had these dreams, with their sameness and variations. "Missing the Bus" is one that I think about. The bus overtakes me when I am a few yards from the stop; I sprint, thinking I'll get in when it stops to admit or let off a passenger, but there are none and the bus goes by without stopping.

Or, number 62 comes by and I tell myself 62 takes a fifteen minutes detour and I'd be better off waiting for a #60 that goes directly home; there is no number 60 for the next half hour.

Or three 60s come by but all are chock full and so don't stop where I'm waiting.

Or, I sprint to the stationary bus but it moves away before I can reach the front door.

Or, I know I can get a seat if I return to the earlier stop, but walking in the wrong direction is ideologically repellent.

Or, I know I can get the bus if I sprint a little way, but my sprinting days are over and I plod on while the bus goes by.

This is not my recurring dream but it could or should be. I have always been a writer, having won awards and published short stories from childhood on, but in Canada I have missed all the buses which would have made me a well-published writer. WHY? Wrong priorities would be the simple answer. I put my academic career ahead of my writing career, Caesar ahead of the Muse; or perhaps I put my home ahead of Caesar, who was ahead of the Muse. Not that I am an efficient homemaker by a long shot, but husband and child, house and kitchen do take up time and deserve attention. And a job outside home has its own demands that I was willing to submit to, saying the Muse was always there, and I did not need to be hawking my wares. So now I have three novels and thirty short stories and a major collection of poems, all waiting in the wings, or getting mouldy in the basement, depending on how I feel about the future at the time I answer the question about why I am not on the bus.

A more complex answer would be that when one moves from one country to another, something happens. I see four phases of immigrant settlement. The first is one of nostalgia for the land left behind, of awe and wonder at the new land; during the second, one is so busy learning survival skills in the workplace and neighbourhood that one is too busy for any artistic efforts; the third phase is one of involvement in one's ethnocentric community; the fourth is involvement in the larger community, or Canadian life. One of my personae in Trishanku, in the secure third phase, says to a fellow-poet who wants to come to Canada:

I have been there, my brother
The land is green but my heart was barren.
Warm are the people but my heart was lonely.
Money flows in rivers but my heart was dry.
Bereft of sorrows and pain, bereft of comradeship,
My heart lost its voice, my brother,
It is not the land for you and me.

But for activists in the third or fourth phase, there is enough of others' pain and tension to write about even if one is fortunate enough not to have one's own.

When I entered the third phase, I wrote some pretty good poetry, some of which found a public space. Having started my writing life as a journalist back in India, deadlines have a way of stimulating my adrenalin flow. Once, when I saw a contest deadline announcing the "Great Canadian Lesbian Contest," I was inspired to write a story but the small print said the contest was open only to lesbians. When I questioned that in my covering letter, my entry came back by return of post, with the organizers explaining how and why it is necessary to be exclusive. So one of my ambitions is to be the Rosa Parks of this issue and find a seat on the lesbian bus because I think one's sensibility and not one's sexuality should be the yardstick.

I am now very definitely in the fourth phase, though others might see only my skin colour and ethnic costume. However, I have realized that single-minded worship at the Muse's shrine is not enough. One needs editors and publishers. When I first came to Canada, editors and publishers were too white-centred; now in the 90s, things have changed and editors want the oomph of marginalization themes. But I have gone beyond that stage. My current fiction celebrates life and laughter; it is laced with sadness and satire but the main fabric is light in tone. I have my Maru cycle of stories – one where Maru, a secretary at a prairie university, is hit by the reality of male menopause syndrome around her and goes through a series of paranormal episodes; one called *Maru and the Maple Leaf* chronicles Maru's life in Winnipeg over the last twenty plus years; and one called "How We Won Olympic Gold" is where Maru comes home from a visit to India the day poor Ben loses his Olympic medal.

The bus route seems to have changed, and I am waiting at the wrong stop. Always a little out of step with the world around me. Which is okay as long as one doesn't need an audience to keep laughing.

Hmmm. Missing the Bus is in a section called "DISpositions: Age and the Arts," the editors too are playing with words I guess. Looks like someone had noticed from what she had published that she should have published more than she did, for they actually asked her to write the essay and paid for it too – the contract is stapled to it!

There is a shopping bag full of conference programme handouts and folders. Baby Vasyl, I have not gone to see him last two days. My shifts are driving me crazy. I know it is not the shifts, I know it is Stephen, but I don't want to think about that. I don't want to think about baby Vasyl. I just want to lie down and sleep. If I could just sleep without dreams. I had no time for Maru but went to her anyway, especially when I couldn't fall asleep.

Maru attended many women's conferences, and I had already seen many of the folders, stacked with programme brochures and names of speakers and panels. Why did she store all this stuff? Really, who cares who these people were, spouting feminist rant as Uncle Siv would say?

I can understand her keeping postcards of the ship she travelled by, S.S.Orsova, programme booklets of symphonies and ballets, I can even understand storing menu cards from her first Air India flight from India for they are quite ornate and pretty, but conference programmes? Sheesh. But here is one with typewritten stuff on lined paper – it must have been a phase – this habit of using lined paper for printouts. And one of the women in this is Ruksana – of course I have to read it, even if it is two o'clock at night.

I've got to get all this down while it is still fresh, let me hope I find the time to do it.

Best science conference I've ever gone to. Made me almost believe that women scientists are almost human.   Siv has introduced me to dozens of women scientists over the years, at various conferences, but they are like any men-delegates, very cordial about superficial exchanges but just scientists, not women, you know what I mean.   When conferences are held in exotic places, there is always a special category of delegates – wives.   We form a group and I quite enjoy myself with them doing touristy things, except if there is a beach.   Beaches are not my cup of tea that is for sure.   Wives can be a bore if the conference is held on the coast.

But Mexico City, wow.   The bus tours were fantastic but what I really must write down first is the evening we had right there at the hotel dining room.   One of the wives had a friend who was a regular delegate, meaning a scientist, and I met a scientist friend, Ruksana whom I'd met once before, she's also from India, and she had told me about how her family fled to India at partition.   We were eight women at the table, of whom four were scientists – who turned out to be regular women as well, opening up with their own life stories!!

Ru spoke first, details I had not known – how she excelled at her college studies but got into an arranged marriage because all her friends were going that way. But it turned out to be a terrible marriage. He didn't want her to complete her M.Sc. He wanted elaborate freshly cooked meals, lunch and dinner. He ran his own business and came home for lunch everyday. Having two babies in quick succession did not help either. At last, when the children were old enough for school, she went back to college, and he bitched about it all the time, and assumed she was flirting with fellow students and professors. When she got pregnant again, he had the gall to accuse her of sleeping around and wanted her to have an abortion. Which she did, because she did not want another child at all and had already planned her way out of his life. She got her Master's, got a scholarship from an American university – in those days it was not difficult to get a scholarship - and upped and left, without her children. But she reconnected with them after some years.

Pr talked about her life. Married young to someone whose family was well-known to hers, they came out to the U.S. and had their family and jobs and slowly drifted apart, a lot of small incompatibilities that led to perpetual tensions in the house. So they decided to split, but since they had a beautiful big house and the children were still young, they decided to separate and to continue to live in the same house. We thought it sounded rather amicable all around but she said that was only so because they were never in the same room at any time. Now that the children were grown up, she was looking for a place of her own. Strange, we said, that neither seemed interested in starting a new relationship. She shrugged, "Too late, there is always work," and her younger son was still a teenager.

I talked about two women I was helping at the time. Both came as brides of men who were in Canada already and both had children born here. One's husband regularly beat her and made sure she never got to see anyone else from their home country. It was only when their son got ill at school one day and the school nurse brought him home that the poor woman got a friend who could advise her, and one day, ten years after coming to Canada, she came into the Immigrant Women's Centre with her children and never went back home. The other was from India, and it was a "love marriage" across language and caste. When they came to Canada, they too had their family and she stayed at home, though wanting to re-train herself for the workforce. Back in India she was from a higher middle class home and had assumed she wouldn't be working but in Canada there were so many opportunities if one could just get a college degree. But her husband wouldn't hear of her educating herself and so she did it on the side, taking a course or two at a time, when the children were at school. Meanwhile, he often brought home a co-worker who loved Indian food and so this poor woman ended up with the other woman at their dining table and soon it was clear she was sharing more with her than food. But there was nothing she could do for the next few years. But at some point, halfway through her nursing course in which she had enrolled after an extended argument of six months, she decided enough was enough and took up her own apartment. She never got a penny when the divorce came through – he managed to make sure of that. But soon she would be earning her living.

Ra opened up next. One thinks arranged marriages are proverbially oppressive, she said, but hers was a love marriage from hell. Ra is a marvellously cheerful woman, not good looking and by now overweight too. She is a great raconteur and kept us in splits of laughter.

She grew up in a quiet Roman Catholic environment and excelled at studies. She was courted by a rich immature brat – these adjectives were her later additions for at the time she was totally infatuated – and her parents were dead against him, for he had not even passed high school, but she went ahead anyway. The date was set, and he had arranged for a horse drawn carriage to bring her to church. It was a rainy day, the front gate of the church was closed, as it always was for a couple of hours in the late afternoon before opening again for evening service. So she and her bridesmaids and party went in through the wicket gate one by one; her wedding gown got all muddied in the rain and the groom was inside arguing with the man who was supposed to have kept the gate open and the priest was waiting inside wondering why the wedding party was so delayed arriving and soon it was apparent the groom was tipsy, and her parents wanted to leave taking her with them but she insisted on staying and the wedding vows were duly exchanged and when they came out, the carriage guy had left and the groom who had his own car took her off on their honeymoon without letting her say proper goodbyes to her family. He turned out to be a boor and a brute through and through and she, like Ru, had fled the country after her Master's and come to the U.S. but unlike Ru had managed to bring her daughter with her.

Ra said all this in what seemed to be her usual fast paced breathless voice, all the while laughing, and we laughed with her, all except Ja who was outraged at the husband's behaviour and kept saying, How did you tolerate it? how did you put up with it?

There was a handwritten postscript:.

Now, three years later I can understand Ja's reaction. That oh-so-charming husband of hers moved out of the house last week during her last conference trip, and rumour has it he has set up with a younger woman. Perhaps I had misread her that time, it was not outrage but a cry for help, really wanting to know what she herself should do with a husband known for his many flirtations. Krishna, dark-hued as the clouds of June, give me the strength to betray myself, so I betray not my home.

I tried to imagine what Ra looked like, what accent did she have? What country was she from? It did not really matter, the common factor was that they were all women, scientists, yes Maru, and many doctors too are women – all women sharing the same cussed problem – men. But then, not all men are obnoxious. I thought of the men in my life, Dad, Uncle Siv, Vithal, Jayant, Arvind... Stephen, I didn't want to add him – he was not in my life any more. Never more, quoth the Raven, Nevermore. But Stephen, what has happened and why? So gentle, so brilliant, so everything any woman could ever want. He was all my men put together – Dad, Uncle Siv, Vithal, Arvind, I fell for him because he is all of them all in one, should I say was all of them? I have changed, he says, in what way Stephen, in what way? Tell me dammit, tell me. Was. Everything is in the past tense, same as Maru's writings. Damn. Perhaps I should phone his parents? No, that would be silly. I doubt he'd have told them how serious we were and even if he had, it would be even worse to tell them we have broken up. He has broken up, how dare he?

Did he have it in him all along that ours was not something that would last? I read something of Maru's the other day where she talks of some other writer's short story, yes it was just a line and I glossed over it because the rest of the piece was more significant, I thought, to one of the stories she has written later and so it proved she often took notes from the lives of those around her. I wanted to tell Stephen of this discovery of mine about Maru's writing habits but never got around to writing the e-mail, and then he throws this bombshell at me. I reread that piece. I wonder if Stephen is like Deepa, with a seed of discontent all along? And Maru, how dare she take up for the guy in the story? Stephen would say, "Does she? Read it again."

Stephen, oh Stephen.

August 16-17, 1993

She has got a job on the west coast and is leaving with her son. He will drive them down, leave the car for them, and fly or bus back. "I just can't function here," she said, "I've been back three months but I haven't done anything. I feel paralyzed... take these sofas for instance, I'd like to throw them out and get some decent furniture...but it is no use... there is so much junk except he doesn't think so...it is going to be good to get far away. I'll come back rejuvenated... here it was too close, the least little thing that he thought was not right with the baby and he was at our doorstep in three hours...."

I thought, there is so much bitterness, so many complaints. Yes, I can understand, can imagine what she has gone through, empathize totally etc. But my heart goes out to him, especially because I feel, I know, I fear I should say, that she will leave him one day, not now, not soon, for she will bide her time and consider and reconsider, but one day.... In Irwin Shaw's *Girls in their Summer Dresses*, the wife bitterly asks/says he will one day leave her, right? And he does not answer but on being pressed, says flatly, yes perhaps he will.

Does he know it? How can one not know it? On the other hand, what do we know about anyone, their feelings, their thoughts, their plans... all this cant about honesty and communication is just that, mere cant, sometimes idealistic, sometimes rationalistic.

He has changed a lot; has given up drinking, smoking. Spends a lot of time with his son, loves him to the nth degree; and he loves her too in his own way, probably with all the jealousy and possessiveness of sexual deprivation, for I am pretty sure she has not slept with him in ages; perhaps even literally even if not with her soul. In this TV soap, Lauren complains about Scott being immersed in his work, they never have evenings together etc. etc. and one day he decides to change and does... arranges to slow down his research, cut his hospital and patient hours etc. and then one night she realizes she has stopped being in love. Soaps, oh the soaps have every situation one can think of.

Yes, I feel for her. Once a writer I love said just that: she had married for love, a foreigner, for whom she left her native land.... We were at her club in London, and she spoke about her daughter, proudly, worriedly as mothers do, wondering what the future holds for their daughters, and when I asked about him, she said, yes they live together but sometimes, "you know, love just ceases to be." It sent a chill down my spine, both what she said and that she should tell me that. I am surprised whenever someone tells me about their private life; my first reaction is to feel immensely flattered, but I quickly tell myself that perhaps most people are like that, they don't mind telling. But perhaps, looking back, perhaps she was not like that; perhaps it was a moment of togetherness that I let pass without reaching out. She was lovely, a translucent-thin-skin, pale pinched proud face that must have been stunning once....

What can a guy do? I am not thinking of the material side, paying for the education, driving a hundred and fifty miles each way every weekend... but of the emotional side; in the graduation pictures he is so happy so proud, he had put in an ad in the newspaper with gown and cap in the "Graduations" column much to her embarrassment, and of course a hundred acquaintances called in... yes he is so happy, but she has withdrawn herself from him, sometimes overtly but always averted from within, I can see, just that pulling away from his encircling arms, and it is not that instinctive shyness of traditional Indian background... or is it only in my eyes?

My heart goes out to him; I wanted to say before I left, be nice to him, after all it is only for another week, and then you are free for four months, please please be nice to him. But I did not. Because all this cant about honesty and communication is just that, mere words.

~~~~~

TWENTY TWO

I had just put all the vegetables on the skillet when the phone rang. It was Uncle Siv.

"Been a while since we chatted," he said, "is everything okay?"

"No," I cried out, "I am losing baby Vasyl. We've tried everything, and we thought he seemed to be responding but not anymore. He is sinking and I think by tomorrow...," I broke down and cried with an intensity I did not know I had in me.

Uncle Siv said, "I am sorry, Priti, I will be there first thing in the morning. Take care, anything that happens happens because it must. Take care of yourself."

I took control of myself. "It's okay, Uncle Siv, last time I spoke to you, I was so pleased we had delivered him just right despite all those complications. Just that it has been awful, day after day to hope against hope and then to find we are going to lose him after all. So how long will you be here? Come stay with me."

"I'll be there first thing in the morning. I am flying into Toronto tonight."

I lay on the sofa and had my cry. Tomorrow is my off-day but I plan to be there all day; I will just sit by him. Perhaps Marika is spending the night there. I wonder how she manages, with two other children, must have a partner that really cares. I was thinking of mine, of course, who clearly didn't care. Was I envying this poor woman for her supportive partner?

If Uncle Siv doesn't come by seven, and I don't see how he can, I'll be gone. Let me write the note for him right now and stick it on the door, never can tell what kind of rush I'll be in.

I took a postie and wrote the ICU phone number so he could page me, and stuck it on the door. I wondered what people do who live in those apartment blocks with a security system, when they need to leave messages. Must be some standard procedure that I have never noticed. I don't notice much, do I? Like what was eating up Stephen when he was here. It must have been there all along. The more fool I. Could I have missed something that could have saved my baby Vasyl? No, when we are at work, we are totally focused; that is what drew me to Stephen. He liked the story I told him about how Dronacharya, when he was teaching bowmanship to the royal princes, asked them to shoot the left eye of the wooden sparrow placed on a branch of a tree. When Drona asked what they were looking at, the others said the sky and the tree and the branch and the bird, but Arjuna alone said he was looking at the left eye of the wooden sparrow and nothing but that.

So he is focused, he says, and where does that leave me? With the sky and the trees, an irrelevant background.

I realized that I was so emotional about baby Vasyl only because of my personal problems. Be passionate about the case, never emotional about the patient. What boots it to know all the rules?

~

Marika was there; she had been there all night, I had found out at the nurses' station as I entered. She sat there, hands crossed on her lap, and looking at the baby.

"You must get some sleep," I said. "I will sit by him while you stretch your legs." She smiled and got up. "Mikhail will be here soon, after he drops the children and before he goes to work," she said. "It is good that he will be able to see our baby today." She rose. "I will be back in a few minutes."

I pulled up the other chair and studied the chart, as though some miraculous entry would have appeared during the night. I took out my text book that I was toting around for the exam next week but did not open it. I put some antiseptic lotion on my hands and then held baby Vasyl's little fingers. My eyes teared. Marika was back sooner than I expected, and I swallowed my tears. "His fingers are so long," I said, "a pianist's fingers."

"I would like to hold him," she said, taking her position in the chair, which I had moved so the monitor was not visible. I lifted him, moved the IV stand closer to her chair and placed him in her arms.

Her husband came. They spoke in their own language. He put his hand under hers and they held the baby together. He turned to me. "Is there any?" he whispered. "One must always hope," I said. "When can you come back?"

He ran his sleeve across his face. "I have to go now but will be back as soon as I can. I dropped the children off at school."

"Do you want to bring them in soon?" I said.

"They were here last night," Marika said. "We made sure of that."

Mikhail bent over the baby and lightly kissed him. He kissed his wife the same way, lightly, on her forehead. Then he left. "I will be back as soon as I can, a couple of hours," he said.

We sat silently for a few minutes.

"Should we have let him go earlier and spared him all this?" she said.

"It is our duty to do all we can to hold on to him," I said.

"A doctor's duty, but is it right?"

"It is the right thing," I said, "he is being loved for that much longer."

"He will always be loved," she said.

I had nothing to say to that.

I persuaded her to take some rest in the recliner in the corner. She shook her head. Her eyes were red with sleeplessness but she did not cry. I had not seen her cry in all these nineteen days.

As she had done so often, she crooned a song in her language. It was always the same song these nineteen days. The tune had been going through my head all night.

She paused to tell me that I could go. "Do you want me to?" I asked, knowing I had to leave if she said so.

"I want you to stay if you can," she said.

Another hour went by. I tried to concentrate on my book but only to keep myself from eyeing the monitor so often. She continued to croon.

I stared at the monitor. As though by staring I could will the heartbeat lines to rise again. She knew he was gone. The nurse came in from the nursing station, and seeing I was there, she went out to do what needed to be done next. The doctor on duty would soon be here. We sat on for a few minutes longer. Then I took out my cell phone and stretched it towards her. She shook her head. I dialled the number on her chart. "Hold him," she said, and gave him to me. I started crying, tears streaming down my face. She made the call.

"Our little angel," she said, taking him back.

We sat silent.

I left when the doctor on duty entered.

As I passed the lounge, I saw Uncle Siv. I got out of my coat, and threw it on a chair as I ran towards him. I buried my face against him and cried. We left after I had composed myself.

Back at home, I told Uncle Siv the whole story from the time I went into the labour room all the way to the very end. It did me good, I suppose, because I was more in control of myself now.

"What time is your meeting?" I asked.

"There is no meeting," he said.

I realized he had come because I needed him. I cried again.

"Now tell me about Stephen," he said.

"How did you know?" I said.

"It came through loud and clear," he said, "but there is no hurry."

I showed him the letter.

"What did you reply?"

"I haven't," I said.

He didn't say anything, but he came to my side, and held my hand. He was smiling.

"So, what is there to smile about?" I said.

"My Priti maid, we love you very much, even though you are such a lousy reader."

"Now what?" I said.

"How often have I told you not to read literally," he said. "*this* is a drowning man calling for help, and all you can see is your own pride danced upon, with hobnailed boots, needless to say."

"Please keep Wodehouse out of this," I yelled, impatiently.

"This is all about Woodhouse," he said, "we can't keep him out of it."

I didn't want to laugh, but I did.

"I am thinking of going to India soon," he said, "next term I'll be on sabbatical. As you know, I have the ashes that…"

"Maru never wanted that," I said, "you know very well the Assiniboine and Red were her Ganga and Kaveri. And you told me that was all taken care of, the time I couldn't come."

"There were two urns," he said, "only one went into the Assiniboine at the Red."

"But you know she wouldn't want that, all that mumbo-jumbo going to India."

A frown passed his face, but his voice did not show it. "The living have to take precedence over the dead," he said quietly. "Do unto others as you would have etc. I would like my ashes immersed in the Kaveri."

"You'd better let Arvind and others know about it," I said.

"The living must take precedence over the dead," he repeated. "They will take care of what they think should be done. Shall we get back to the matter at hand, if you don't mind, and let me say it before you interrupt again. I might be going there soon, and I think you should go in person to see what this is all about. If you wish, we could go together."

"I can't be flying half way around the world to go see him wallowing in some woman's lap."

"Priti, pull yourself together, young lady. You know very well that is not likely."

"Why not?" I said.

"Do you really think so?"

"No, I don't, but I can't think of any other reason for this letter."

"Think again."

~

We had lunch, old lasagna I had frozen godknowswhen and had left on the counter to thaw. Then, over coffee, still at the table, Uncle Siv gave me a talking-to.

"If you do decide to go, remember to have a clear picture of what this is all about. You have to be prepared for one of several possibilities:

One, he might have changed, as he says, and you may not like this changed person. This changed person might not like you.

Two, he might be in need of more help than you can give him, in which case you must not carry a weight of guilt for the rest of your life.

Three, he might really want to stay on in India, and you have to figure out if you'd be willing. Love alone is not enough. Man does not live by love alone but also by bread."

"India isn't that bad an alternative" I said, "lots of young people are going there, the whole IT world from what I can gather."

"I think every child should grow up in India and even if they come away after that, they'd be okay. So I would absolutely encourage you to live in India if the fourth alternative works – namely that both of you find you love each other enough to get married and live happily ever after, or even the fifth, which is that you commit yourselves to each other and live unhappily ever after here or in India." He smiled.

The way he listed everything, his confident charting of the situation, everything was so like Stephen, I told him as much.

"When a young woman falls in love with her father's clone, usually things work out all right," he said, "if the father is an okay guy, of course. Do you remember the discussion about women of abused mothers falling for abusive men and abusive men being sons of abusive fathers? I always thought that was weird but you two almost convinced me with statistics etc."

"Why only almost?"

"I have always kept out of your feminist ra.. I mean talks."

"You were about to say 'rants' weren't you?"
"Of course, I was."

I found it such relief to be arguing again.

He said, "Now can we get back to the main issue?"
"Wait," I said, "if one falls for one's father's clone you said, so don't you buy the unhealthy iffiness of the Oedipal complex?"
"No, I don't. If the parents are happy with each other, the sons end up marrying their mothers' clones and daughters their fathers' and all is well. And may be that is why so many arranged marriages turn out okay. The parents look for their own clones when match-making. Point made."
"You are assuming arranged marriages work."
"I already mentioned the caveat – if the parents are okay people, arranged marriages are likely to work. Likely is all I said. Likely. Now, can we get back to the main issue?"
"And what was that?" I asked, overly-sweetly.

~

The finals are here. I don't think I am going to pass. I am a basket case. No mail from Stephen. I run to Maru. How lucky she was to have so many women friends. They seemed to have shared such strong bonds, by the sheer fact of being women. And her connections with women from the subcontinent was quite something. There is this piece published in *Kala*, one of the short-lived Indo-Canadian magazines, about the time she was at some women's conference in England - *Going beyond the Hyphen without erasing it* – her titles were usually so catchy, I doubt I can ever come up with anything half as catchy but Stephen can – I guess I am too literal or something.

I experienced a moment of celebration. The conference was a wonderful coming together of women in academia and the arts. I shall concentrate on one experience, the experience of joyful community that happened when the women of the Indian diaspora converged by happenstance in one corner of the delegates' lounge at the end of a long day of panels and workshops. And what a group we were - each a name that should be recorded in the annals of diaspora ground-breakers, alphabetically: translator Lakshmi Holmstrom, freelance lecturer Ranjana Ash, Kathak dancer Rina Singha, poets Sujatha Bhatt,

Suniti Namjoshi and Uma Parameswaran, storyteller Vayu Naidu. We requested Rina to dance and it was typical of Rina to agree without standing on formalities. That she was not in costume and was without any makeup and that the floor was carpeted did not bother her a bit; she had her ghunghroos and cassette player and tapes that she carried around with her in her backpack and she needed nothing else. At the sound of her ghunghroos, more and more delegates came to our corner and the lounge became a dance floor. But even in that crowd, we, the original group, felt we were a strongly bonded unit. We are domiciles of different countries but we felt bound through filigreed threads of memory and affection to a motherland that would never be other-land, though each of us has woven our different loyalties into our variegated tapestries. On my return I wrote to the others about this feeling and they wrote back that the evening had been the highlight of the conference for them also. In short, there is much in our collective life to weep about, but there is also much to celebrate, not the least of which is joyful diaspora consciousness.

Maru had so many friends, I do envy her. Me, I don't have anyone except Stephen and now I don't have him either. Curious, Maru doesn't seem to speak or write about men much. Sure, they appear in passing, but just cameo appearances, though she wrote about Ranjit rather insightfully in that Deepa story. I found so many life stories of so many women, all in notes, fodder for her fiction. Did they know she was forever weaving possible plots around their stories? There is this steno-notebook with women's life stories she garnered from a single conference – she seems to have gone with Uncle Siv to one of his conferences and there too a group of women seem to have had a whale of a time sharing their pretty horrific stories with so much laughter! It must have been soon after that conference in England or that other conference with women scientists.

~~~~~

TWENTY THREE

Uncle Siv called me this morning while I was still in bed. He told me he had booked his flight. Are you trying to blackmail me, I asked, why are you pushing me against the wall? He said it had nothing to do with me, though he would be glad to have my company, and that he was going because he had to. But he followed up the phone call with an e-mail of his itinerary.

I too have changed, Stephen. I don't hang out with the crowd, I go to work and work is work, just work, not an emotional roller-coaster. I was on Dr. Rafter's team this morning when we lost one of the twins, and I didn't let myself get all tangled up. Thinking about it, I wonder if it was good or bad. If one becomes objective and removed from one's work, isn't that most regrettable? How can one be a good doctor if one doesn't cry? I have hardly started my professional life and already my heart is hardened? I remembered those friends of Maru's at the Y. whose life seemed to have closed within five years of getting married. No, I am being theatrical. Of course they would have gone on to live a full life, had children, and a career if they wanted one, and bossed over their husbands and a houseful of domestics and what not. Life in India can be fun for those with money.

Stephen. Has Stephen got a taste of how the rich live in India? Not a word from him. Bloody hell, what does he think this is all about? Throwing me off without a word of explanation. I wrote him that nice letter, didn't I? Crock, Uncle Siv's clone diagnosis is all crock – and now he wants to take me there and humiliate me further. Huh.

I riffled through one of the cartons and came up with something that gave me an escape from my hell. It is a bit of that biography Maru wanted to write about Chittammai. Wow, it is a continuation of what she wrote in the *M.M. Syndrome*.

Chikkamma's voice hovered over me, though, and her snort, the sarcastic one I remember from childhood days, broke my concentration everytime I tried to get back into my writing about Canada. So why did she do what she did? I doodled on the computer screen with the graphics software I had discovered quite accidentally. Indeed, the computer had all kinds of secret software that would pop up on the screen like an india-rubber toy as I ran my fingers over the keyboard waiting for the Muse.

Chikkamma's nagging worked and one day I started a new file: *Chikkamma*, I typed in fourteen point Book Antiqua, and doodled with it until it was highlighted, underlined, shaded, edged with a border... But what appeared on the screen when I went into a freefall of writing was about Chittammai, the way her stomach heaved and rolled when she laughed as she recounted to me anecdotes from her sixty years of charismatic existence, during one of the many summers I as a teenager spent with her in Bangalore.

"You can never really understand a person," she said, "my father, for instance, was so wonderful in every way but I never could figure out the many contradictions in him. Did I ever tell you how he ran away to Ceylon and came back a year or two later?" She laughed, and then she stopped and wiped away tears. "That is why I was misled into thinking my sons would come back."

Another time she said, "I never have understood my father's paradoxical views. So radical in his own life and so conservative when it came to mine. One sometimes wonders if it was the same person..."

She had told me so many details about her life, her early days, her father and grandfather, her sister and brother-in-law, her own intersectal wedding that had been once postponed, of how the elders of the Brahmin community had entered the furor over the differences that seem so trivial now, and how it hit the newspaper headlines at the time. Years later, I went to the office of the newspaper and dug out the exact wording. Along the way, I myself had got married across subsects, which by this time in social history did not matter much to anyone. She had a special affection for Sivaram, who is from her subsect. She said to him, "You and I, both naïve, were led down the path by these cunning *others*." Sitting on the huge leather upholstered chair from the age of dinosaurs, she laughed, her stomach heaving with mirth.

Because she had told me so much of her memories and experiences, the words came easily to me. The words are mine, transformed as all oral stories are transformed and translated as they flow through another mind, another language, another generation. But this is her story, and as I typed it over the next few weeks, somewhere along the way, I changed the file name to *Chitammai.*

He was born in 1856, in his father's ancestral house in Madurai. Seven children had been born before him, of whom one, a girl, lived to adulthood. The others died at birth or soon after. He was the eighth child, and so his father named him Krishna and prayed that this child, like the eighth child of Devaki and Vasudeva, would survive all dangers of infancy and grow to manhood.

His father died soon after, and he was brought up by his father's younger brother, Sundaram. Himself childless, Sundaram adopted his brother's children as his own. He sold his house and moved into his late brother's, that was a little bigger, and moreover was their ancestral home.

Sundaram Iyer was *akattar* at MeenakshiTemple. His duties included general supervision such as looking after the preparation and distribution of the *prasadam*, and the overseeing of any entertainment that took place. He was fond of music. He was also interested in classical dance and had himself studied Bharata Natyam. He enjoyed the pageants and festivities organized at the temple, and he brought in musicians and dancers whenever he could.

For performing these duties, he was given a modest salary and a measure of rice twice a day.

Infancy on, Krishna was quick at numbers and memorization. Sundaram Iyer was of a generation that had to break ground. English education held danger. Sons sent to English schools might give up Hindu scriptural studies and turn to western literature and sciences. They might break away from the Hindu code of social conduct, from orthodox conventions and traditions that had held the community together for centuries. On the other hand, they might be able to serve the country. And they could make money. Earning a regular salary that did not depend on the vagaries of the elements was a dream that few could realize. English education seemed to hold great promises of security. Even so, it needed courage to send one's sons to schools opened and run by the British. Sundaram had the courage. He sent Krishna to the local English-medium school.

[When Chittammai told me all this, she added, "This was, you will remember, the third quarter of the last century, a time when Britain was consolidating its power. Macaulay's imperialism had imposed English as the medium of education as early as 1833, and the flow had reached South India as well. Brahmins, predisposed to learning, were the first to take up English education. They selectively memorized Macaulay's words, do you remember any of it, Maru?" I, fresh from my history exam recited, "The sceptre might pass away from us... but there are triumphs followed by no reverse. There is an empire exempt from all natural causes of decay. Those triumphs are the pacific triumphs of reason over barbarism; the empire is the imperishable empire of our morals, our literature and our laws. But," I added, "Macaulay also said we Indians 'are sunk in the lowest depths of slavery and superstition' and it was the white man's burden to awaken the colonial subjects blah blah..."
Chittammai said, "We now know all that, but at the time, English education seemed a great thing. An opportunity for action and service without upsetting caste conventions was being offered and they took it, not recognizing the cunning of the British who wanted to train a class of Indians to help them rule the country."]

Krishna was duly prepped to take the 'accountant exam' as it was called. Can you imagine, the exams were held in Tiruchi and not in Madurai and the students had to travel the sixty miles by bullock cart; the journey took them three days each way, but no one regretted it because even those who failed were seen to have reached some level of praiseworthy education.
It was 1874. Krishna was studying for the exam. The whole family, indeed the whole Brahmin street that stretched from the temple outward all the way to the peasants' fields, was proud of him. He would soon receive his school certificate, and how many families could boast of such brilliance?

Krishna was under great pressure. He knew the school certificate was a milestone in more than one way. It was not just as academic feat; it was a gateway to life for the whole family.

By November, it was clear that a severe famine was inevitable. It would starve not just Madurai and the adjoining districts but the whole province, perhaps the whole peninsula. The rains had failed. They often did, and December even in good years was a lean month. The harvest came in only the middle of January, and provisions were always low in the preceding month.

Most Brahmin families could draw from their stores to tide over a difficult period, and rice would come from distant districts even if at a high price. But now, with the spectre of famine over the whole south, the atmosphere was heavy with anxiety. Krishna knew that his school certificate would be a passport into the secure world of government service, and he realized the tensions behind his family's references to his exam.

When the results were announced, they were overjoyed to find Krishna had done even better than he had expected. He was immediately rewarded with a government job. While he waited for his first posting, his wife came home.

~

Krishna received his first posting. He was appointed to the famine relief section as a gruel-shed clerk. For most others, a government job was a gate to lifelong security to good living and a steady income. For Krishna, his first job was his first major lesson in life. All that he had studied during his school years seemed irrelevant in the face of this experience.

He was in charge of supervising the distribution of free rice gruel. The people he now saw filled him with a new reverence for the human capacity to survive. True, there were incidences of corruption, aggression, insensitiveness and cruelty. But these receded to insignificance when one considered the sheer accumulated abundance of human fortitude that was present under the thatched sheds.

Krishna walked home every evening, and as he turned into the temple street, he seemed to enter a different world, sheltered and remote. They had always lived in the shadow of the Meenakshi Temple, but the figurative description of their way of life seemed to take on a literal dimension. They were protected, secure, the goddess always there, always bestowing grace, benediction.

~

Krishna's first assignment ended with the end of the famine. The gruel sheds were pulled down, and in the presence of green fields, people shelved away in their memory the worse-than-usual famine. But Krishna was not to forget or ignore that experience. From then on, he spent more time with the peasants, and he tried to improve their lot.

After the famine, Krishna was posted to Sea Customs Service. His duty was to keep watch over incoming and outgoing ships, to collect custom duty in the name of Her Imperial Majesty's government in India. It was mostly routine work. The bigger ships usually waited offshore and unloaded the cargo into boats, just as the smugglers did, except that there was no secret midnight unloading. He, as Sea Custom officer, would go on board, inspect the cargo as it was unloaded, and assess the customs duty to be levied.

Krishna and Rukku set up house on the coast. In 1876, their first child was born. Rukku, as was the custom, had gone to her parents' house in Madurai for the confinement. The child died at birth. Rukku returned to her husband. Their second child was born in Madurai in 1880. She was named Lakshmi, after her grandmother. Rukku went to her parents' as usual for the third baby. The baby, a girl, was born in 1882, and named Meena, after her aunt, who doted on her brother's family. When the baby was two months old, Rukku as per custom, prepared to leave for her husband's home on the coast. As was the custom, her father settled on an auspicious date, and wrote to his son-in-law. There was no reply. He took a trip to Devipatnam, where he was posted, and was told at his office that Krishna was on leave. Thinking that Krishna was on his way to Madurai, he came back. Days passed, and there was no sign of Krishna. There was only one conclusion to be drawn – Rukku had been deserted. Desertion was not common, though infidelity was. A man did not abandon a woman he had wed, no matter how often his visits to the devadasi district. But even that he had not expected from

Krishna. So upright, with all that education and talk about social reforms.

Several months later, he received a letter from Krishna that he was in Ceylon and wanted to bring his wife and children. He was earning good money, much more than his salary at home.

Sundaram Iyer, a man seldom perturbed, was completely lost. He was greatly relieved to know his son was alive and well. Nevertheless, as he read his son's brief letter, he was inclined for the first time to keep it secret until he had thought a little longer on it.

But there could be no secret within the community. Half the street already knew he had received a letter from Ceylon.

To all those who wondered how this was going to be received by the community, Sundaram's answer was, "Time will tell." Krishna's wife and children continued to live with him.

Krishna returned to his post before the year was out. He rejoined his job and moved back to his old house by the sea.

He had taken a boat to Ceylon on an impulse and had experienced in all its intensity the excitement and guilt of his situation. He had boarded a boat back home on a similar impulse, suddenly one day, but now he realized that the impulsive act both times had been the culmination of an inner process, and external execution of something that had been rehearsed in the subconscious.

He had set out to prove something of himself to himself. He had wanted to concretize something that had permeated his being with vague desires, distant aspirations.

He had longed to see the sun set into the sea.

In Ceylon, he had seen the sun sink into the sea day after day. What had filled him with fear and excitement on his way out seemed purposeless on his way back. The sea without land held no meaning. There was no basis for his former fascination with fishermen and sailors; or for the Portuguese, French and British, who had crossed the seas and taken over his country. To do them justice, no doubt they held some reverence for the elements. Whatever it was, theirs was an attitude that led them to catch fish, to conquer countries. He himself had wanted to be a fisher of men. Now he did not.

He had seen the ball of fire sink into the deep and now he wanted only to see the sun rise from the deep and set behind the green fields along the Coromandel Coast. He had paid his debt to youth.

Krishna sent word to his father. His father was with him within two days of getting the message. He arrived one evening. Krishna saw him coming up the path, and he hastened out, meeting him a few yards in front of the house. He prostrated himself full length on the sand at his father's feet, and the older man's eyes filled with tears at the gesture.

They spoke of the family, Sundaram answering Krishna's questions about each one, about neighbours and relatives. Then they went to bed.

Next morning, when Sundaram came in after his ablutions, he saw Krishna standing at the window.

"I slept well," he said. "Now tell me about your travels. Are the people there very different from us? Did you learn their language? I hear there are quite a few Tamilians there. And that the landscape is beautiful. Did you enjoy yourself?"

Krishna replied, "One owes youth a debt."

Sundaram Iyer turned the words over in his mind. He wanted to ask if the debt had been paid in full, but he held his peace. No one would know yet, perhaps no one could know ever.

"One owes youth a debt."

Looking at his son, Sundaram Iyer knew he was home for a while, if not for always. He could set about preparing for the purification ceremony. Father and son stood silently until the sun rose out of the sea.

Later, standing knee deep in sea-water, Krishna repeated the mantras of atonement and rededication, donned afresh the sacred thread, and returned home to Madurai, where he went through the same and other rituals before returning to his post at Devipatnam.

Rukku and the children were brought to Devipatnam by her father, and they set up house once again. Krishna was posted to various coastal towns. His family grew, one more daughter and two sons, a still-born child between the two boys, and then on Saturday, in the year Vijaya, in the month of Kartikai, under the star Uttara, on the tenth day of the waning moon (December 2, 1893,) their eighth child (Chittammai) was born in Kizhaikkarai where he was posted at the time.

Though it was a story of long ago, about people I don't know and don't care about, it spoke to me, told me something I needed to hear. One has to pay one's debt to youth. Stephen.

~~~~~

TWENTY FOUR

Two days later, I got a call from Ma. She asked me if I had heard back about where I had been accepted. I told her nothing was happening and nobody was likely to reply for another six weeks, and I'd let her know if and when I heard from any of the half dozen places to which I had applied. Then she said something that threw me off track altogether. "I am so glad you have volunteered to go to India with Siv, that is really nice of you and good timing too. As you say, all these responses will come at the same time later. I am not saying you should go with him, but in case you do, let me buy your ticket."

"No," I said, "I will take care of that. I may not go and I don't want any hassle of you booking it from there."

She must have caught my impatience with her, for she said, "I wouldn't want to take charge of any booking, sweetheart, not with someone who takes so long to make up her mind as you do. But, I could upgrade it for you with my Aeroplan points – really, I don't want you to be all wilted by the end of the flight. Even just being together on the flight would be enough help for poor Siv. These pilgrimages are always so difficult, sweetheart."

As usual, she spoke fast, and she went on to talk about how she'd love to hop down for a weekend with me but they were hiring and she was on the committee etc. etc. As soon as she hung up, I tried to figure out what all this meant. Why had Uncle Siv told her about me? To pressure me? What else had he told her? I was getting pretty het up about what Uncle Siv was up to, but there was no time. I had to rush to work.

It was a busy day, and I didn't have time even for lunch. On the walk back, I picked up some salad vegetables and bread from the convenience store. The fridge had been pretty empty in the morning, except for milk and orange juice. But who wanted to buy regular stuff after a long day. I was tempted to buy salad from the deli, but I liked having something mindless to do when I had to think. So I bought the raw stuff and hoped I had some dressing left in the fridge. May be a stir fry would be better any way. The bread smelt good.

As I chopped the vegetables for a stir-fry, I thought things over. I figured I'd give Uncle Siv the benefit of the doubt. May be, knowing how I never told Ma anything, he was paving the way for me springing it on her after I'd booked the ticket, in case I decided to join him. I guess you could say he knew me well. Probably that's what I would have done – just told Ma and Dad I was going instead of telling them now I was thinking of going. Why was I like that? Really, I was pretty mean with Ma most of the time.

Would it really help him to have me tag along? I assumed he was just saying so because that would eliminate the need for bringing Stephen in. Uncle Siv had such a clear head for things. Like Stephen. Or rather the way Stephen used to be. Who knows what he is now. Stephen, what was he doing this minute? Paying his debt to youth? Youth, hah, I feel old as the hills.

The more I thought about it, the more sure I was that Uncle Siv hadn't said a thing about Stephen to Ma. Just as Maru hadn't written a word about me in all the stuff I've read so far. I was so afraid she would have. I mean, it would make a great story. May be it is somewhere; there's a lot to read yet. Under a "Story-lines" sheet or floppy disk file that I have not opened at all. Rich girl gets entangled in fast life; lives in two worlds, druggie and Wellington Crescent. Narrator has to be someone who could realistically come across the girl – make her a social worker who is in charge of one of the other girls in the sorority?

Well, if nothing, I am getting the hang of how Maru writes her stories. If Stephen were here, he would say I am all wrong, and it would be a first person narration or some such thing. Oh god, if only we could go back to where we were six months ago. What is he up to? Why doesn't he write? May be I could call his parents. Nah, one just has to wait it out, or go there and check in person.

Ma talked of this as a pilgrimage for Uncle Siv. How weird it sounds, coming from Ma. A pilgrimage. Maru uses it too somewhere I am sure. I remember seeing the word, because it was in a font that was very different from any other Maru used or on a kind of sheet that is different. I've got to look for it. I am pretty sure it is in the early-works carton.

~

Just as I kind of decided I would go after all, I get this phone call that's freaked me out. From Arvind, saying how glad he is I was going with his Dad. That he had called my Dad about his neighbour's mother who wanted to know about her son who was at the University of Manitoba, and that Dad had told him I was going with Uncle Siv. We had a long chat, and it was like old times. Why don't we ever hold on to people we really care for? A phone call once in a while is all it takes. He said he had been feeling awful, not being able to go home as often as he would like to, but his youngest was only a few months old, and work was killing him. He was disappointed that Uncle Siv had taken the house off the market, but as he talked it was clear he was on a guilt trip, as though he had abandoned his dad to misery. Then I was there holding his hand long distance and saying his dad was quite okay, he had his lab and his research etc. And he said, but it would be nice if he would retire and spend some time with his grandchildren etc. etc. So we had a long chat about everything under the sun, and he kept thanking me for being there for his dad.

So where does it leave me? I feel a bloody hypocrite having everyone think I am going with Uncle Siv to help him. And then it hits me – in all my vacillating about going or not going, I never once thought I could/should go because I owe it to Maru, for heaven's sake, I owe it to her to see her off to the other side, and to help Uncle Siv for her sake, if not for his, oh god, what a perfect creep I am.

That is when I decided I was going.

~

I can't believe this! She has written out her own funeral service, and stuffed it away in this carton, as though it too is part of her writing.

When I die, do not mourn for long,
For in having my children
I have held the joy of the world
In my arms.

This is to be read aloud:

From Bhagavad Gita:
2:20 The Atman is never born nor dies; for it is unborn, eternal, everlasting and primeval; even though the body is slain, the Atman is not.
2:22 As a man discarding worn-out clothes takes new ones, likewise the embodied Atman, casting off worn-out bodies, enters into others which are new.

2:25 This Atman is unmanifest; it is immutable. Therefore, knowing it as such, you should not grieve.

2:27 The death of one who is born is certain; and the rebirth of one who is dead is inevitable. It does not therefore behove you to grieve over an inevitable event.

18:54: Having become one with the Eternal, and cheerful in mind, one neither grieves nor desires; treating all beings alike, one attains supreme devotion to Me.

18:61: The Lord dwells in the hearts of all beings, whirling by Maya and causing them through His illusive powers to revolve according to their actions.

18:62: Seek refuge in Him alone with all your being. Through His grace you shall obtain supreme peace and the eternal abode.

From Bhaja Govindam: Bhagavad Gita kinchidadhita, Gangajalalava kanikapita, sankredapi yena Murari samarcha, kriyate tasya yamenana charcha (Take but once the name of Krishna Murari and when the time comes, you'll never need to quarrel with Yama)

Final words at some point:

The sheaths have been removed.

She was Annamaya, but now she is free from body.

She was Pranamaya but now she is free from breath.

She was Manomaya but now she is free from mind.

She was Vijnyanamaya but now she is free from knowledge.

Like her grandparents Seshiah and Sreemati, Subrahmanyan and Seetha, and her parents Ganesan and Rajalakshmi, now she is Anandamaya, and she is filled with bliss.

Music: M.S. Bhaja Govindam and Meera songs to be played in the background.

This is nothing like the service we had for her. Why, oh why, don't people tell those around them just what they want done at the end? Why don't they leave it on the computer table or some place where it will be seen right away? Stashed away in a carton, for pete's sake. But who ever thinks of dying so suddenly? I can't get over the way she left us, all of a sudden, all by herself. I will put it in my India suitcase and give it to Uncle Siv for the rites in India.

~~~~~

TWENTY FIVE

I found the Pilgrimage story – it was typed on the back of those posters again – with Latha looking so splendiferous back in 1979. Why don't I just find out about her and her mother and phone them for old times' sake? She is probably old and fat by now, and may be her mother is dead. If Maru can die at the age she did, there is every possibility that others older to her are gone. Death, geez, I have to get out of this Thanatos fixation. That is a word I got from Stephen, and I hope I am using it right. Stephen. He is the one who is on a pilgrimage, not I. So what does Maru have to say in this story?

The Pilgrimage

Rishikesh Rishi kesh, Rishikesh Rishi kesh, the words chanted in her brain to the clang of the wheels as the train steamed through the fertile greenery of Uttar Pradesh. The words had been clanging in her brain for several days now. She had connived to get to Delhi ostensibly to visit her best friend and with her complicity had taken the train. All the way to Delhi and now, the clanging in her brain had outdinned the din of the platform, outshouted the shouts of porters and hawkers, outclamoured the clamour of bells and whistles.

Shanti stood up, adjusted her sari and sat down again on the hard wooden seat next to the window. The carriage was crowded, with villagers. The air smelt of their tobacco and clothes. Next to Shanti was an old woman who alternately mumbled over her beads and talked aloud to herself. From her disjointed sentences, Shanti gathered that she had lost all her children, the last of whom had died a month ago, and whose ashes she was carrying to immerse in the Ganga.

At every station, the new passengers looked curiously at Shanti. She was an alien among them, with her silk sari worn the modern way, her heeled shoes, her long black hair hanging in a braid, her head uncovered instead of being covered like the other women's. She was from the city, a place of which they were suspicious, with its people who made them feel they were worms of the earth. But the quiet, subdued expression on the young woman's face, and the very aristocracy they hated, made them pay her the tribute of silence. They left her alone. She, though, wished she could talk to someone about something inane, and so forget her own problems. She quietly observed the people around her.

This was a slow train, but she had taken it because she wanted to be at her destination in the morning and not in the evening. The train stopped at all wayside stations, and often enough it stopped in the middle of nowhere, waiting for the signal light to turn green. Running an hour late, it had to stop at sidings to let faster trains go by.

The engine wheezed to a halt at a small station. Shanti, who had been leaning against the window shutter, sat up and opened the window. It was a station for sure, not a siding. There stood the waiting hall of corrugated iron sheets, flanked by the ticket office and the public convenience; half a dozen painted signs on lamp posts proudly proclaimed the name – Belipur. The tea vendor walked past with a bucket of water filled with cups, and an aluminum kettle of steaming tea; a hawker with a flat basket on his head and a cane-woven stand under his arm cried out, "Aloo-puri, do anna plate, do anna." With a tray strapped from his shoulders, a boy shouted, "Pan-beedi-cigarette-matches." Village tramps peeked into the compartments and passed lewd comments directed at women. Their laughter with villainous undertones made the young women in the compartment bow into their veils. The platform and tea-stalls were soon crowded. The tea vendor dipped used cups in a pail of water and poured fresh tea for new customers all in one smooth flow. While the men in the carriages got off to stretch themselves, the women made use of the space vacated by the men to stand and fan themselves with the edge of their saris.

A family of villagers came to Shanti's compartment and loaded themselves and their baggage in. A young man in the group pushed them in one by one, first a veiled woman in a blue sari and a girl of six, then a steel trunk, several cloth bundles jangling with the sound of utensils, and a kerosene tin of grain. Then the man lifted a four year old boy with one hand and a surahi of water with the other. He stretched the jug towards the woman but the boy reached out for her arms at the same time and as she took a hold of the boy, his leg kicked against the jug, breaking it. The water showered on another passenger who was clambering up. The man threw away the neck of the jug that was still in his hand, and the woman cried, "Ram, Ram, the children will have to remain thirsty."

"Curse you, clumsy son of a dakoo," stormed the wet man as he wiped himself.

"Check your evil tongue, you son of a syphilitic," said the father with equal venom.

The woman's voice came placatingly from under her veil. "Forgive me, brother, it was my fault."

The aggrieved man was all apologies. "Oh no, no, sister, it is this frantic hurry on everyone's part. The train is not going to run away." He climbed in and wiped the sweat off his face with the tail of his turban.

Shanti turned her eyes to the door at the front of her carriage. A wedding party had come to see off a bridal couple. Although there were as many men as women, bright saris and tinkling glass bangles made the women dominate the picture. They were clustered around the bridal pair. The groom stepped out of the centre, sheepishly self-conscious. Chaplets hung from his goldthread-wrought cap. His forehead was smeared with kumkum powder. His shirt could hardly be seen for the garlands round his neck. His dhoti was transparent in its newness. He awkwardly stared at the betel leaves and coconut in his hands, and moved towards the carriage. The lamentations of the women grew louder. They blew their noses on the edge of their saris and cried. The bride, completely hidden under a heavy pseudo-tissue sari embraced each one of them and touched the feet of the older men, who gruffly gave their blessings. "May you live a hundred years." "May you die a wife," "May you gladden your husband's home with sixteen children." The engine whistled. The farewells grew tearier. "Ah, our little beti has to go now," "Woman is born to leave her parents' home." The bell rang, and the chorus grew – Our little one, our child, be happy.

Meanwhile, an assortment of bundles and trunks had been piled into the carriage by the younger men in the party. The couple stood on one of the trunks at the door and looked out as the train heaved itself out of the platform.

Shanti could not help imagining what the scene would be like when she got married. There would be no confusion about the baggage. She would be standing at the door of an air-conditioned coupe in a real tissue sari, waving out to people dressed in the latest fashion and to the inevitable photographer. She would be standing proudly and happily by the side of, and here her thoughts stopped. Was it going to happen?

The bridegroom put his hand around the bride and she, abashed, swivelled around and landed among a group of women. One of the women made a little boy give up his seat for the bride. Shanti motioned him to sit with her, but he hid his head under his mother's pallu.

"It is a sad thing to be born a woman," an old woman said, chewing betel nuts with her toothless gums.

"Aye, aye," said another, nursing a baby."

"Oh, shame," said a widow, "don't speak such inauspicious words. It is a gladsome thing, is marriage."

"A child a year and the grain drying in the drought," said a middle aged woman, rocking her baby.

"Come, let us see your pretty face, child." The woman next to the bride lifted her veil. At the words, some men turned, ready to have their share of the picture. The groom fidgeted, shredding one of his garlands till the brown thread peeped out naked.

Her face lay open now – small, clear skinned face, frightened eyes, tear-stained cheeks. Her intricately painted hands, with silver rings and heavy silver bangles, hastened to cover her head, but the sari slipped in her nervous fingers, uncovering her bosom, which beneath the red satin blouse was flat and thin. She covered herself.

"Pretty face," a young man said.

"Ach, she is still a child," said another.

"She'll grow, aye, she'll fill out quicker than mustard sprouts up," laughed a woman who was all of seventeen. There was an infant at her full breasts; the shine of her bracelets showed she had not been married more than a year. The groom blushed and nervously kept shifting from one foot to the other.

A man snapped his fingers at him. "The door is right behind you, boy, stinks but serves the purpose." All the men laughed, and another added, "Bladders are bothersome things o'nights for sure." The laughter grew louder, the jokes coarser.

The women did not join in, but they snickered behind their veils. Shanti had no veil to hide her embarrassment. She looked out the window, pretending she could not understand them. One of the men made a pass at her, and another recited a couplet on the disdain of fair women. The old woman near Shanti spit tobacco juice out the window and then gave Shanti a lecture on the impropriety of travelling alone, and if one had to travel so, why not take the ladies' compartment?

The next station was a big one. Half the compartment alighted there but the carriage filled up as quickly. The first to enter was a young man. His white trousers and starched shirt showed that despite his unshaven face and uncombed hair, he was of the upper class. He pulled in a five-year-old boy, and seated him on the groom's steel trunk. He had no baggage except for a small leather bag, which he hung on a hook over the near-opaque mirror. He looked at his watch. He tallied it with the clock on the platform. The boy ran his fingers over the leather strap. "When I grow up, you will give me a watch, won't you Bapu?" he said.

"Yes son, sure."

The boy looked at the huge clock outside; for a minute and a half he sat watching the black hand, fascinated by the sudden click with which it moved.

"What is the time on your watch, Bapu?"

"Two minutes to seven."

"And on that clock?"

"Same."

"But that is so big and yours is so small."

"They are made that way," the father said, absently.

"But how?"

"You are small and I am big. But we both have two legs, don't we? And walk together don't we?"

"But Bapu,"

Just then a toy seller passed by with a wheelbarrow of toys. The boy looked out eagerly, and the quick eyes of the hawker caught a prospective customer.

The father shook his head. "Not now, Sohan, please."

"Just one?"

"Later, boy, later."

"Bapu," the whisper became conspiratorial, "just one big blue drum, not for me, for the new baby." The man bowed his head and swallowed a sob. The boy at once stood up and caught his father's arm in both of his. "Yes, Bapu, later, not now. I don't want it now." The last words were swallowed in tears of spontaneous sympathy.

The train steamed on into the darkness. The compartment smelt of potatoes-puri as passengers had their dinner.

"What's the time, bapu?"

"Eight o'clock."

"When will we reach Ma?"

"Four o'clock."

"When will it be four o'clock?"

"When you wake up in the morning, now sleep."

"And will Ma come to the station?

"We'll go to her."

"Will grandpa come to the station."

"We'll see him soon."

"Will ma be all right?"

"Gods grant she will."

Shanti turned her eyes away. She could see he was crying inside.

"Poor child," said a woman, "is something wrong?"

The young man closed his eyes.

Through the night, Shanti heard the same words. Is it morning yet? Is ma all right? Are we there yet? Is ma okay? Gods grant she is.

Once, the man said into his son's sleeping head, "The gods are kind. Did I not go to Rameswaram before you were born? Son, pilgrimages are never in vain. Love will win over death. It has to."

The clanging suddenly stopped. So many around her were on a pilgrimage, as was she. Each with a prayer, a special prayer to a special deity with a special promise. Do this for me and I will do this and this and this. Except for the old woman, who had nothing to ask, and was only going to the river to give back what had once been a son. Only her prayers would be answered but she had none.

Shanti suddenly felt that the boy would never feel his mother's arms around him again. And she herself?

When she planned this trip, she had fully believed that when Ramesh saw her, he would know he was a builder of bricks and mortar, not of abstractions. He would return to the world of drawing boards and architecture, and not continue to sit at the feet of a Master, who surely knew he did not belong there.

The engine gave a tortured scream into the night. Shanti leaned against the bars of the window. How stupid she had been, how naïve, and with all that conniving to get away from home on this journey that she had thought of as a pilgrimage of love.

She wouldn't even leave the platform at Hardwar. She would just take the next train back. Better that than

The page ended there. I frantically searched through the carton for the other poster-page that had to be there, somewhere, but I could not find it. I was in a sweat. I had to find it. But it was not anywhere in the carton. All the sorting I had done, by date and by theme and what not, had got messed up. I went to the sofa and lay down, my feet on the arm, and I covered my face with the crook of my arm, and started counting aloud. I counted to two hundred and forty three and then stopped.

I was being stupid, I realized, reading everything like it was an oracle, a personal oracle written just for me. It was so clear that this story was the same as that little piece about that woman in the college hostel, the one who left her home and went off to the Ramakrishna Mission. Maru had changed things around, having a young man leave home and go off to an ashram. She was always doing that kind of fictionalizing, rehashing real stories into fiction. Only that and nothing more.

Quoth the raven, Nevermore.

~~~~~

TWENTY SIX

We are leaving Friday evening. Uncle Siv will be here by the morning flight and we will go together to the airport. We did not get seats together, because with all that vacillating, I ended up barely getting the last seat on his flight. I will probably get the seat next to the toilet, way back in the tail of the plane. May be someone would trade seats so we get to sit together. May be I should have taken Ma's offer to upgrade me to business class. I did okay in the exams. I will soon be home free. But free for what? I don't want to think. Is Stephen still there? I don't know. I don't want to think about ifs and if nots.

Perhaps I should have talked to Dad, like, really talked to him instead of all those weekly calls about nothing. About Stephen, and that I was not going with Uncle Siv just to help him but for, what was I going for? Perhaps I might have talked to Dad if I did not have Uncle Siv. I don't know how I did so well at the exams. I was a basket case. Still am, I suppose, but booking my ticket helped me take the turn. I read Krishna's story again and wondered if it perhaps had a hand in my decision to join Uncle Siv. I don't know, I don't want to think why we do what we do or whether we do it on our own or whether there is a hand that guides our hand. Everything Maru has written seems to have been written for me, everything strikes a chord, some chord or the other. May be that is what reading is all about, it is all in the reader, not in the story. One owes youth a debt. Will I find that Stephen has paid his debt to youth, or will I find something else? India. Who would have thought I, Priti Moghe, would ever lose my lover to India, would ever fly to India to try get back my lover? We carry India with us and within us wherever we go, Aunt Savitri often says, but that was for her generation, not for mine. India for me might well turn out to be the other woman. I wish Maru were here with us. But of course she will be, has always been. I pick up and read again what I'd read twice already.

I miss Chikkamma. It is months since she came by. What could have happened? Why hasn't she come?

Of course I know the answer. I should. I have not kept my pledge to her, haven't written a single blessed thing about her, swimming around in my own little fishpond, preoccupied with my own little trivia. Why do they go away? My boys, all took wing in different directions by the time they were nineteen. Because they were too good for this stagnant fishpond, Sivaram said. Let them go, let them all go before they themselves become blackguards, Uncle T said thirty years ago when he heard Siv and I were leaving for Canada. And so also with them. There was no place for them here in this fishpond, they were just too brilliant, and so they went, to Harvard, and Berkeley, and Carnegie Mellon; now why did they go to such different places? Why not nearer each other? I've never wondered about that. And Priti.... But they are still here with me as I with them. But Chikkamma, I thought I'd have forever; maybe I took her for granted, obsessed with my own fishpond. Yes, I have turned out some good work, told a few women's stories, and some men's; I can't get the men out of my mind, especially the ones who find themselves hit with a brick and laid flat, like poor Ranjit. Thambi, thambi, where are you? And Chikkamma, I need to hear what you have to say about the icicle, and the freeze frame. And what am I to do with the frozen frame I carry of you? What am I to make of it? It isn't as though I haven't tried. I went on this trip in my van across the country; and made friends with women campers and asked them what they thought of it. After all, women are women and our common womanhood should be able to jump borders. But no one could really understand, and how could they? They don't know anything about India, about life in your times; some think of it as the dark ages, some that India is still in the dark ages, some are simple in their reading, and there are so many Meeras in this world. And some literalists - bigamy is wrong, some fanatically feminist, like Purna of *Freeze Frame*. Some think he was an okay man, some that you were no better than Hardy's Tess, bamboozled by a man. But their answers are too simple, too one-dimensional. I want someone to see you my way - as a feminist who went out on her own, and who did what had to be done, both before and after getting what she knew was her inheritance, a child. And you, Chikkamma, who can give me more factual details, just won't. And now you have gone.

So where could she have gone to? Could it be her time was up? That she had been given a lease, a conditional lease in which

I had a role, a role that I did not fulfill... despite my pledge? And so she had been forced back into the other world. I had condemned her, she who loved to travel and see this world, get into people and places, yes even into my computer, gone now to the eternal silence. The clock has struck twelve and the carriage has become a pumpkin again, all because of my negligence. Keeping one's word. I never thought much of Dasaratha for keeping his word to Kaikeyi, but may be that is what life is all about. If you don't, some other cycle is set in motion. Time is up.

Mortals were supposed to honour their forebears - that is what life is all about, that is what civilization is all about, to give continuum to all that is worth preserving. And the spirits have to depend on us humans. And I have failed Chikkamma.

Find out the details, dig around, that is what biographers are supposed to do, she said. But I am not a biographer, just one who wants to tell stories, women's stories, so we can know ourselves through others. Yes, I must go. Back to people who knew her, to get them before they too go on and away. India.

~~~~~

Acknowledgements

(In this novel, there are several excerpts, with some variations, from Uma Parameswaran's earlier publications, including the following, which are acknowledged in order of their appearance in the book)

Chapter 2: "The Day I met Attia" first appeared on <sawnet.org> on the Sawnet Bookshelf pages under the Attia Hosain entry.

Chapter 3: "Curling…" A slightly different version appeared in *Winnipeg Free Press Leisure Magazine* (Sunday Supplement) dated April 22, 1967.

Chapter 4: "The Fate of the Fair" appeared in *The Deccan Herald*, Dec. 23, 1961
"Tuesday Nov. 4" appeared in *Outofprint*. Issue3, March 2011.

Chapter 6: "VIII" excerpted from "Maru and the MM Syndrome" in *What was Always Hers*. Broken Jaw Press. 1999.
"Cancer simple as a Flower" appeared in *Close to the Heart*, edited by Mary and Paul Knowles as a fundraiser for Breast Cancer Research. 1996.
"Chittamai wedding story" excerpted from *Lady Lokasundari Raman: Reflections of her Early Life and Times*, Manipal University Press. 2013.

Chapter 7: "Panchali's Hour of Choice" first appeared in *The Illustrated Weekly of India*. Jan. 18, 1970.
"Come Ambike" appeared in *Sisters at the Well*. Indialog Publications. 2002.

Chapter 9: "Cultural Appropriation/Misappropriation: Journal of an Ongoing Journey." Excerpted from "I see the Glass as Half Full" in *Between the Lines: South Asians and Postcoloniality*, ed. Deepika Bahri and Mary Vasudeva. Temple University Press. 1996. It was later included in *Writing the Diaspora: Essays on Culture and Identity*, Jaipur: Rawat Publications. 2007.

The letter from the uncle appeared in *S. Chandrasekhar: Man of Science*, edited by Radhika Ramnath. Harper Collins. 2011.

Chapter 11: "We have always had a Volvo" excerpted from story of the same title in *Atlas 02*, edited by Sudeep Sen. Aark Arts. 2007

Chapter 13: "Pinto sees the Light" appeared in *South Asian Review* (28:3) 2007.

Chapter 17: "When the Time Comes," appeared in *The Deccan Herald*. May 21, 1961.

Chapter 21: "Lie" appeared in *The Deccan Herald*, 25 June 1961.

Chapter 23: Excerpts from *Lady Lokasundari Raman*. Manipal U. Press. 2013.

About the Author

Uma Parameswaran was born and educated in India, and has
lived in Canada since 1966. She retired as Professor of English
from the University of Winnipeg, and is the author of ten books
and numerous articles on postcolonial and women's literatures.

Her works of fiction include *A Cycle of the Moon, Mangoes on
the Maple Tree,* and award-winning *What was Always Hers.*
Her other fiction titles are *Riding High with Krishna & a
Baseball Bat and Other Stories, The Forever Banyan Tree,
Fighter Pilots Never Die, The Sweet Smell of Mother's Milkwet
Bodice,* and *Pinto sees the Light.*

Most of her works are available from
<larkumapublishing@gmail.com>